# THE ARMAGEDDON CHOICE

*STRUGGLE FOR EXISTENCE OR
COOPERATION FOR CONSCIOUSNESS*

A NOVEL BY DON CARROLL

ISBN: 0982926553
ISBN-13: 978-0-9829265-5-0

THIS IS A WORK OF FICTION

# DEDICATION

For Dante and Liam

# ACKNOWLEDGEMENTS

I am indebted to Lisa Trotter for taking time out of her busy schedule as Expedition leader on a trip to Antarctica aboard the *National Geographic Explorer* to talk with me about her experiences in Antarctica as station master at the United States Palmer research station on Anvers Island.

Helen Palmer is a spiritual pioneer in the landscape of the Enneagram. I am indebted to her research, learning and intuition for the ideas developed in the novel about the Enneagram and the night sky.

I am grateful to Susan Whiteman for her love of many of the ideas explored in the novel, to Reita Pendry for her kindness and skill in reviewing the original manuscript, to Charles Hedgepath for his last minute assistance and to Cristy, for her sharp proofing-eye, encouragement and forbearance when I would disappear into a writing reverie. I am again deeply indebted to Buffy Holt for her skill, creativity and diligence in the often arduous process of bringing a novel to publication. Buffy is an imaginative writer herself and her passion for and commitment to the writing life makes working with her a joy.

*Your separation from God has ripened.*
*Now fall like a golden fruit*
*into His hand.*

*Hafiz*

# LIST OF ILLUSTRATIONS

Dear Reader,

Your perseverance in spite of my warnings is of no small moment. Some would say your degree of tenacity is admirable, others would say profound rebellious stubbornness. I shall not inject myself into that question, but you know who you are. Regardless, I must say that I am impressed that you are back again, having read my warnings in *Hacking Toward Consciousness* and *The End of Democracy*, and assumedly somehow completed those two works.

So having failed twice in my efforts to dissuade you from reading the first two novels in this trilogy, I must at this point change tacks. To start with I would encourage those who read the earlier works to continue. If you are a true spiritual seeker then you have survived the assaults on your beliefs in the earlier books by the musings and general shenanigans of the characters, yours truly, of course, hopefully excepted. In reading the first novel you risked undermining your beliefs about the Christian faith and, in reading the second, the collapse of the illusion of American democracy.

Of course by now, as a true spiritual seeker, you also realize that your beliefs and three bucks will get you a cup of coffee. That is you are aware that your beliefs are a part of your ego, small-self-based security system and have nothing to do with your experience of and the meaning in your life of faith, hope and love. I assure you, as a character in the book, that it is precisely these latter characteristics that are my concern in each book. Faith, hope and charity are not only the three cardinal theological virtues but they are also the main characteristics of cooperative evolution which at a Newtonian level seems poorly outfitted to win out in the evolutionary tug-a-war against the more primitive survival energy of competition. However, the deck is not nearly so stacked against faith, hope and love at the quantum level, where in fact these qualities seem to live.

Given that you have come this far and that I have abandoned warning you not to read this book out of fear you will lose the grounding beliefs we all need early in our journey, I still must warn you. If beliefs about the Christian religion and American democracy took it on the chin in the first two books, my warning is that your chin is exposed in reading this one.

The characters in the book, including myself, will be making their choices as you turn the pages, but in some way so will you. These are gut wrenching decisions both for you and those you love, presumably, in fact, collectively for the entire planet. A recent bumper sticker I saw said: *Mother Nature Bats Last*. No doubt. And you, my dear reader, are walking to the plate and it is the top of the ninth. So, whereas you could come to the other two books armed with rebellious stubbornness or simply a beguiling naiveté, neither of those will serve you here. Your usual small-self psychological coping mechanisms will avail you of nothing. Not only must you bring a clear mind and an open heart, you must bring courage. Then how you will proceed, how our mutual destiny will unfold, is, as you will see, your choice.

Very Sincerely yours,

Father Charles F. "Cloudy" Hay

# Chapter 1

"Change your energy field and change the world?" queried Norris under his breath to Will Dawson as the two emerged together from their last class for the week at the University of Arizona's Center for Consciousness Studies.

"I think it was more like, unplug from your little ego energy field and plug into the big one and the world shifts," said Dawson in reply. "But a little visit to our local might provide more clarity on this subject."

Going to a bar, the archetypal home of unconsciousness, to explore the meaning of consciousness might be perverse, thought Will Dawson, but the road to greater consciousness was never what he expected.

Norris nodded to his new friend, "Sure I'll meet you at CJ's in a bit. I have to run a quick errand first," said Norris, as they both headed down the hallway toward the main exit.

Will Dawson was struggling with becoming a student again. But, as the days passed, the material he was studying at the University of Arizona's Center for Consciousness Studies excited him more and more. In addition, a budding friendship gave him an emotional connection to his new learning experience.

At first, Dawson and Norris were wary of speaking with each other. Gradually over time, as the only middle-age students in the class, they began to sit next to each other in the back row. Dawson began to realize there was something uncannily familiar about Norris. Dawson could not quite put his finger on what it was, but a friendship started developing and the two began meeting after their late afternoon classes on Wednesdays and Fridays at Calamity Jane's, one of the many local student watering holes, to discuss the material they were learning. Over the early months of their friendship, they carefully avoided sharing anything about their personal lives.

On the weekends Dawson commuted back to the monastery, where the pace of his instruction from Father O'Donnell in contemplative exercises with the other monks picked up significantly. Father O'Donnell extended the length of time each day when the monks were practicing centering prayer meditation. Each period of centering prayer was followed by a work session which had two goals: the first was to get work done necessary to keep the monastery functioning—everything from repairing the old farmhouse that served as the main building, to chopping celery and onions for the next meal; and second, to develop an inner awareness of their emotional and mental reactions to the work and to the other monks. The physical work was easy compared to the inner awareness practice. With any given task one person's perfectionism would rub up against another person's need for productivity or procrastination. The result was a developing awareness of how the psyche's programmed responses to life were triggered.

Maybe it was Dawson's many years of serving as a CIA officer that drove him to focus compulsively on getting a task done as efficiently as possible. His urgent need to finish an assignment was one of his first realizations from the awareness practice. Over and over again, he would catch himself becoming compulsively attached to getting a job done in a certain way, completely losing connection with himself and, as Father O'Donnell put it, the Mystery of Being.

Because Dawson was studying science at the University of Arizona's Center for Consciousness Studies, Father O'Donnell was also giving him talks on the different approaches of science and Christianity or, as Father O'Donnell repeatedly emphasized, mystical Christianity. Father O'Donnell stressed to Dawson the difference between Christianity as a mystical experience of faith and Christianity as an institution of power in the world. One is experienced only in the present moment, the other a testament to the unceasing ego needs of humankind.

Dawson realized that the reason Father O'Donnell sent him to the University of Arizona Center for Consciousness Studies was because Father O'Donnell was convinced that modern quantum biology was affirming the ideas that the mystics of the church had experienced for centuries. At the same time, Father O'Donnell was anxious for Dawson to understand the fundamentally different starting places of science and faith.

Dawson had never thought about the ideas that Father O'Donnell was presenting to him. Science, as Father O'Donnell explained, was focused on the idea of understanding and controlling power.

Dawson could see that his entire life was an expression of commitment to the power perspective of science. Everything he had ever done as a CIA officer was about using force. In fact, the agency loved exploiting the most cutting edge technology to achieve its goals by force. The more clever the stealth technology used by the agency, the more satisfaction it seemed to bring, and along with that, a sense that the successful exploitation of science to achieve the goals of the agency made those goals right. Power validated power.

The scientific perspective of power as a way to view life was so inculcated in Dawson, that the teachings of Father O'Donnell about the mystical Christian perspective were at first downright frightening to him. Dawson soon realized that the reason for his parallel studies with Father O'Donnell was that, although Father O'Donnell wanted Dawson to learn as much as possible at the University of Arizona about the science of consciousness, he wanted Dawson to learn about consciousness, not from the perspective of how to use that knowledge to dominate, but rather from the perspective of surrendering to the experience of that knowledge.

Father O'Donnell was convinced that Heisenberg's theory about the relativity of subatomic particles to an observer applied similarly to the perspective of the student of consciousness. In other words, Father O'Donnell felt that if Dawson learned the structure of consciousness from a Christian mystical perspective, his experience of that learning would in some real way be different from the experience of learning from an ego-based perspective of wanting to understand consciousness in order to control it.

Dawson's intuition was that Father O'Donnell was right about the importance of the perspective from which knowledge was learned, but he had grave doubts about whether he was the appropriate student to learn this new information from a mystical Christian perspective. How could he, Dawson, after so many years as a CIA officer operating from the perspective of power, begin to learn from a place of powerlessness?

Father O'Donnell was quick to remind Dawson that he had had several experiences of powerlessness. Dawson minimized those experiences of powerlessness because they all had to do with his failure to be able to respond in an authentic way to women he loved. Melissa Dowling was the first and the most haunting experience. He met Melissa when he was a young CIA officer in Afghanistan, back before the Russian invasion. She was a young Peace Corps worker. He soon learned that she had had a mystical experience at a place not too far from Kabul called St. Issa's Pond. Following that experience she learned to develop her psychic abilities, especially her ability to control her energy and to enter the thought fields of others. After Dawson's twenty-year stint in the CIA, he received word from Melissa's mother that Melissa was missing.

Moved by his earlier failure to follow his heart, Dawson sought to find Melissa. He came close. He was even in her presence without knowing it. But he had not been able to actually talk with her and the lack of any re-connection with her added intensity to the twenty-year long loss.

His other experience of powerlessness of the heart was with a young computer hacker named Blaine Astrid, whom he had chanced to meet at an Enneagram conference in Italy. Dawson had fallen for Blaine immediately. But rather than follow her invitation to explore being with her in Berlin where she was living, Dawson returned home to pursue Melissa. The result was that Dawson ended up without either relationship.

Father O'Donnell told Dawson that what he experienced with Melissa and Blaine was the exact kind of heart suffering that often causes a man to seek the monastic life. Dawson did not feel he had sought the monastic life as much as the chaotic storm of his life had figuratively thrown him up on the shore of the monastery emotionally and spiritually empty.

It was no small weight in his decision to commit to Father O'Donnell's monastery that he was being actively pursued by the CIA for reasons that so far eluded him, unless the Company hoped he would lead them to Melissa. Just the thought of being on the Company's detention list made his stomach knot. He knew all too well what would be in store if he were caught.

Father O'Donnell assured Dawson that it was these experiences of loss and powerlessness that would give him the right perspective from which to understand the scientific information he was studying about the quantum biology of consciousness.

*            *            *

Dawson was the first to arrive at Calamity Jane's. He headed for the booth in the back of the bar that Norris and he both liked. It gave a wide unobstructed view of everyone coming and going. Dawson plopped down on the cracked Naugahyde. He was glad to be here. It had been a particularly long week. He nodded at the bartender and held up two fingers. Soon the waitress placed two double-Wild Turkey bourbons directly in front of him. He glanced up and saw Norris coming through the front door. Dawson raised his hand and waved. This was not necessary. Norris was already making a beeline for the back corner booth.

"Welcome, I'm glad to be here," said Dawson. "This has been a tough week for me."

"I know what you mean," said Norris. "It's been a long week for me and in more ways than one. Actually, a long few months. Are you going to drink both of those?"

Dawson pushed one of the bourbons toward Norris. "Got it special for you."

It wasn't long before Calamity Jane's began to fill up with students ordering beer and pizza. By the time they were on their second round, Dawson and Norris began to relax.

"Norris, what did you think of all the stuff that got dumped on us in the brain biology class?" asked Dawson.

Norris paused before replying. "It does seem to me that

everyone is a little too carried away with the neuroplasticity of the brain. Maybe I'm just coming to the lecture hall late on this, but I have a hard time imagining why people ever thought the brain didn't grow and change. Scientists can now show that when we learn there are basic cellular changes that occur in the brain. It doesn't seem so astounding to me. Also, I worked in a pretty stressful environment most of my life and I am not so sure about the professor's thesis that stress is what blocks our ability to learn. I know that he said it was a matter of degree, that some stress can be helpful in learning, but she emphasized that stress and anxiety decrease learning."

Dawson thought to himself: *I wonder what work Norris has been engaged in most of his life? I sure don't want to ask him, because I know he would simply ask me the same question.* "Hey, you know, I thought the studies were very interesting which showed that kids who did best in high school were also involved in fitness programs during the school day. I've had my share of stress at work and had times when I spend long hours sitting behind a desk, but I've also had physical exercise as an integral part of my day each day."

Norris and Dawson were having similar thoughts. Norris began to wonder what Dawson had spent most of his life doing before ending up here in school at middle age. He would try to find out in the manner a Company officer tries to find out everything: indirectly. "Yes, that was fascinating," said Norris. "I think really that brain derived neurotropic factor, BDNF, or, as the professor called it, Miracle Gro for the brain, is actually more interesting. Scientists don't seem to know how it works, simply that there is this substance which turns on genes and

THE ARMAGEDDON CHOICE

helps brain cells be more vigorous."

Norris smiled at Dawson and chuckled. "Doubtless there will be biotech companies selling this as a brain nourishing product before too long. Top shelf, next to the Botox."

Caught in the middle of a sip, Dawson suppressed his grin so he could swallow more easily. He leaned back against the booth and nodded at Norris.

"Yep," said Norris. "It is a cinch our culture will want BDNF in a pill, rather than exercising our minds so the brain will actually produce it."

"Switching gears," said Dawson. "What did you think of the lectures on interpersonal neurobiology?"

"To be quite frank, that was a little scary for me," said Norris. "The idea that the way we relate to one another shapes who we become is a bit far out, but I must admit the lectures on this made a very convincing case. I did like the study which showed that a person who has an empathic visit with the doctor gets over the cold at a faster rate, with an improved immune system response, versus the visit with the un-empathetic doctor who simply asks about the symptoms and says, 'Here take this pill.' The scary part is my interpersonal life leaves a whole lot to be desired."

Dawson realized that Norris was being more forthcoming about his personal life than he had been in their Calamity Jane discussions. He decided it was worth risking a more probing question. Glancing down, and noticing again that Norris did not wear a wedding ring, he began. "So, you must have a girlfriend somewhere?"

"Yes, but I guess you could say my girlfriend is in cold storage right now and you would be more right than you know," said Norris. "I've never been the kind of guy to make any commitments, and you pretty much get back what you put out there. I was thinking things might be different for me with this woman, but then I ended up having to be here."

Dawson decided to take a little risk himself. "I am probably in the same camp as you. I never knew this information that we are learning now, that relationships affect the physiology of the brain. But looking back on my life, sure seems to be true. The professor also said something like *relationships are energy information sharing*. What do you think he meant by that?"

Dawson looked at Norris, who had drifted off into a world of his own.

Norris was flooded with memories of being in the hospital at the Palmer Station base on Anvers Island on the Antarctica Peninsula, when the station manager, Terry Shaw, was nursing him back to health from frostbite and dehydration. He had not thought of her good-natured humor as energy information sharing, but maybe it was. What he was most aware of now was that she was a long way away, and in what was a new experience for him in a relationship with a woman, he missed her. He missed her a lot.

His memory of Terry Shaw was immediately followed by the image of the new section chief, who replaced Charles Redman. Redman retired suddenly. Maybe too suddenly, thought Norris. His replacement was a zealot, who raged about the need to preserve the free world by capturing Melissa before someone else did. His logic seemed to be—if the Company got to Melissa first, it would be able to control the thoughts of everyone. If a rogue state or terrorist group got her, then it would be all over. Norris didn't like the new section chief, but it was familiar ground. Perhaps he should simply focus on the mission and forget Terry Shaw. Maybe the disastrous either/or choice the section chief believed the world faced was true. Maybe Norris should be the loyal Company man he always had been and forget about this new heart stuff.

Norris turned, blinked and focused back on Dawson sitting across the table from him in the back booth of Calamity Jane's.

"Not sure what it means, Dawson. Maybe it is simply the specialized language of these academic researchers, but I'll tell you one place the nail was hit on the head—the rat research about touch. You remember that bit? How they figured out that the amount of touch the young rats received shapes the structure of their brain, and the unfolding of certain molecules that control gene expression." He paused. "I got some genes that would like to get expressed with a little touch," continued Norris with a glare. "What do you say we get another round of Turkey?"

Dawson nodded.

"Yes, I liked the example that was given. That a gene is folded up in double helix DNA, just sitting there like a book on the shelf. As long as it is on the shelf it has no impact, it is not expressed. And these things like touch and interpersonal relationships are the librarians that decide if you get to check that book out. I think I must've grown up a few librarians short, at least those librarians that let you check out books that have to do with women."

"I'll drink to that," said Norris catching the waitress's eye and pointing toward their glasses. "If you believe our neurobiology professor, when a part of our brain is underdeveloped—not destroyed but underdeveloped—it can still change. So I have the feeling that there is a part of my right hemisphere that never got checked out of the library, and the truth of the matter is that not having it taken off the shelf has allowed me to be very efficient at what I've done for most of my life. Somehow this woman I met a few months back is asking me to check out a few new books. You know the kind that allow you to experience life not as doing, but as a way of being, with a different focus of awareness and connectedness to others." Norris' expression changed. He'd probably already said more about his personal life that he intended to. He looked down at the empty glass in his hand.

Norris's thoughts were resonating with Dawson.

Dawson paused, as the waitress brought their fresh drinks. "It really is complicated. I mean I thought the experiments they told us about, relating to learned non-use were amazing. You remember those? Where the researcher cut the nerves in a monkey's arm and after the initial period of creating stability from the nerve trauma tried to teach the monkey to reuse the arm with limited success. Then the experimenter cut the nerves in both arms of a monkey. He stabilized the arms in casts to allow for a period of non-use to let the monkey's nervous system adjust to the trauma and then, when he took the casts off the monkey's arms, the monkey was able to learn to use both arms. The bottom line is the brain's plasticity will not rewire to help a limb, or an organ, if the brain can rely on another limb or organ to do the job. If there is no alternative, the brain will rewire itself. I think I have been subject to learned non-use in regards to emotionally connecting on an intimate level with women. However, having this information sure doesn't solve the problem."

"You'll have to be a little more specific," said Norris. "Are you telling me you got a honey out there and you haven't figured out yet how to be a meaningful partner? Or is this a time in your life where you have no meaningful female relationship and you are just adrift?"

"I guess you could say I'm adrift," said Dawson. "I've had a couple of real opportunities with extraordinary women, but I never seem to be able to rise to the occasion to form a deeply meaningful long-term relationship. Even my marriage was a hollow affair." He took another sip and set his glass back down on the table.

"The one thing that is clear from all this research is that it's a use-it-or-lose-it brain. Our brains require an ongoing active engagement with what we're interested in to really stay tuned up." Norris paused. "The key seems to be our focus of attention. Or, put another way, our brain is shaped around what is important to us. Our behavioral rigidities and emotional inflexibility are just as much a product of the brain's plasticity as the good things we would like our brain to learn to do. So I hate to get overly dramatic, Dawson, but if we've learned anything about the brain, it boils down to understanding that if we are interested in getting what we want in our lives we need to develop our intention in that direction, so that the brain's neural plastic molding can grow to get us there." He paused. "So what do you want, my friend?"

Dawson was stunned that the conversation so quickly took such a personal turn. The question was right on target. A target which had eluded him for most of his life, and one that he felt frankly should be left for his work with Father O'Donnell. Dawson looked at his watch. From the awareness exercises that he was doing at the monastery, he could feel uneasiness churning in his stomach. He sat up straight in the booth.

The truth was he was rebelling against being too conscious at this moment. After all, it was Friday afternoon, and he didn't feel like utilizing his awareness practice to work through the automatic operation of his avoidance response. Better to retreat, he thought, and he pushed himself up from the booth.

"I got to get moving now," said Dawson. He looked directly at Norris. "This has been an interesting conversation. I look forward to continuing it with you."

Norris understood all too clearly the nature of the sharp

anxiety within Dawson. He raised his half-filled glass. "Anytime, my friend. Anytime."

# Chapter 2

After the Conficter gangsters shot up the storage room where Rat lived in Berlin, Blaine, Aasia and Rat—along with Manuelito the young Navajo, and his Plott hound, Ooljee—made the trip together to the convent of the Sacred Order of the Sisters of Mary of Magdala's (SOS) in northern Sweden. Rat kept the two young women laughing most of the way telling self-deprecating jokes and twitching his nose is his disarming and rat-like way. When Rat was not entertaining everyone, Ooljee was center stage, gaining the attention and affection of Blaine and Aasia.

The troupe of travelers were exhausted when they finally got to the convent, but a celebration immediately took place. Sister Maria, who had been Blaine's mentor during her first trauma release and energy training period there, led the celebrations. The Minnesota sisters who fled their convent because of CIA surveillance in pursuit of Melissa, were delighted to see Blaine again. She was a heroine to all of them since she was the decoy that enabled Melissa to return to the United States for the funeral of her mother without capture by the CIA.

After Rat's initial excitement at escaping alive from Berlin and enjoying the warm reception Blaine and Aasia received among the sisters, Rat began to get restless. Aasia wanted him to stay, and he did for an extra week.

Despite his growing affection for Aasia, and his complete devotion to Blaine, his urban hacker roots could not be denied. Rat arranged for a place to live with a fellow hacker in Berlin, which was equipped with high tech security devices.

Before he left the convent, Rat's last task was to help Manuelito communicate with Father O'Donnell. After this was done, Sister Maria took him to the closest train station to make his way back to Berlin.

*  *  *

Man, as he was called by all his friends, was not sure of his next step. He had followed Father O'Donnell's instructions in helping Blaine make her escape from Canada through Iceland to Europe, after Dawson and Man had smuggled Blaine out of the U.S. Though Blaine was a few years older than Man, he was aware she had grown to have real affection for him. She teased him like an older sister, which was the only way she allowed anyone, including herself, to see she was attracted to him.

Blaine knew from her discussions with Man that though he had only seen the tattoos on her left arm, he accepted the cuts and tattoos she had all over her body in a way that dignified her. He was not judgmental of her in the way that she suspected all white men would be; or, in fact, in the way she was of herself. Man was barely eighteen and still young in many ways, but he had a sense of calmness that made him seem wise beyond his age. Given the turmoil that Blaine had experienced in her life, she could not help but be attracted to the equanimity she felt in his presence. Plus, as one of the younger Swedish nuns confided to Blaine, Man was hot. Blaine definitely did not want Man to leave, but she feared Father O'Donnell would not want him staying in a convent of young women who were oohing and aahing over him nonstop.

Her fears were well-founded. But, it could've been worse. Blaine was afraid Father O'Donnell would instruct Man to return to Father O'Donnell's monastery in New Mexico. She had not considered that Father O'Donnell's Order might have brother houses in Europe. They did, and Father O'Donnell instructed Man to go to such a brother house in northern Germany. Father O'Donnell wanted Man to be in a place where he could be guided in deepening his spiritual warrior practices, as well as other more traditional monastic spiritual practices. He also did not want Man to be too far away from Blaine. If CIA officers in Europe, or European operatives of the CIA, sought to pick her up, despite all the SOS spiritual resources available, Blaine might need some old-fashioned warrior help.

After Rat left to return to Berlin and Man went to northern Germany, the atmosphere at the convent took on a more sober note. The Mother Superior set a new schedule for all the novitiates and nuns to follow to deepen their spiritual practices. It was as if a big game was coming up and every spare minute was to be spent training. Blaine and Aasia were treated just like all the other sisters and were expected to keep up with the new regimen.

For the first time, Blaine realized that the purpose of spiritual practices was not to gain spiritual knowledge, but to develop a new way of perceiving reality. They were not being taught new ideas about the spiritual life, but being equipped to acquire greater spiritual understanding from their experience. This new way of seeing was not something that they could actually make happen, rather it was opening to a new way of being. They practiced focusing their intention to be open to this possibility of new seeing. The guiding scriptural text was found in the eleventh chapter of Luke verse nine: "Ask, and it will be given to you; seek, and you will find; knock and it will be opened to you." This was the touchstone synthesis of work and Grace.

Their spiritual practices were teaching them how to ask and how to seek. They were not being taught dogma or creeds, but were becoming capable of knowing how to know. They were not being instructed about God or human nature, but were learning how to be present and open to the moment. They were being given opportunities to arrive at an experience of openness to receive inner insight about God and human nature by perceiving the great and subtle reality of God in everything.

Blaine's perspective on spiritual growth was changing. She had thought spiritual growth was something one did to transcend the abuse and trauma of the kind she suffered as a child and teenager, but her spiritual practices were teaching her the opposite. She was learning to be more present in reality. She was glimpsing that the more one becomes truly human, the more one experiences an inter-abiding with the divine within all human nature. She was at first confounded when Sister Maria told her that she would only become more spiritual by becoming more human. Once she had gotten away from trying to understand this intellectually, she was beginning to experience what Sister Maria meant.

Blaine was seeing that the abuse and mistreatment she suffered early in her life could, if she contracted around these experiences, cut her off from life. If she opened to them, so that her life force was not trapped by the trauma, then she began to experience a deeper sense of her own humanity. In short, as Sister Maria was allowing her to experience, when she was abiding, not in her ego protections against her trauma experience, but in God—in those moments she experienced truly being alive.

Blaine began to feel she was making the same kind of rapid spiritual progress that Aasia was making. At twelve Aasia was thrown into one of the Serbian rape camps during the Srebrenica genocide. She was so mentally and emotionally overwhelmed that all of her ego defenses for coping with life were destroyed. She had not even had the dubious luxury of being able to withdraw into a shell of anger like Blaine had. Because Aasia's ego structure was destroyed, and her desire even to live so tenuous, when the nuns began to focus their unconditional love on her, she soon made rapid spiritual progress. The ego, which needs to be surrendered for one to be born again, had already been stolen from her. There was nothing left inside Aasia but the glow of that coal of divinity that lies buried in everyone. It was this treasured coal that the sisters knew, through their energy practices, how to connect with, blow on and ignite with their unconditional love.

Aasia did so well during her first stay at the convent recovering from the effects of the abuse and trauma ordeal she suffered in Srebrenica, that when Blaine went to the United States as a decoy to help Melissa attend her mother's funeral, Aasia, after getting much encouragement from the sisters, made the decision to receive plastic surgery. Even with all the support she received from the sisters, this was very difficult for Aasia. Getting repairs to the scars and mutilations inflicted on her body, especially her breasts, literally and figuratively opened up the old wounds.

Rat found a foundation on the web that specialized in underwriting the costs of medical treatment for war victims. Aasia got her treatment in a hospital that was more like a country club spa, as this was where the doctor who volunteered his skills did most of his medical practice. The surgery went well. Two sisters stayed with her around the clock, engaging in energy practices of sending her love, and Rat visited every day while she was recovering. All the patients at the facility intensely prized their anonymity, and this suited Aasia fine. It was a source of many good laughs between the sisters and Aasia that most of the patients at the facility were movie stars and jet setters getting nips and tucks for their egos, while Aasia, supported by the visits she was getting from Rat and the sisters, was there getting repairs to her soul.

Now several months after the surgery, two of the younger

sisters at the convent asked Aasia if they could see how the healing of her breasts was proceeding. Aasia, as she often did about anything that worried her, went first to consult with Blaine who by this time was back at the convent.

"Blaine, you remember when I first met you in the Turkish café in Berlin? What I feared more than anything in the world was anyone ever seeing my body exposed."

"Yes," said Blaine. "I remember those long-sleeved, high collared blouses you always wore."

"I know the two young sisters who asked to see how the healing from the surgery has progressed are totally innocent in their request, but I'm not sure what I should do. What do you think? I am just now getting halfway comfortable seeing my own body, much less showing it to anyone else."

Blaine, as she had learned to do from the practices taught at the convent, focused her attention on her heart-center and waited to experience what her answer might be. "What comes to me," said Blaine, "is that your body needs to answer this question. If you get in touch with your gut, and it feels like it is time for the rebirth of your physical body, to go along with the rebirth of your spiritual body, then it seems to me you might want to go for it."

Aasia smiled at Blaine. She could tell how her friend was also changing and growing, and she knew, more than ever, she could always count on Blaine for thoughtful advice. "Great suggestion," said Aasia, "and as I sit here now and focus my attention on my gut, my body feels perfectly okay to share the progress of its healing with the sisters, who are so responsible for the emotional and spiritual healing that has made the physical healing possible."

"You may also want to check with Sister Maria to make sure that she sees this the same way we do," said Blaine. "You know what we have learned, any decision made alone is never as good as one made in consultation with a spiritual friend."

"I will do that right now," said Aasia, and she got up from the chair where she was sitting and headed down the corridor to Sister Maria's office.

Soon Aasia was back with a big smile on her face. "Sister Maria thought that it was a great idea, but that we should celebrate my physical healing progress as a part of our weekly Friday celebration, because the Friday celebration always focuses on how we, as a community, have gained more than we could have possibly gained as individuals during the week. You know Sister Maria is absolutely right—the extent to which my breasts have been repaired is solely because of the love I have received from you, Blaine, and the sisters. Sister Maria thought it was important that all the young sisters should feel proud of my breasts, because the truth is, except in the most literal sense, they really are not mine."

"Hey, you really are getting this stuff we're learning, aren't you?" asked Blaine.

"Much of the time I think I am," said Aasia. "But then I

occasionally have thoughts that maybe I would be willing to have a man see me naked. A thought which I would have dreaded before. I wonder if that is too much of my ego beginning to come out."

"Remember what you just told me: that they are not your breasts, and I think you'll be okay," said Blaine with a smile. "We better get a move on, it's time for us to be in the chapel. Let's go."

*       *       *

At the Friday celebration of community in the main convent meeting room, an opportunity was provided for any sister to speak about what she received that came from the love of the community. Several sisters spoke before Aasia. When her turn came, it was a little easier because she was not going first. Then she modestly removed her blouse and bra. No surgery could have completely corrected what was done to Aasia, but the change was dramatic. No longer were there the white ropey scars and mutilated nipples. And while there was redness and shadows of lines from the surgery, the beauty of her once perfectly proportioned breasts was again apparent.

There was a murmur of approval and awe from the sisters. Then clapping and hugs.

When the Friday community time was over, Blaine said: "You did good, Aasia. Here, it is a bit cool without a top." Blaine put a prayer shawl over Aasia's shoulders.

Aasia pulled the soft wool around her breasts. "We did good," said Aasia. "Thank you, thank you, my dear friend."

# Chapter 3

Father Hay realized Godfrey was late for his monthly spiritual direction appointment. Father Hay was also aware, with a sense of amusement, that he was not experiencing impatience because of his directee's lateness. In fact, Father Hay was enjoying the opportunity to recall the wonderful progress that Godfrey had made since he first started spiritual direction. This recollection confirmed for Father Hay that real progress in spiritual direction never occurs except in the context of real human struggles and challenges.

The challenge Godfrey initially started with was how to explain his spiritual longing to his fun-loving partner Jeff. Jeff didn't mind Godfrey's interest in spiritual things; it was just that getting a good tee time seemed much more important to Jeff than a discussion about anything to do with God.

Then, as usually occurs at least once or twice in a person's lifetime, events happening in the outer world came crashing in with a huge blow to Godfrey's inner world. For Godfrey this was the realization that the ideal of American democracy, which he had so cherished all his life, was a fraud. Of course, American democracy was not a fraud when it was born over two hundred years ago. Then, there was an underlying commitment to a form of government without a king that preceded all partisanship interests in power. That ideal eroded quickly in the late twentieth century.

After the generation that fought for the ideals of freedom in World War II passed on from leadership, there was no firmly held collective American experience that made the nation a community. Instead, democracy became not a form of government that brought people together to promote community interests, but a sacred ideological cow that allowed every person and partisan group unrestrained permission to pursue power in the name of their own brand of political truth. What was labeled "democracy" became a form that promoted anti-community and fostered dualistic thinking, and was about somebody's ideas always defeating someone else's. Democracy became a system of winners and losers, where almost half of the electorate was always feeling bitter and cheated, the other half smug and superior. Power itself became the only legitimate king.

The crowning blow that destroyed Godfrey's naïve idealism about democracy was the election of a corporation as President of the United States. Corporations are legal fictions created in order to be vehicles to create power and wealth. Through fluky Supreme Court decisions, corporations were given the same rights as citizens and it should not have been all that surprising that eventually a corporation would run for office. What was perhaps surprising was that the office would be the presidency of the United States and that the corporation, whose acronym was GOD, would win.

The prevailing civic theology was that, while the American

version of democracy may not be that good—and frankly everybody would admit this—that there were simply no better alternatives. Godfrey had become dreadfully depressed about the whole situation until Father Hay helped him to understand that the prevailing civic theology, about there being nothing better, might not be correct. And, while Godfrey had clearly gotten to the place where he understood that just because the original American framework of government, which among other things initially enshrined slavery in part of the country, worked more than two hundred years ago, did not mean that this form of government was the last and best model of government in the evolution of humankind. Godfrey could understand what Father Hay was saying—something better might be just around the corner. But because Godfrey could not envision what that was, he found the existing ambiguity extraordinarily disconcerting.

A majority of Americans voted for the corporation, after an intensive media campaign by GOD's parent corporation, which was a news and media conglomerate. Once GOD was elected President of the United States, public pressure was brought to bear, forcing the corporation to change from a private corporation to a public one. This did not mean a lot practically.

There were only a few dozen shareholders of GOD, including its privately held media parent, with enough shares in GOD to have any meaningful say in who the president of GOD was, even after the company's stock became publicly traded.

The bottom line was that the curtain hiding reality had fallen and the great ideal of American democracy was exposed for what it had become: not a medium for the reconciliation of shared values and creation of community, but a system that brushed aside any values except those which allowed the promotion of power and, as required by the laws governing what corporations were to do, only allowed decisions that promoted the creation of wealth using that power.

Father Hay heard a knock. He got up from his reverie and opened the door. There stood Godfrey. Father Hay surveyed Godfrey's demeanor. Father Hay quickly digested the clues on Godfrey's face. Something was not right.

"Welcome," said Father Hay. "It is good to see you Godfrey. You look a little worried. Come on in and tell me how you're doing?"

"Jesus, am I glad to see you," said Godfrey. "Oops, I didn't mean any offense, Father."

"Don't worry, none taken, but you won't get anywhere by name-dropping," said Father Hay with a twinkle in his eye.

Fathers Hay's good humor seemed to allow Godfrey to lighten up a bit.

"Do you want to come into the kitchen and get a cup of tea as is our usual ritual, or are things so pressing you would prefer for us to sit down now and talk?" asked Father Hay.

"Let's skip the tea," said Godfrey. "I cannot believe what is happening to our country." Godfrey looked at Father Hay and saw that Father Hay's expression did not change.

"Father, I guess you've read the newspaper?"

Father Hay shook his head *no*.

"You are not going to believe what is happening. If someone had told me five years ago that the United States would have a corporation as its President, I would have thought they were totally insane. Now, not only do we have a corporation as president, but the latest news is that a Chinese government controlled company has made a tender offer for all of the stock in GOD. And one commentator is saying that the price offered is so good, that given the fiduciary duty of the members of the Board of Directors of GOD to do what is in the best interest of the corporation to make money, they will have to take the offer. Another commentator is saying that because the Chinese own so much American debt, if the Board of Directors of GOD does not accept the tender offer, the Chinese will dump their American debt and our economy will go back to the Stone Age. That commentator thinks most people would rather have the Chinese running our country, than risk not having cheap Chinese electronic products to buy at Walmart."

Godfrey always admired the equanimity of Father Hay. But Godfrey could tell that the elderly priest was stunned by the news.

Maybe Father Hay regained some of his serenity, or maybe it was just out of habit in the way that he worked with directees, but he spoke to Godfrey in a calm voice. "In a way, what you're telling me, Godfrey, is simply confirmation of the reality of the demise of the American ideal of democracy that we have discussed so much. The truth is—the American version of democracy as a way to achieve the common good has not worked for a long time. I guess this recent event shatters any illusion that might be left."

"I'll say," said Godfrey. "Even Jeff who hardly ever lets anything interfere with his golf was half an hour late leaving for the course this morning because he couldn't get away from watching this."

"Yes, I guess we all will have to move to Myanmar," said Father Hay.

"What is that?" asked Godfrey.

"Just kidding," said Father Hay. "You know the country that used to be Burma, which has been, until recent signs of change, one of the most repressive in the world."

"Oh," said Godfrey, clearly not quite able to appreciate Father Hay's sense of humor.

"Well, I guess that means we have to get to work," said Father Hay. "We really have no time to lose. The American version of supposed democracy thrives on dualism. It is a system of government that thrives on differentiation, of us versus them. It is not a form of government that is going to save the species. There will not be a better form of government to replace it until more people move to a non-dual level of consciousness. At that level, I expect there is democracy that really works. Achieving greater consciousness is something we must each strive for in ourselves, and you sure have done your share of work on yourself. Obviously, there is more that needs to be done by each of us. Can you tell me how your contemplative practices have been going since we met last month?"

Talking about how his centering prayer practice and his *lectio divina* practice were doing was little consolation to Godfrey. The country was literally falling apart at the seams, but then again he did not know what else to do. Still, he had a question for Father Hay from their last discussion.

"Before I get into giving you an accountability update on my practices," said Godfrey, "could you please explain to me a little bit more about what you meant last time when you said that choosing the door to the spiritual life was always one of choosing willingness rather than willfulness?"

Father Hay paused. It was a great question. Discernment around this question was often essential for spiritual progress and journeying through problems life presented. He decided that it was best to give Godfrey a bit of background.

"Fundamentally, it is a question of whether the will is bound to the ego or is surrendered into service of something greater outside of self, which, because I like the term and it is the long-established one used, I call God. Traditionally, the ego-centered will has been understood to have five strands: the desire for personal greatness, the desire to take, the desire to keep, the desire to advance and the desire to hold on to, to the resulting detriment of others. Each of the five strands of ego will has been understood to come from a specific location in the body: the desire to take things is bound to the right-hand; the desire to retain things belongs to the left; the desire to advance at the expense of others belongs to the right foot; and desire to hold onto at the expense of others is bound to the left foot. The desire for personal greatness is often expressed through the head, and occurs when the head is not nested in the heart.

"The experience of the spiritual life is the process by which these five aspects of ego will, or collectively willfulness, are changed to willingness.

"Christian monastic communities developed three paths to transform the five strands of willfulness into willingness. These are reflected in the classic monastic vows of obedience, poverty and chastity. Let's look at each of these in turn.

"Obedience starts from the very practical realization that recognizes and experiences the existence of something higher than oneself. Obedience is the corollary of this recognition. If we experience that there is a higher authority, then we naturally obey that authority. We would not obey something if we did not intuit that it had more wisdom than we have. And we would be foolish to be aware that there was a higher source of wisdom than ourselves and then neglect to use it. Obedience then is a step into greater freedom, by having one's life guided by a source of greater knowing.

"You with me, Godfrey?" asked Father Hay. Godfrey nodded his head affirmatively.

"The vow of poverty is often misunderstood. The vow of poverty is about practicing inner emptiness. It is about letting go of attachments to our thoughts and feelings, and the objects upon which our thoughts and feelings are projected. The process of letting go is eloquently described by St. John of the Cross in *the dark night of the senses*. Once the soul is empty, then it is capable of receiving from a higher authority what is new and unexpected, both revelation and illumination."

"This is kind of a Buddhist idea isn't it?" asked Godfrey.

"Yes, Buddhism has some beautiful articulations of this idea."

"Okay," said Godfrey, "but I can tell you I'm not all that fired up to hear about chastity."

"You may like chastity better than you think," said Father Hay. "Chastity is the state of living from the heart. The heart lives only when it loves. A person is chaste no matter whether he or she is married or celibate, if they live from the heart. Chastity triumphs, on the one hand, over indifference, and, on the other hand, over aggression or violence."

"Godfrey, can you see how the classic Christian monastic vows are designed to turn our ego willfulness into soul willingness? It is not a matter of actually achieving the virtues of humility, poverty and chastity, which is probably impossible anyway, but because willingness is a state of being, it is the sincere effort to practice these virtues that counts. This state of being is one of receptivity to Grace and a conduit for Grace. From this state of receptivity to Grace, or purity of will, we both recognize and reflect the presence of the true, the beautiful and the good."

"I think I get it," said Godfrey, "and somehow the reference to truth, beauty and goodness reminds me of the Enneagram. Am I missing something?"

"Not at all," said Father Hay with a huge smile. "You hit the nail on the head. From the place of purification of will, or willingness, one has integrated the three Enneagram centers: mental, emotional and somatic; or as Plato would say: truth, beauty and goodness.  Obedience is the remedy for somatic ego attachment, chastity is the remedy for emotional ego attachment, and poverty is the remedy for mental ego attachment."

"Father, you have given me an enormous amount to consider. I think I am full for now."

Father Hay continued, "Here is a chart that sets all this out."

**Enneagram of Monastic Vows and Plato's Virtues**

"What we have talked about is important," said Father Hay. "But remember it is just words. What goes in the mind comes out of the mind. What goes into the heart through experience stays. So while it is extremely helpful to have this map of the spiritual terrain when we are on our journey, just remember it is only a map. The danger of having a map is that we can be seduced into thinking we can make some shortcut to get ourselves further down the road. This desire for a shortcut always arises; it is an ego willfulness assertion or action, and it is one that is bound to set us back. There are no human shortcuts on the journey of this life of the Spirit, but there are many shortcuts by Grace if we constantly open ourselves up by willingness to the mysteries that our life brings us.

"We will talk about contemplative practices in detail next time. They are what will open us to the mystery, not our head knowledge, which is usually about trying to control the first whiff of anything we don't understand. Okay, I can see I am starting to get wound up again. Let me let you get out of here."

Godfrey stood up to go and then turned back to Father Hay. "You know it is still next to impossible for me to talk to Jeff about Jesus. It is like when I just say the word 'Jesus' he immediately turns off."

"Remember we are Christians, followers of Christ, not Jesusians. Within that difference lies everything."

"I have one other rather personal question," said Godfrey.

Father Hay nodded for him to proceed.

"Did you have some kind of personal experience that got you started on this path willingness?"

Father Hay smiled. "Yes, I guess so. Like most good things in life it started with love, with love for a fellow priest. A man whom whenever I was around him, I was always about to laugh or cry. His name was, well still is, Father O'Donnell."

Father Hay smiled and looked at his watch. "Enough of this for now."

With that, Father Hay got up from his chair. He and Godfrey walked to the door. They parted with a silent hug. As Godfrey settled into his car, before he turned the key, he felt this strange sense of warmth, a feeling of openness almost like joy. He paused. Maybe, he thought, this was what willingness actually feels like.

# Chapter 4

Gordon Slade had not seen Joe Carroll since Slade got back from his honeymoon. With the baseball season opener just a couple weeks away, it was high time for the two friends to get together at their local near Fenway Park. He wanted to talk with Carroll about whether or not he should retire as a private investigator. Since he'd married Joy, Slade had lost his appetite for chasing unfaithful spouses. He didn't have a huge nest egg, but he thought maybe it was enough to retire on if he could also produce some other small stream of income.

Before they got married, Joy had been moonlighting in the fortune cookie business, writing the sayings in several specialty lines of new-style fortune cookies, including, Sufi, Kabbalah and Christian mystic, and these new lines seemed to be doing exceptionally well at restaurants and coffee shops. Slade and Joy had discussed going into this new, alternative fortune cookie business themselves. He was delighted with the thought of anything that would allow him to spend more time with Joy.

Slade believed he had some culinary genes somewhere on his Italian side, plus he had a cousin in a monastic order, who might be a valuable marketing contact. If Slade and Joy could produce a line of contemplative fortune cookies that monastics all over the world—and Baby-Boomer spiritual seekers— started buying, Slade might be able to create a fairly profitable business. He wanted to run all this by Carroll for a reality check.

Carroll was a professor of creative writing at one of the many local universities. One of the reasons Slade and Carroll were such good friends was that they both grew up in ethnic communities in Boston. In addition, despite the fact that Carroll was in academia, he was one of the most practical, down-to-earth guys Slade knew.

Not that creative writing programs were really academia, but at least they passed for that on the outside. Inside, if Slade could believe Carroll, graduate creative writing programs were simply refuges for adults with difficulty outgrowing childhood fantasies and adolescent narcissism. In addition, the teaching faculty at these institutions were even more stuck in adolescence than the students. Carroll told Slade he had only managed to survive in such a childish, ego-driven environment because an alumnus had heard one of Carroll's poems read at commencement and was so taken by it that he had given the university a large gift. The Dean, with hopes of a stream of such gifts, promptly appointed Carroll department chair.

This was a windfall for Carroll. Now a tenured professor, he was able to spend much more time at his favorite bar. Indeed, Carroll hadn't written a poem in years. As far as Slade knew, no alumnus had ever again given the school another dime because of a poem that Carroll had written. In fact, Carroll told Slade one night after their fourth round of single malt Scotches that several prominent alumni sent letters saying they would no longer give to the school after Carroll's first and last book of poems, <u>The Infanticide of Higher Education</u>, was published. For Slade, Carroll was just the kind of hard-drinking, straight-talking friend that he could not do without.

Plus, it was at Carroll's urgings that Slade had gotten off his duff and asked Joy to be his bride. Slade knew Carroll's persuasive advice to seek Joy's hand was the kind of advice that he could give to Slade, but could not, despite himself, incorporate into his own womanizing life. Still, Carroll would be the first to admit the double standard, and yet it did not diminish a bit the value of Carroll's friendship to Slade. Slade owed Carroll a lot.

The first round of double single malts was sitting on the table in the booth in the back corner of the room when Carroll arrived.

"Gosh, it's good to see you," said Slade, standing up from the booth and giving Carroll a bear hug before they both slid into the booth and raised their glasses together.

"*Long may your lum reek,*" said Carroll, after tilting up his glass, but before knocking back the better part of the double Scotch.

"What the hell does that mean?" asked Slade, grinning at his friend.

"I was trying to think of a good Irish blessing for you now that you're married," said Carroll. "This one is Scottish, but it seems perfectly suited for a married guy like you. Plus whatever is Celtic is all you Americans care about anyway. I don't know who got the notion to market Celtic as a brand in this country, but they sure scored a huge success."

"You have got to be the most cynical guy I know, Carroll. Don't you think it's possible that people just like Celtic stuff without there having been a marketing campaign?"

"I can see the delusion of marriage has not allowed your vision to clear, to provide sight or insight," said Carroll with a chuckle.

"I can tell you are probably going to hammer me for this idea," said Slade, "but let me run it by you."

"Take your time," said Carroll waving his arm "Where is the barmaid?  Service around here is like expecting someone to pay attention to what you are saying at a faculty meeting."

A mini-skirted young woman, just out of her teens, came over to the table. Immediately his impatience turned to a Carroll-esque mixture of honey and vinegar.

"Sweetheart, I know you are just doing this gig to idle away your time while you're waiting for that big break on Broadway, but if you could possibly stretch those beautiful arms back across the bar toward the bartender and gather up a couple more double single malt Scotches, I would roll on the floor and bark like a dog, or do most anything else you wanted me to do."

"Talk to the hand," said the barmaid waiving her palm at him, before she abruptly turned back toward the bar so that her ponytail whipped through the air in a defiant I-will-have-the-last-say gesture.

"Like most young women these days," said Carroll sighing. "Yes, beautiful bodies, but no ability to have any type of meaningful repartee. The sex might not be boring, but anything else with her would totally put you to sleep. Slade, you sure are lucky that you talked Joy into marrying you."

"You're right about that," said Slade. "And part of the reason that I wanted to talk with you comes because of that good fortune. I have lost all motivation for my work as a private detective. I would like to be able to spend more time with Joy. I have been thinking that I might retire and go into the alternative fortune cookie business with Joy. I wanted to get your thoughts on whether this would be a viable way to make a little income."

"Damn, you sure are smitten. It's a good sign, too, when you're talking like you are, even after you're married. Sure, you need to retire, that's a good idea. You've been doing the gumshoe stuff way too long anyway. I don't have a clue what the alternative fortune cookie business is. Sketch that out for me."

"Okay," said Slade. "You may remember that some time back Joy took on a second job, besides her librarian job, helping to write fortune cookie fortunes. The reason her boss needed somebody smart like Joy to help him was that he does fortunes like the little quotes that are on the boxes of Celestial Seasonings tea. I know he has introduced a line of Sufi fortune cookies, Kabbalah fortune cookies and Christian mystical ones. They have all been a huge commercial success."

"Doesn't that beat all," said Carroll. "I bet the yuppies just love to read these little whiffs of wisdom, which of course is the closest they'll ever get to any real wisdom in their lives, which you and I both know is only obtained through suffering, and certainly not by breaking open a cookie."

"Great, I can see that we will need to hire you as our marketing director," said Slade with a grin.

"Right, just as long as I don't have to work on commission. Where did that barmaid go?" asked Carroll looking out across the barroom. "Ready for another round?"

"I don't know why or how, but marriage somehow slows your drinking down. But, hey, don't let me hold you back. I'm just not ready for another one yet," said Slade.

"No problem, I will get us a couple more Scotches and if you dry up on me, I will do whatever suffering I need to do to take care of what you can't finish."

"I am serious, Joe, tell me what you think about the alternative fortune cookie business? Joy thinks we should do a line called contemplative fortune cookies."

"What do you mean, contemplative fortune cookies?" asked Carroll.

"I don't know exactly," said Slade. "But it is some kind of movement in Christianity that has been going on for a few years, just below the general radar. Joy has a lot of insight into spiritual development in our country and she thinks that we are at a critical time when progress by everyone on the spiritual front is essential. She believes that there have been three critical events in the development of spirituality in our country in the last hundred years. The first was the founding of Alcoholics Anonymous in 1935.

"This took spirituality out of the domain of the church hierarchy and into the lives of people struggling to survive a deadly disease. Essentially, this brought spirit back into matter. The second major event occurred in the early 1970s when knowledge about the Enneagram became public. This ancient map for guiding people on their spiritual journeys, that has been used in Sufi, Jewish and Christian mystical traditions for centuries, was now available for everyone. The third major event has occurred in the last ten or twenty years with the emergence of the contemplative movement. The contemplative movement is simply the return to ancient spiritual practices, such as centering prayer and *lectio divina*, which help people align the inner core of their being with God.

"Joy believes that the cumulative impact of these three events has the potential to save the human species from its increasingly individualistic competitive race for power and possessions at the expense of the human community."

Carroll suddenly got serious. "I have a good number of friends in AA, and I know some of them think that I probably qualify for membership. Yet, so far the illusion of the benefits of drinking outweigh the negatives of quitting. I know I am probably a candidate and I sure am glad it's there for those people who really need it.

"You told me all about the International Enneagram conference that you went to in Italy. I see the powerful potential it has for those willing to really use its insights. I am less sure about the impact of the contemplative movement. I do see the potential. If people are able to tease apart all the crazy Catholic baggage from the actual practices of mystics like Teresa of Avila and St. John of the Cross, then maybe there is promise in the contemplative movement to bring a new orientation to being human.

"I was reading an article recently about how the Christian population has shifted away from North America and Europe to Asia, Africa and Latin America. My theory about Christianity is that it really has three facets reflecting three different levels of need and consciousness: the first is what I call refugee Christianity—its appeal is to those in distressed societies, much as was true at the time of Christ with the Roman occupation in Palestine. The second is cultural Christianity—its appeal is to those in affluent societies like America and its content reflects more cultural values than Christian values. Inevitably it declines as it has in our country because it is simply a belonging group that embodies cultural mores, not real spiritual truth. The third occurs in what I call post-affluent societies—pockets in societies like ours where the meaninglessness of rampant materialism and ego-driven power, as exemplified on Wall Street, has resulted in back-to-the-spiritual-basics movements like we see historically with the Quakers and the Mennonites. I'm guessing this is the group that is energizing what you call contemplative Christianity."

Slade was stunned. Carroll could at times, seemingly without knowing it, be brilliant. His three facets of Christianity each reflected an overemphasis of one of three centers of intelligence of the Enneagram: refugee Christianity appealing to the bodily need for security; affluent Christianity appealing to the emotional need to belong and to have approval; and post-affluent Christianity appealing to the mental need to know truth. Slade was just about to ask Carroll whether he thought Christianity could ever possibly integrate all three in the same way that a few enlightened individuals seem to have been able to integrate these three centers, when Carroll continued.

"My gut feeling is that your beautiful wife, Joy, may be on to something. If you're actually going to get your fingers in the cookie batter dough, and if you can make them dark chocolate rather than bland little vanilla jobs, then I would say—*Go for it*. Let her do the mystical fortunes part. If you're in there making the dough and baking the cookies, then you may live an extra ten years. Unless you end up eating too much of your own stuff. The older we get the more we need good honest physical work if we wish to stick around. Oh, and by the way, I think you should call your brand of fortune cookies Delectio Divina."

Slade smiled realizing it was impossible for Carroll to be serious for too long. But Slade appreciated that Carroll gave the proposal serious thought and his thumbs up would not be given unless he really thought it was a worthwhile venture.

Slade could hardly wait to get back home to Joy. She would love Carroll's suggestion that the brand name for the fortune cookies ought to be Delectio Divina. For a long-lapsed Catholic, Carroll still knew the religious terrain.

# Chapter 5

Melissa had left the SOS's dark-retreat hermitage, near the Canadian border, in the middle of a brightly lit, full-moon night. Objectively, it was very hard to leave Blaine there alone without explanation. But subjectively, her own inner guidance told her overwhelmingly that this was what she should do. Weeks of sensory deprivation in the dark retreat took Melissa into the depths of a greater consciousness and expanded knowing. Her inspiration was that she needed to leave the hermitage before the CIA closed in and picked her up. The urging was so strong for her to leave immediately she left in the middle of the night. If the CIA got to Blaine before Dawson, it would be best if Blaine had no idea what had become of Melissa.

Once in Canada, a series of fortuitous events led her to a chance meeting with a professor at the University of McGill with whom she worked at the environmental organization where she was employed when she first went missing. He was on his way to Antarctica to participate in several scientific experiments to measure global warming. A lab assistant had dropped out of the research team at the last minute, and Melissa readily agreed to take her place. There could not possibly be a better place to hide out on the globe than a scientific colony a few degrees from the South Pole. The

Canadians used research space at the American Palmer Research Station on Anvers Island on the Antarctica Peninsula.

Before leaving North America, Melissa got in touch with Mother Mary, the Mother Superior of the Sacred Order of the Sisters of Mary of Magdala. Mother Mary gave Melissa specific instructions on how to continue her energy practices to further raise her consciousness. She was very frank in telling Melissa that the practices she would be doing, especially if she did them alone, in the sensory deprivation environment of Antarctica, could actually result in her leaving her body and not being able to come back. From where Melissa was on her spiritual journey such a possibility seemed of minor importance. Mother Mary agreed to send Melissa a number of esoteric spiritual classics about the mystical experiences of various saints for reading while she was in Antarctica.

Fortunately, Melissa was able to buy a Canadian passport on the black market in Montreal. The professor was a bit embarrassed that he remembered her last name as Dowling, rather than Darling as it appeared on her new passport. But all Melissa had to do was unveil her soft, warm, loving energy in his direction, and the very proper professor was unable to be self-critically embarrassed for long.

The research team traveled as a group on a chartered plane to Ushuaia, Argentina. Melissa had no problem leaving through Canadian customs and none entering Argentina. Since nobody really owned Antarctica, and all claims of ownership were suspended under the Antarctica Treaty, there were no customs to go through upon arriving at Anvers Island. She was essentially back on American soil, yet in the one place on the globe where she could do that without having to go through American customs, where her identity was right up at the top of the CIA watch list.

Melissa avoided experiencing the tiresomeness of the long flight by sinking into a deep contemplative state. Her colleagues, thinking she was asleep, left her alone, though they were somewhat amazed that someone might be lucky enough to sleep so much of the flight.

The living arrangements at the research station were dormitory style for the most part, however Melissa managed to get a single room so that she would have space alone to engage in meditation and other spiritual practices. Her agreement with the professor, when she took the place of the research assistant, was that while Melissa would contribute to the research team efforts, she would also have a substantial amount of time on her own. Given this setup, Melissa quickly saw her arrangement as ideal.

She felt a real connection with Terry Shaw, the young American woman who was in charge of the research station. Terry told her there were a couple of ice huts out on the continent that had been used recently by two American researchers, ostensibly studying the Ross seal, but were actually ideal for sensory deprivation experiments if Melissa ever wanted to use one.

This was exciting news. Having just spent several weeks in a sensory deprivation hermitage in the northern part of North America, Melissa was now going to have the opportunity to do the same thing in a location close to the South Pole. Her bodily vibration in meditation was fine-tuned enough now that she could tell from her first meditation at Anvers Island that the energy of the magnetic field in the southern hemisphere went in the opposite direction from the magnetic field in the north. She was extremely curious about the potential for this change in direction of the Earth's magnetic field to be something that would help her go deeper in a sensory deprivation retreat. She had read that the magnetic field in the Northern Hemisphere strengthened the left side of the brain and that the magnetic field in the southern hemisphere strengthened the right side of the brain. And, of course, it was the right side of the brain that carried the capacity for a person to enter fields of consciousness outside of their own.

As it was, Mother Mary warned her that there probably was not that much further for Melissa to go in her current incarnation in expanding her consciousness, and to be patient and go slow. However, a sensory deprivation retreat away from the research station had other advantages besides allowing her to continue her spiritual growth. Around the research station, Melissa had to be very careful to keep her energy cloaked, or those around her would have immediately detected the warm halo light of consciousness that glowed around her when her energy was not disguised. Even when her energy was fully cloaked, it was hard for others on the research team to be around Melissa and not feel excited and openhearted. This meant Melissa had to rebuff the awkward romantic attempts of more than one of the male members of the research team. She of course realized the men were not really attracted to her as much as to what her higher energy vibration stirred up in them, something that they had probably never before experienced.

Between the tedious detail of recording scientific measurements when she was working with the research team and the constant need to keep her energy veiled, Melissa was only at the Antarctica research station a few weeks when seeing Terry Shaw one day coming down the corridor she quickly hurried over to her.

"Terry, would it be all right for me to go out to one of the ice huts over on the mainland?" asked Melissa. "I know I haven't been here that long, but I already feel like I need a break from all the people. Is this common?"

"Well, not really," said Terry. "Usually it's the reverse, people get so tired of being with the same folks all the time that they want to get out of here and go where they can be with more people, not less. But I always thought you might be a little different in that regard." Terry smiled and looked at Melissa levelly.

"Well, I don't want to be any trouble," said Melissa, "but if it would not be too much of a strain on you as administrator of the station, I would love to go to one of the ice huts at the next opportunity. I can be excused for a few weeks from my duties on the research team."

"I think it can be arranged without any problem," said Terry, "but tell me, why are you interested in being out on the ice alone?"

Direct questions that might have put other people on the spot, were handled in a different way by Melissa. She always went for the truth. In fact, she was not really capable of proceeding any other way, but when she told a hard truth she also opened her energy field a bit. The medium was the message. Regardless of what the hard truth might be, receiving it in a wave of love meant that most people immediately accepted Melissa's answer without question.

"I want to have a chance to settle into a really deep meditation practice, and being out there in an ice hut would give me that opportunity," Melissa said as she opened her energy field to Terry.

Terry could not help but smile. Though she was young, she was a seasoned administrator. She inclined her head in a serious way. "I think I understand, Melissa, but one thing you need to know. I cannot allow you to engage in anything that would endanger your life. You are here on my watch, and I am responsible for your safety. If you choose to engage in any activities which put your life at risk, I will have you on a plane back to the good old U.S. of A. in no time flat. Do we understand each other?"

Melissa was surprised at the directness and authority with which Terry spoke. She knew that she would have to do her silent, sensory deprivation retreat on Terry's terms, but maybe that was the best anyway. She remembered Mother Mary's warning. "Yes," said Melissa. "I understand."

And then suddenly Melissa felt this energy rising up her spine in the core of her body and expanding in the center of her chest. She thought she should be used to it by now, but its freshness and immediacy were always surprising. This wave of love came out from her heart and surrounded Terry. And with it, Melissa's consciousness went deep into Terry.

Melissa was not surprised to find there a primal drive in Terry to do a good job and the need to look good in the process. Melissa could see the ego-driven part and she could also see the pure essence of Terry, which was just a beam of pure light from which came the grace that allowed her to work so well with crotchety old scientists, helping them get their research projects done.

Then Melissa noticed in the corner of Terry's heart center was this golden spot of pure longing. Gosh, thought Melissa, Terry is in love, and her beloved is a long way away from here. Melissa could see that Terry's love was deeply protected behind her competency and ability as an administrator; and, as far as Melissa could tell, knowledge of it was not shared with anyone else at the research station. But, there it was, as love always is, innocent and vulnerable.

As best she could, Melissa let love from her heart tell the tender spot of love in Terry's heart that all would be okay, that risking for love was always good. The intuitive message that Melissa got back was to thank Melissa and to tell her that while Terry's love was very tender it was also resilient, and fear would not prevent her from risking for this person she loved. Melissa gave a virtual hug, a sort of somatic *You go girl* and then began to withdraw her consciousness from Terry.

Terry's body gave a little instantaneous quiver and she re-focused on Melissa as if for a second she had been caught in a daydream.

"Okay," said Terry, "then we'll make it happen. Be down at the small meeting room near the kitchen tomorrow at ten a.m. and we will start putting you through the mandatory ice survival skills course required for anyone who is going to be out on the ice."

"Fabulous," said Melissa. "I will see you then."

The two women parted and Melissa headed back down the corridor toward her dorm room. She chuckled to herself thinking how crazy it was that the CIA was pursuing her for what just happened. Yes, she was able to experience what was happening deep within Terry. It was not like she was able to control Terry's thoughts as the CIA believed. Rather, and more significantly, she was able to read Terry's heart. But though Melissa could not, as the CIA thought, control another's longings, Melissa sure could use her love to give them a pat on the back.

The one thing the CIA seemed not to understand was that Melissa's ability only came about as a byproduct of her feeling this deep love for another. The entry point for the use of her psychic gift, if indeed it was a gift, mused Melissa to herself, was that it was only accessed at a higher vibration level that was synonymous with a deep love that was not under her ego's control.

Love is at its core a form of energetic knowing. Melissa's love came from such a depth it allowed her to know the thoughts of others. Those who felt Melissa's love energy experienced this wonderful sense of being loved, which is only possible when another person sees *you totally and accepts you just as you are*. Remembering what Will Dawson told her years ago in Afghanistan about Company training putting a premium on an officer always being in control made Melissa realize that the CIA would never be able to use the gift they were chasing her to get. Dawson told her how officers would spent weeks and months rehearsing an operation just to try to be able to control every possible variable. Accessing the gift she had, which involved letting go of will and a sense of self, was something that CIA officers spent years of training learning how *not* to do.

Melissa realized now how the CIA might have drawn the wrong conclusions about her abilities. When she was working with an anti-nuclear environmental organization and met with the leaders of New England First, an organization to promote the development of a new nuclear reactor in New England, everyone was surprised at the results of the meeting. Melissa opened up her energy field to the stressed-out businessmen and something within their consciousness shifted. They began to view the challenges of getting electric power in New England in a more nuanced way. They saw the accident in Japan from a fresh new perspective and went back to study all options. They came to the conclusion nuclear power was not the best or most economical choice. Melissa had not so much changed their minds as she had opened their hearts, so that they saw the power issue in a less dualistic way.

Melissa walked to the end of the corridor and opened the door to her room. She looked at the icon of Mary of Magdala that she had hung on the wall above her bed. Immediately the thinking voices in her head began to subside and she could feel this sense of peace at her heart center. She was doing exactly what she needed to be doing for some much larger reason than she understood. She was profoundly aware that the skill she was developing was about something much greater than her. Her job was simply to hone the skill and be ready when the weary world said, Y*es, let's learn more about this mystery called love.*

*          *          *

Terry Shaw was reading the *New York Times* on the Internet as she did every morning. She was used to reading articles about the chaos of the American political scene with the election of GOD, as President, followed a few months later by the tender offer of a Chinese company for GOD. For the most part now she just skipped over these articles. What was drawing her interest for the past two weeks was a series of articles about a woman named Melissa Dowling from Minnesota. Presumably, some former CIA agent had gone to the press and leaked this bizarre story of how the CIA was trying to capture Melissa because she had the ability to control the thoughts of others.

The story was tragic because the CIA, in trying to find Melissa, had harassed her mother to such an extent that the elderly woman died. Evidently, the former officer could not get this off his mind and told all. Melissa returned to Racine, Wisconsin for the funeral. Then she foiled what should have been a routine CIA operation to pick her up. Now nobody knew where she was.

Terry looked at the check-in chart that she kept above her desk regarding people out on the ice. Melissa had been out on the ice by herself for three weeks and knew nothing about the articles running in the *New York Times*. Terry thought the names Melissa Dowling and Melissa Darling were just too close. Besides, it was clear that Melissa was not much of a research assistant. Melissa told Terry directly that she wanted to be out on the ice by herself doing some kind of meditation. That sounded to Terry exactly like the kind of practice that would go hand-in-hand with mind reading. Terry also vividly recalled the time Melissa approached her in the corridor asking her about going out on the ice. It was an unusual encounter that left Terry feeling warm and happy inside, but also a little unsettled. Terry could not quite put her finger on what it was, but there was something very different about Melissa.

Melissa was scheduled to call Terry for her daily check-in in ten minutes. Terry decided that she would not say anything to Melissa about the *New York Times* Internet articles. There was no hurry. Melissa said that she wished to stay out in the ice hut as long as possible, but it was beginning to get colder and Terry would have to go get Melissa before long. When Melissa got back to the research station, they would have a heart-to-heart.

Terry wondered if she should say anything about Melissa to her boyfriend who was studying at the University of Arizona School of Consciousness Studies. Terry emailed Norris every day. Since there was not a lot of other news to talk about, she was usually telling him virtually everything that was going on at the station. But Terry hesitated to tell Norris about Melissa. For one thing, if there was any truth to the articles in the newspaper that the CIA really was looking for a Melissa, and that her Melissa Darling really was the Melissa Dowling, then just this possibility could change Terry's whole career.

Terry had been around the intersection of government and research academia long enough to know that with the wrong administration it only took a slight hint that one of your researchers was a security risk and all of a sudden government funding completely dried up. In these difficult economic times, funding for the Anvers Island Palmer research station on the Antarctica Peninsula was already tenuous. Who knew what the new GOD administration might do. The Holy Grail of running a research station was to do everything possible to minimize any negative impact on your funding. She did not want to give some bureaucrat in Washington any excuse to cut funding.

The easiest excuses were always the simplest ones, like the project or the personnel were too risky. Other than her natural good-heartedness, her understanding of the administrative need to have a clean record to avoid funding cuts was the reason Terry was so scrupulous in being sure that everybody who went out on the ice got back safely. That was exactly the concern which had allowed her to get to know Norris.

Of course, who Norris was, or who he might really be, gave her another reason not to bring up Melissa with him. He came down to Antarctica with his buddy as a Ross seal researcher, but then they really didn't do any research. He got stranded out on the ice in one of the ice huts after a storm.

Wait, thought Terry, that was it: Norris was out there doing the same thing that apparently Melissa is doing. "Holy Cow," she said aloud. "I don't know what exactly they're up to, but Melissa and Norris are doing something very similar."

What made who Norris really was even murkier was that before Norris could even finish his experiments, he was abruptly transferred from Antarctica to the University of Arizona Center for Consciousness Studies. Before he left Anvers, while he was recuperating from the frostbite, Terry had teased him mercilessly about working for the CIA. He had never denied her assertion, but always deftly bantered it away.

Just then the old-fashioned CB radio squawked to life. "Just checking in, per usual," said Melissa in a syrupy voice.

"Roger that," said Terry. "Melissa, are you doing okay? Are you eating properly and staying warm?"

"Sure," said Melissa.

"Okay, you behave out there. I will be out to check on you in a few days. If you're not doing well I will bring you right back.

Do you understand?"

"Gotcha," said Melissa. "Bye for now."

"You call any time if you need anything. Over and out."

Just talking to Melissa confirmed all of Terry's suspicions that Melissa was engaged in some kind of consciousness research and using herself as the guinea pig.  Terry felt a wave of exhilaration go through her. You didn't become a research station administrator in Antarctica without being a bit of an adrenaline junkie. She did not want to do anything to imperil funding, but this was going to be fun. The first order of business, before Melissa got back, was to find out more about Norris.

She had other reasons, too. Certainly to figure out his connection with what Melissa was doing out on the ice, but above all, to find out whether he was the man who might figure into her future. Terry realized that she and Norris were a lot alike in their ability to be engaging with others while keeping themselves very protected. Their relationship started getting traction when Norris was in the infirmary with frostbite.  Terry would come by several times a day to tease him. They each protected themselves with humor. But despite that, over the weeks of his recovery, their hearts began to open to each other and, for the first time in her life, she developed a real love and caring for a man.

*I got it*, thought Terry. *Maybe the best way to bring this all to a head is to email Norris and ask him, as strongly as possible, to come visit.*

She slid out the computer keyboard at her desk and pulled up her email. She typed in his address and began to compose her email.

*Dear Norris,*

*It has been almost six months since you were here. One of the things about being in this beautiful and barren environment is that there is plenty of time to think. You know how I like to distract myself by busyness, but more and more I have been thinking about us, the meaning of our relationship, the timing, the possibilities. The whole deal about what we must do if we want to risk it going somewhere.*

*I want you to come back down to Antarctica to be with me so that we can see where things might go. I'm not sure I really understand why you had to go back to school just when you did. But they did away with indentured servitude at least a century ago. Even if you have to skip a semester, come on down and be with me through the winter. There are a few more weeks during which travel here should not be a problem, before winter sets in hard. You can skip your spring semester, and, if things work out, I promise you I will go back with you so you can complete whatever you're doing at the University of Arizona. But you know when I signed up as the station manager of the research station I agreed that I would complete my tour. I cannot leave in midstream, there is simply no backup for me down here. Sweetheart, the ball is in your court. Please come be with me.   Love, Terry*

Terry clicked on the save as draft button. The letter seemed right, but she would think about it. She was not used to asking for what she wanted in her personal relationships, though she did it very effectively as an administrator. The truth was she had never felt much desire for something in her personal life that involved a man.

There seemed to be little downside to sending it. All he could do was say *no*. At the least maybe he would get off the dime and tell her why he had left her in the first place, to rush off to the University of Arizona to school. He was way past the usual grad school age and she was sure he hadn't gone to something called a School of Consciousness Studies to research the Ross seal.

She pulled up her draft email and hit Send.

# Chapter 6

"See you at CJ's?" asked Dawson, as he and Norris left their last class on Friday afternoon.

"Absolutely, great timing," said Norris. "I should be there in thirty minutes."

"Okay, I'll try to score our booth in the back. See you shortly."

Dawson headed directly for Calamity Jane's. Though he and Norris had developed a friendship, Dawson was uneasy about their upcoming conversation. He felt uncertain about the new ways of trusting he was trying to develop since he left the Company. Suddenly, his well-honed sense of paranoia got the best of him and he could feel his stomach churning. After all, he was on the CIA's wanted list. Norris seemed like so many other Company officers that Dawson had known during his tenure at the CIA.

Dawson did not think that Norris was at the University of Arizona to shadow him. If he had been, Dawson would have been picked up last semester. But, if Norris was a CIA officer, Dawson needed to know. There were big implications. He would need to tell Father O'Donnell. So Dawson got back in touch with Rat, the Berlin hacker who helped him assist

Melissa in her Minnesota escape.

Rat previously set up a chat room for Dawson to connect covertly with him. It only took Rat a short while to get back to Dawson after he inquired about Norris. Dawson's suspicions were correct. Norris was a Company officer, who was assigned to work on a project code-named 1776. This project sent him to Antarctica to engage in experiments to learn how to control his energy field and the thought fields of others. From there, he was re-assigned to the University of Arizona Center for Consciousness Studies to supplement his field experience with an academic background. Norris was just about the same age as Dawson and, like Dawson, had completed twenty years of service with the Company. This was the normal retirement age for a field officer. Norris was not an officer who ever wanted to move on up the administrative ladder, where the prospects of a longer career were. Apparently Norris was asked to extend his time with the Company to complete work on the 1776 project and he agreed.

Rat did not know how much Norris knew about the Company's efforts to find and detain Melissa, but Rat was aware that knowledge of this effort was recently leaked to the newspapers. Rat's advice to Dawson was to be very careful of any interaction with Norris.

When Norris arrived at Calamity Jane's, Dawson had already staked a claim on the back booth and there were a couple of double Wild Turkey bourbons sitting on the table.

Norris slid into the seat opposite Dawson, picked up a glass and raised it in a prayer-like gesture and took a long sip. "We sure have covered a lot in class this week," said Norris. "Have you been able to keep up with all that reading?"

"From what I have read the experimental evidence seems to be in—that meditation practices alter both the structure and the functioning of the brain," said Dawson with a gesture that seemed to imply, *of course everyone knew that.*

"The information that your cerebral cortex thins out just like your hair, was not too much comfort," said Norris, as he reached up and ran his left hand through his thinning hair-line.

Dawson smiled. "We are used to the 'use it or lose it' philosophy, but I never knew until now that use it meant meditation. The experiments by Dr. Sara Lazar at Mass General Hospital in Boston seem pretty conclusive."

"Yes," said Norris. "That was amazing. Her experiments showed that people who meditate lose less gray matter than those who don't, and I thought it very significant that those who meditate have positive changes in the brain stem area that's involved in the production of serotonin. Her research seems to bear out some other less scientific studies that show that people who meditate are less likely to have depression than those who don't."

"Of course the $64,000 question is which types of meditation pinpoint which specific areas of the brain in a more positive way. The scientist who figures that out will have it made, or maybe not if she can't figure out how to put it in a pill."

Dawson laughed. "You would think with my efforts to stimulate my right and left prefrontal cortex in the biofeedback lab I would be getting less cynical, but I guess I have a long way to go."

"What strikes me is the paradoxical nature of how meditation improves the brain structure," said Norris. "The evolutionary problem seems to be that the emotional part of the limbic brain is designed like Velcro for negative events and Teflon for positive ones. This survival instinct has given us a tenacious memory for dangers and sharpened our sense of anxiety with any slight appearance of a threat. But, the research is showing that those folks who meditate actually tend to have more enlivened emotional lives, and at the same time, they aren't controlled by their emotions. They seem to feel things vividly by having contact with the limbic system, but not so much so that they are compelled to act on their feelings as opposed to simply experience them. All this sure rings true for me, Dawson. It was not until I fell into this relationship with my girlfriend down in Antarctica that I had any notion that our emotions were good for anything but warning signals. What a surprise for me to learn, when I'm around Terry, I can actually enjoy my emotions. I had thought that a sarcastic sense of humor was the highest form of emotion I could feel."

Suddenly Norris looked startled. "You know, I had not thought about this before, but at the time I met Terry I was meditating for long periods of time for the first time in my life. Geez, this is getting a little heavy. Want another drink?" Norris looked around for the waitress.

"Sure," said Dawson. The conversation was edging into what Norris said he wanted to talk about when they had left class: his Antarctica girlfriend. But at that moment, Dawson realized all he could think about was that he could not wait to tell Father O'Donnell about one piece of research they just learned. One of the specific areas activated by different meditation practices was the dorsolateral prefrontal cortex. The interesting thing he had discovered from the research, which would intrigue Father O'Donnell, was that not only was this area of the brain activated by different forms of meditation and Tibetan Buddhist practices using images, it was also activated by chanting the Psalms, one of the mainstays of monastic life for centuries. But his life at the monastery was not something to share with Norris.

"You know," said Dawson, "the other thing that struck me was the degree to which these scientists have charted the neurobiology of narcissism. It seems to be defined by this idea of how we experience our sense of self. For most folks it's a narrative focus; I'm this kind of person, and I construct a story that I tell myself about what happens to me. This narcissistic sense of self is supported by certain brain structure activity. On the other hand, there is another way to experience the self called the *experiencing self.* From the perspective of the *experiencing self,* it's not about a particular story, or particular positive or negative attributes that tells me who I am, but an experience of identity through what is being experienced moment to moment. The research data seems to confirm that meditation practices support this second kind of identity, which is less narcissistic. Remember that the professor said that everything that goes wrong in a couple's relationship results from our experience of our identity from the first perspective. If we miss some emotional cue and our girlfriend is in a narrative sense of self, then she gets her feelings hurt. So tell me, Norris, what's up with the girlfriend? Have you missed a cue?"

Norris did not respond immediately. "Amazing how all this scientific research we are studying can be acutely personally relevant. Well, the cue is my girlfriend Terry wants me to leave school before the next semester starts and come to Antarctica to be with her during their winter. Basically, to see if our relationship might go anywhere. Dawson, this is the first woman in my life I have ever felt anything special for. I am forty-nine years old and I'm not sure how many opportunities I will get at the chance to have a really meaningful intimate relationship.

"It's for sure I am totally inexperienced on how to proceed. I don't usually talk to others about stuff that is this personal, but it seems like I am at a crucial crossroads and I appreciate your listening to me. What's your advice, my friend? And one more thing—this is a big deal in many ways. I would have to quit my job that is underwriting my being in school. But again, the economics are not critical; I am eligible to retire, and maybe it's more than time for a change in my work life."

Norris began to reflect on the reason he could not go to Antarctica, which he could not express to Dawson. He knew what happened to CIA officers who tried to leave the Company in mid-assignment. Somehow their post-CIA careers met innumerable obstacles. He could walk out on the plank of discovering the meaning of an intimate relationship with Terry and overnight the Company could make his life so difficult that even if Terry fell for him, she wouldn't want to stay around. His new section chief was one of the new GOD zealots—little chance he would be dealt with kindly if he up and went back to Antarctica, unless somehow he could break open the Melissa case so he would deserve an honorable exit.

Dawson remained quiet. From his work with Father O'Donnell, Dawson realized that he could be most helpful to Norris by listening and not giving advice. Some time passed.

"I'm afraid I'm not a good person to give you advice about relationship matters," said Dawson. "I have a spectacularly unsuccessful record in that area myself. But what I can tell you from my experience is I failed on a couple of occasions to pursue women with whom I felt a real heart connection; and I think it's fair to say that my failure resulted in nothing but heartache and loneliness. If we have learned anything about the limbic brain, it is that we are an inter-relational species. I can't say this because I've done it right, but it is my belief that the failure to follow my heart at critical points in my life resulted in my living a much narrower, constricted life."

"Thank you for telling me what I already know," Norris said grimly. "Don't get me wrong, I really mean it in a non-sarcastic way. I really need to hear what I know, because I am so unused to living life from that heart perspective." Norris sighed. "Don't guess it would be a very meaningful decision if it wasn't hard."

"I expect you're right about that," said Dawson. "You may not want to wait around till next semester when we take that course on the neurobiology of compassion. Reminds me of the old joke about the man getting up to heaven and he sees two directional signs: one points toward heaven, the other points to a lecture about heaven."

"Yes," said Norris. "I'd be going to the lecture too. Maybe I ought to try to learn about my life from living my life this time, rather than trying to control everything under the illusion I can create the kind of life I think I want."

Dawson raised his glass. "Novel idea. Go for it."

Norris knocked back the remainder of the bourbon in his glass. He nodded at Dawson as he thought to himself, *I think maybe I would if only I could figure out a way.*

# Chapter 7

This was just the excuse Rat needed. The new information he had received from Dawson was so important he would have to go back to the convent in northern Sweden and talk with Blaine about it. Rat missed Blaine and Aasia.

After packing the essentials he needed for travel, which consisted primarily of three laptops, Rat decided he might as well go by way of the town in northern Germany where Manuelito was staying. Perhaps the young Navajo could get leave from the Abbot for a little road trip.

Man had been working hard at his spiritual warrior practices at the monastery in Germany and he was deeply homesick for the American Southwest. While he loved coming to Europe to look after Blaine's safety, once he was relocated away from her, the strangeness of the new European environment weighed heavily on him. The weather was miserable and he was just not used to spending so much time indoors. He was delighted when Rat showed up at the monastery, asking him to go visit Blaine and Aasia at the Swedish convent. The novitiate master, knowing how homesick Man was, readily obtained the Abbot's consent for Man to travel with Rat.

Rat loved surprises more than anything else, so of course he showed up at the convent without letting anyone know ahead of time. Blaine and Aasia were delighted to see him, as were the rest of the women there. They were all especially glad to see Man and Ooljee.

It did not take long before Rat found a way to speak privately with Blaine.

"Rat, it is so great to see you. And, I am guessing you are up to something. What brings you back up here to this isolated place?" asked Blaine.

"*Liebste, du siehst schön*," said Rat. "I could not stand going any longer without seeing you."

Blaine looked at Rat ruefully. "I expect it is thoughts of darling Aasia that have contributed to your journey to see us, but I can tell something else is up. Give me the scoop."

It was hard for Rat to be serious about anything. Still, he got right to the point. "I had not thought it necessary to go into detail with you earlier, but before you escaped from Canada and made your way to Europe, Melissa showed up again and I was able to help her leave Canada. Fortuitously, it happened that there was a Canadian scientific expedition leaving to go to Antarctica. Melissa was able to go as a part of this research team. It just seemed like the easiest way to get her out of North America and the safest place on the planet for her to hide out."

This was a lot for Blaine to take in. She had not even been sure that Melissa was alive. She nodded for Rat to continue.

"Melissa has been down in Antarctica for awhile. Your old friend Will Dawson, after he went back to Father O'Donnell's monastery, was sent by Father O'Donnell to attend the University of Arizona Center for Consciousness Studies. Dawson meets this guy named Norris, who I discovered is a CIA officer. For some reason, the CIA sent him to school there, probably, come to think of it, for the same reason that Father O'Donnell sent Dawson. Anyway, Norris is there. He's not assigned to find Dawson, and does not know that Dawson is the former CIA officer that the agency is searching for. Searching for, we suspect, in order to find Melissa.

"So now, Dawson has become good friends with this guy Norris and Dawson finds out that Norris has a girlfriend, Terry Shaw, who is the station master in Antarctica where Melissa is. As you know from your experience with Dawson, authentic relationships for Company officers are always problematic. Either because of this problematic trait, or in spite of it, Norris is considering going to Antarctica to be with his girlfriend."

Blaine nodded. Gosh, she thought, a lot has been going on while I have been pursuing healing and consciousness work at the convent.

Rat continued. "Oh, another thing you might not know is that the CIA's search for Melissa, and the fact that they apparently caused the death of her mother, have both been leaked to the American press. There is a possibility that Terry Shaw has put together who Melissa really is from these press reports. Regardless, if Norris gets to Antarctica, her identity will be clear to him, and even if he has left the Company, he may be under some obligation to let them know. So that is the reason I have come to see you. Once again Melissa's freedom and well-being are imperiled and we need to figure out what we need to do to help her. Of course, any excuse to come see you is more than enough to bring me." Rat wrinkled his nose at Blaine in his most beguiling rat-like manner.

"Oh, Rat, quit acting so.....uh....rat-like. This is serious. And, I don't have a clue what we should do, but obviously we need to get Sister Maria involved. This is really something for The Sacred Order of the Sisters of Mary of Magdala to figure out, not us. Let's go see if we can find her now." The two got up from where they were sitting in the library and headed down the corridor toward Sister Maria's office.

When they approached the door to the lounge, they glanced in and saw that Man and Ooljee were holding court with all of the younger nuns. Rat and Blaine paused and looked in. It appeared they were again playing the Navajo dog-version of spin the bottle. The young sisters were sitting in a circle around Man and Ooljee. One of the sisters would ask a question. Man would then ask Ooljee the question in Navajo. Ooljee would answer the question by raising his paw and counting on the floor, one for yes or two for no. Each answer by Ooljee was followed by gales of laughter from the sisters. After Ooljee's last answer, the young sister who asked it blushed a bright crimson.

"Rat, only in a place like this would you get sex ed from a Navajo dog," said Blaine with a sigh. "But somehow it all seems to work here. It would sure be a lot more fun to stay and watch this, but I guess we better go talk with Sister Maria."

Rat mumbled something in German and nodded affirmatively.

They walked on down the corridor and knocked on the door of Sister Maria's office.

"Come in."

"Rat, welcome, it is so nice to have you come visit us. We have not forgotten your help in safeguarding Blaine and Melissa." Sister Maria smiled. "As much as it is a pleasure to see you, I have been wondering to what do we owe this pleasure."

"Right you are," said Rat. "I have just been explaining the situation to Blaine, who, under your care, gets more beautiful each day." And he smiled at Sister Maria and twitched his nose in an absurd way. She did not return his smile.

"As I expect you know, Melissa escaped to a research station in Antarctica. I have just learned that a CIA officer is on his way to that research station to visit his girlfriend. Given the press stories about Melissa, there is little doubt in my mind that once he arrives, her cover is going to be blown. My belief is that Melissa needs to leave immediately. The real problem is communicating with Melissa. I know this is my specialty and I'm usually very good at finding a way to communicate with someone. But I'm afraid I'm stumped."

"I can see the problem," said Sister Maria. "And this is the kind of problem I don't think we can solve alone. I believe we need to bring the Mother Superior of our Order into the loop and get her direction on how we should proceed."

"Right," said Rat. "What I have always said: 'if it isn't one thing it's a mother'."

Blaine could tell that Rat's unquenchable need to add humor to everything was about to get on Sister Maria's last nerve. "We will leave that to you," said Blaine. "I think Rat will be delighted to try to help us in any way the Order feels is needed. Won't you?" she said turning toward him.

Rat did another rat-like grin at Blaine and gradually modulated it into a grimace for Sister Maria.

With that, Blaine and Rat stood up and left Sister Maria's office, leaving the matter of rescuing Melissa to her and a higher authority.

Except for the slight grimace, Rat seemed totally unfazed by Sister Maria's reaction to his humor. "Let's head back down to the lounge," he said. "Maybe we can get in on the rest of the spin-the-Ooljee game."

Blaine took his arm as they walked down the corridor. Rat sure was a dear, and he definitely was one of a kind.

In the lounge they saw Aasia seated on the other side just outside of the circle of young sisters who were seated on the floor. Rat made a beeline for Aasia with Blaine in tow. He would not be able to be away from Berlin for long, Blaine thought, but while he was here with her and Aasia he clearly was in his version of cheese heaven.

*     *     *

The next day after lunch, and after getting permission from Sister Maria to take the afternoon off, Blaine invited Man to go on a walk. Man and Ooljee were delighted with the invitation. Even at this northern latitude, there were signs of spring in the air.

Blaine knew most of the trails near the convent, but she was so delighted at being with Man and Ooljee, and having the whole afternoon free, that they had soon hiked far beyond where she had ever gone. The landscape was rugged and beautiful. Their hike was invigorating, though the harshness of the Swedish winter lingered on the land even in early spring.

Man was the first to experience a message in their encounter with the presence of the natural world. "There is something about this land that seems to press for a decision," he said. "There is an insistence. Maybe it comes from the harsh winter, this sense that there may not be enough time. Quite a contrast with the open spaces in the Southwest, where the very openness seems to say to me, *Man you have all the time you need for everything.* I wonder what this northern land is asking us to discover?"

"I think I understand what you are saying," said Blaine. "I too feel this urgency coming from the land, but for the life of me I don't know what the question is. Do you know what I mean?"

"The urgency is very real to me," said Man. "I think I know the question it is asking. I feel the pull to go back to the Southwest. We see our land as our mother, and I have been away too long from the nurturing the land gives me. But I am concerned, Blaine. I don't want to leave you here in Europe. You might need my help."

They paused by a stream charged with fresh spring runoff. Blaine turned to look at Man. His black hair was even longer now, cascading over his shoulders. Her gaze into his dark eyes seemed to take her into the innermost reaches of her own soul. As she looked at him, she felt this wave of heat move from the base of her spine upward. She remembered the heart-opening exercises that she had spent hours practicing at the convent. As soon as the heat got to the center of her chest, she flung herself off the cliff of her own ego as she had been taught to do.

There is probably no way a young man can resist the full outpouring of love from a woman who surrenders a cloistered heart. Especially, a woman who has been abused sexually when she was young like Blaine—who, even after much healing still carried a strange erotic magnetism left by her wounding. When Blaine put her hands around his neck and pulled him toward her, Man did not resist. They moved from a slow caressing tenderness to what from a distance might have looked like a wrestling match and then back again to a slow dance of touch. If the ground everywhere around them was not so wet, it is impossible to know where the ballet of undammed passion would have taken them.

As it was, they were soon shirtless, and only much later did Blaine realize that never for a second had she experienced the dreaded shame from having the scars on her torso from her cutting seen by Man.

In their total presence with each other, time flew. Suddenly, it became apparent that they would need to turn around and start the hike back if there was to be any chance of getting to the convent by dinnertime.

For Blaine, the simple act of turning to go back, the change of direction, was hard. It threatened their idyllic, in-the-moment experience with the question of what would be the ongoing meaning of their shared intimacy.

Blaine took a deep breath. "Man, I want us to figure out a way that we can be together."

Man looked at the slim young woman by his side with her collage of scars and tattoos. He could feel the heat coming toward him from the center of her chest and off the top of her head. He felt simultaneously the warm sun on his skin and the cool breeze. He recognized that this was also how he felt inside. He wanted to share the heat of Blaine's passion and yet he felt a strong command to heed the cool call of his warrior training.

"Blaine, I want to but I don't know that the time is right. It is not that I think it is wrong. I just don't know if it is right. It is the teaching of our wise Singers that any big decision in life involves more than just the person making the decision. To get a larger perspective, it is necessary to seek wise counsel. I shall go back and meet with Father O'Donnell and ask him to help me discern what I should do. Do you understand?"

"Yes," said Blaine. And that was all she could say, feeling the tension of the wisdom of this young man and the compelling urgency of her passion for him.

Man smiled. "You should do the same thing. Seek counsel from Sister Maria about where your future lies. It is one thing to come with me to be with me, but that will not be enough. There is not much computer software work on the rez."

Blaine nodded. They both needed to understand more deeply the arcs of their individual lives. Once they had this understanding, they would be able to discern if their arcs intersected.

# Chapter 8

Dawson was feeling nostalgic. This would be the last time he and Norris would get together at Calamity Jane's, as they had done after class on a regular basis for over two semesters.

Norris was anything but nostalgic. He was tense with anxiety and excitement. He resolved to play the Company the same way it played everyone else. He would entice it with information, to give himself time to explore his relationship with Terry. As soon as he got to Antarctica he would let his section chief know he had returned there quickly to follow a lead that might break open the case to find Melissa. By the time he followed up on the alleged lead, winter would have closed in and he would be ice-bound with Terry until Spring.

Playing the Company's own game was the easy part. The tough nut was himself. He was feeling for the first time in his life that he was using his intention to step into his own life. Having never done this before, he was scared, and that was hard for a man to admit who was a twenty-year veteran of the CIA and prided himself on being able to walk into the middle of any kind of situation no matter how potentially hostile.

Once he was in Antarctica he would resume the meditation

practices he had been required to do, when he was first sent there. Maybe the Company would be excited about this and throw him into the briar patch by leaving him alone. He realized that it had been his meditation practice which allowed him to experience his own emotions in a way he never had experienced before. And those emotional feelings for Terry Shaw were what this trip was all about.

He only had a brief window to get there between the end of his classes and the Antarctica winter. His arrangements were quickly made. He would fly from Tucson to Dallas, Texas and from there to Santiago, Chile. After an overnight in Santiago, he would catch a four-hour flight to Ushuaia, Argentina and from that drab and rainy town he had passage on the last supply ship for the year going to Anvers Island.

"You know, Dawson," said Norris, "It is very odd. I don't think I would have ever made up my mind to do this if it hadn't been for that research on obsessive-compulsive disorder."

"Say a little more about that," said Dawson, as he lifted his glass. Both men settled into their habitual habitat in the last booth in the back of Calamity Jane's.

"The research started way back in the mid-80s trying to figure out how to treat obsessive compulsive disorder. The researchers figured out that our mind is a non-local thing and that we can use it to control how the brain thinks and to heal the brain when it has defective circuits."

"Yes," said Dawson. "I am still trying to wrap my brain around that fundamental principle that our mind, or, if you will, our attention, is not a material thing. Actually, it seems intuitively obvious, but it is an impossible perspective from the frame of reference of Newtonian cause and effect. On the other hand, if you apply orthodox quantum physics to biology, it's a no-brainer."

"Right," said Norris, grimacing at Dawson's attempt at humor.

"The quantum Zeno effect is the first cousin of Heisenberg's uncertainty principle, and says that when you observe something repeatedly you stabilize the thing that is being observed. I know we're going to have this on the exam tomorrow. Tell me if I have got it right. Once you stabilize your observation of the repeated hand-washing, for example of OCD, you can recognize that the urge to hand wash is a function of a broken brain neural circuit. You then can disregard this information and change the focus of your attention onto something else beside the defective information feed. Over time your symptoms of OCD subside."

"Bingo," said Dawson. "Now tell me how learning this helped you make the decision to go to Antarctica to see your girlfriend? I'm thinking the decision had to do with another vital organ, besides the brain, that depends on having a large blood flow."

"You sound like how I would've thought a year ago. But, it's really very simple. The class has taught me to not believe everything I think; and not to act on everything I feel. I have to evaluate the source of the thought or feeling data before responding involuntarily as I've done all my life. My brain doesn't give me clearly wrong data, like the OCD patient, but it does give me skewed data. My brain has told me all my life that it is unsafe to get into a close relationship with someone of the opposite sex. That they are unsafe and I'll get hurt. The brain data has always said, *sure, sex is fine*; and, thank goodness, sex for most of us guys is easy enough without forming any emotional attachment.

"But after that experience of long periods of meditation the first time I was in Antarctica and learning what we have learned here, my mind is now able to analyze that data and see that it is skewed. I don't need to make decisions based on it. And, I'm damn well not. Let me buy you another drink, Dawson."

"Absolutely, let's make it official by drinking to your trip and your girlfriend," said Dawson. And as soon as the barmaid had re-filled their glasses, the two men solemnly raised their glasses in the air.

"You just sketched a beautiful answer to the essay question we will probably get. The difficulty for me is what you call this thing that is non-local: the mind, or the focus of attention, or an energy field or God. I realize this language conundrum has been a way to avoid the huge impact and responsibility of this knowledge by my getting hung up on what the label for it is. Watching you come to the decision to take greater responsibility for your life, by consciously choosing to make a decision based on understanding how your brain operates is a powerful lesson for me. The hard reality is that once you know about this stuff, the old fashioned word "responsibility" brings it home much better than the wimpy term the professor used, calling it self-directed neuroplasticity. Norris, I will be eternally in your debt." And Dawson again raised his glass in tribute to his friend.

"I am realizing that it is an extremely subtle understanding," said Norris. "You could tell from the questions of a couple of those New Age types that always sit on the front row. They are thinking that this explanation says that your mind creates your own reality. I am glad the professor went out of the way to stress that this is a mistaken view. What this view does say is that your mind gives you choices to make about what you focus your attention on and this influences the way you experience reality. You kinda create your experience and you kinda don't."

Dawson nodded, but he did not reply. He was thinking of Father O'Donnell. 'Kinda creating it and kinda not' was a sort of country music sounding version of exactly the kind of non-dual perspective Father O'Donnell had been trying to get Dawson to understand. Well maybe, just maybe, thought Dawson, I am beginning to get it.

*      *      *

Father O'Donnell was indeed gratified with the progress that Dawson was making. Father O'Donnell kept telling Dawson he was making great strides, but it was harder for Dawson to see his own gains as opposed to the changes those around him could see.

The training regimen that Father O'Donnell set up for Dawson had three aspects. First, there was the daily focus on contemplative practices. Second, there was a focus on gaining a perspective of learning from the heart—that is, learning not to have knowledge for power and control, but learning from open surrender. And, of course, the third focus always took Dawson back to the trip he and Father O'Donnell had made to Turin, Italy to the International Enneagram conference. Despite all that Dawson had learned at the conference, Father O'Donnell was convinced that continued study of the Enneagram was essential for Dawson to be able to obtain the three great gifts of Enneagram studies: awareness of when he was stuck in his false-self, awareness of when he was living into and surrendering to the virtue of his type, and knowledge of when he was integrating the three centers of knowing: mental, emotional, and somatic.

Father O'Donnell was delighted to get new little tidbits from what Dawson was learning, such as how a scientific study showed that the recitation of the Psalms produced a positive improvement in the neural circuitry of the brain.

But so far after two semesters, Dawson's studies had not produced any breakthrough insights to give to Father O'Donnell, which might suggest new practices that would improve the classical monastic program of training in mystical Christianity.

Father O'Donnell's reaction was not to be discouraged by the lack of new training methods or materials, but to push forward even harder with the existing program. Always Father O'Donnell pushed forward with love. Always he was so delighted when Dawson returned to the monastery for the weekend.

After the semester was over and Dawson saw Norris off on his trip to Antarctica, Dawson made the long drive back to the monastery feeling like his best friend had graduated from elementary school while he was repeating the last grade over again. Once he got back to the monastery, the sheer delight in Father O'Donnell's eyes when he greeted Dawson with a big bear hug gave Dawson a feeling, which had eluded him all his life—that he did belong.

"Father, I said goodbye to my buddy Norris this morning. I took him to the airport and put him on the plane headed to Antarctica. I know this is bad news for Melissa, but it sure has been remarkable to watch the change in Norris over the past two semesters. It has been a hundred and eighty degree-turnaround. He has gone from Mr. Cool, CIA officer, to someone who really cares about another human being in an emotional way. I never could get him interested in a Christian mystical path to raise his consciousness, but after his experience in deep meditation on his first trip to Antarctica, he continued to keep up his meditation practice at the Zen Center in Tucson."

"It is so good to see you, Brother Isaac," said Father O'Donnell, addressing Dawson by his order name. Father O'Donnell with his arms extended on each of Dawson's shoulders looked at him intently with his piercing blue eyes. "I think I would have really liked your friend. And I have heard from the SOS Mother Superior that she is planning to communicate the danger of Norris' visit to Melissa by prayer. Once I get the schedule from her we can join in the effort. Should be a real opportunity for you to see whether this prayer stuff works."

Well, that is interesting news, thought Dawson, that some spiritual-type effort is being made to communicate with Melissa. "You know I enjoy participating in these prayer practices," said Dawson. "But I must admit that I am really scared for Melissa. The thought of actually having to depend on prayer to let her know what's going on seems a bit dodgy to me."

Father O'Donnell smiled. "I am afraid that for most people prayer is sort of a nice-to-have plaything, sort of like a little parsley garnish on the entrée of your life. Nice to have it there, but most people just leave it on their plate. Brother Isaac, as your training gets deeper, you will see that prayer is the main course."

"I was afraid you would say something like that," said Dawson. "The good news—or the bad news—I am not sure which it is, is that I think I am far enough along that I see there are no real alternatives. Either this stuff we have been working on works, and will help us find a way to succeed, or competition among people will not only wreck any viable means of human self-governance, but ultimately wreck the planet itself. Not so hard to choose a diet of prayer under these circumstances."

"Brother Isaac, there has actually been a lot written on the efficacy of foxhole prayer and how it can change willfulness to willingness. Sometimes we need an emotional jarring to get our internal compass reset. I guess I believe it doesn't matter how we get there just as long as we do. And in that regard I want us to focus more on some of the Enneagram material this weekend."

"Sure," said Dawson. "The Enneagram material is rich stuff. What else do we need to cover about it? Professor Gallagher's presentation at the conference which showed the Enneagram logic of the Lord's Prayer and the Sermon on the Mount was incredible. I cannot see how anyone would not be convinced that Jesus was a master teacher of transformation of consciousness using the knowledge we call the Enneagram."

"Brother Isaac, you know it's not so much about learning information, as about becoming centered in a new perspective. Here, I have a handout for you on some of the key ideas from Prof. Gallagher's presentation: the Enneagram of the Lord's Prayer; the Enneagram of the Sermon on the Mount; the Enneagram of Spiritual Discernment based on Galatians 5; and, the Enneagram of Love based on Corinthians 13.

# Enneagram of the Lord's Prayer

**Amen - Our Father** — 9

**For thine is the kingdom, and the power, and the glory, for ever** — 8

**Which art in heaven** — 1

**And lead us not into tempation, but deliver us from evil** — 7

**Hallowed be thy name** — 2

**Forgive us our trespasses, as we forgive our trespassors** — 6

**Thy kingdom come** — 3

**Give us this day our daily bread** — 5

**Thy will be done on earth, as it is in heaven** — 4

# Enneagram of the Sermon on the Mount

Blessed are the poor in spirit: for theirs is the kingdom of heaven — 9

Blessed are ye, when men shall revile you, and persecute you, and shall say all manner of evil against you falsely, for my name sake. — 8

Blessed are they that mourn: for they shall be comforted. — 1

Blessed are they which are persecuted for righteousness' sake: for theirs is the kingdom of heaven. — 7

Blessed are the meek: for they shall inherit the earth. — 2

Blessed are the peacemakers: for they shall be called the children of God. — 6

Blessed are they which do hunger and thirst after righteousness: for they shall be filled. — 3

Blessed are the pure in heart: for they shall see God. — 5

Blessed are the merciful: for they shall obtain mercy. — 4

# Enneagram of Spiritual Discernment
## Galatians 5:22

Peace
**9**

Gentleness **8**

**1** Long-Suffering

Temperance **7**

**2** Meekness

Faith **6**

**3** Goodness

Joy **5**

**4** Love

# Enneagram of Love
## I Corinthians 13

Love is kind.
Love never fails.
**9**

If I have the gift of
prophesy...I am nothing.
Love always protects.
**8**

**1**

Love keeps no record of
wrongs. Love does not
delight in evil.

If I speak in the
tongues of men or of
angels...a clanging
cymbal.
Love is patient
**7**

**2**

Love does not
dishonor others. Love
is not self-seeking.

Love is not easily
angered.
Love always trusts.
**6**

**3**

If I give all I possess to
the poor...I gain nothing.
Love does not boast, it
is not proud.

Love rejoices with the truth.
Love always hopes.
**5**

**4**

Love does not envy.
Love always perseveres.

THE ARMAGEDDON CHOICE

"What I would like you to do during your study time over the next few days is see if you can discern whether or not the miracles of Jesus and the monastic vows of obedience, chastity and poverty fit into an Enneagram pattern in some way. The miracles I am referring to are the seven archetypal miracles described in the Gospel of John: the miracle of the wedding at Cana, the miracle of the healing of the nobleman's son; the miracle of the healing of the paralyzed man at the pool of Bethesda; the miracle of the feeding of the five thousand; the miracle of walking on the water; the miracle of the healing of the man born blind; and, the miracle of the raising of Lazarus at Bethany. You probably know the stories of these miracles from childhood, but go back and reread them in a contemplative fashion and see what emerges. Remember we are in silence for the rest of the weekend. I will meet with you Monday morning before you go back to Tucson to see what has emerged for you."

Dawson could tell his session with Father O'Donnell was over. He rose from his chair, nodded toward Father O'Donnell and turned and left Father O'Donnell's office. Dawson walked through the central passageway of the old farmhouse and out the front door into a beautiful day in the high desert. He felt exhilarated, overwhelmed and just simply amazed that his life was what it was.

Images of Melissa and Blaine flashed through his mind as he looked at the rugged mountain-scape all around him. He sensed that after running away from what the images of these two women represented all his life, maybe, just maybe he was beginning to turn in a new direction back toward his own life.

He looked at his watch and then headed toward the kitchen. He walked in and looked at the chore chart posted on the wall. He picked up a cutting board and grabbed a ten-pound bag of carrots out of the fridge and began chopping away. He glanced up at two other brothers moving silently and efficiently around the kitchen and realized that in addition to the tumult of emotions he was feeling, he felt content, even happy, to be exactly where he was.

*       *       *

On Monday morning at exactly 9:30 a.m. Dawson walked back into Father O'Donnell's office for his instruction session feeling like he'd made some progress on his assignment.

"Greetings, Brother Isaac," said Father O'Donnell. "I hope you had a good weekend of study, prayer and work."

"It is a funny thing—being here is always so much more fulfilling than I ever expect. I had a great hike on Saturday afternoon with Brother Will. We went up to check on your hermitage. And, I feel I made some real headway on the assignment. Should I go over that with you now?"

"Excellent, please do."

Dawson proceeded. "To start off with, it seems clear that the three monastic vows of obedience, poverty and chastity are representative of three points of the Enneagram making the corners of the central triangle. Similarly, the seven archetypal miracles fall on Point Nine and the other six points. The monastic vows represent the remedy for the false-self energy at the three points of the equilateral triangle. At Point Nine falls obedience; at Point Three chastity; and at Point Six poverty."

"Because the false-self trap for the Nine is to fail to see what really is important in life, obedience becomes a way out of that trap. Because the false-self trap for the Three is deceit, and the three is a heart type, who is out of touch with the heart, then chastity, or seeing with a pure heart, becomes the way out of the Three's impasse. Because the false-self trap for a Six, like me, is grasping at ideas because of my lack of faith, then the solution is poverty or emptiness, to admit that I do not know. It is from this unknowing that faith emerges."

"Excellent," said Father O'Donnell. "What about the miracles?"

"They were a little tougher. But this is what I got. The miracle of the wedding at Cana falls at Point One. The false-self of the One is seeking a skewed human view of perfection. Everything is perfect in God's world and in God's timing, including providing wine for the guests at the wedding.

"The miracle of healing the nobleman's son falls at Point Two. The problem for the Two is pride and pride is exemplified by the status of the nobleman. Yet he was able to let go of the barrier of that self-image in order to have his son healed.

"Point Three we have already covered.

"The miracle of the healing of the paralyzed man at the pool of Bethesda falls on Point Four. The false-self trap for the Four is to get caught up in the Four's intense emotional inner world, just as the paralyzed man was trapped at the pool for years but never able to get into it. The miracle for the Four is getting outside of the inner turmoil and into the pool of life.

"Well, this next one was easy. The miracle of feeding the five thousand obviously falls on Point Five. The false-self issue for the Five is feeling that there is not enough, a feeling of insufficiency that leads to greed. Jesus' miracle shows to the Five the crucial lesson that there is always enough when what you have is shared.

"Point Six has already been covered.

"The false-self issue for the Seven is wanting more. The image of walking on water is a perfect image of how following Jesus provides everything. The ultimate option of getting out of any storm is always open. The need to have new options is unnecessary when the ultimate option of following Christ is present.

"The miracle of healing the man born blind falls on Point Eight. The Eight is blind to the energy of his false-self asserting itself in the world so the Eight can feel okay. The blindness of this compulsion is healed in this miracle.

"At Point Nine we have already seen that we have the monastic vow of obedience, and, in addition, the miracle of raising Lazarus from the dead. This miracle illustrates that we all need Grace outside of ourselves to help get us out of our trance of ego self-determination.

And with that, Dawson handed Father O'Donnell an Enneagram image containing what he had said.

Enneagram of Jesus' Miracles and the Three Monastic Vows

| One | Miracle of the wedding at Cana |
|-----|-------------------------------|
| Two | Miracle of healing the nobleman's son |
| Three | Chastity (pure heart) |
| Four | Miracle at the pool at Bethesda |
| Five | Miracle of feeding the 5000 |
| Six | Poverty (clear mind) |
| Seven | Miracle of walking on water |
| Eight | Miracle of healing the blind man |
| Nine | Obedience, Miracle of raising Lazarus |

**Enneagram of Jesus' Miracles**

Miracle of Raising Lazarus from the dead
Obedience
**9**

Miracle of healing the man born blind **8**

**1** Miracle of the wedding in Cana

Miracle of walking on water **7**

**2** Miracle of healing noble man's son

Poverty **6**

**3** Chastity

Miracle of feeding the 5000 **5**

**4** Miracle of healing of the paralyzed man at pool in Bethesda

"Very well done, Brother Isaac," said Father O'Donnell. "Excellent, I mean you've really done a great job. We will defer more discussion of this until our next session. I see that time is getting on and you need to hit the road to make it back to Tucson in time for your first class." With that Father O'Donnell got up from behind his desk and came around and gave Dawson another of his fatherly bear hugs.

"Thank you, Father," said Dawson. "I will be back to see you again in a few days. With my buddy Norris gone I want to be home as much as possible."

Both of them realized Dawson had called the monastery home for the first time. The moment was too precious to embellish with words. The two men nodded at each other. Then Dawson turned and walked out the door.

# Chapter 9

Melissa had no desire to be a saint. Yet, her experience at St. Issa's pond and her contemplative practices had deepened her experience of compassion for the Earth and all people to the point where, if her life could be given to save the green and blue planet and all its creatures, she was ready to make that sacrifice. Of course, it would not really be a sacrifice, but rather simply living out who she had become. While she spent her time in the ice hut out on the frozen Antarctica continent, she experienced that her devotion was both reckless and, in a way, the most conservative thing, perhaps the only thing, she could do.

When she was not deeply in meditation, she was reading some of the books that Mother Mary sent her. At times she felt as if her desire to save the world was a kind of mania that would land her in some baroque psychiatric ward when the CIA caught up with her. Mother Mary cautioned her that following a path of faith was always uncertain. *Only those who do evil have certainty*, she said.

She realized from her reading that most saints, if they had lived in modern times, would probably have been hospitalized with psychiatric diagnoses. The saints really did seem to be nut cases in many ways, but most mental illness is characterized by a withdrawal into the isolation of the self. What seemed to separate the saints she was reading about from real looneys was a deep, authentic humility and a sense of profound connection with others.

The books she had gotten included a copy of the voluminous revelations of St. Brigitta who was, naturally enough, a favorite of the sisters of the SOS Order living in Sweden. St. Brigitta had grown up in Sweden in the 1300s and she was of special importance to the SOS because she articulated a second, more feminine Trinity: Mary, the mother of Jesus, John the Baptist, and Mary of Magdala, as being the most important people in Jesus' life. In St. Brigitta's revelation, Christ speaks directly to her, over and over again. Melissa read and pondered a key passage: "The Son speaks: There were three saints who were most especially pleasing to me. These were Mary, my Mother, John the Baptist, and Mary Magdalene."

In this Trinity, in Enneagram terms, Mary, the mother of Jesus, represents receptive energy, John the Baptist represents assertive energy and Mary of Magdala represents reconciling energy. If the Father, Son and Holy Spirit is the trinity of otherness and maleness; then St. Brigitta's trinity is one of personal interconnection and femaleness.

Melissa owed her escape from the CIA to Rat, Blaine, and the sisters of the SOS. But how could she save anything, or be much use to anyone, as long as she was underground and on the run? And, what got her into trouble in the first place was speaking out in a prophetic, assertive way like John the

Baptist. She had no idea how she might play some role that was both prophetic and one of reconciliation like Mary of Magdala. Still, she was sure the Mother Superior, in giving her the book on St. Brigitta, had some vision that this dual role of prophecy and reconciliation was to be her destiny. Melissa realized that, paradoxically, she would never be able to fill that role unless she completely surrendered the egoic part of herself that wanted to save the world. To do this, she needed to find a way to no longer be moving from place to place. She needed to be back in community, the kind of community which allows humility and connection to evolve.

The egoic surrender was what her work out on the ice was all about. Terry Shaw warned her over and over about frostbite, and Melissa was extremely careful, as her body temperature dropped significantly during long periods of meditation.

Everything seemed to be going well in her efforts until one night she awoke from a deep sleep, startled by a lucid dream. She dreamed St. Brigitta came to her and told her that she must leave Antarctica and go to Sweden. St. Brigitta was insistent. She must leave immediately, and she was to journey back to Sweden slowly, on a ship named Jonah. Melissa was not able to go back to sleep after the dream.

Adding to her dream anxiety, Terry Shaw was telling Melissa she must soon return from her icy outpost to the research station. The Antarctica winter was coming and Terry could not have Melissa out on the ice when weather conditions were so difficult that it would be impossible to reach Melissa in an emergency. Melissa kept arguing with Terry that her meditation practices were deepening to the point of being extremely helpful, and that she needed to stay out on the ice at least one more month.

At first, Melissa wondered whether her St. Brigitta dream simply represented Terry Shaw's admonition that Melissa needed to return from the ice to the research station. But upon reflection, Melissa realized this could not be a correct interpretation because the dream was clear—she needed to leave not just the ice hut, but Antarctica.

The following morning when the radio crackled to life for her daily check-in with Terry Shaw, Melissa did not protest when Terry told Melissa that she was coming to pick her up the next day. Melissa told Terry she would be ready and set about packing her meager personal belongings and putting everything in order in the ice hut.

Three days after Melissa got back to the research station, she was still haunted by her dream. The dream seemed to have a presence that would not leave her alone.

There was a lot of activity at the research station. Most of the research group were not committed to staying during the winter in Antarctica and were packing their gear and getting ready to leave. Only a few of the scientists were staying. Because of her time out on the ice, Melissa had not been a significant contributor to the research effort, and had previously told the leader of the research team that she would be glad to stay over the winter. She was one of the few assistants to express any willingness to stay and he had encouraged her to do so. Now Melissa was sure that her dream was telling her she had to go.

When she talked with the research team leader about leaving, she was relieved. She was such a last-minute sign-on for the research team, that though he hoped she might stay over, he never expected she would want to overwinter. She was free to return with most of the research team on the last supply ship heading back to Argentina.

*       *       *

The wind was howling. It was a particularly bleak, cold blustery day when the last supply ship arrived at Anvers Island. Melissa and Terry had grown quite fond of each other and walked gloved-hand-in-gloved-hand down to the pier together.

"Terry, you have been so good to me, I really do not know how to thank you enough," said Melissa. "I know I was nothing but trouble and worry. Thank you so much for putting up with me. I really do feel deeply refreshed by my time out there in meditation."

"Melissa, you have been no trouble at all. Given the narrow confines of the routine down here and the grumpy scientists I usually get to look after, you have been a breath of fresh air and it's been delightful having you. You know I would be totally gloomy with your leaving, if I was not so excited about my boyfriend arriving. I am so sorry that you will not have a chance to get to know him, but because of weather conditions, after the supplies are offloaded, the ship is going back to Ushuaia as soon as possible. But come, the few passengers coming to stay are unloading right now and I want to introduce you to Norris."

"Sure," said Melissa. "I can't wait to meet this guy who means so much to you. I know he must be really special." Melissa could feel the warmth and engagement in Terry's energy as she talked about her boyfriend.

The two of them walked quickly the last few dozen yards to the pier. Terry bolted forward when she saw her boyfriend and ran into his arms.

Melissa was headed in that direction to meet Terry's boyfriend. But almost immediately she got a metallic taste in her mouth as if she had eaten something horribly disagreeable. She felt a wave of nausea. A sailor was hurrying the passengers who were leaving the research station forward onto the ship.

Well, thought Melissa, maybe I just need to give my friend Terry this special time of reunion with her boyfriend. I better get on board and into my cabin before I throw up.

Melissa was soon up the gangway and aboard. Just as she was turning to go below deck to her cabin she looked back across the pier. She could see Terry looking around for her, to introduce her to Norris. But it was too late for that now. She ducked out of the snow and through the door leading to the cabin deck below.

Melissa was dreading the passage back to Ushuaia after she boarded the ship not feeling well. However, as soon as they were out at sea she immediately began to feel better, and even that part of the voyage through the notoriously rough Drake Passage was not bad. She often found herself standing out on the deck watching the storm petrels dance atop the waves. She had been told that they got their name from St. Peter for the way these birds faced into the wind, stretched out their wings and appeared to walk on water. Melissa never tired of watching them. She was struck by the notion that the storm petrels might be a koan for her life. But try as she might to experience what the storm petrels embodied that she needed to learn for her life, the meaning eluded her.

Once the supply ship arrived back in Ushuaia, Melissa spent less than half a day making inquiries to discover that there was a Norwegian icebreaker named a *Thousand Fjords* leaving at the end of the week for Scandinavia. The ship was just completing a season of showing tourists the penguin colonies and other wildlife on the Antarctica Peninsula and was headed back to the Northern Hemisphere to take tourists into the Arctic for the coming spring and summer seasons there. She tried to hire on, but the ship had no need for additional crew. Since there were very few tourists on board, she was able to book passage at a modest rate.

Though the ship was not named Jonah, she did feel a sense of relief when the ship set sail from Ushuaia. She soon found that traveling aboard ship in the off-season had real advantages. There were no scheduled social events other than the first lifeboat drill and no enforced table sitting times at meals. She was able to spend as much time as she wanted in her small cabin doing contemplative meditation and reading. After the first few days, she decided that it was probably okay for her to send a coded message to Rat using the public computers onboard to let him know that she was safe and on her way to Oslo. She wanted his advice on getting through Norwegian customs and his help in traveling to the SOS convent in Sweden.

In no time, she had a message back from Rat. He believed that she should not try to go through customs. Rat told her that the Norwegians were just as efficient as the Germans, but without caring so much. And even if they didn't care, they would be on top of looking for anyone the CIA asked their help in finding. He would come up with a plan. First, he would find out the date that the ship was supposed to arrive. Before she got to Oslo, he would let her know the details.

Melissa's meditations at sea became deep and serene. The pace of shipboard life was relaxing. No place to go and no place to be. Melissa had been on the run since she went to Racine, Wisconsin to visit her mother's body before she was buried. The slow rolling motion of the ship was balm to a bodily weariness which she had not realized she carried until it began to soften in the rhythmic living of shipboard life. The ocean was Mother Nature's giant cradle gently rocking her weariness away.

Melissa had space in her life for the first time to pull out the paper written by Professor Gallagher which Blaine had given her. The highly acclaimed paper was presented to the

International Enneagram Conference in Turin, Italy the year before. It presented the results of Gallagher's research on the life of Jesus during the years not mentioned in the Gospels. Melissa knew that Blaine's research—hacking would be a more accurate word—was the key to the evidence Gallagher presented in this paper that outlined the travels and life of Jesus as a spiritual teacher of transformation based on an understanding of the Enneagram.

Melissa also knew that her own mystical experience at St. Issa's pond in Afghanistan was in its own way a confirmation of Jesus' travels. She was fascinated to read the part which suggested that through the skill of his uncle, Joseph of Arimathea, Jesus may have survived the crucifixion and escaped underground through the network of Essene communities. She could relate her own experience of being on the run from the CIA to Jesus' experience of being on the lam from the Jewish authorities and the Roman state. Just as Rat had become her way to communicate with her supporters at the SOS, Jesus had met Paul, a gay man who immediately fell in love with Jesus, who became Jesus' scribe for Jesus' communications to the early Christian communities. No wonder, Melissa thought, over a third of the New Testament is made up of the writings of Paul. Though Paul occasionally throws in a few of his own ideas, he is for the most part simply conveying the heart of Jesus' message directly from Jesus about the path of transformation of consciousness.

On this particular morning, Melissa went back to read the portion of Gallagher's paper about Jesus' trip to England, with his uncle Joseph of Arimathea, a copper merchant, and

Joseph's son, Joshua, Jesus' cousin and best friend. Only twelve, the two young cousins persuaded their families to let them go along on the year-long voyage across the Mediterranean sea and up the coast of present day Portugal and France to the copper mines in the Cornwall area of the British Isles.

As she was sitting, propped up on pillows on her bunk in her cabin reading, Melissa noticed that the motion of the ship was beginning to dramatically increase. She looked out her small porthole streaked with raindrops and watched as the scene changed from a massive wave of water to a framed portrait of a majestic, dark foreboding sky.

She tried to continue to read. She got to the part where the ship that Jesus was on shipwrecked in a storm off the southern English coast and he was nearly drowned before finally being washed ashore. This was not the kind of reading she needed right now, as the motion of the ship continued to increase.

It was impossible to do anything but try to hold on. She got dressed as best she could, while sitting on her bunk, and made her way out of her cabin and down the passageway.

Because there were so few passengers on this voyage, the captain announced the first day at sea that they would observe an "open bridge" policy during the voyage. Melissa had taken full advantage of this, especially late at night when all the other passengers retired. She enjoyed going to the bridge and talking with the officer on duty and observing the comforting glow of the navigation instruments. There was a sense of rapport and right relation with the ocean as the ship cruised confidently through the night across the ocean's huge expanse.

As she struggled up the stairs at the end of the passageway going to the bridge, she felt anything but serenity and rapport. She had already bruised her left thigh rather severely when she was thrown off balance into the railing running along the side of the ship's passageway.

She opened the door to the bridge. The tension in the air was palpable. The Norwegian Captain, a man named Aaronson was at the helm. The first mate was from Croatia and was referred to as Brog. The second mate was apparently from Russia since he was called Russkie. Luckily for her the language of the bridge was English. Except everyone seemed to swear in their own native tongue.

Captain Aaronson was attempting to keep the ship heading into the wind. They would head up a huge wave with nothing but an angry sky visible in the two-paned, thick glass, wraparound bridge window and, if their timing was right, slide down the other side. If their timing was wrong, the bow would drop headlong with a thud into the trough between two waves. Often the ship would be almost immediately covered with water by a breaking wave. Melissa had been standing watching for only a few minutes when, just after they crested a huge wave and slid down into a trough, another monster wave came crashing down on the bow submerging the bridge windows in water as the entire ship shuddered and fought to regain the surface.

Captain Aaronson didn't appear to be fazed but continued to give short commands which were relayed to the engine room by the First Mate—to slow or to accelerate the ship as quickly as possible—whatever was necessary to put the ship in the best possible position to take the next wave.

Russkie reported to the Captain that all hatches and doorways had been battened down and all passengers and crew instructed to remain below deck with their life jackets on. As this report was being given, life jackets were passed out to everyone on the bridge and Melissa pulled hers over her head.

Captain Aaronson even put one on. He asked the First Mate Brog in a flat tone, "What is that weather radar showing as the closest perimeter of this storm?"

"Sir, I can't see any immediate perimeter. The bulk of the storm is coming out of the north, and it seems to have engulfed us completely in the past few minutes. The closest fringe seems to be eastward, but if we head that way we risk taking the big storm surges on the beam."

The Captain winced and nodded tersely. Clearly the First Mate's explanation of the risk involved in taking the shortest route out of the storm was unnecessary.

"We will try to keep directly into the storm as long as we can before we consider trying to thread the needle out to the side. I want a full report immediately from the First Engineer on any leaks and the extent to which we are taking on water."

"Yes, sir," said Brog.

Captain Aaronson focused his full attention back on climbing the ski slope of the next giant wave.

Melissa took a deep breath. Even with all her energy training, she realized she was hardly breathing. But, despite the storm, she felt that place of inner calm that connected her directly to the Mystery that most people call God. It was particularly good, she thought, to feel this connection at a time like this.

The more she focused her attention on her heart-center and her breathing the more deeply connected she felt. As the moments passed, she felt connected to herself and God and to Captain Aaronson and the other sailors on the bridge, indeed even to the huge walls of water the ship was struggling to get over, or through, or sometimes beneath.

Her connection continued, as if by no effort of her own, as the storm seemed to go from bad to worse. She remembered the first time she had experienced a titanic struggle within herself years ago at St. Issa's pond—the struggle between fear and faith. Not faith, as an idea or concept, but faith as a lived experience. Just as she did then, she found herself letting go into the oblivion of faith, and as she did she heard within herself a voice say. *Tell the Captain to turn back south.*

She was shocked to hear such a clear command, and also apprehensive about having the temerity to say anything at all to the Captain in the midst of such a storm. Probably he did not even know she was on the bridge and would have preferred that she was below with the rest of the passengers and crew.

Just then another huge cliff of water came crashing down on the bow. This time large cracks appeared in the thick bridge window on the port side. Without deciding to do so, she spoke: "Captain, I know this sounds bizarre but I have been told by God we should turn and go back south."

Captain Aaronson turned sideways to look at her. His lips curled as if in preparation to hurl an epithet her way. Melissa fully uncloaked her heart energy on the Captain. The bridge window on the left side burst open and the ocean came pouring through. Gear and papers swirled about in cold sea water that rose to everyone's chest.

Melissa gasped at the coldness of the water and when the weight of the surge hit her, she was pushed to the floor. Just as she was trying to pull herself up a blunt object hit her in the head. She was unable to stifle her startle reaction. Her mouth immediately opened and she took in an enormous gulp of seawater. Dazed by the blow to the head and groggy from the seawater, she groped on the floor around the steel stanchion of a deck chair and, with the help of her lifejacket's buoyancy, she was able to pull herself upright. Standing erect her head was just barely above the roiling, dark water.

The Captain, who appeared not to have moved, looked at her and said in a loud voice so he could be heard above the roar of the storm that was now inside the bridge, "Your advice is a bit late, but given the storm's breach of the bridge there is not much alternative. Brog, open a door to get this damn water out of here as soon as the ship gets back fully upright. I will bring her about. Then get me a full damage assessment. And see if you can get the ship's carpenter to find some plywood or something to plug that damn hole."

"Aye, aye, Captain."

Melissa hung on for dear life as the water began to drain out of the bridge in one huge sucking roar. Then, just barely in time, she turned sideways away from the Captain and projectile vomited against the side wall. It was as if all her ego's desire for enlightenment, all her years of striving in her practices to control her energy and increase her consciousness, were released from the bottom of her gut and went draining out of her onto the wall and into the seawater covering the floor.

She felt a sense of utter calm and peacefulness in the chaos of the storm. Life and death were right there next to each other, fiercely next to each other, and at the same time all of one cloth. Melissa realized that once again she was asked to surrender, or more accurately, something greater than her had led her to a point of surrender in her life and she said *yes* to it. She felt her life about to be taken away from her, just as she had read about Jesus when the ship he was on foundered in a storm off the coast of Cornwall. In the moment of supreme danger, rather than being destroyed, the magnificent splendor of life opened up before her.

Just as she experienced this inner change, the ship came about, and everything changed in her outer experience. The storm continued just as violently as before, but now they were going with the wind and the storm surge, not against them. The tension on the bridge broke. They were a long ways from being out of the storm, but somehow they were released from its stranglehold.

The Captain smiled toward the First Mate and said, "You know, I have been asking the company for a year to replace that window. You could tell by the frosting that the seal was broken. Guess we will get it replaced now. If we make it to Oslo, that is. What is the damage report?"

"Most of the electronics are ruined. We have no damage to the engine. The Chief Engineer will have to implement your engine commands manually, but it is all workable in the old-fashioned way. Most of our electronic communication with the outside world is knocked out, but we may have some back up possibilities once we get out of this storm. Anything else right now, Captain?"

"No, let's just get that hole plugged as soon as possible. It is freezing in here."

"Yes, sir."

"Oh, one other thing. See if you can take our navigation assistant below so she can wash the vomit off her face and find some dry clothes." The Captain nodded toward Melissa. She smiled the best she could for someone with a trail of vomit and seawater still trickling from her nostrils. Brog took her arm and guided her to the door leading below.

"Right you are, Captain," he replied.

As he led Melissa down the passageway from the bridge Brog turned to Melissa. "Don't worry Missy, even in a big storm like this you have nothing to fear with Jonah at the helm."

Melissa stopped. "With who at the helm?"

"Oh, Captain Aaronson," said Brog. "I am afraid the crew call him by his first name behind his back. Lucky name for a captain I think, Jonah. Well, here we are at your cabin." And with that Brog turned and headed back for the bridge.

Melissa opened her cabin door and slipped inside. She stripped off her wet clothes and washed her face the best she could with a wash cloth in one hand and holding to the sink with the other. With the storm still in full gale, it was too treacherous to risk taking a shower. She got a towel, sat on her bunk and wiped off as best she could. Then she slipped under the covers. As her head settled against the pillow, the pounding and hurling of the waves above sounded like celestial music rather than the raging of a huge rogue storm.

*        *        *

When the ship was a day out of Norway, communication was restored and Melissa got an email from Rat. He instructed her that she should remain on board when the other passengers disembarked, but pack all of her things and leave her cabin. He suggested that she find some place like the small workout room sauna, which would be turned off and unused, and hang out there for the night. The ship was arriving late in the afternoon and normally all passengers would disembark by 6 p.m. The customs office closed at 8 p.m. and most of the crew from the ship would have left by that time. There would be no easy access to the ship until the next morning. A laundry supply company vehicle would arrive early in the morning to pick up the ship's laundry.

Melissa was to be on the lookout for the driver of the laundry truck, who would be wearing the colorful red jersey of the Norwegian national football team. He would ask her how many times the Norwegian team had qualified to play in the World Cup and she would tell him the answer, which any Norwegian school lad would know: three—the first in 1938, the most recent in 1998. He would help her escape in a large laundry basket that he would roll into the back of the laundry truck.

Rat's plan went off without a hitch. When the laundry truck pulled up to the customs gate, Melissa was resting comfortably in a laundry basket with a sheet lightly over her head. She immediately sensed the energy of the customs agent standing right beside the driver's side door.

You don't usually get a job as a customs agent without having a natural predisposition toward suspicion. But all Melissa needed to do was direct the warmth of her natural heart energy in his direction and any thought he had of searching the back of the truck immediately vanished.

By nine o'clock they were heading north up the E6 and she

was seated comfortably in the front seat. Her driver spoke a bit of English, but he was a taciturn man and said little when Melissa tried to make conversation about the weather. Two hours later Melissa was in Trondheim, Norway's leading technology center. The driver dropped her off at an Internet cafe as Rat told Melissa he would. There she ordered a latte and sidled up to a computer and logged onto the chat room that Rat designated for further instruction.

The instructions didn't come in the form she expected: over the computer. After she had been logged into the chat room for a while, a young woman with purple hair came over and asked her if she knew when the Norwegian national team last went to the World Cup. Upon receiving the answer of 1998, the young woman nodded her head toward the door.

In a short time they were in a small car headed west. The woman informed Melissa they were headed toward Ostersund in Sweden where she would be delivered to the Froso Church. Except to stop to pay a toll, the trip was uneventful and the car didn't even slow down to enter Sweden. Rat warned Melissa not to be too chatty with the people who would help her on her journey. The young woman was intent on driving and Melissa kept her energy closed as tightly as possible so that later the young woman would hardly remember what Melissa looked like.

After she was dropped off in Osterund at the Froso Church, Melissa barely had time to join a few tourists gawking at the pagan-looking church structure before a young sister from the SOS walked up and introduced herself. The two immediately headed for the sister's car for the last leg of Melissa's journey to the SOS convent up north.

When Melissa arrived at the convent, there was a grand celebration. A celebration was in the works already, but after Melissa sat down with Mother Mary and described in detail what had happened to her on the voyage from Antarctica, the celebration went from being a celebration about her successful journey to the convent to something much grander and more profoundly meaningful.

Mother Mary knew Melissa had profound spiritual gifts. But after what everyone thereafter would refer to as Melissa's Jonah experience, it was clear to Mother Mary that this woman had experienced a profoundly deep awakening, just as she had years before at St. Issa's pond. Two such awakenings in a lifetime are rare, and a sign of extraordinary Grace. Now in the serene environment of the convent, where she did not have to worry about cloaking her energy, a golden glow of love hovered around Melissa everywhere she went.

The sisters of the Sacred Order of the Sisters of Mary of Magdala had an esoteric tradition. Over many years since their founding, every century or two, a woman was initiated into the Order who had such exceptional love, piety and devotion that she was given the Order name of Sister Magdalen. The sisters at the convent unanimously voted to have Melissa initiated into the Order as Sister Magdalen.

The initiation ceremony for a Sister Magdalen was ancient. Even Mother Mary did not understand all of the archetypal imagery involved. The principal image came from Revelations 12:1:

*And there appeared a great wonder in heaven; a woman clothed with the sun, and the moon under her feet and upon her head a crown of twelve stars.*

The ceremony was delayed for two weeks until the rising of a new moon occurred at the end of the day at the time all the sisters entered the chapel. Melissa was adorned in a centuries' old dress made of golden thread. At dusk, as the ritual commenced, Melissa stepped to the altar of the convent chapel. The silver crescent of the new moon shown through the clear window behind the altar and was visible at her feet. Mother Mary recited the ancient ceremony, then she invoked the Sophic Trinity—Mother, Daughter and Holy Soul—and placed a crown of twelve stars on Melissa's head.

Melissa recited from the eighth chapter of Proverbs:

*The Lord possessed me in the beginning of his way, before his works of old. I was set up from everlasting, from the beginning, or ever the Earth was. When there were no depths, I was brought forth; when there were no fountains abounding with water. Before the mountains were settled, before the hills was I brought forth: While as yet he had not made the Earth, nor the fields, nor the highest part of the dust of the world. When he prepared the heavens, I was there; when he set a compass upon the face of the depth: When he established the clouds above: when he strengthen the foundations of the deep: When he gave to the sea his decree, that the water should not pass his commandment: when he appointed the foundations of the Earth: Then I was by him, as one brought up with him: and I was daily his delight, rejoicing always before him; Rejoicing in the habitable part of his Earth: and my delights were with the sons of men. Now therefore hearken unto me, O ye children: for blessed are they that keep my ways. Hear instruction, and be wise, and refuse it not. Blessed is the man that heareth me, watching daily at my gates waiting at the post of my doors. For whoso findeth me findeth his life, and shall obtain favor of the Lord. But he that sinneth against me wrongeth his own soul: all that hate me love death.*

From then on, Melissa was known as Sister Magdalen.

After her initiation, the sisters all prayed a novena for Sister Magdalen. The practice of the novena—a formula of prayer which one devotes oneself to for nine days—is so ancient in the church that its origin is unclear. The sisters, at Mother Mary's instruction, used it as way to pray for the restoration of the divine essence of each Enneagram type, which Mary Magdalen carried in fullness and are hidden in each human soul. One type was prayed for each day. Each day the sisters of that particular type led the novena in the late afternoon chapel service. On the last day, Sister Magdalen, wearing her crown of twelve stars, sat with Mother Mary in the front of the chapel. Mother Mary explained to the sisters of the Order that the twelve stars represented the twelve levels of consciousness, nine exoteric and three esoteric, that it was possible to obtain through God's Grace. The stars were set in the crown in a spiral, reflecting the spiral path of the classic journey of transformation. From then on, Sister Magdalen's very presence magnified the glory and presence of God.

Although Mother Mary remained governing head of the Order, when the nine-day initiation ceremony was completed, Melissa became the spiritual leader of the Order. Not that this gave her any special privileges.  For although Mother Mary gave Sister Magdalen the maximum time allowed for an individual to pursue individual spiritual practices, she was also assigned the most menial of the convent chores. Mother Mary knew that great spiritual depth and great humility always went hand in hand.

Of course, the youngest initiates, who were also given some of the most menial convent chores, loved this arrangement. Now they were delighted to be basking in the golden energy of love that poured from Sister Magdalen while they were on pot-scrubbing duty or slopping the pigs.

# Chapter 10

Gordon Slade was glad to see his old, buddy Joe Carroll, and even gladder they were meeting at their usual, the Rhythm and Booze, near Fenway Park.

"Joe, why so glum on a game night?" asked Slade.

"You are spoiled rotten, Slade, now that you have found Joy. But some of us don't have that comfort. Some of us have come to the realization the political process in America is broken and that, far from helping us solve problems, our political process is leading us down an ever-increasing path of human alienation. Of course, most of us gave up on religion long ago. I sure did. And, you know, for a long time I was able to feel secure simply by virtue of my ability to be creative. But the truth is I haven't written a decent poem in ages and my writing students are for the most part lost in their own navels for four years as undergraduates and I don't see much hope there. And I hate, I mean I hate to admit this, but I actually have gotten a bit tired of chasing broads."

"Whoa, you are suffering," said Slade. "The next round is on me." And he signaled the barmaid to come over to their back corner table.

"But, you know the fortune cookie you gave me the other day from the new company that you and Joy got going?"

Slade nodded.

"Well, this is what it said: '*You wander in a spiritual bazaar, touching a hundred items; buy something!* Rumi.' And I have been thinking, if the political process doesn't work, religion is long dead and gone, and as a certain country music singer was famously quoted as saying, 'I have outlived my dick,' then the only place to turn is to this path of transformation of consciousness which that cookie fortune is pointing to. I can't believe I am saying this, but I need to get—really the whole delusional country needs to get—beyond the stuck place we are in and, if I am honest, I don't see any other way out. But, except for the change in you, Slade, brought about by Joy, I am pretty damn pessimistic about me and the rest of the country."

"Hearing you articulate so clearly the place our culture is at this time in history gives me a breath of hope," said Slade. "The way Joy sees it also gives me hope. She believes that the Creator is in love with creation and that the more the creation *groks* this, to use the old sci-fi term she likes, and returns the love, the greater the energy load we humans can handle and therefore the higher the level of consciousness we can get to."

"Slade, if you are going to get that heavy on me, I am going to need another drink."

"Well, I avoided referring to this greater consciousness as a higher level of vibration just because I didn't want you to go off on a cursing tirade that might make your ulcer start multiplying and dividing." But Slade could see he was about to lose the humor battle to keep Carroll from getting caught up in a harangue against dope-smoking New Agers.

Then Carroll suddenly reversed course. "Of course, I know it is easy for me to stay stuck by staying in this aloof place of cultural critic. You know it is the way I have always criticized most of my colleagues in academia. I have never thought about myself as wandering in a spiritual bazaar, but I see for the first time that, in a way, that does describe me. I never quite thought of the desire to get into a good-looking woman's pants as wandering in a spiritual bazaar, or for that matter, writing self-indulgent poetry that doesn't rhyme, to be that kind of journey, but maybe it has been."

Slade smiled at his friend. They'd talked together through most of the difficulties in their lives, but to Slade it seemed like they were at a new, more authentic place. Talking through whatever was on their minds had given them a deep friendship, but it had never solved anything for Carroll, who always seemed to keep his own life at arm's length. Slade knew his friend needed a new experience of life as Joy had given him. What that might be for Carroll, Slade had no idea. It seemed impossible to know what would jar Carroll out of the ivory tower of the cynical observer. Carroll was so knowledgeable and so jaded by his knowledge. It was not like he could walk through the beautiful spring flowers growing on the Boston Commons and see the exotic surprise of a hummingbird for the first time. Or, walk along the Charles River and be awestruck by watching a mother goose and the fluffy little puffs of her newly hatched goose family swim up to the bank where he was standing.

Suddenly Slade had an idea. "Carroll, did you see the news about the Pope dying?"

"Of course, the less important something truly is the more time it gets in the news. Sure, I saw it, and I didn't miss the news about the last royal wedding either. So what?"

"Well, it seems that a small group of American Catholic bishops is calling for a meeting of lapsed Catholics. They want to explore what could occur in the process of this election of a new Pope that might bring the lapsed back to the church. You are about as lapsed as anyone I know. Why don't you get involved?"

Slade could see the twitch in Carroll's brow, which fore-shadowed a sizzling sarcastic response, but then his demeanor relaxed. Carroll spoke with unexpected candor, "Slade, I know what you are trying to do—you are fishing to find out how to get me interested in something outside of my own cynical self, but really! Me going to a Catholic meeting about electing a new Pope would be like throwing my piggish cynical self into a huge mud hole. It would not be pretty. People would be getting pig shit all over themselves, if you know what I mean."

Slade was not about to let his friend off the hook. "The reason I make the suggestion is I think it represents most of the things you don't like: organized religion, the church, sanctimonious people, and so on. If you are going to find a new way to experience life, the best way to start is with something that you find most distasteful. Everything else is just going to bounce off you like rain. Why don't you give it a try? Something that far out of your comfort zone might bring new meaning in some unexpected way. Go act like it matters to you and see if something new really does matter. Plus, the meeting is going to be right here in Boston."

Carroll winced, "You have single-handedly destroyed all of my recent thoughts about giving up chasing women. The idea that I could actually find excitement and meaning in trying to influence who the next Pope is makes me want to throw-up. I much prefer to come here and complain about whoever the unlucky bastard is."

Even though it was negative emotion, Slade could tell that Carroll was at least having a powerful response. Slade kept pushing. "Well, that is one of the purposes of this gathering— to get women involved since women make up almost 70% of the membership of the Catholic church in the United States. So with all these spiritually deprived women showing up, you ought to be able to keep all your options open for personal growth."

Carroll flipped him the bird. Slade grinned. Carroll was taking the bait.

"Okay, old pal, put my name in the hat. Just let whoever is organizing this gathering know that I fall into the most lapsed group, the real Dionysian goats, but if they want me I will go. Not saying I will stay, or anything like that, but I will go.

*         *         *

*The Lapsed Catholics Conclave for a New Kind of Pope* took place at one of the downtown Boston hotels. It was an unexpectedly large gathering. There were people from all over the United States and a fair smattering from Europe. There were far fewer from Asia, Africa and Latin America, the most populous centers of Catholicism. But, of course, those were places of the new conservative Catholicism, not the home of lapsed Catholics.

One of the few remaining liberal bishops presided over the opening of the conference. The opening plenary session was over quickly and people were divided into a myriad of small groups. Out of his natural perversity Carroll signed up for the small group entitled, *Electing a Woman Pope.* The idea sounded far out even for Carroll, so he thought it would keep him awake and maybe even be good fun.

He had no idea who would be the other participants in his small group, and Carroll was intrigued by who showed up. Several really impressed him: a woman not dressed as a nun, but typical of the stereotype of nun teachers in parochial school with a stocky frame and assertive demeanor, whose name tag identified her as Mother Mary, abbess of the Sacred Order of the Sisters of Mary of Magdala; an elderly man whose name tag said—Father O'Donnell from New Mexico; a lovely blonde whose name tag identified her as Sister Ingrid from Sweden; and, another priest who was a friend of Father O'Donnell's named Father Hay. The common denominator of all four was the quality of their relaxed way of being, and a certain fullness and warmth of energy that made him want to sit close to each of them, particularly the young blonde from Sweden.

Carroll understood quite clearly that the group was united in their belief that the next Pope needed to be someone who did not have a dualistic perspective, starting with not having the kind of dualistic outlook that divided people into Christian or non-Christian. Yes, they all wanted the next Pope to be a woman, but above all they wanted the next Pope to be someone of unitive consciousness, who, because he or she was not divided internally, would not divide people, but bring them together.

Carroll had heard Slade talk about this idea of non-dual or unitive consciousness, but he was not about to fall for something that sounded good without really knowing what the term meant. He put on his most professorial persona and pushed back hard to get the group to tell him what unitive consciousness meant. There was a bit of surprise at his tone and no one spoke in response immediately. But after a minute, Father O'Donnell did.

"Professor Carroll, it is a fair question, but to understand the answer I must ask you to relax. Rather than look directly at the sun just squint your eyes a bit."

"Father," asked Carroll, doing his best to be civil. "What has

THE ARMAGEDDON CHOICE

squinting my eyes got to do with anything?"

"I am talking about changing the way you see," said Father O'Donnell. "Part of understanding my answer is you must look at what I say differently. Sometimes if you squint up your eyes you see what is familiar differently, in a truer way."

Carroll furrowed up his brow and squinted at Father O'Donnell in his most madman, Jack Nicholson manner. "How is that?" he said.

Father O'Donnell ignored the leer. "I am not sure it will change your perspective, but maybe it will help a little. So let's give it a try. Relax, breathe deeply. Would you say that the best things in life are free?"

If Carroll hadn't automatically followed Father O'Donnell's suggestion and taken a deep breath, which caused him to relax a bit, his reputation for sarcasm would have been well served. As it was, all he said was, "Yes, I would agree to that."

"And," said Father O'Donnell continuing, "that everything in life has a price?"

As Carroll's brow began to contract, Father O'Donnell repeated his instructions, "Relax, breathe into the question, just let your most authentic response come."

Carroll nodded, and, despite himself, breathed deeply. "Yes, I would agree with that also."

"So, if you combine these two true statements what you get is the conclusion: the best things in life are free at a high price."

Father O'Donnell waited. It did not happen often but Carroll had no quick facile rebuttal. Father O'Donnell continued. "At the literal level we see that the third statement is simply a combining of the other two statements. But at a literal meaning level, it makes no sense for something to be free and also costly. Yet we know instinctively that both parts of the third statement are true. Non-dual consciousness, or unitive consciousness, is a perspective that sees the inconsistencies in life: liberal versus conservative, or capitalism versus socialism, and understands the greater truth that is inherent in the two limited truths. The greater truth is experienced, more than simply received as information. For us as Christians, we see what appear to be the greatest opposites, life and death—that even they are held in an even larger truth." Father O'Donnell paused. "But more of that for another time. I am side-tracking us from our task." He stopped and looked directly into Carroll's eyes.

"Is that helpful?"

Carroll nodded. He was thinking of a T.S. Eliot poem he often taught in class about returning to the place of beginning for the first time. He exhaled, realizing that he was holding his breath in amazement because he was not understanding the poem as much as experiencing its meaning for the first time.

The group seemed to candidly realize that much of the church was dualistic in outlook, both church leaders and parishioners, and that while this made the need to have a Pope with a unitive outlook even more essential, the chance of many in the church accepting this kind of leader was slim and none. There was talk among the participants about the historical precedent for having more than one Pope.

When his small group completed its first day's meeting, Carroll was unsure what had happened. He realized, walking back across the Commons, that somehow the deck chairs in his mind had been re-arranged beneficially. He no longer felt cynical about being a part of this meeting and its purpose.

At the end of the second day the small group prepared its report to the whole conference. The report was presented on the third and final day to the conference by Mother Mary. It petitioned the cardinals at the Vatican to elect a woman Pope. The report recommended that if the papal conclave failed to elect a Pope unitive in outlook, who understood Christ's message of transformation of consciousness, all those churches and orders who believed this was the true message and way of Christ were welcomed to withdraw from the authority of the church at Rome and to join in abiding in the authority of a new Pope duly elected by them.

Carroll loved the report. It was the kind of in-your-face report he thought the Catholic hierarchy deserved. However, he was quite amazed that it was delivered with such love and nuance by Mother Mary, without any sense of holier-than-thou judgment. Carroll was so taken by Mother Mary that he spent one evening at dinner with her and Father O'Donnell. Taking nuns to dinner was not his habit, was the way Slade would jokingly put it later. But something had indeed shifted in Carroll, and he was taken by the compassion and lightness of being that both Mother Mary and Father O'Donnell displayed. Their dinner together was great fun. Carroll could not remember when he laughed so much. And for sure he could not remember when he laughed so much when he was not in the process of making fun of someone else.

As the conclave was breaking up, Mother Mary pulled Carroll aside. "Joe, I have been praying for you."

Carroll winced. "Jesus," he muttered under his breath.

"Joe, it did not cause you any pain did it?" asked Mother Mary with a grin.

"No, but just the thought of being prayed for gives me the creeps. It is a personal invasion and I resent you sending your hocus-pocus beliefs my way."

"Point taken," said Mother Mary, "but to be more accurate, I was praying for guidance about the next step to be taken after this conference. The message I kept getting back is—take Joe with you back to Sweden. It is the end of your semester isn't it? Would you like to come?"

"Holy shit, Mother Mary, I'd just as soon go to Fenway and pull for the visiting team. What in the world would I do in a Swedish convent with a bunch of nuns?"

Carroll had been around Mother Mary long enough that he was

aware of the tractor-pull of her energy field as she focused on him. He was not about to give in without a fight. "Plus, if you have more nuns in that convent like that blonde, buxom jailbait you brought with you, well, I can tell you Mother, you do not want me in your convent."

Mother Mary continued to look directly at Carroll. "Do you have plans for the summer?"

"Well, not really. I'm not teaching, if that is what you mean," said Carroll, resenting that he was being pulled into a civil conversation.

"Joe, I understand your fear. We have all been there. I am sure a literary guy like you knows the Grail story. You remember the story teaches that in life we only get one or two chances to ask the question. My offer for you to come will give you the chance to ask the question, 'What does your life serve?'"

Carroll could feel her heart energy pouring over him like warm sunshine. For once he could feel his rebellious personality rebelling, not in a cynical way against something outside of himself, but against his own inner survival way of being and stuck-ness. Without even knowing what he was going to say, he began to speak.

"We need to get one thing straight, Mother Mary. I am not going to act like some damn goody-goody-two-shoes Christian. I will not be anything other than my asshole self, and if anyone, especially you, doesn't like it, that's too bad. And one other thing: I am leaving any time I damn well please."

"Joe, I am so, so glad you are going to come. We wouldn't want you any way but the way you are. And I expect you will find out, there is a lot more to who you are than you presently know. So the more of you the better. We leave from Logan tomorrow evening on a direct flight to Stockholm."

"Well, I may sort of be agreeing to come, but I can't go tomorrow and I am sure at this late date it would be hard for me to get a seat on your flight."

"Don't worry, we have already made a reservation for you. We did at the start of the conference. You will be stuck in a seat by that—what did you call Sister Ingrid, blonde bait?—for the flight over. Do you think you can handle it?"

"Jesus, I cannot believe this," said Carroll staring wide-eyed at Mother Mary. "If you give me that smug little look again, I assure you positively, I will not go."

Mother Mary smiled. "The flight leaves at 6:45 p.m. See you at the departure gate."

# Chapter 11

Dawson's spring semester was very different from his earlier terms. The things that made it different were in themselves very different.

First, Norris was beginning to understand what Father O'Donnell had expressed to him from the beginning about the difference between the approach of faith and science to the material Dawson was leaning. Science, as Father O'Donnell explained, was focused on the idea of understanding and controlling power.

The corollary assumed in this focus was that power was truth. Because of its focus on power, the nature of scientific inquiry is largely a destructive one; how do you break matter down in order to control it? The scientific ideal is the domination of nature by breaking it down to understand, to control and to make it subject to man's will.

Much of the history of science has focused on creating energy to do tasks to make man's life easier. The science of creating energy always involves the destruction of matter. This is seen in the history of how humankind has created energy: from burning wood, to consuming petroleum in a combustion engine, to smashing the atom to create atomic energy.

On the other hand, Father O'Donnell explained, the ideal of faith moves in the opposite direction, toward construction rather than destruction. Instead of trying to have power over the forces of nature by destructive means, faith aspires to conscious participation in the constructive forces of the world on the basis, not so much of understanding, but of being in communion with the spark of divinity in everything. The efforts of science are to force nature to conform to the will of Man; while the approach of faith is to purify the will of Man in order to bring humanity into harmony with the creative principle of nature as a part of divine reality. In this state of collaboration the human being experiences rapport with all of life.

The two approaches are diametrically opposed. The scientific attitude is one of acquiring knowledge to have power, and the Christian mystical approach is an opening of mind and heart in order to receive. One is an effort to gain control, the other is a surrender to powerlessness in order to gain unity. The ideal of science, since the time of the Renaissance, has been about man achieving power over both visible and invisible nature so that nature can be subjugated to the human will. The mystical reality is that authority comes from the divine and only by surrendering to divine will is a human being able to mediate the authority of this wisdom.

Father O'Donnell assured Dawson that the path mystical monastics have pursued over the centuries has been a path of renunciation—renunciation of power, violence, and the need to know as a way to control; and, finally even renunciation of a personal identity. It is this renunciation that is found in the beatitudes of the Sermon on the Mount. "Blessed are the poor in spirit, for theirs is the kingdom of heaven" is saying that those who are rich in their own egos, who are not empty, have no access to the Kingdom of Heaven—their way of knowing is not the kind of knowing that brings access to the Kingdom of Heaven. The mystical Christian tradition seeks emptiness or powerlessness in order to receive divine purpose. God governs the world by authority of divine love, not by power. Only those who are empty can be filled by the fullness of God's love.

Secondly, in addition, to his finally understanding the mystical faith perspective, the spring semester was different because his buddy Norris was no longer there to go with him to Calamity Jane's a couple of times a week to discuss their course material. He was getting frequent emails from Norris, but in a way these made things even worse, as the emails were full of Norris gushing about being with his girlfriend, Terry. Dawson missed Norris but hearing from Norris led to his re-experiencing his grief at the loss of his relationships with Melissa and Blaine.

Thirdly, Father O'Donnell's health was deteriorating and Dawson was regretting the time he was in Tucson away from the monastery.

Fourthly, for the first time in his life, Dawson was not turning his head at the next pretty girl who walked by in class. He was more animated by his desire to do his inner work to find himself within than the need to be distracted by a woman in order to avoid how he was feeling. And finally, fifthly, and perhaps most important, the material that was being presented in class was getting to the heart of the question of the quantum biological structure of consciousness. Dawson was beginning to understand this material was a path to surrender not control.

Father O'Donnell, even though he was clearly not in good health, had insisted on going to a conference in Boston, convened after the Pope's sudden death. Dawson was so excited to tell Father O'Donnell about his first quantum biology class that he failed to get details about the conference. When Father O'Donnell left he insisted Dawson follow up with email about the details of what he was learning about the biology of consciousness.

Dawson could only guess that the conference Father O'Donnell was attending must be totally dullsville, since it involved church politics. So Dawson, glad to get back to the monastery from Tucson late on Thursday after his last class for the week, immediately sat down at the computer to outline his notes in an email that would keep Father O'Donnell updated.

*Dear Father O'Donnell,*

*I cannot begin to tell you how fortunate I am that you sent me to the University of Arizona's Center for Consciousness Studies. Your insight is just dawning on me. When the professor reviewed how scientific paradigms change, it became clear to me that changes in scientific paradigms only develop in tandem with changes in spiritual paradigms. Ptolemy's flat Earth model lasted for hundreds of years, until it was replaced by Galilean astronomy and Newtonian physics. This happened about the same time the Protestant Reformation occurred. Quantum physics has been around for almost one hundred years, but quantum biology has only developed recently. At the same time traditional church membership has been shrinking, while the contemplative movement has been gaining momentum in the United States. I see that historically greater consciousness about science also leads to greater consciousness about the spiritual reality of life, or maybe it is vice versa.*

*Despite all the enthusiasm about the material that we are learning among the students in the class, it is very apparent from our class discussion today that most students are caught unawares in two completely different paradigms of reality. They are still heirs to the spirit versus body division that the church has fostered in since the time of Augustine in the fourth century.*

*In chemistry class they accept a very Newtonian view of biology—they see the body as a machine that follows Newtonian physics. But, when they go to church and pray, or go to an energy healer for pain relief, they readily accept the paradigm that spirit is not separate from matter. This doesn't say as much about the models being different, as it does about us as human beings being willing to accept conflicting models, when we can compartmentalize our lives in order to avoid seeing the conflicts.*

*Early quantum physicists, like Neils Bohr, recognized that descriptions of how quantum particles behave were very* similar to the way Taoists describe reality. In the 1970s a book came out by Fritjof Capra called the Tao of Physics, which explicitly made the connection between spirit and science. But despite this similarity between the way Taoists describe reality and descriptions of energy and matter used by quantum physicists, up until recently there has been little effort to describe how spirit works biologically. No one has figured out how to connect descriptions of inner spiritual experience with how quantum particles like photons, electrons and quarks operate.

You could say that for many of the students here, bridging this gap is what the Center for Consciousness Studies is all about. One of our professors thinks the reason this gap has remained largely unexplored is because the medical-pharmaceutical industry is threatened by it. But while Western science has held back from exploring the inner human spiritual experience, that has not been true of other cultures. The Taoist and Buddhist cultures have accepted descriptions of inner spiritual experience as valid measurements of these states. In the West, we have discounted the relevance of such descriptions of the human inner state because they weren't scientifically quantifiable.

No one has said this in class, Father, but it seems to me that what has been lacking is an approach to understanding reality from the type of unitive consciousness perspective which you talk so much about. Somehow we need a perspective that eliminates the dualism between Western science and the non-material and non-local aspects of our human spiritual experience.

*Well, you can see I am very excited what I am learning. I hope your conference is going well and that your health is holding up. Send me an email when you get a chance.*

*In the bonds of obedience to the gift of God's love,*

*Brother Isaac*

Father O'Donnell read Dawson's email and smiled. He remembered when Will Dawson first came to the monastery alone and lost. Father O'Donnell was unsure whether or not to take a chance on this former CIA officer. But Father O'Donnell had learned over the years to practice in himself a willingness to be open to whoever showed up needing help. His willingness was rewarded. Not only did Dawson become a fervent student of the science of the spiritual life, he also became a leader with the other brothers at the monastery. His email to Father O'Donnell was not really telling the elderly priest anything new, but Dawson's enthusiasm was itself a joy.

Only a hunt-and-peck typist, Father O'Donnell wrote a short note to Dawson thanking him for his email and encouraging him to continue to provide detailed reports on the most important things that he was learning. He was delighted the next day to get a return email.

*Dear Father O'Donnell,*

*I think my classes are beginning to hit pay dirt. The key is this change in perspective to the realization that all living things, indeed everything, has non-material, non-local and non-*

*temporal connections. This is fascinating and undermines the heart of the Newtonian view of reality.*

*The biggest Newtonian assumption that we have to give up is this idea that we are separate objects that think and feel on our own, independent of being impacted by the reality of other people and things. The quantum view is that our thoughts and feelings originate in the quantum field, the same place that subatomic particles like electrons and protons originate. These thoughts and feelings are then projected into material reality through our senses.*

*The dazzling thing about applying quantum mechanic principles to life is that once we understand how we think and feel from a quantum perspective, then by analogy we can understand how the universe thinks and feels. This may sound heretical, Father, but we are talking now about understanding God in a new and deeper way.*

*So the challenge in class that the professor is trying to get us to confront is how do we reconcile the two versions of reality that we participate in—on the one hand, this sensation we have of ourselves as isolated material objects moving about, and, on the other hand, being connected across time and space with each other in our feelings and thoughts. Again, it seems to be the dualism that gets us in trouble because we see things as being only here or there, not really here and there. In the spiritual world, we know prayers are answered, we know that we can experience an encounter with a person who lived 2000 years ago right in the present moment during the Eucharist. We intuitively understand that reality is much greater than*

THE ARMAGEDDON CHOICE

*what we perceive with our five senses.*

*While quantum mechanics is a very complex subject, there are two key factors our professor has emphasized that we need to understand: the holographic nature of the quantum field and the probabilistic behavior of quantum level events. The scientific, non-dual understanding of reality is exemplified in the hologram.*

*I must say, Father, that I am having trouble getting my arms around this idea of what a hologram actually is. I think it is because I never did that great in math and the underlying dynamic of the hologram is explained by sine waves. I remember the term from algebra, but sure couldn't define it for you now. This same math is used in modern cell phone transmission design and other electronic applications and now, get this, as a way to understand how spirit works in matter. This sine wave math describes how information can be spread out and not in one place. It also does a great job of describing the behavior of light.*

*So even though I am not sure how holograms work, I do see from our professor's explanation that they work in a very specific, scientific way and that they are able to contain non-local information and that they can contain a lot of information. In real, linear life, I am separate from you out here in New Mexico while you are in Boston, but holographically, the information about the connectedness of you and me is everywhere; and because of this it is possible for me to experience a deep connection to you during prayer time.*

*The reason this hologram stuff is important is because the quantum field is a hologram of our material world. While things with lots of mass act just like Newton predicted, at the very small scale of protons, neutrons and photons, matter acts very un-Newtonian like. At this level, particles that appear to be separated by space and time are actually connected and influence one another instantaneously. So the Newtonian world exists, like one of those little Russian dolls that lives in another larger quantum doll, in a larger field where all matter and energy exists.*

*What has prevented us from making the shift from the cause and effect world is that quantum equations do not give cause and effect outcomes. What they do give is predictable results that occur based on probability distribution.*

*So the quantum field is two things at once. It is the expression of data that is the material world in waves, just like the waves of a hologram that contain data. You could say these waves are the spiral DNA of our material world, and the field is also the waves that determine what happens in our material world, or—to stay with the DNA analogy—which genes get expressed. The waves also mathematically represent the probability distribution for the outcomes potentially available to any given expression. Thus the quantum field of all reality is nowhere and timeless and everywhere and every-when.*

*Well, I hope I expressed this in some manner that is understandable. It is time for me to go to the chapel for evening prayers. Every time I go, I miss you and Man.*

*In the bonds of obedience to the gift of God's love,*

*Brother Isaac*

Father O'Donnell appreciated Dawson's enthusiasm for the science of quantum mechanics, but for Father O'Donnell it was all much simpler. He did not need a scientific explanation of what it means to abide in Christ. With his health failing, it was simply enough to have the benefit of many years of spiritual discipline so that it was easy for him to enter that non-dual space with God. However, he did wish to support Dawson's new learning, even though he also knew that head knowledge about the spiritual life was often an obstacle to full participation in that life. He wrote out a quick email.

*Brother Isaac,*

*Thank you so much for your email. Your description of material reality being everywhere and timeless reminds me of mystical descriptions of living constantly in the presence of God. God is that non-local reality that is available to us anywhere, anytime. Prayer is the word we have used for centuries to describe the process of communicating between the objective Newtonian reality and a quantum or spiritual reality. Try to experience this reality just as much as you are learning about it.*

*Blessings, Father O.*

# Chapter 12

Blaine was shocked. Sitting in her email in-box was an email from Professor Gallagher. She had not seen or heard from Professor Gallagher since he delivered his sensational paper at the International Enneagram conference in Turin, Italy in which he showed how the Enneagram was the basis for Jesus' wisdom teachings of transformation.

Without even opening the email, she could tell from its size he had a lot to say. Without knowing why, she was anxious about opening the email. Professor Gallagher was so instrumental in her leaving the pain of her past behind, first by hiring her as his research assistant and then through his personal kindness and caring for her. But in some way, he represented a part of her past that she did not want to go back to. The part of herself when she lived on the dark side as a computer hacker, using every ounce of her hacking ability just to survive.

Her cursor hovered over the Delete icon. Still, she owed Professor Gallagher a lot. Finally she took a deep breath, realizing she had more tools than she had ever had in her life to deal with difficulties. She was in the process of creating a great problem in her mind, without even knowing what the email was about. Maybe Gallagher was just sending her a funny cartoon or some new article he had written. She smiled and opened his email. A moment later, as she plowed through, she wished she'd hit Delete.

*Dear Blaine,*

*I hope your life is going well in Germany. Everything is okay here. You know nothing much upsets the small-town life of small-time professors.*

*I have continued to work on the origins of the Enneagram and even though I thought I found the seminal origins in the message of Jesus, which you so wonderfully helped me uncover, I have been digging deeper and finding even more.*

*I am writing you because your talents for finding out information were so incredibly helpful. Without your assistance, I am sure I would never have been able to produce a credible paper for the conference, much less one that was so highly acclaimed.*

*Here is my dilemma!*

*I have discovered what I call the Enneagram of Creation. Like the discoveries we made of the Enneagram of the Lord's Prayer, the Enneagram of the Sermon on the Mount, the Enneagram of Spiritual Discernment, and the Enneagram of Love, the Enneagram of Creation is hidden in plain view. It is found in the first chapter of Genesis.*

Images of each of those flashed in her mind.

*After reading the creation story over and over for a week, one night I dreamed that there were nine utterances of God starting, "Let there be..." Sure enough, when I looked the next day, there they were in plain view. I was immediately able to chart out the Enneagram of Creation. There could be nothing more dynamic than creation, so the order of creation given in Genesis follows the Law of Seven, that is, it follows the order of the quotient of seven divided into one, and therefore goes from Point One, to Point Four, to Point Two, to Point Eight, to Point Five, to Point Seven. Then the Law of Three: Points Three, Nine and Six.*

*Here is what it looks like:*

Let there be light — Point One
Let there be firmament, Heaven, matter — Point Four
Let there be waters gathered together — Point Two
Let there be dry land, the Earth — Point Eight
Let there be plants — Point Five
Let there be stars, sun and moon — Point Seven
Let there be living creatures in the water and the air — Point
       Three
Let there be living creatures on the land — Point Nine
Let there be mankind — Point Six

Here is the presentation in a diagram:

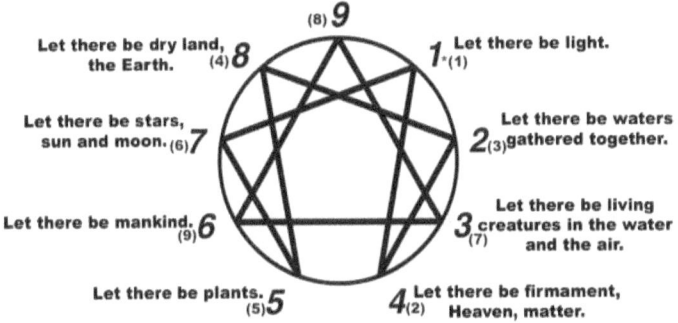

**Enneagram of Creation**

Let there be living creatures on the land.

(8) *9*

Let there be dry land, the Earth. (4)*8*

*1* Let there be light. (1)

Let there be stars, sun and moon. (6)*7*

*2* (3) Let there be waters gathered together.

Let there be mankind. (9)*6*

*3* Let there be living creatures in the water and the air. (7)

Let there be plants. (5)*5*

*4* (2) Let there be firmament, Heaven, matter.

*number in parentheses is the order of movement

Blaine paused. Despite the worry triggered by his email, she was nonetheless intrigued by Professor Gallagher's new discoveries.

*I was getting ready to publish a paper about this new discovery when I got wind that there is a professor at MIT who has discovered something called the Enneagram of the Sky and my old nemesis, Professor Walter Blalock, has now discovered something called the Enneagram of Early Christianity. You will remember Professor Blalock is the man you talked to in the Vatican Library.*

Blaine felt a tenseness in her shoulders just remembering the anxious moments as she had downloaded on a zip drive two years of Professor Blalock's research notes off his hard drive, while Will Dawson had taken him up to the Vatican library coffee shop.

*I have tried to talk to my two colleagues about their discoveries, and told them I would be glad to share my new findings if we might work together and do a joint article; however, they both are still very upset about my paper at Turin presenting information that they feel was in their proprietary domain of research.*

*The bottom line is I think all three of us are finally focusing in on unraveling the Enneagram of History. I do not want to have the importance of this message diluted by academic infighting and obfuscation.*

*Blaine, I need you to find out for me what these other two professors have found. I know this is a lot to ask, but I did not know where else to turn. You have already made a huge difference in my life. Help me if you can.*

*Professor G.*

Blaine was about to hit the Delete button. But she hadn't been doing all of this consciousness training to act without thinking and feeling things through. She would have to talk to her sister mentor and Rat. She was trying to leave her old hacking ways behind. She was discovering that the process of advancing her consciousness required greater and greater degrees of honesty, both internal honesty and honesty in how she acted in the external world. She did not want to turn back her progress, even at the request of someone who had helped her so very much and whom she cared about.

*       *       *

The day after Blaine told Rat about Professor Gallagher's email and how distressed she was by his request, Rat sent her an email with the answers, quite literally all the answers to the questions that Professor Gallagher posed. Rat had no scruples about hacking into anyone's information; in fact, it was the source of his greatest pleasure in life. So, rather than try to counsel Blaine about whether she should hack into these two professors' files, he made it easy. He did the job for her. She studied Rat's email again.

*Liebste,*

*I couldn't resist taking a peek to see if there was anything there for you to actually worry about trying to get for your old buddy Gallagher. I will leave it to you to decide if this is meaningful information.*

*This is what the professor at MIT has figured out—which he calls the Enneagram of the Sky. He has tried to work backwards from what Gallagher presented about the insights of Evagrius, the great Desert Father who lived 300 years after Christ. Evagrius referred to eight habits of the mind which block the Enneagram virtues.*

*Evagrius believed in the wisdom precept of "As above, so below." What the MIT professor has done is look back at the astronomy of the sky as it existed at the time of Evagrius. What he found was that the sky presented a dynamic pattern of interaction between the sun, the full moon, the waning moon, the waxing moon and the five planets known at the time. Contemplation of this pattern, like contemplation of an icon, reveals the imprint of the Enneagram in the reality of the sky in several provocative ways.*

*Start with the moon.  The moon has three phases: waxing, waning and full, representing the three domains of the Enneagram.  The moon takes twenty-seven days to complete its cycle in the sky. The twenty-eighth day represents the night when the moon is completely dark and not visible. If you plot this graphically in a circle, it gives a chart with a gap in the bottom. The gap represents the night the moon is not visible. This is what it looks like:*

## Moon Phases in the Night Sky

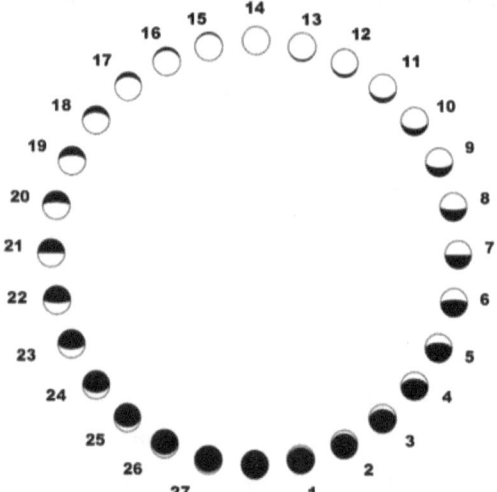

THE ARMAGEDDON CHOICE

*Then if you connect the moon phase every sixty degrees this is what you get:*

## Enneagram of the Night Sky

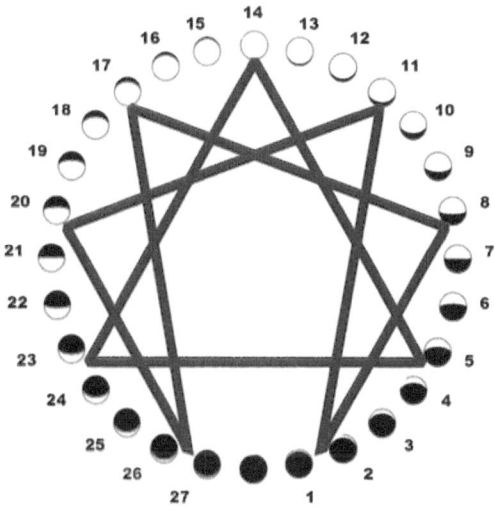

*In ancient times, people thought that the gods and goddesses were up in the sky. So there was an implicit relationship between the dynamic pattern of the night sky and the Earth's inhabitants. Each god or goddess had a human trait, which, carried to the extreme, was the negative side, or passion, of that god or goddess. Later these archetypal faults were designated as points on the Enneagram and seven of those points correspond to the Seven Deadly Sins. Ponticus Evagrius would have recognized eight of them as follows: Avarice, Pride, Acedia, Anger, Sadness, Gluttony, Lust, and Vainglory. Missing from Evagrius' list would have been the primal energy beneath all the passions—Fear/Doubt.*

*When Evagrius looked skyward at night he would have observed nine moving elements visible to the naked eye—the planets Saturn, Jupiter, Mars, Venus, and Mercury; plus the Sun and then the Moon in each of its three cardinal presentations: half-full, full, and half-empty. Of course, these objects in the night sky were each named for gods by the Greeks: Kronos (Saturn), Helios, (Sun), Selene (Moon), Ares (Mars), Hermes (Mercury), Zeus (Jupiter), and Aphrodite (Venus). The vices of each of the Greek gods mirror the habits of the mind that Evagrius noted as blocking the way to God.*

| | |
|---|---|
| Avarice | Saturn |
| Pride | Sun/Helios |
| Acedia | Full Moon/Selene |
| Anger | Mars |
| Sadness | Mercury |
| Gluttony | Jupiter |
| Lust | Venus |
| Vainglory | Waxing Moon/Artemis |

*Missing from Evagrius' list and the primal energy beneath all the passions:*

| | |
|---|---|
| Fear/Doubt | Waning Moon/Hera |

*Or, if this information is placed on the Enneagram image, this is the result:*

## Enneagram of the Planets and Passions

*The imprint of the Enneagram was found in the ancient night skies and in the nature of the gods and goddesses thought to inhabit this realm.*

*The research of the other professor shows the imprint of the Enneagram is also found in the early Christian communities and in the message Jesus tailored for each of these communities.*

Okay, thought Blaine, so the ancients believed they saw the pattern of the Enneagram in the interactions of the heavenly bodies, so what? This is just more Enneagram trivia, which if I provide it to Professor Gallagher will simply be an amusement for him, which might prevent him from becoming an even grumpier old man. Give me a break! I don't want something like this to pull me back into my old hacking ways.

Blaine had come to realize through her work with the SOS sisters that hacking was a reaction out of fear of the world, and what she was trying to do now in her life was respond to the world from love. That place of love was still very new and tender, and thanks to her work with the sisters and one long afternoon hike with Man, it was the place where she wanted to live. She had hacked her body and hacked the information of those who controlled her. Hacking could be intense, providing the thrill of a pseudo-aliveness, but she now knew it was not a way to live.

She would finish reading Rat's email explaining what he found out about Professor Blalock's research and the Enneagram of Early Christianity, and then figure out a way to respond to Professor Gallagher that was a polite and firm no. She read on.

*Professor Blalock's research is straightforward. While the other professor was looking at the skies at the time of Jesus, Professor Blalock was looking at the ground, or, rather more accurately, the geography of the early Christian communities. Revelations Chapters Two and Three contain letters to seven of the early Christian communities that grew up in Asia after Jesus' life. These communities were at Ephesus, Smyrna, Pergamum, Thyatira, Sardis, Philadelphia, and Laodicea. If you chart these on a map, you see that they form a seven-pointed circle with an opening at the bottom. From an Enneagram perspective, the points that are missing are Points Three and Six which are the same two points missing in the churches later declaration of the Seven Deadly Sins. Points Three and Six, representing Deceit and Fear, can be seen as the underlying emotional and mental springboards for the remaining seven points.*

## Enneagram of Early Christian Communities

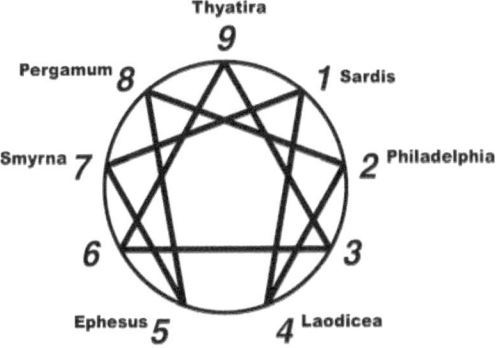

*If you line up the messages to each of these communities found in these two chapters of the Book of Revelation, then you see that the wisdom message of Jesus, spread throughout what was then called Asia, today Turkey, in the form of an Enneagram of the Seven Deadly Sins in Early Christian Places.*

*Here is Professor Blalock's outline of the messages contained in the letters to each Christian community, starting on the left side of the Enneagram circle at Point Five and moving clockwise as the towns are named in Revelation (and including with each point the particular Seven Deadly Sin or block to transformation of that type):*

Point Five (Avarice) — Ephesus — "you have great theological understanding but not sufficient love"

Point Six (Fear)

Point Seven (Lust) — Smyrna — "you will be thrown in jail and have no options and because of that you will be born into new life and freedom"

Point Eight (Gluttony) — Pergamum — "do not fall into the excesses of the pagan religions of eating food sacrificed to idols and the immorality of pagan sexual practices"

Point Nine (Torpor) — Thyatira — "you will be given to because of your dynamic good work that comes from your heart and mind"

Point One (Anger) — Sardis — "your works look perfect, but you are just invested in the appearance of perfection and substance is missing underneath the appearance of perfection"

Point Two (Pride) — Philadelphia — "you are praised for going with humility through the open door I have set before you"

Point Three (Deceit)

Point Four (Envy) — Laodicea — "you are lukewarm about matters of the Spirit, your envy is misplaced on material things, not on the gold and purity of living in the spiritual Kingdom"

## Enneagram of the Seven Deadly Sins in Early Christian Communities

**(Torpor) Thyatira**
"You will be given to because of your dynamic good work that comes from your heart and mind."

**(Gluttony) Pergamum**
"Do not fall into the excesses of the pagan religions of eating food sacrificed to idols and the immortality of pagan sexual practices."

**(Anger) Sardis**
"Your works look perfect, but you are just invested in the appearance of perfection and substance is missing underneath the appearance of perfection."

**(Lust) Smyrna**
"You will be thrown in jail and have no options and because of that you will be born into new life and freedom."

**(Pride) Philadelphia**
"You are praised for going with humility through the open door I have set before you."

**(Avarice) Ephesus**
"You have great theological understanding but not sufficient love."

**(Envy) Laodicea**
"You are lukewarm about matters of the Spirit, your envy is misplaced on material things, not on the gold and purity of living in the spiritual Kingdom."

Interesting, maybe even astonishing, thought Blaine. She could see how a Five Enneagram type like Professor Gallagher might latch on to this information as really important, since Fives' compulsive device for knowledge was a way they avoided opening their hearts. She also saw that she would be doing him no favor by strengthening his compulsivity, by affirming his greed for knowledge, even if it was amazingly interesting knowledge. On the other hand, it would be easy enough to send him what Rat had found and since she had not hacked it, she could rationalize that it would not be a step backwards for her.

Blaine soon became aware that her muddled thoughts about what to do meant she needed spiritual discernment help from Sister Maria. Even through her confusion, she felt a warm surge in her chest. She would so love to talk to Man about this. She knew he would have some great insights from his ability to tap into the energy and thought fields of the wisdom tradition of his people.

Maybe the timing of Professor Gallagher's email was just right for reasons totally unrelated to its contents. She had been distracted from her practices at the convent ever since Man went back to the monastery in Germany. Rat seemed to be the communication bridge with everyone, and he told her recently that Man requested permission to go back to the Southwest to see Father O'Donnell.

Blaine knew Man was not happy being away from the Southwest. He had a bodily connection to the land of his people. She also knew that, like her, he was not happy being relatively close to her, while unable to visit her regularly. She felt Man shared the same feelings—so close, but so far. In addition, Rat indicated that Father O'Donnell was having health issues and this was another reason Man wanted to return.

Blaine realized that if Man was going to be heading back to the States—if she were going to see him before he left—she better act soon. Maybe her need to talk to Man about Professor Gallagher's email was exactly the excuse she needed for the Mother Superior to let her go to Germany. Blaine had fought for everything she ever had in her life, starting with her sanity. She did not want Man to leave without at least fighting for the chance for their relationship to grow. She knew there was no chance for them to stay together right now, but maybe if they could actually spend a bit more time together, what began to happen when their energy fields dissolved into each other would deepen even further. If she gave this a chance to happen, then maybe, just maybe, she could surrender to whatever the great mystery of life might ultimately bring them.

# Chapter 13

Brother Isaac was deeply distressed. He and the other brothers were advised by Mother Mary that Father O'Donnell was admitted to Mass General Hospital in Boston when the conference concluded. After a series of tests the diagnosis came back—fourth stage lung cancer. A cloud hung over the brothers at the monastery. How could this be happening to Father O'Donnell? Though he was in his early seventies, he seemed young, and it was impossible for Brother Isaac and the other brothers to think about being at the monastery long-term without the guidance and love of Father O'Donnell.

Mother Mary assured the brothers that it was indeed fortunate that Father O'Donnell traveled to Boston for the conference. The opportunity for the best treatment for his cancer was much better in Boston than what he might receive in rural New Mexico. The brothers could understand this intellectually, but it did not ease their emotional longing to be with Father O'Donnell in his time of suffering. Mother Mary encouraged Brother Isaac to continue to email Father O'Donnell with updates on the progress of his studies, since it would be the one thing he could do to support his beloved mentor from a distance. Although Father O'Donnell might not be able to reply, Mother Mary knew that it would be comfort to both the student and the teacher.

For Brother Isaac, this was the least he could do.

*Dear Father O'Donnell,*

*We are all very grieved by your illness. Please know that we hold you in prayer each time we are in the chapel.*

*I would like to continue to update you on my studies. Things are moving along. I am beginning to understand how the quantum field allows things with little or no mass to be distributed across time and space. The next step is the realization that something can exist in the quantum field across space and time and also be observed in a particular moment of space and time. Those on a spiritual journey have long been comfortable with this idea of us having both a timeless aspect and a material aspect at the same time—our physical bodies and our immortal souls.*

*The difficulty is in using the quantum field to account for the non-material phenomenon that humans experience when the scale of biological systems is so much greater than the subatomic scale in which subatomic particles function in the quantum field. Because living organisms operate on such a larger scale, most research has assumed that Newtonian cause and effect applies and that there are no quantum effects in living systems. But the application of Newtonian cause-and-effect to living systems is slowly unraveling, as experiments have begun to show that thoughts, perceptions, and feelings have a holographic form and a subatomic existence.*

*One challenging aspect that scientists here are trying to*

*understand is, assuming that our thoughts and feelings exist as holograms, how does this information communicate with a larger thought field outside itself, and how does the larger thought field communicate back to the individual? Or, how do fields communicate, particularly fields involving living things?*

*First, it's important to wrap the mind around the idea that we do not see or hear like a camera or tape recorder. Rather, sensory data is converted into holograms before being processed by the brain. Then the raw inputs from the environment are interwoven with familiar holograms drawn from sensory memory. This sensory data hologram is then projected out. This is all fairly well established in experiments by Carl Pribram and Dennis Gabor. What is amazing, and what makes so much sense, is the insight that our perception of non-sensory information—that is intuitive or spiritual experience—works the same way. We think and feel in holograms.*

*Our thoughts, feelings, ideas—our entire interior life occurs in holograms. In other words, our interior life has the same structure as the quantum field. Our thoughts and feelings originate in the field and operate as holographic structures. Said another way the structure of the field consists of subatomic energy that characterizes thoughts and feelings.*

*So we understand that the structure of our interior life parallels the way some subatomic particles work in the quantum field. The big challenge is to understand how our biological system, which appears to only have this macro structure, also communicates at a very different micro scale.*

THE ARMAGEDDON CHOICE

*I'm going to a lecture about that tomorrow and I will try to send you a follow-up email.*

*The rest of the brothers and I pray for you constantly and hope that your recovery from the chemo treatment is progressing well. We are anxious that you will be able to return to the monastery soon.*

*In the bonds of obedience to the gift of God's love,*

*Brother Isaac*

Father O'Donnell read Brother Isaac's email and sighed. There was a time in his life when he would have delighted in the scientific exploration of consciousness that Brother Isaac was immersed in. Now it all seemed a bit trivial. He asked the nurse at his bedside to type a quick email reply to Brother Isaac, thanking him for his report on the lectures and asking him to be in touch with Rat, so that Rat could let Man know of Father O'Donnell's condition.

At the mention of Rat's name, the nurse's eyebrows lifted. But she had spent many years on the cancer care unit and not many things that patients asked for, or what their friends were named, fazed her. Even though it meant more work for her, she could tell that the new hospital policy of allowing patients to receive personal emails improved patient morale and well-being. The policy did not include transmitting replies, but she was glad to do it for Father O'Donnell.

The following day, she printed out the next email from Brother

Isaac and brought it to Father O'Donnell.

*Dear Father O'Donnell,*

*You are in my prayers and the prayers of all the brothers here. We have been informed that the Provincial of the Order requested a special day of prayer for you all day next Thursday. I hope this will be a blessing. I believe from what was presented in class today I can explain to you how it will help you recover.*

*Oh, and I did email Rat and let him know your situation and asked him to convey that information to Man. I also asked him to let Mother Mary and the members of her Order know, and he advised me that she and the rest of the Sacred Order of the Sisters of Mary of Magdala were already aware of your condition and would be joining the special prayer vigil for you next Thursday.*

*Back to the lecture. It seems spirit really does live in matter. We start with the fact that our brain is made up of approximately 35,000,000,000 neurons, with each neuron having as many as between 1000 to 10,000 nerve endings or synapses. The synapses carry electrochemical signals between two neurons. The holograms exist in the micro voltage oscillations between the synapses. These waves that make up our interior state have no mass, they just carry information.*

*One of the things that the Center for Consciousness Studies is proudest of is their theory that microtubules in our cells are the basic units of conscious awareness. Microtubules are made* out of a protein called tubulin. Each microtubule is a tube made out of rings of 13 tubulin molecules. The microtubule is essentially the link between matter at the macro level and subatomic particles. The microtubules act like quantum particles, and also like macro matter. When the microtubules cycle into the quantum state, they carry information in a hologram into the quantum field. When the microtubules cycle back into a macro state they carry information from the field to the holograms existing between the synapses. In other words communication is two-way.

What we see from this operation of quantum biology is that we have a mechanism in each cell by which our thoughts, feelings, and all the non-material spiritual aspects of our being originate in the field. They are both non-local and non-temporal, or, in other words, they are everywhere and every-when. What this means is that when we talk about losing our memory, we aren't actually losing anything inside our heads, we are simply losing access to part of the field.

In trying to understand this, one of the things that our professor keeps stressing is that the state of our language itself makes it difficult to explain this because our language is so cause-and-effect, or so non-quantum. What she is trying to convey to us is that the quantum field is not some shadowy aspect that follows the material body. It is not something separate that we are connected to; rather, it is the origin of us and our reality. We are each a projection of information living in the field. In other words, spirit comes first. Matter is a manifestation of spirit in time and space.

*Our prayers for you, Father, move from the microtubules of our thoughts and feelings into the quantum field and from there into your body for your healing. Prayer may not be cause-and-effect. But hopefully our prayers create a greater likelihood of a positive outcome. For now, I rest assured in that.*

*In the bonds of obedience to the gift of God's love,*

*Brother Isaac*

The nurse remained by his bedside as Father O'Donnell read Brother Isaac's email. He looked up at her with an animation she had not seen in the past several days. He let the paper on which the email was printed rest on his chest, as he struggled to fill his lungs with air. "You know, I think this man is going to do all right. Not just by me, but maybe even by you too," he said, looking at the nurse with a light in his eye. "When I say doing right by you too, I mean by all of us. May I give you a brief reply?" The nurse smiled and jotted down Father O'Donnell's reply. She returned to the nurses station, sat down at her computer, typed in his words and sent them off.

*Brother Isaac,*

*You are learning good stuff. Thank you and the other brothers and our Order for your prayers.*

*The quantum field your prayers take you into is an aspect of the consciousness of God and will determine my outcome. All prayer is a way of wrestling with God in the quantum field. I*

THE ARMAGEDDON CHOICE

*am afraid God wants you to wrestle with him, even perhaps over me. I thank you deeply for that.*

*Love and blessings,*

*Father O*

# Chapter 14

Father Hay heard the knock and went to his front door. He opened the door and there stood a smiling Godfrey. It had been two months since the two men sat together in spiritual direction. Given the long gap, Father Hay was concerned that Adams might have slipped backwards into greater anxieties about the state of democracy in America, which had been the focus of their last conversation.

Since their last meeting, a Chinese company, controlled by the Chinese government, had successfully completed its tender offer for GOD. The unreal state of affairs now was that not only was the United States ruled by a corporation as its President, that corporation was controlled by a communist country.

All these thoughts flashed through Father Hay's mind in an instant as he sensed from the smile on Adam's face that his directee was in a good place.

"Welcome," said Father Hay. "It is good to see you."

"Likewise," said Godfrey. "It is amazing how good I am feeling, particularly in light of the fact that the country seems to be in a self-induced trance. Just as long as the drug of consumerism is available, I guess an addict nation is not about to fret." He breathed deeply and grinned again at Father Hay. "Yes, despite all that, I am doing great."

"What do you attribute that to?"

"I was thinking about that on the way driving over here. It is new. I think it must simply be that I am into a very regular rhythm doing my contemplative practices. I am doing centering prayer at least twice a day. Then I do the daily examen at night with Jeff. He wasn't so keen about participating at first, but this is a ritual that has really strengthened our relationship. And I have been practicing welcoming prayer to the extent that it automatically comes to mind when I start to contract out of anxiety or fear."

"That is wonderful," said Father Hay, beaming as he handed Godfrey a cup of steaming hot tea. He led the way into the room where they would have their session together. After both men were seated, they sat silently for several minutes, as was their customary practice.

Father Hay inquired, "So what seems to be most up for you that would be helpful to explore—to discover where the Spirit is or is not present?"

"I am feeling so grateful," said Godfrey, "not only is Jeff participating with me in one of my contemplative practices, I am trying to learn golf so I can play with him. You know, it was the challenge to our relationship caused by my spiritual journey that first got me here. Then external events kind of took over my inner psychic landscape and I got caught up in the struggle to understand what was happening in our country as dualistic democracy was destroying it." Godfrey paused, sat back in his chair.

"It is not that this issue has in any way been resolved by our country, or even that there is any collective understanding of what is happening, but the contemplative practices have allowed me to feel like I am doing the one thing I can do, and that is work on the evolution of my own consciousness. That, in turn, has allowed me to be able to tolerate the anxiety of this huge political change, which frankly, looks apocalyptic. I guess the one thing that still seems to be a spiritual separation for me is that the church's beliefs are at such odds with reality. This causes me great discomfort.  I am ashamed of being connected with much of what the church professes to believe."

Father Hay nodded. His directee was consolidating in his psyche much that he had experienced. He was making good progress without regressing. Father Hay waited silently, knowing it was best if he simply allowed Godfrey to continue at his own pace.

"Like you said last time, I really get that we are not Jesusians, but Christians. I like your idea that the Shroud of Turin evidence suggests Jesus survived the crucifixion. And I do believe that Paul, who does seem to be a gay man like me, and who included his own misogynistic remarks in letters to early churches, was the person who took dictation directly from Jesus that gives expression more clearly than anywhere else in the Bible to what it means to live in Christ." Godfrey paused

THE ARMAGEDDON CHOICE

again. Different feelings within him seemed to be competing for a voice.

Father Hay simply focused his energy attentively and silently on Adams.

Adams continued. "I'm not sure how to put this—working with you to have a realistic interpretation of certain biblical events has helped my faith so much, but at the same time I seem to have lost something. I really want to experience Christ in the Eucharist, but if he didn't actually die from the crucifixion, how is that possible?"

Father Hayes smiled. The waiting had been fruitful. Godfrey was finally able to articulate what was bothering him most.

"You know, Godfrey, this was among your first concerns, which we discussed early in your direction. One of the things that was pushing you away from the church back then was that you could not stomach the scapegoat theory of the crucifixion. I think your rejection is supported by a lot of scholarly research, which suggests that after the Christian church became the state religion, it theologically regressed back to embrace the scapegoat mythology that dominated the thought and practices during much of Hellenistic times, and on which the Roman empire was built.

"In fact, the scapegoat theory of the crucifixion is more solidly based in a pre-Christian theory of projection than any reality.

"But I hear your question: If we understand that the purpose of

Jesus' life was to bear away our sins by being a scapegoat, where does that leave us with this idea of resurrection? Perhaps it means that the question of whether or not Christ survived the crucifixion physically doesn't really matter. Maybe in the fourth century, Christians in this new state religion needed to believe that Jesus was killed for their sins on the cross and did not survive the crucifixion in order for them to make a meaningful connection with his Spirit. But we have something today that those Christians in the Roman state church did not have. We have this unfolding knowledge of quantum biology. The great reality is we know through our understanding of quantum biology that Christ is everywhere, every-when.

"It is fascinating what the Shroud of Turin suggests, but the truth is we don't need to get caught up in the whole debate about whether or not Jesus survived the crucifixion. Why? Because resurrection is the great reality of the law of conservation of matter and energy. Resurrection is a not-too-scientific word to describe the law of conservation of energy at the subatomic level. Christ is as fully alive and next to you as your next breath. All you have to do is be willing to open the window of longing for the divine so you can enter the quantum field where He exists right next to you.

"Your salvation depends not on scapegoat theology, but upon whether or not you identify more with what is not you, that is, with the greater reality that is all around you, or whether you identify more with what you think is you. The latter is the ego, small-self you, which seems to be so vividly who we believe we are. But I am afraid if you identify with that you, then you stay stuck in matter. Without sufficient love in your life, sufficient longing for the divine, then not enough of your matter gets changed to energy to allow you to also be the non-local you. Like resurrection, love is another word for the law of conservation of energy at the subatomic level.

"Ultimately, whether or not we choose to identify with the small self, separate self or that part of our self connected through the transfer of energy in subatomic particles to the rest of reality, is a choice we all make, consciously or unconsciously. Because it is such a momentous decision, I call it the Armageddon Choice. Your current life is just an eye blink. The Armageddon Choice is about your essence for eternity.

"But, as we have discussed so often, this knowledge and three bucks will get you a cup of coffee. We all both make the choice and we don't. We practice the contemplative practices that are going to give us a chance to be conscious enough for the window of the subatomic energy flow of love to be open. Then you might say that the greater reality comes through the window and takes you with it. God longs for you just as you long for God. As Rumi says, the moon, our conscious and unconscious longing for connection with the Mystery of life, *won't use the door, only the window*. The door is Newtonian cause and effect; the window is subatomic probability.

"What I would suggest to you, Godfrey, is that you spend some time reading aloud the *Song of Solomon* to Jeff. This little book in the Old Testament is packed with an articulation of this tremendous energy of longing for God. Bring that energy more into your life and I expect the weight of the church's dysfunctional beliefs will ease. Faith, hope and love are all higher energy experiences. In contrast, belief is like a concrete block, overwhelmingly stuck in matter. As your heart-feltness grows with the rhythm of your contemplative practices, your experience of faith, hope and love will also grow. At the same time, your need for any particular beliefs will diminish. Only when we are caught up in fear do we cling to beliefs. We can't be in a state of love with the divine—allowing the non-local reality of Christ to be within us—and also be in a state of fear.

"The church as an institution is by definition stuck at a lower level of consciousness where it needs beliefs and doctrine to feel secure. You are growing beyond that, and yet at the same time in a very non-dualistic way, we still need the church to be where the community of those seeking to live in Christ can gather. Admittedly, that is not most of the people who are at church on Sunday celebrating civil religion, but it is the place we are most apt to find that remnant who sincerely and devotedly crave a life of Christ within."

A long pause ensued. The air was still, but a candle on the table between the two men flickered and danced in a celebration of light.

"As usual, Father, you have given me a lot to ponder. I will do that, and I will do it lightly as you have suggested before, knowing how easy it is for me to worry anything into a mental obsession. And, of course, I will continue to focus on the practices.

"I don't understand everything you have told me, but I do experience the joy with which you have shared these ideas. Even though I was feeling good when I first got here, I feel even lighter in spirit now. And yes, I won't forget to read the *Song of Solomon* to Jeff."

There was a glint in his eyes.

# Chapter 15

Blaine was delighted. Mother Mary approved a week's leave for her to go see Man so she could talk with him about what to do about Gallagher's email. Man was also able to get leave. Though Blaine did not know for sure, she suspected that her Mother Superior and Man's Abbot had discussed the whole thing. What she did not know was that the Abbot resisted Mother Mary's insistence that the couple have a chance to see if there lives might merge together. The Abbot saw it as a threat. His hope was that Man might remain in the Abbot's traditional celibate order. Mother Mary saw the chance for Blaine and Man to pursue a relationship as an essential step on their spiritual journey that might ultimately provide Blaine with a desire to be a part of the SOS. Happily for Blaine and Man, Mother Mary won out.

Mother Mary was not a permissive cupid. She insisted that someone go with Blaine. Of course, Aasia was more than willing. After consulting with Rat by email, Blaine decided that they should all meet in Copenhagen. Rat suggested they spend the week at Tivoli Gardens.

Rat and Man found a B & B for a decent weekly rate not far from Tivoli, where the owner allowed Man to keep Ooljee for a slight additional charge. Blaine and Aasia also found digs nearby.

Rat came to Copenhagen with three laptops, and was on them most of the first day. That changed after their first night together at Tivoli. Somehow the intrigue of the electronic screen was supplanted by the lights and magic of Tivoli Gardens.

They often spent time together as a group. But while they remained a foursome, they also became two couples. Blaine and Man were soon walking everywhere hand-in-hand and Rat seemed to be watching Aasia as intently if she were a computer screen.

Both Blaine and Aasia had done enough work at the convent to begin to be able to control their energy fields. They were each in their own way—with Aasia helped by her surgery—more confident as women. When Blaine opened up her energy field for Man, literally and figuratively he walked right up to her heart—their fields meshed. Aasia commented to Blaine after the first night, when the two women were back at their room, "Blaine, your and Man's energy fields tonight looked like double-dipped scoops of ice cream melting in the sun." Blaine just laughed. How sweet it was to have Aasia as a girlfriend whom she could trust and love.

Even Rat, who was oblivious to most non-computer things, sensed that Aasia's healing had changed her appearance and, more remarkably, the way people perceived her. A radiance poured from her. Every man who walked by her involuntarily turned and gazed. Aasia wore brighter, more femininely tailored clothes, and the men who gazed after her seemed oblivious to the scars on her arms and the healing pink ones exposed just above the curve of her shapely breasts.

The first night they went for dinner at Groften's, a traditional Danish restaurant right near the main entrance to Tivoli. As they left the restaurant, Rat pointed out the secret of Danish cuisine, "I have never had so much butter."

"Yes, let's do something to clear the arteries. Why don't we go on that ride over there?" Blaine pointed toward the Ferris Wheel with its brightly colored balloons hovering above each car.

"Sure, Blaine," said Man, watching the fairyland play of twinkling Tivoli lights dance across her face and light up her eyes. He turned and looked back. "Rat, do you and Aasia want to try that ride?" asked Man pointing.

"Of course," said Rat and he grabbed Aasia's hand and they came running behind Blaine and Man to get in the queue.

The first time their car came over the top of the Ferris Wheel, Blaine's body tensed and she instinctively grabbed Man's hand. Then she relaxed as the lights of Copenhagen dazzled below them and their car dropped smoothly through the night air like a slow exhalation of breath.

The next day was spent wandering among the beautiful gardens. Never in their lives had Blaine and Aasia seen so many beautiful flowers, especially roses. It was a sensory paradise. And everywhere couples of all ages were walking hand-in-hand or cuddled together on a bench overlooking a bed of flowers.

For all the extraordinary wonder of Tivoli Gardens during the day, night was the special time. With each evening came a new ride. The second night was the Golden Tower. It was seductive. Locked securely in the chair they rose slowly into the night sky, as if all they paid for was a view of the city. Then the bottom dropped. Suddenly Aasia found her voice. Blaine was next to Man and could not see her and Rat who were in two companion chairs, but Blaine could sure hear Aasia. Aasia screamed the whole way down, a scream that started in the high register of fear, but by the time their free fall ended, came from down deep in her gut.

Blaine was worried. Had some war trauma been re-triggered? After the ride she immediately ran over to Aasia, but she need not have worried. Aasia was clinging to Rat, who seemed not to know what to do. Aasia's cheeks were flushed so pink she looked like a young Dane. Fun had overridden fear. Somehow the adrenaline of fear had become the adrenaline of wild surrender and joy.

Aasia turned to Blaine, "That was incredible. I was so afraid at first and then something happened and I let go to the unknown joy of it and it was sooo beautiful." She was jumping up and down and pulling at Rat's arm.

And so the ritual continued—each night a new more daring

ride, and then later delicious ice cream.

It was on the third night when they were riding The Demon, a roller coaster that soared to heights above the city and then went into three incredible upside down loops, that Blaine lost it. She began to scream and she couldn't stop. Man, who seemed to handle all the rides with gentle amusement, became concerned about her. She went from looking white as a sheet to glowing like a beet.

When the ride was over and they were unloaded from their car, all three of them looked at Blaine expectedly. Blaine tried her best to look grim, then burst into laughter.

"Damn, that was good," she said. "At first I felt like I used to when I wanted to cut myself, then the circuits seem to overload and I just let go. I will have to tell the nuns back in Sweden they need to include Tivoli in their healing practices."

"Easy does it," said Man, as he felt this intense energy pouring off of Blaine. Her energy was strong, intense, fierce, and seductive all at the same time. He couldn't get enough of it. To her surprise, although Man was shy about showing affection in public, he pulled her close and gave her a long kiss. They finally broke when Ooljee began to growl. "Maybe we ought to do that ride again," Man said.

Aasia and Rat stood there looking at their friends with bemused expressions and then at each other. They too could feel the love spell of Tivoli. It was hard to resist.

The next night they were on the Star Flyer, the newest ride at Tivoli. Over two hundred feet high, it had them spinning and falling high above the city. But even though the Star Flyer was a more glamorous ride, followed later by the special excitement and fun of the Monsoon and the Odin Express, it was those first rides for Aasia and Blaine that they would always remember—where they gave voice to their terror and that voice turned to joy.

The week went by more quickly than any of them could have imagined. The last night they had a wonderful dinner at the Faergekroens Bryghus, sitting at a lakeside table looking out on the light and fountain show that emerged from the lake.

As they were watching, Aasia looked at Rat. He was a funny guy, but when Blaine first introduced Aasia to Rat, back when she was living a life of resolute despair, he treated Aasia as if she was the most important person he had ever met. Rat never seemed to notice how emotionally and physically disfigured she was. Now Rat was enchanted when she opened her energy field to him, and yet he appeared not to notice how her beautiful radiance turned the head of every guy she walked pass. He just looked at Aasia in the same awestruck way he always had, his nose quivering in its rat-like way, as if she had suddenly stepped out of his laptop into his life.

It was hard to believe this was their last night at Tivoli. The two couples, ever so tight, decided after dinner to go on their separate walks and meet later for dessert. On this last night there was no longer the need for some terrifying ride to allow them to surrender old, stored fear.

Man and Blaine walked down to the lake and curled up on a bench next to each other. There was silence between them. Neither wished to start the conversation that they both knew had to come.

Finally Man, ever courageous, began. "Blaine, one summer when I was about twelve I made a long trip from the rez to Minnesota with my dad. He had been sober for several months and so gotten a bit past the guilt and remorse of the last drunk and was so much fun to be with."

"We went to Pipestone National Monument in southwestern Minnesota. It seems that when the white man made a treaty with the natives, the chief insisted on a clause in the treaty giving native people the right to mine in the pipestone quarry for all times. Since the treaty was taking away all their land, giving native people access to a small quarry was a throw-away right.

"Now native people have to wait years to quarry, but my father had a relative who had a permit. So we went to quarry with him. For native people, the red stone is the compressed blood of our ancestors. We carve into this red stone these hollow shapes in which the flower fragrances of the prairie are smoked, and, in the process, we connect with our ancestors and their experiences of our land over the centuries. We experience that the idea we are separate from the land is an illusion."

Blaine began to get a little restless and worried. She feared that the circuitous nature of Man's story was leading up to his telling her that he would be leaving her. Welling up within her chest was the same tightness she felt when Will Dawson left her in Italy. Before the feeling took over, she remembered to use the breathing technique the SOS sisters had taught her so that she could stay present.

Man stopped. He sensed that Blaine's energy had gone somewhere else, but when he felt it return and connect with him, he continued.

"You must quarry deep to find the blood of your own ancestors. The long, horizontal layers of red stone are all maternal lines. Our understanding is that men bleed quickly and die, but women bleed often over many moons of their lives, and because of this, most of the time, the stone talks to women first.

"That summer my father and I had a wonderful time digging every day and staying up late at night talking to our relatives and new friends. My father told wonderful stories and sometimes he would get so tickled at his own tale that he wouldn't be able to finish the story because he would be laughing so hard.

"But even though we dug all summer, we never found stone that spoke to us, that told us it was the blood of our tribal ancestors. For hundreds of years native people have come from all over North America to quarry at Pipestone, it is a sacred place to many tribes, so maybe it was not surprising that we never found the vein of our family's blood."

Blaine snuggled even closer to Man. She put her hand on his shoulder and wove her fingers through his long, black hair. She had been so worried about this conversation, which she knew they had to have about their future, but from what Man was saying she did not have a clue what he was trying to tell her. But, she could tell his heart was open to her and she could feel her heart breaking open to him more deeply than she ever thought possible.

"When we got back home, my father started drinking again. I thought it was just time for the next bender, but later my uncle told me my father felt deeply disappointed that he was not able to find the layer of red stone that was the blood of his ancestors. This was a soul wound to my father. To us soul is like after you drink a glass of milk and a little white rime is left on the glass. Do you know what I mean?"

Blaine, her head only inches from Man, was not sure, but she nodded *yes*.

"We all drink experience, and like that white rime left on the glass, the residue that builds up in the blood between the heart and the kidneys is soul. I mean, you put people on dialysis and they have no soul, no emotional depth. Maybe you have heard the story of when Carl Jung went to the American Southwest in the early 1930s and visited with Chief Mountain Lake of the Taos people. I memorized their conversation in grammar school on the rez for a school play.

"Chief Mountain Lake told Jung: 'See how cruel the whites look, their lips are thin, their noses sharp, their faces furrowed and distorted by folds. Their eyes have a staring expression; they are always seeking something. What are they seeking? The whites always want something. They are always uneasy and restless. We do not know what they want. We do not understand them. We think that they are all mad.'

"When Jung asked why he thinks they are all mad, Mountain Lake replies, 'They say they think with their heads.'

"'Why of course,' says Jung, 'What do you think with?'

"'We think here,' says Chief Mountain Lake, indicating his heart.'"

Man paused and looked at Blaine. He could feel her openheartedness and her worry and fear of what he might say to her. He smiled and touched the side of her face with the tips of the fingers of his right hand.

"So I must go back to Pipestone. We are more ensouled—we live and think more deeply from our hearts—when we are in touch with the blood of our ancestors, the blood that ran through their hearts." He looked directly into Blaine's dark eyes. "I want you to go with me. I never thought much of white people. Really I didn't think much of them one way or the other. Kind of like Mountain Lake, I felt they were out of touch with themselves and the great flow of life. So I never thought I would want to be with a white woman like you, but your work with the sisters has made you different from the kind of white people that Mountain Lake was talking about. I can see that you have begun to think with your heart. And I believe that you might be able to help me find the red blood stone of my ancestors. If I can find that, then I will know what shape my life and our lives are suppose to have. I will know what the Great Spirit wants of me."

Ooljee, who was sitting patiently under their bench, as if on cue, issued a plaintive little whimper.

Blaine put both arms around Man's neck and moved her breasts against his chest. She could feel his hand pressing against the base of her spine and she was immediately aware of a surge of tingling between her legs. "If I go with you, Man, I do not want to be left by you. Are you sure you want a woman like me? With all my cuts and scars? I am afraid that once you see them all you will change your mind about me."

Man smiled at Blaine.

"Of course, I want you to be with me because I see that you are a warrior of great heart spirit. That you have many battle scars, where your spirit has counted coup over what would destroy you, only honors you. You are not a washed glass, I know that. Father O'Donnell has told me that our elders back at the time of Chief Mountain Lake participated in unconscious heart-thinking. Jung was a modern scientific explorer of consciousness, yet he was amazed when he encountered the reality of the real essence of heart consciousness. Jung could tell that the wisdom of the heart must be retrieved if mankind is to survive with his overdeveloped head knowledge, but even he was not sure how to consciously develop heart-thinking. What I have learned from Father O'Donnell is that Jesus, and the mystics who followed him, taught how it could be done. According to Father O'Donnell, Jesus knew that it would be marginalized people like my own who would have to do the teaching."

There would be time to talk about the details later—the impossible details of how in the world she could even travel back to the United States without being detained. But now Blaine allowed her body to feel the same surrender it had on The Demon as Man kissed her deeply. She let go of thought, and surrendered to the opening of her heart. She abandoned her restless mind to the gentle web of love she was experiencing pouring out of and into her heart. She stopped protecting her heart in order to live from it.

The next morning over breakfast, Blaine and Man told Rat and Aasia that they were both planning on going back together to the United States. They wanted Rat's help in trying to figure out how Blaine could get back into her home country. Rat was full of ideas and suggestions, but in the end the plan boiled down to simply what they knew. Rat would get Blaine a new passport, though that in itself was difficult. The problem with fake passports these days was that unless they matched the identity of someone already in the homeland computer who had left the country, they were not much help. Without a match in the homeland computer with someone already abroad, a huge red flag would pop up on the immigration officer's computer, which would be sure to get Blaine detained. Getting a forged passport that was based on having stolen someone's identity, before that person discovered it was stolen, was a dodgy matter.

Rat was convinced he could figure out how a stolen-identity passport could be obtained and Blaine's photo inserted in it. But he cautioned that even with a proper stolen passport it would be safer to go to Canada first and infiltrate back through the SOS convent border wilderness. Rat did not have to spend a lot of time trying to sell Blaine and Man on this idea. When he told them the safest route would require a couple of weeks hiking together with Ooljee through virgin forest, they simply looked at each other and smiled the sort of silly smile people have who are pictured in travel ads for exotic honeymoons.

"Okay," said Man. "Blaine will go back to the convent in Sweden and get ready for this trip by going on long hikes each day, while you are working on the passport, Rat. I will let the Abbot know that I plan to go back to America to see Father O'Donnell and to accompany Blaine. The Abbot knows that my assignment from Father O'Donnell was to accompany Blaine and make sure she was safe in her travels to Europe. I think he will feel he has no alternative but to accept my plans, even though I know he would like me to stay. So that takes care of us. What are you guys going to do?"

Man and Blaine looked directly at Rat and Aasia. Man and Blaine were so caught up all week in their own emotional whirlwind of feelings for each other and their possible futures with or without the other, that it was the first time they focused their attention on what might be happening to their two best friends. Rat and Aasia looked as if they had each been caught with their hands in the cookie jar.

Rat, who always had something to say, seemed unable to utter a word. Aasia, who was becoming more and more the talker she must have been as a young girl, said nothing, but the skin wrinkled around the corners of her eyes.

Geez, thought Blaine, Aasia really has grown up. She is now way too smart a woman to respond to a loaded question like the one Man gave her and Rat. Then Blaine realized why it was almost impossible for Rat to answer. She, Blaine, was the problem. She was Rat's first love and he was being asked to say, even though he had lost her to Man, that he was forsaking her for another. For once he could not joke and make a rat-like gesture and have everyone laughing. She knew his heart was torn.

"I think this conversation has gone on long enough," said Blaine. "I realize that whatever our next steps, that the four of us will probably not be together for awhile and that is terribly sad. We need to do the best we can to look after each other. Aasia, though I will be going back to Sweden, will you go with Rat to Berlin? I know you have been thinking about joining the SOS, but you know at some point the SOS is going to insist that your spiritual journey must be lived with a partner. I would be so happy to know the two of you were looking after each other while we are trying to get out of Europe."

Aasia looked shyly at Rat and nodded *yes*.

"Well," said Blaine, looking at Rat. "Will you look after Aasia in Berlin? You guys can stay at my apartment. It is about time you stopped bumming off your buddies and it would not be safe for you to go back to the storage shed." She paused.

Everyone looked at Rat.

Finally, Rat found his tongue. "Blaine, you know I would do anything you asked, and I cannot think of anything I would rather do than look after Aasia, though I cannot fathom why such a beautiful woman as Aasia would want to hang out with a geeky dork like me. Nonetheless, when duty calls, the Rat obeys."

Blaine had given Rat the perfect way out, to be true to his love to her and to open to his love for Aasia. She was amazed when she realized that non-dual consciousness even had its place in romance. Rat turned to Aasia and wiggled his rat-like nose and all four friends burst into laughter.

*          *          *

After spending the week at Tivoli, it seemed fitting that they should leave Copenhagen via the Copenhagen Central Station Tivoli Gardens entrance. As Blaine walked into the station, she realized she had completely forgotten to ask Man to help her decide what to do about Professor Gallagher's email. From the first moment they met in Copenhagen, any thought unrelated to Man had vanished from her mind.

After saying good-bye to Rat and Aasia, who caught their train to Berlin, she and Man were waiting midway between the two different platforms—hers to Sweden, Man's to northern Germany—and all she could think about was Gallagher's email.

THE ARMAGEDDON CHOICE

"Man, I forgot to ask you earlier, but I am troubled by a request from Professor Gallagher. I am not sure whether to send him some information Rat hacked."

A lighted sign flashed above their heads indicating that it was time for Man's train to board.

Man could feel the sudden surge of tension in Blaine. He wrapped his energy around her as best he could and concentrated his energy field on pushing the energy firing from its survival base at the seat of her spine, up her core to her heart.

Blaine relaxed and her whole body seemed to smile. There was nothing so powerfully intimate as two people being able to participate consciously in each other's energy fields and she and Man had been able to do that all week without ever seeming to try.

"Thanks, Manuelito," she said, letting his full given name roll sensually off her tongue. She pulled him toward her. She put his left hand over her heart as he put her left hand over his. As she kissed Man the boarding light above them pulsed again, as if the whole world was signaling the rhythm of their beating hearts.

# Chapter 16

Not only the monks living at Brother Isaac's monastery, but monks of his Order from all over the country and even a few from abroad, made their way to the Southwest to be present with Father O'Donnell. It was scary for Brother Isaac that so many people had come—it made him think they knew for sure Father O'Donnell was dying.

The dozens of gathered brothers meant that Brother Isaac was busier than ever trying to see that everyone was fed and had a place to sleep. Still, he reserved time for himself to be with Father O'Donnell each day, and Brother Isaac was the first one to go in and be with him each morning. Father Hay would usually have been there all night keeping vigil for his beloved brother.

The brothers moved Father O'Donnell's bed into the largest room in the monastery, the old living room of the farmhouse. It was not all that big. Today, Father O'Donnell asked Brother Isaac, when Isaac awoke him, to gather as many of the brothers as could fit into the room at ten that morning.

By 9:30 a.m. the room was already crowded. By 10:00 a.m., Brother Isaac had strung up a little amplification system and placed a speaker in the window, so those who could not get into Father O'Donnell's room could listen to him talk out on the porch.

Unlike so many days, when by ten in the morning Father O'Donnell looked desperately tired, today he seemed to have summoned strength from some hitherto untapped source. He allowed himself to be propped up on a few pillows. It was his habit his entire life to be punctual. Right at ten he picked up the mike and started talking.

"Brothers, sharers in the sweet joy of our fellowship, thank you for being here.

"Let me talk frankly. I am not down for the count yet, but my days are numbered. I hope I get to speak to you all individually over the next week or so, but what is most important to say should be said collectively, for we have staked our lives on the power of our collective fellowship." He stopped to catch his breath.

"We live in difficult times. In point of fact, those of us living in the U.S. have seen the dissolution of meaningful political process in our country because our countrymen have put fears for their own security and greed above the gospel's call to love one another. I know it is bizarre. We would rather have our young people die in foreign lands than share our own abundance with each other; give a life for killing, rather than give a helping hand.

"Yet, we have seen this huge expansion of the contemplative movement across our country and beyond. Further, we have seen, on the one hand, the dissolution of meaningful church authority in the Roman church; and, on the other, the expansion of individual spiritual growth by many people using the ancient wisdom of the Enneagram.

"Dearly beloveds, indeed we are witnessing the rending apart of our dear Roman church, while we also see the possibility of this new integration of masculine and feminine power with the call for a female Pope. It is not too much of a stretch to call this a time of Armageddon.

"Armageddon has traditionally been thought of as the time preceding judgment, but the word judgment, as used a couple thousand years ago, can more accurately be translated as choice. We are not punished for our sins as much as we are punished by our sins. It is not so much that God judges us, as He gives us a choice. It is the same as it was 2000 years ago. It is our choice—do we stay stuck in our fear or are we willing to let go into God's love?

"Beloved brothers, it seems like an easy choice, and it would be if we were all sufficiently conscious to make the choice. I am reminded of the passage in the thirteenth chapter of Matthew: 'By your words you will be acquitted, and by your words you will be condemned.' We are the defendant sitting in the docks and we are the jury that passes sentence on ourselves. So even though this is a fearful time, we are the ones who choose what happens to our lives, and we can either choose fear or step out in faith."

Father O'Donnell paused again. "Let me read you a bit of this

Kabir poem:

*The idea that the soul will join with the ecstatic*
*just because the body is rotten —*
*that is all fantasy.*
*What is found now is found then.*
*If you find nothing now,*
*you will simply end up with an apartment in the City*
        *of Death.*
*If you make love with the divine now, in the next life*
        *you will have the face of satisfied desire.*

"As Kabir says, we choose now. What we choose now, we have in the next life. It is daunting. But we do not make this choice alone. We are brothers in a long lineage. The essence of our spirits is entangled with those who came before and those who come after us. The prayers of those given for us hundreds of years ago and the prayers to be given in the future are all available to help us make our choice right now.

"What I want to talk to you about is not falling into the trap of either/or choice. We can slide into it so unconsciously. There is the trap of retreat. We can see so clearly that our country, and all the world, is caught up in such fear that this can compel us to decide our only choice is to retreat to a hermitage and stay there and work on evolving our own consciousness and control of our energy and our thought fields. This was in fact a needed choice in the Dark Ages for monastics to keep alive not just their faith, but a tradition of wisdom that was copied over and over again in monastic libraries. It is a choice that has a lot of appeal, but it is not a non-dual choice.

"The other primary choice trap is just the opposite of retreat, it is full throttle engagement with the world. This is the trap of those who seek traditional political reform in our dualistic political system, and who either burn out in their idealism or, if successful in their political efforts, become a newer, often more oppressive version of the power structure they once opposed. We can do that in the religious life also. We can be so engaged in helping to create the conditions for the Kingdom that we lose the inner connection our own conversion brings to God in everything.

"So the choice is not either/or, but both. We must redouble our contemplative spiritual practices so we become even more centered in Christ, in the inter-abiding of the energy field that is God in energy form, the true form. We must also not shirk our duty to step forward to embrace all those driven by fear and help them experience the love of Christ. The command to love your enemies was never easy, and it is even harder today because fear has given some people pretty grim and ugly faces."

"Father, I have a question," said a young monk standing over near the window. "What if we end up with two popes? What if the authority in the church splits? What are we to do? How do we engage in this, but not get upended by our engagement?"

Father O'Donnell's face tightened. He knew that most of the monks in their spiritual journeys were to the point where they were free of the fear arising from the secular turmoil in the world, but they were not free from fear. Fear about what church authority to follow was the biggest issue for monks in the Order, young and old alike. He recognized that this fear, at least in part, was the reason that so many members of the Order had showed up for his wake-before-the-wake.

He smiled. "I hoped to dodge that question for a day or two. But I am glad you asked me. As you suspect, the answer is both/and. The question will force us all to use our contemplative practices to go deeper into God. Like so many discoveries on the spiritual journey, the answer is not a this or a that, but the answer is the process of allowing yourself to open deeper in your own spiritual process by wrestling with the question." He paused.

"I think there is a reason this question is up for us as brothers in an Order sanctioned by the Roman church. For too long we have let the hierarchical model of the church control what we said and what we did. Our Order itself is a model of self-government that emerges from a kind of consensus we would call unitive consciousness. But it only exists as a microcosm in a hierarchal church structure, which has allowed terrible abuse by priests to occur. Whatever the outcome of the external power split in the church, you are each being asked to reclaim a deeper level of inner authority within yourselves. Your struggle with this external issue will allow you to claim that greater internal authority. I wish there were short cuts I could give you, but I don't know of any. We do however have a little map that St. Teresa of Avila gave us many years ago."

Brother Isaac looked closely at Father O'Donnell. He could not believe that the dying priest had the strength to talk this long and with such force. He didn't seem to want to stop.

"Since this has come up, let me go over this map with you. Even though I know you all know it, many of you may not have thought about this map in terms of how you wrestle with this question of finding where God's authority lies in your life. So I will outline St. Teresa's template focusing on this issue.

"St. Teresa sees the spiritual journey as the process of moving through a series of rooms in the castle of the soul. In the first, we see that our attachment to the church's images of success and power allows us not to feel fear. In the first room we are going to identify with the external hierarchical authority of the church. At this point, it is not that the authority of the church is bad, but rather that our preoccupation with that authority deprives us of an inner connection to God. We only get out of the first room by becoming aware of the ways in which patterns of fear have shaped our life and caused us to cling to external authority, whether it is being a loyal American or a good Catholic.

"We enter the second room when we become aware of a stirring that tells us there is a greater vitality and possibility to our experience of life. We make decisions sometimes from our inner connection with God and there is a certain lightness to them that is not contained in decisions simply dictated by the church. We probably still make most of our decisions based upon external authority, but there is awakened within us the desire to connect with our own inner authority with God.

In the third room, we have internalized our own values. We picked and chose the things that we believe from the church's teachings and we have become at home with those beliefs. The danger in the third room is complacency. We have taken our beliefs from the church, but we have become our own moral authority. Many Christians get to this point on their spiritual journey and stop. In the third room we can become a Pharisee. In this room it is easy for one to cling to rigid conservative or conventional liberal views; it is a safe place to be stuck.

"At some point, however, if we remain open to Grace, we become humble enough to let go of our hard-earned views and step into greater uncertainty. When we do, we enter the fourth room. In the fourth dwelling place, we are asked to give up our church beliefs, even our notions about God and what God wants of us in this life. We are asked to surrender to the Mystery of God's love. Many of you are probably already in this room of uncertainty about what God's will for you is in responding to this division in the church. It is a tough place to be. In the fourth room, the key is that we seek God in the wisdom of the heart in deciding what authority to follow and do not just rely on the head. We use the mental function, but the head must first be nestled in the heart. Occasionally, in this unknown and uncertainty that we are suffering, the reality of abiding in this heart Mystery will be experienced as freedom.

"If we keep on our path, if we keep doing our practices, we will finally get through the dark night. We will emerge in a room where we live moment to moment in touch with what God wants us to do about the split in church authority, as well as any other issue before us. We accept that God is not a fortuneteller, a source we contact so we don't have to suffer the experience of the unknown. Rather, we become intimately conscious of God's presence with us in every decision we face.

"My beloved brothers, if you remain loyal to your practices and keep centered in your hearts, you will be in the inter-abiding with Christ from which your life will be a profound response to the split in church authority. Delight in the journey. Delight in knowing you are making the journey with so many other brothers who love you and God. The answer will take care of itself."

Father O'Donnell slumped back on his pillows. Brother Isaac hurried forward to check on him. "I am okay," he whispered. He looked anything but okay to Isaac. But Isaac believed what Father O'Donnell said, and given Isaac's belief that Father O'Donnell was speaking from his own inner authority, there was nothing else he could do but ask him to save his energy and rest.

# Chapter 17

Only after he got his seat belt on for the flight to Stockholm did Carroll have the chance to text Slade and let him know that he was going to a convent in Sweden with Mother Mary. As he completed the text, Carroll could feel the enormity of the unknown he was stepping into. He could not for the life of himself describe to Slade exactly why he was going. He titled the text 'Northern Beaver Hunting Trip,' but for once his salacious humor did not seem to provide any sense of coherent reality. He ended the text thanking Slade for enticing him to go to the conclave and admitting it got him to thinking more deeply about his life. He ended by telling Slade he hoped the trip would restore some *joy de vivre,* just as Joy had in Slade's life.

As he finished the text, Carroll got up from his aisle seat to let Sister Ingrid wiggle into her seat next to him. Carroll let out a long breath. What a blonde bombshell! But in language he would only learn later, she sat beside him with her energy tightly cloaked. After dinner, she pulled out a heavily underlined, dog-eared paperback entitled *The Cloud of Unknowing.* She had only read a few pages when she was asleep, her head against his shoulder. For the rest of the flight, as he squirmed in his seat to get comfortable, he did so as gently as possible in order to avoid disturbing the blonde head on his shoulder.  He had never had a daughter, but as he looked at the young woman sleeping against him, he thought he was experiencing what it would be like to have a daughter, to want to hold someone fiercely with love in a protective embrace.

*          *          *

Carroll was at the SOS convent in northern Sweden for only a week when he discovered that he had been put in the pre-beginner class.  He immediately confronted Mother Mary.

"Look, Mary," he stammered.  In his anger he was not about to call her Mother anything. "I did you a favor by coming on this jaunt to this God-forsaken frigid wasteland. I don't like that I'm getting second-class treatment. I understand that most people start at the beginner's class. Why am I starting in something called pre-beginner.  No bullshit, what's the deal?"

Mother Mary opened her heart energy to Carroll.  "Joe, you are not getting second-class treatment, you are getting preferential treatment. Most people at your level of consciousness would not get an invitation to come to the SOS convent. Sister Magdalen, who is somebody you will meet later, insisted before we even went to the conclave in Boston that we should invite you to come back with us. For some reason known only to her and her discernment, she believes it is important for you and us that you are here in training. Because the mental center is your forte, she wanted you to start your work with Sister Angelina. Normally beginners start with the purely experiential. But I am sure you will be on the fast track before too long," she said with a smile. "Tell me, did you find your spiritual direction time today helpful?"

Carroll's anger began to recede. "It was very interesting. I told Sister Angelina that I was willing to concede there was a possibility of belief in an abstract idea of God. Frankly, I thought I was being very charitable in conceding that. In all honesty, I could go that far. I do believe that.

"After being that honest with her, I was quite surprised when she helped me to see that the more abstract an idea is, the more superficial it is. I was familiar with the philosophical idea of the Absolute as explained by Hegel. But I had not thought about the fact that something that signifies everything becomes empty of anything.

"She brought this home to me in raising the question—What would it mean to die for the Absolute, or for that matter, to live for the Absolute? To die for the Absolute amounts to dying for nothing. She explained to me that the prohibition of the First Commandment of 'having no other God before me' is that we must not substitute an intellectual abstraction of God for the spiritual reality of God. You could have knocked my little bitty mind over with a feather.

"Frankly, I don't know where you come up with these sisters that are such babes. I was expecting to get stuck with some bimbo, Blondie type and you throw me in the briar patch with a Latin goddess who is smarter than most of the faculty PhDs I am forced to hang out with at work. I mean, I love this warped spiritual sense of humor you must have, which allowed you to invite me to this briar patch." He stopped talking for a second. Then Carroll concluded, "I just hope I can get laid before I am converted," leering at Mother Mary with his best Jack Nicholson imitation.

Having regained a sense of being defended in his intellectual self, Carroll was comfortable again and ready to go back on the warpath. How much could he goad Mother Mary?

She didn't take the bait. She simply opened her warm, accepting energy even more. Carroll couldn't resist. He went back to the discussion of what he had learned.

"I realize now that my image of God as an idea, or the First Cause, is really a graven image created by my intellect. Sister Angelina suggests that this is a far cry from the luminous vibrant reality of the living Christ. Hell's bells, I sure don't know what that is. So I think I am making great time going backwards."

"Wonderful, wonderful," said Mother Mary, who seemed almost gleeful. "You will soon be through the intellectual traps that gum up Western thinking and on to experiencing what that vibrant reality might be. Keep up the good work. You should be out of pre-beginner shortly." And with that she turned and headed down the corridor.

Carroll, of course, had no desire to be out of anything that would take him away from Sister Angelina's tutelage. Complaining loudly was simply his primary way to ease his discomfort with the unfamiliar. For one thing, he liked that

Sister Angelina was older than many of the young sisters, probably somewhere in her forties, which put her just a few years younger than him. It was Carroll's habit to process everything from an intellectual perspective. The night before he wrote Slade a long email explaining to Slade the difference between the beauty of a young woman like Sister Ingrid, with her innocence and sparkle, and the more embodied beauty of a mature woman like Sister Angelina.

He also included a long paragraph on how female figures from the rear could be classified as either apples or pears, and that while young Ingrid was an apple, there was something so languorously beautiful about Sister Angelina's pear shape that only Rubens might be able to come close to expressing it.

But putting the philosophy of beauty totally aside, Carroll had to admit he was captivated by Sister Angelina, who was tall with long dark hair, luminous gray eyes and a winsome pear figure. When she talked, her hands moved like hummingbirds. Carroll was mesmerized watching her long sensuous fingers weave through the air.

Carroll looked down at his watch. He was delighted. It was time for his next session with Sister Angelina. At his insistence she agreed they could use a session to talk about the history of consciousness. Carroll wanted to fit what these sisters were doing into a wider historical context. He was realizing from what he had learned from Slade about the Enneagram that his need to have this intellectual understanding was a psychological coping mechanism, but it felt completely natural and necessary to him. He headed down the corridor.

"Good morning, Sister Angelina. You look more radiant than the Virgin Mary, I mean absolutely stunning this morning." said Carroll, asserting himself as always with a verbal barrage.

Sister Angelina looked up from her desk. Her expression was one of such compassion and seemed to say: *This poor man is so trapped in the hallways of his own mind.*

"Buenos días, Joey. I am glad to see you. How are you?" Sister Angelina got up from the desk. Spanish words often made their way into her vocabulary in a fashion that added a sensuous quality to her conversation. The sun shone brightly through the widow and light danced on her hair. She walked around her desk up to Joe and one of her fluttering hands landed on his right shoulder.

"Holy cow, Angelina, I am all of a sudden so good I don't know what to say." No one in his life had ever called him Joey, and it was hard to imagine that anyone had ever considered calling him by such a charmingly innocent name. All his life he had struggled to assert a persona that was anything but charming.

She smiled a beautiful, dazzlingly smile at him. "Joey, when you do not know what to say, we are making great progress. So today we will try to learn with the mind, but first we must have the mind nestled in the heart. You have a big mind, Joey, so you must also have a big heart."

"Okay," said Joe, still a bit wide-eyed and unable to put a full sentence together. "Sure." Joe sat down in the chair opposite the desk. Sister Angelina sat back on the desk and crossed her long legs. A sound like a small animal crying came from his lips.

"Joey, do you sense how you are not just up in your head right now trying to figure things out, but more centered and more here?" she said and her right hand fluttered over her left breast.

Joe nodded.

"Good. That is the place we want to learn from today, and what we have to talk about is extraordinarily interesting. You have already learned something about the Enneagram haven't you?"

"Well, not much," said Carroll.

"You get the basic idea, don't you, that the Enneagram is a symbol that provides a map for us of how to achieve greater consciousness?"

Carroll nodded again.

Sister Angelina continued, "I know you are familiar with the great intellectual heritage of the Greeks. We believe that the expansion of human knowledge achieved by the Greeks was based on certain individuals having had an experience in which they achieved greater consciousness. They believed that greater human understanding was only possible from a place of greater consciousness, and so they set up schools of consciousness. You could say that the SOS Order and this convent are modern-day imitations of the schools of consciousness-raising that the Greeks first developed. The most important of these were the schools of Mithras and Eleusis.

"Although I use the term school, the approach to raising consciousness was more experiential than academic. The idea was, in fact still is, that people are initiated into greater consciousness by an experience, rather than just some ideas that they understand. Because this experience involves the whole person, we would call it a spiritual experience. Now we do not know the details of the Greek initiatory experiences, but because of our present knowledge of the Enneagram and its universal application we have some good ideas."

Sister Angelina shifted her position on top of the desk and crossed her legs in the other direction. She looked at Joe intently. "Are you following me?" she asked.

Joe swallowed hard and nodded *yes*.

"We know that the ancient wisdom teachers believed in the maxim: 'as above, so below.' So all we have to do is look at the ancients skies to see their template of initiation into greater consciousness. We now know that astrophysics, the way the stars and galaxies work, has more in common with quantum physics, and the way the smallest particles work, than anything to do with this Newtonian reality we walk around in and think is what is. Lo and behold, the ancients were more right than they had any reason to ever believe.

"Okay, that is all very interesting," said Carroll, "but I still don't get how looking at the heavens provides a path for spiritual growth."

"Good point," said Sister Angelina. "The emphasis today in using the Enneagram is on the particular point that most defines the gifts of a person and the person's personality blocks. The ancient Greeks were concerned in their initiation process that one move through all the self-defensive barriers of each point in order to achieve greater consciousness."

"That makes sense to me," said Carroll. "From what little I know of the Enneagram, I can see parts of me in all of the nine points."

Sister Angelina nodded. "So where did the ancient Greeks find the process for moving through all of the points of the Enneagram in order to be initiated into greater consciousness? In the sky, of course. There is a celestial phenomenon that suggests this process. There are references to it in both the writings of Euripides and Sophocles. It happens that at a particular time of year key planets of the zodiac align in a particular way. When an initiate was brought from the darkness of a cave below ground to see the night sky, it revealed a golden pathway, a celestial staircase, leading to the divine.

"The planetary staircase involved bright Saturn at the bottom, reddish Mars in the middle, and sparkling Venus at the top. At the time of this alignment, myriads of dust particles that circle the sun along the path of the planets become visible in the solar glare and create a golden haze that illumines this pathway to Heaven.

"Coming after an experience underground that would have involved the exploration of one's own shadow—a necessary part of the initiation process—the initiate then emerges into a physical experience of the reality of a pathway to God. This is the jolt that allows the initiate to be set free of the defenses of the false-self and enter into a greater realm of consciousness.

"The grandeur of Rome was built on the glory of Greece, and symbols of the planetary ladder were carried on the standards of Roman legions, to inspire the soldiers with a promise of heavenly ascension as they marched into battle. It is from the experience of being initiated into a realm of greater consciousness that the first Roman Emperor Augustus achieved deification. While the ritual of deification continued with succeeding emperors, its origin was the reality of the greater consciousness that came from this first emperor experiencing a pathway to God in an initiatory experience into greater consciousness."

"That is extraordinary," said Carroll, "that the concept of the divine right of kings, which continued to exist through the Middle Ages, had its origins in the experience of one emperor who really might have experienced the divine."

"Exactly," said Sister Angelina.

"Good for the Greeks, and I'm happy for Augustus, but what does that have to do with a Christian path to greater consciousness?"

Sister Angelina smiled. "We do not believe that the experience of greater consciousness is defined by a particular religion. We believe that all great religious traditions offer insight into the process of transformation from the unique spiritual experiences of their founder and followers. And we don't throw out what has gone before just because the greatest insight into the process of transformation comes from Christ. There are lots of interesting overlaps. In the Judeo-Christian tradition, the seven branches of the great Menorah in the Temple in Jerusalem is asserted by the Jewish writers Josephus and Philo of Alexandria to represent the lights of the seven known planets. In esoteric mystical Judaism, the seven branches of the menorah reflect the Tree of Life with all its Enneagram symbolism.

"But you don't have to look to the esoteric to find connection with the ancient template in the night sky. In literature we see in Dante's *Paradiso* a description of a climb through the planets.

"However, the most obvious reflection in our daily life of this planetary pathway to the divine is seen in the order of the days of the week. There was a sublime auditory experiencing of the music of the spheres that occurred in the initiatory process.

It is these musical intervals that determine the sequences of the days of the week. The Roman historian Dio Cassius noted that. Starting with the Moon, Monday, we skip three planets, the musical interval of the fifth, and we arrive at Mars. In French this is *Mardi*, which we translate into English as Tuesday. We go next to Mercury which in French is *Mercredi*, or in English, Wednesday. Then we go on to Jupiter, which in French is *Jeudi,* or in English, Thursday. Venus follows, which in French is *Vendredi,* or Friday in English. Then to Saturn which of course is Saturday. Finally we arrive at the resting place of the divine, the day of the Sun.

"Here is a summary of this," and she handed Joe a list and a chart with an Enneagram image on it.

Type Nine - Moon - Monday
Type One - Mars - Tuesday
Type Four - Mercury - Wednesday
Type Seven  - Jupiter - Thursday
Type Eight - Venus - Friday
Type Five - Saturn - Saturday
Type Two - Sun - Sunday

**Enneagram of the Planets and Days of the Week**

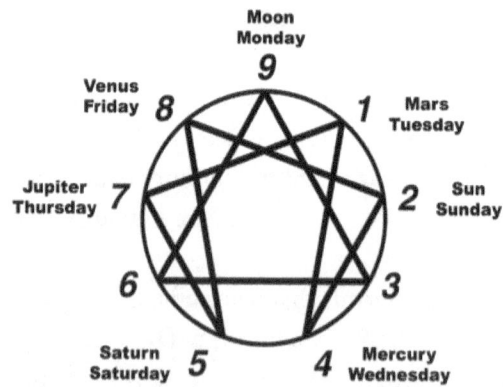

THE ARMAGEDDON CHOICE

"The experience of moving up the celestial stairway along the planetary path was the great secret of the ancient mystery religions, including those at Mithras and Eleusis. Our modern knowledge of the Enneagram shows us that this planetary pathway is actually a reflection of the wisdom of the Enneagram. Since the planets must also travel beneath the Earth, a journey of initiation as I mentioned earlier also included the descent into the underworld, where the shadow issues of the false-self were confronted.

"This gives us the Enneagram of the planets and the passions of the false-self identified with each planet:

Point Five -Avarice - Saturn
Point Two - Pride - Sun/Helios
Point Nine - Acedia - Full Moon/Selene
Point One - Anger - Mars
Point Four - Sadness - Mercury
Point Seven - Gluttony - Jupiter
Point Eight - Lust - Venus
Point Three - Vainglory - Waxing Moon/Artemis
Point Six - Fear - Waning Moon/Hera

Sister Angelina handed Carroll another chart so he could get a visual idea of what she was saying.

## Enneagram of the Planets and Passions

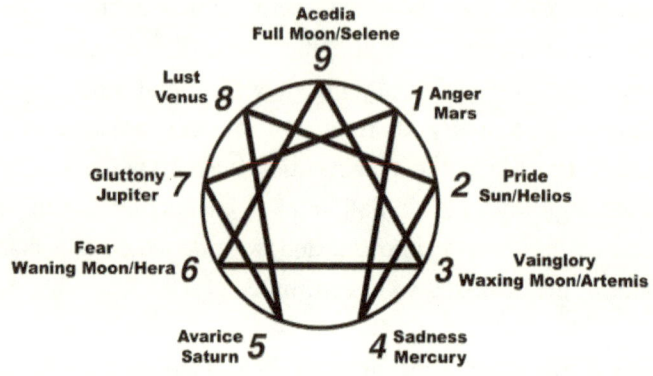

"We know that the great mystery rites at Eleusis were celebrated at night, in the spring and fall of the year at precisely the times when the alignment of planets and solar dust best illuminated the pathway to Heaven.

"You must admit, Joey, that it is all very stunning in a way that must appeal to someone with a brilliant intellect like you." Sister Angelina smiled at Joe. "As our level of consciousness increases, our ability to see reality exactly the way it is, without projections or idealizations, grows. We think the lesson from the ancient Greeks is that our consciousness level is enhanced by how in tune we are with the universe, particularly as reflected in attunement with this great reality of the planets moving in our solar system.

"The consciousness map the Enneagram provides is found in the ancient night skies, the early Christian communities, and the message Jesus tailored for each of these communities, the Lord's Prayer, the Sermon on the Mount, the First Corinthians

13 Sermon on Love, in the miracles Jesus performed which are described in the Gospel of John—and this map even charts the passage of the story of creation as reflected in each day of the week."

Carroll was overwhelmed on many levels. First, at the brilliance of what Sister Angelina presented to him, the clarity of her presentation, and the fact that she and Mother Mary respected his need for intellectual understanding. Secondly, as she slid off the desk at the end of her presentation, her skirt slid up her legs, and he felt an incredible longing for this beautiful woman. For once, he thought it was more than simply lust. But, he was not used to knowing what longing for a woman was that was not lust. His mind, trying to understand, ground to a halt. His heart-knowing was woefully undeveloped. It was more input than he could handle. For once, Joe Carroll did not know what to say.

Then suddenly he got a thought out of left field. "Sister Angelina, one time I got a fortune cookie and the little piece of paper in the cookie said: *The last apostle will be first; follow her.* I don't know why this comes to mind, but all of a sudden I think you might know what it means, and whether in some strange way I am here to follow some unknown person?"

Without missing a beat, Sister Angelina responded. "Don't worry, you will get to meet her later. But you have a good bit of work to do first, for that to happen." She turned and started toward the door.

He got up and, without thinking, touched Sister Angelina from behind on the shoulder. She turned and as much as a surprise to himself as to her, he pulled her into a gentle embrace. He could feel his wildly beating heart calmed against the even steady pulse of Sister Angelina's.

# Chapter 18

Blaine's head rested gently against Man's shoulder. How different this trip was from the first flight they made together escaping from Canada to the SOS convent in northern Sweden. They were on the same airlines, Icelandic, but that was the only similarity. This trip was more like another visit to Tivoli Gardens than a clever strategy to avoid detection by the CIA.

Blaine, as she described it to Man, was given a talking-to by Mother Mary before she left the convent. Mother Mary was delighted that Blaine was in love. Blaine's ability to fall deeply in love was a testament to the healing and love that she received from all of the sisters at the convent. Still, Mother Mary warned Blaine that being in romantic love was a way to lose some of the gains in consciousness that she had worked so diligently to achieve.

It was a paradoxical thing, being in romantic love. On the one hand, it was the primary way people have always first learned to experience being a part of another, escaping from the routine experience of oneself as a separate, isolated self. On the other hand, the emotional feelings that come with romantic love are so delightful, that it is easy for the ego to identify with the necessity of having those feelings. Once the ego identifies with anything, then it filters and narrows the range of perception to try to keep what it wants. In short, we can lose consciousness whenever the ego becomes attached to something. Mother Mary gave Blaine the classic warning: *Whatever you must have you will lose, whatever you surrender you will keep forever.*

Blaine understood on an intellectual level what Mother Mary was telling her, but at an emotional level she was simply overwhelmed by the delicious feeling of being in love with Man. Blaine felt as if she was riding the crest of a huge emotional wave. Most of her life she experienced spinning in the undertow: from the first time she was sexually abused, through using her computer skills to hack herself out of a mental institution, and even up to just a short while ago, when she viewed the world as a cynical and hostile place. Being in love with Man and traveling with him on a trip to re-enter the United States, life simply seemed a daring adventure.

Rat came up with a forged passport for her in the name of Candace Bergman. To go with her new identity, Blaine dyed her raven hair blonde. She startled herself every time she looked in a mirror.

There was no problem when she passed through immigration in Copenhagen to board the Icelandic flight, which took them first to Reykjavík. She and Man decided to spend an extra couple of days in Reykjavík as tourists, to see a little bit of the Icelandic countryside. Later, Blaine would tell others that their time in Iceland was fascinating, but she would not be able to remember any of the details of what they did or saw. All she would remember is how wonderful it was to be exploring some strange new place with a strikingly handsome man at her side. There were no immigration problems when she boarded the flight to Winnipeg. She didn't know how Rat got her the forged passport, but she fully trusted in his competence and ability. Her own passport was carefully sewn into one of her undergarments by one of the sisters.

The captain's voice came over the public address system. Blaine opened her eyes and saw that Man was carefully watching her awaken. She reached her right hand into the tumble of his long, dark hair and pulled him toward her. They kissed long and hard. She pushed up the armrest between them and slid her left hand up the inside of his left leg.

"I like it when you wake up mischievous," said Man. "The Captain just said we have only fifteen minutes until landing. Do you think you can wait maybe thirty minutes till we get through immigration? Then we can find a hotel room for a couple of hours before we head out to Sister Darcy's and Sister Josephine's dairy farm."

"I don't think I can wait at all," said Blaine teasingly, and she took his right hand and slipped it under her indigo blue top. "We have never made love in North America. We have a lot to celebrate today."

"You know, if I remember right, I think Rat said that he asked Sister Darcy and Sister Josephine to pick us up at the airport. We may have to wait for a couple hours. That will be rough."

said Man as their hands began to play the same minuet of caresses.

"And, I am sure Sister Josephine is going to give you a hard time too, Blaine. There is no escaping the fact that despite the blonde hair you look so beautiful, and what do you white people say, 'like you just got off the love boat?'"

Blaine, who most of her life felt she was a non-person, never expected to be teased about being a white person, but, of course, she never expected to be in love with someone like Man. Before she could reply, Man gave her the immigration form that the flight attendant had passed out. She pulled out her forged passport to fill in the form. *I need to do a little better job of remembering who I am supposed to be*, she mused.

In a matter of a few minutes the plane landed, the passengers disembarked, and Blaine and Man were standing in line waiting their turn at the immigration desk. Man had already cleared Ooljee, whose shots were all up to date, and who would be able to re-enter Canada without quarantine.

Admittedly, Blaine and Man were a curious couple—Man, tall with his long, black hair cascading over his shoulders, and blonde Blaine, diminutive in size with dark eyes and tattoos creeping down one arm. Man stepped up to the immigration officer's desk first. The officer looked at his passport and slipped it through the scanner. He then looked over Ooljee's papers, glanced at Man, and gave a cursory nod for him and Ooljee to proceed on through. Man headed over to pick up his luggage. He unzipped his bag and pulled out his long-bladed folding knife and dropped it into his boot. He re-zipped his bag and left it on the carousel and returned to wait for Blaine.

Blaine walked to the immigration officer's desk. She handed him her Candace Bergman passport and he slipped it through the scanner. Immediately he sat up straight in his chair.

"Please, wait just a minute, Ms. Bergman, I'll be right back," he said.

*Oh no*, Man thought. *Just what we did not want to happen.*

In a matter of less than two minutes, three immigration officers appeared and escorted Blaine down a hallway. Man followed at a distance. When he got to a doorway that said Immigration Personnel Only, he waited until Blaine and the officers escorting her were almost out of sight down the hall. Then he slipped into the hallway and ran to where it intersected with the next corridor. Just as he got to the corner, he saw Blaine being led into a room labeled Interrogation No. Four. He looked around for the nearest men's room. He was in luck. A unisex handicapped bathroom was just across the hall from No. Four. He slipped in with Ooljee and locked the door.

Rat had insisted Man take an iPhone with him. Now he was relieved he had. He immediately texted Rat and told him the situation. Rat, as always, seemed to be ever accessible. He replied immediately.

While Rat was pulling up a Google map of the immigration

building, he was also getting in touch with Sister Josephine. Piecing together Man's description of the general layout of the building as he experienced it from leaving the airplane with the Google map's photographic image, Rat was able to get a good idea of exactly where the interrogation room was. While Rat was working on an escape plan, Man slipped out of the restroom, went back down the hallway and retrieved both his and Blaine's luggage from the now stilled carousel. He returned down the hallway undetected and slipped back into the restroom. He piled the luggage on top of the toilet seat, locked the partition door of the toilet stall, and fluidly pulled himself over the stall partition wall.

Rat was able to get Sister Josephine on her cell phone. She and Sister Darcy had just arrived in Winnipeg to pick up Blaine and Man. They were parked in the Arrivals cell phone parking lot. Rat described to them the route to a small parking lot at the end of the immigration building. This parking lot was for immigration personnel only, but it did not appear to have any entrance barrier. If the nuns got questioned, they were simply to indicate they were lost. This parking lot would be the closest accessible point for the two sisters to pick up Blaine and Man.

After about five minutes, Man got a text indicating that the sisters were now in place and their car was in the immigration employees parking lot. He slowly opened the bathroom door. There was no one in the hallway. Just beside the bathroom was a small alcove containing a water fountain and a vending machine. Quickly Man, with Ooljee following, moved to the alcove. He found a few quarters in his pocket and put them in the vending machine. He turned the knob for gum and out dropped a pack. Quickly he wadded a couple of sticks in his mouth and chewed vigorously. Then he moved down the hallway till he was under the hallway surveillance camera. With a running jump, he put his right foot on a window ledge and rose high enough so that he was able to apply the gum to the lens of the camera before falling back to the floor.

Man put the rest of the gum in his mouth and hurried back down the hall to Interrogation No. Four. He turned the doorknob. The door was not locked. He thrust the door all the way open. The room was small. In the center was a Formica table. Blaine was sitting on one side of the table. On the other side was an immigration officer, who looked up, startled.

In one smooth move, Man reached into his boot and switched open his long-bladed knife. "Please take off your ID badge and your pocket radio and place them on the table." Man instructed. "Then sit in the corner right behind you. If you do as you are told, you will not be hurt."

As soon as the officer was sitting on the floor in the corner, Man jumped onto the table and plastered the remainder of the chewing gum on the camera globe at the top of the wall right below the ceiling.

Man then spoke a few words to Blaine in Navajo. She had no idea what he said, but she played along, smiled, and said *yes.*

Man picked up the radio and put it in his pocket and grabbed the officer's ID badge off the table. He motioned Blaine to get behind him, next to the door. He pushed the table to one side of the small room so that Ooljee was directly in front of the officer seated in the corner.

"If you move, or make any effort to communicate with anyone, this dog will kill you. Do you understand?" As if on cue, Ooljee bared his fangs.

Man spoke to Ooljee in Navajo. Then Man said, "Hold or kill! Hold or kill!" Ooljee growled as if he completely understood his orders.

Man then opened the door slightly and looked out. The hallway was empty. He grabbed Blaine by the hand and quickly ran to the end of the hallway. He took the officers personnel badge and swiped it through the door scanner. The electronic lock opened. He and Blaine both looked out. There in the bright sun, not a hundred feet away, sat Sister Josephine and Sister Darcy in their car with the engine running.

"Tell Sister Josephine to pop the trunk for me and Ooljee."

Blaine nodded and ran to the car and jumped in the back seat, where she snuggled under an overcoat and an old lap blanket. Man returned to the restroom, picked up their luggage, brought it out to the sisters' car, and wedged it in on the floor behind the front seats.

Man returned to Interrogation No. Four. Quickly he opened the door and slipped inside. Nothing had changed. Ooljee was standing tense as a drawn bow. The officer on the floor did not appear to have moved. "Come with me," said Man. They exited Interrogation No. Four, and Man motioned the officer into the unisex handicapped bathroom just across the hall.

"I am going to leave you in here, with the dog outside the door. He will stay there for thirty minutes. If you make any effort to leave this room before thirty minutes are up, the dog is instructed to attack and kill. Do you understand?"

The immigration officer nodded *yes*.

Man read the immigration officer's energy. He was scared, but not enough to stay in the bathroom for thirty minutes without opening the door slightly and hollering for help. Man shrugged his shoulders, *I guess we need a little more fear*, he thought.

"Hand me your wallet."

Slowly the immigration officer reached into his back pocket and pulled out his wallet. He handed it to Man.

"Sit on the floor against the far wall."

Man opened the wallet and looked through the contents. From between two credit cards, he pulled out a picture of a woman and two children. He threw the wallet on the floor.

"If you try to call for help or leave before thirty minutes are up," said Man and he stopped speaking and reached into his boot for his long knife pulled it out, flicked it open and cut the picture diagonally in two.

"It would not be good for your family. Am I clear?"

The officer, on the floor in the corner, nodded *yes* and said, "Please, please do not do anything to hurt my family."

Man could tell that the officer's fear had escalated. "If you do not do exactly as I have told you, then *you* will hurt your family. Do you understand?" And with that, Man slowly folded his long-bladed knife and slipped it into his boot. He turned and opened the bathroom door until he could see down the hallway. There was no one there. He and Ooljee slipped out of the bathroom and dashed to the end of the corridor. He slid the officers ID badge through the door scanner and opened the door.

The sisters' car was still sitting there, just a short distance away. He could see that the trunk door was ajar. He and Ooljee ran for the car, jumped into the truck and he pulled the trunk door down until it clicked shut.

Sister Josephine pulled the car into gear and headed out of the parking lot. Rat told Man they would have to pass a couple of airport surveillance cameras before they got off the airport grounds, but even if the cameras picked up the car's interior, nothing should reveal Blaine's and Man's presence.

Soon Man sensed they were on the freeway. He remembered that, thankfully, Sister Josephine had a heavy foot. It was cramped quarters, but this was not the first time Man had ridden in a trunk. The time before was in his father's old Crown Vic, back before his father got the pickup he died in.

His father had been on a bender for a couple of weeks, and Man was so tired of hearing his father argue with his mother that, when they went on a trip to Tuba City, Man told them both that he would just as soon ride in the trunk. His father quickly obliged. Of course, Ooljee was with him then also, and riding in a trunk was never too bad when he was curled up with the best dog anyone could possibly have. Particularly now, when he could sense Blaine's energy and her desire for him lying across the backseat just a few inches above his nose.

Ooljee let out a sound like a small squeak. Blaine, in response, moved her pelvis back and forth on the seat above them. Man sighed. It wouldn't be too long before they would all three be hiking deep into the Canadian woods.

# Chapter 19

Rat was eager to get to the small Turkish café in the Berlin neighborhood where he and Blaine often went to eat. He was going to meet Aasia. He had much to tell her.

When he arrived, she was already there. She was seated at the table in the front corner by the window, the table that he and Blaine customarily gravitated to. Rat was oblivious to most things that he was not viewing on a screen. But as he pushed open the café's front door and his eyes came to rest on Aasia, he was struck by what an extraordinarily beautiful woman she had become over the past several months.

"Aasia, I hope you haven't waited long," He pulled out a chair and plopped down next to her at the table. "You look so beautiful," he said looking into her sparkling, brown eyes. She evidentially had just come from the gym where she and Blaine started working out together a few months earlier. She was wearing a tight-fitting, stretchy gym suit that was light purple with pink trim. There were little beads of perspiration still around her temples. Her top was unzipped halfway revealing her generous cleavage. The pink trim of her workout bra danced against her perfectly white skin and the healing pinks of her cosmetic, scar-removal surgery.

"I mean so, so beautiful," said Rat wiggling his nose at Aasia in his most rat-like manner.

Aasia smiled and put her finger gently on Rat's nose. He beamed and then continued.

"I have been anxious to give you an update about Blaine. I heard from Sister Josephine in Canada that Blaine, Man, and Ooljee made it to the sisters' safe house. Blaine was detained when she went through immigration. Man and I were able to work out a plan to spring her. Man is the man. Of course, yours truly masterminded the whole plan to defeat the minions of state power." Rat stretched out his arms and puffed up his chest.

Aasia's smile turned into laughter.

One of the wiser, older hackers once told Rat that when a woman is beautiful, her beauty can be a barrier to connection with others. It is easy for her to slip into her own myth of only seeing herself through her appearance. Others conspire and reinforce this illusion, seeing the image and not the person. Rat realized that for Aasia to have been becoming a beautiful woman and have that beauty completely taken away meant she was forced to give up any emotional attachment to the idea that her appearance was who she was. Now that she had been through an extraordinary healing and the outward beauty was restored, she wore her beauty like a loose garment. It was as if an angelic presence peeked out from behind her beauty and knew that her appearance was not who she really was. For Rat, her carefreeness about her beauty and the fact that her energy practices were allowing her inner warmth and gracious essence to shine through left him awestruck.

"So what will be happening to them now?" asked Aasia.

"I guess they will be stumbling through the woods together, having to sleep on the ground with all the bugs. No Internet access. I mean I guess they will be miserable," said Rat with a huge grin.

"It's sure a delight living with you in Blaine's apartment, but you know, Rat, you work all the time. Maybe we ought to get away and have some time together, just us, like Blaine and Man are doing. What do you think?"

"Aasia, you know you are my WiFi signal. Wherever you want to go, I will go. But you know, if I get too far away from a computer, I am a fish out of water, and you may not like me too much, flopping around on the beach."

Aasia bent forward and kissed him on the forehead. "I know, Ratie-pooh. I got an email last night from my mentor at the convent. I don't quite understand what is happening. But it seems like there's a lot going on. Whatever it involves, it sounds like they could use someone with the computer skills you have. There is a hermitage a little ways from the convent. She said we could stay there together. Although, as you know, the sisters do not believe in celibacy, they also do not allow folks to shack-up at the convent. This would give us a way to spend more time together, and also allow you to help out the sisters on whatever the big project is they are working on. And while you are working for the SOS, I would like to spend time doing more energy work as an novitiate. What do you say?"

"Sounds like I could have broadband access to you," said Rat wriggling his nose, poking out his chin, and waving his hand beneath his chin. "What more could a geek like me ask for?"

Aasia gave Rat a gentle kick under the table. "Can't you ever be serious about anything?" she said in a mocking tone. She paused. "At least half-serious?"

Rat did his best to look serious. "I think we have a plan. Tomorrow, we'll go buy some warm clothes."

# Chapter 20

Brother Isaac, you know why the desert Fathers and Mothers, like Ponticus Evagrius, went to live in the desert?" asked Father O'Donnell, his voice coming out in a raspy whisper.

Will Dawson shook his head *no*. He was trying to be as quiet as possible, hoping that by his being silent, Father O'Donnell would not feel the need to talk. The strategy was not working. Tired and drained though he seemed to be, there was an insistence in Father O'Donnell's voice.

"Because there is no place quieter than the desert. I chose this place years ago for the monastery, because I experienced a bone-chilling quietness here the first time I visited. I can still feel it. Particularly now that the other brothers have left." He paused to get his breath. "I am glad they all came to visit, and I'm glad they're gone. A man needs to die in quiet stillness."

"Father, enough talk about dying."

Father O'Donnell gently wagged his finger at Dawson. "Don't try to distract me from what is happening. Death is what is happening. It is, after all, a pretty big deal. I may not be quite over the hill, but I am getting close and I sure don't want to miss anything."

"I just mean, don't you think it's best that you conserve your energy. There is no need for us to talk right now."

"Brother Isaac, I know how good you're trying to be to me. But there is something I need to tell you. I had this dream last night."

Dawson nodded. He was in no position to argue with Father O'Donnell. Dawson was, in fact, grabbing onto his dying mentor's every word.

"Remember what you told me you learned this semester: Thought and memory have the same form as particles in the quantum field. The difficulty has been in showing the connection between our internal human processes and the quantum field. Your professor presented to you the idea that our interchange with the quantum field is made possible by the microtubules in our cells. The microtubules are the heretofore missing connection between our seemingly much more real Newtonian world and the quantum field.

"If the brain then is simply a translator of our sensory experiences into the quantum field, and a translator of information back to us from the quantum field, then the problem of how to achieve greater consciousness is simply a problem of what field we are accessing and the bandwidth of our connection. If we are only accessing a limited personal field, for example, a narrative of intermixed thoughts and feelings of how we grew up in our dysfunctional family, then our level of consciousness is going to be defined by that field.

"All new perceptions, as our lives move forward, are going to have meaning only within that field of experience. It is like the story that is told about when Columbus arrived in the new world—Native Americans did not see the sailing ship he arrived on. They could not see his ship because it was not an image within their quantum field of memory experience. Only after a certain period of sensory exposure did the image of a European sailing vessel become part of the Native American quantum field, and once it was, it was immediately accessible given the right sensory input.

"In our search for greater consciousness, we are like Native Americans when the European sailing vessel arrived on their shores. Greater consciousness may be right next to us, but we have no way to enter the field it exists in—that is to experience it because we are stuck in a different field. This is one of the reasons why for centuries, going back to the mystery schools, the path to greater consciousness has always been an initiatory path of creating a liminal space where there is the opportunity to experience reality in a new way, to break into a new field.

"But I am getting astray. Let me get back to my dream. In my dream, I enter into a magical city of light. As I walk down a street that seems to be paved with golden stone, I notice that all of the buildings are supported by round columns. I stop in a city square. There is a well in the middle of the square, a well with a circumference consisting of thirteen stones. I look closer at the buildings around the square and see how the columns are all made of rings of thirteen stones. Then a beautiful woman comes toward me with a large earthen jar that it appears she wishes to fill with water from the well. The jar I see has been formed with rings of thirteen segments of clay. As the woman gets closer I see light emanating from her. The light is most visible above her head and here I distinctly see it is formed in a ring of thirteen segments. Her body appears to be made up of twelve rings, each consisting of thirteen segments.

"You know we teach in the Enneagram system that there are nine different levels for each type—that is what is taught in the public, secular understanding. In addition, our esoteric teaching says there are three further spiritual levels. In my dream last night I believe that when the woman appeared consisting of twelve rings that she represented all twelve levels—she represented the experience of human enlightenment.

"I began to form a question in my mind to ask her. I was going to ask her: *What is consciousness?* Before I could ask her, she changed into a cloud of mist. I gazed, surprised and puzzled. Suddenly, she changed back into the form of a woman more beautiful than ever. Then I awoke.

"I immediately remembered what you told me your professor said about microtubules being the translator of our experience from the material state into the quantum state. Didn't you tell me that all of the cells in our body have microtubules?" asked Father O'Donnell insistently.

"Yes, that is right," said Dawson.

"And didn't you say that each microtubule is made of rings of thirteen molecules in circumference?"

"Your memory is good, Father. Yes, each microtubule is made of rings of thirteen tubulin molecules which form the circumference of the tube. Microtubules are continually forming and dissolving in all of our cells."

"I was reminded of the Gospel of Mary Magdalene where she quotes Jesus saying: *All that is born, all that is created, all the elements of nature are interwoven and united with each other. All that is composed shall be decomposed.* I think the Master Teacher might have been talking about this process of going back and forth between linear reality and the quantum field. Tell me more about this tubulin, and perhaps I will be able to understand my dream a bit better," said Father O'Donnell.

"Well, tubulin is a protein, which means it is a chain of amino acids. How a protein functions depends upon how it is folded. If it is folded in a certain way it performs a particular function, and if it is folded in another way it may perform another function. In the case of tubulin, there are two different ways it folds, and it goes back and forth between these two forms."

"Yes, thank you, Brother Isaac, I think I'm getting it. What your professor is describing about microtubules is what we call the Trinity. The Trinity is the name we give to the three forces of being—the assertive, the movement into manifestation, which would be when the tubulin molecules create a sense of material awareness of what is; the withdrawing, the movement out of manifestation or, more accurately, into the quantum indeterminate state of all possibilities that are in the field; and the reconciling force, the power that we call the Holy Spirit, that nudges the pattern into material existence or into the quantum indeterminate state. Our ordinary experience of cause and effect is a grain of sand inside the large ball of quantum reality. As I say, historically the name the church gives to this larger understanding of reality is the Trinity."

Father O'Donnell let his head sink back into his pillow. He smiled. "Yes, it would be a woman at the well who would come to tell me this. I must sleep now." He looked up at his student, who gazed back at him anxiously and with love.

"Thank you for being here with me. Maybe I will have a chance to finish the dream before I die."

*  *  *

First thing in the morning, as he did always, Dawson brought a cup of hot Irish tea into Father O'Donnell's bedroom, still located in the living room of the old farmhouse.

"How did you rest?" asked Dawson.

Father O'Donnell grunted. He was not a morning person and was not much for conversation prior to his first cup of tea. He sipped away on the steaming brew. After a moment he spoke.

"I was restless and had difficulty going to sleep. But I awoke feeling contented. The excitement about understanding the science of consciousness faded but I think I am clear on how the scientific explanation fits logically into a mystical Christian understanding."

Dawson perked up. The scientific understanding was the day in, day out of his ordinary schoolwork at the University of Arizona. Understanding the mystical implications were, he knew, something he could only learn from Father O'Donnell. "Father, tell me how it fits together."

"We start with a contradiction between two perspectives, which are both true but conflict. It is what we called in seminary an antinomy. The antinomy here is between consciousness and matter. Consciousness is the idea of something prior to its manifestation. In the field of your life experience, all your thoughts and emotions derived from all your life experiences exist in your field in a quantum, un-manifested state. This comports with the philosophy of Hegel, the idealist, who considered everything first to be a form of thought, an idea.

"However, from the perspective of realism—the thing itself, the *res*, exists prior to any abstract idea of it. In other words, matter comes first. Objective matter must exist first before there can be any sensory idea of it, which then becomes a part of the quantum field. The realists, like English philosopher Herbert Spencer, would objects of knowledge exist independently of thought or consciousness. The realist would say that the notions which exist in the field of consciousness are derived from the realistic objects themselves. The idealist, in contrast, would say that objects are 'created' by the projection of ideas.

THE ARMAGEDDON CHOICE

"Why is this important? To understand the barrier that either path creates. So, with realism, the thing, the *res*, becomes an idol existing prior to thought. With idealism, the idol is the human intellect, whose ideas are then responsible for the things of the world. In mystical Christianity, we learn that we do not bow either before the things of the world or before the human intellect—either would be idolatry. It is the greater quantum field that is the source both of the ideas and the objects, or as we call it, the Mind of God or the Word of God.

"Thus from a mystical point of view, reality is neither realistic or idealistic, but it is the meshing of the two. This meshing of the two is what we call Logos. It is the third force, which your professor would see as the way the microtubule protein shapes itself to manifest either concrete reality or an idea within all possible reality as yet un-manifested, existing in the quantum field.

"That's a lot on one cup of tea. Can you give me a refill?"

"Sure," said Dawson, his mind still reeling, trying to take in everything that Father O'Donnell had said.

# Chapter 21

Joe Carroll could not get over the sensation that he was the fox loose in the henhouse. Prior to arriving at the convent in Sweden, he was under the impression that convents had largely become assisted living residences for the diminishing numbers of elderly nuns who survived in them. Not so here. He guessed that the median age of the nuns at the convent was twenty-five. Even though he had a bad case of puppy-dog love for Sister Angelina, which he was trying to convince himself was just lust, every time he turned the corner there was another young sister whose energy glow immediately ignited his *eros*.

He was intrigued by what he was learning about the Enneagram, even though he was convinced he was still being kept in what he called the retarded class. He was also skeptical. His mind was working overtime, as he was spending mostly sleepless nights in the small convent guest room. Too much time in his mind was never a good place for Carroll to be for too long. Trying to put the time to good use and to take a little of the wind out of Mother Mary's Enneagram sails, Carroll had come up with the idea of the Enneagram of Snow White and the Seven Dwarfs. He scheduled an appointment with Mother Mary just so he could spring it on her and, though he would not have admitted it, assert his authority by his cleverness.

Mother Mary looked at Carroll intently. "I am glad to see you, Joe. How have you been?"

"I must admit that I'm doing some adjusting," said Carroll. "I am still not sure why you insisted that I should come here. But being the college professor, I thought I should try to help you in the way I am best suited. So I have taken the liberty of working out a new Enneagram scheme for you, based on the story of Snow White and the Seven Dwarfs."

Carroll cleared his throat in the way he would before starting a lecture. In this case, more as a way for him to get a tighter grip on his emotions. The last thing he wanted to do was spoil his presentation by breaking into a leering grin.

"Snow White represents the archetypal Adam and Eve, who are thrown out of the garden of Eden. She ends up alone in the forest." Carroll paused. "I thought you would like the biblical spin I'm putting on this. Are you following me so far?"

Mother Mary nodded for him to proceed. What she was thinking about his explication of the fairy tale he was unable to read.

"Once we are lost in the forest, our ego defenses come to our rescue as our survival mechanisms. In this case there are seven. There is Doc who is probably a One. He is always mixing up his words and is a classic picture of the perfection of imperfection. Then there is Grumpy, the Two. He is a rescuer, but of course always grumpy because he is doing for others to feel okay for himself and feels unappreciated. Then there is Happy the Seven. It is hard not to like these people who strive to keep their mood elevated by always seeking new options. Next we have Sleepy, the Nine, who is always tired and very laconic. Then there is Bashful, the Four, who is also a withdrawal type, withdrawn into the interior world of his own emotions. Sneezy is the power type, the Eight, whose power is represented in his sneezing. What a great way to say that all power is illusory! And finally there is Dopey, the Five, who is clumsy and who has never even tried to speak because he is withdrawn into his own inner world of observation and fact-searching."

"It seems like you have way too much time on your hands, Joe," said Mother Mary, intrigued just the same. "What about the stepmother?"

"I guess she is the easiest figure of all. She has to be a Three, since she spends all of her time looking into the mirror asking who is the fairest."

"Yes, that makes sense. And it makes sense that the seven dwarfs would in fact represent the Seven Deadly Sins. That just leaves us with the question of Point Six. What about it?"

"I understand the energy from points Three and Six, our underlying egoic fear and need for approval, are what drives the compulsion of the other seven points. So in ancient times, and also in church literature with the focus on the Seven Deadly Sins, points Three and Six are often omitted. But I do think we can find Point Six in the figure of the Prince."

"Good observation," said Mother Mary. "I like the fact that in the fairy tale, as is true for all of us initially, Snow White is asleep. She precisely describes the kind of trance we walk around in, and in our sleep, the seven dwarfs, our ego compulsions, look after us."

"She is awakened by the Six, the Prince, because he is attracted to her beauty," said Carroll. And you know Sixes have this thing for beauty." He gave her his most beguiling smile.

"Joe," said Mother Mary, "you have done good work. But while it may have been Snow White's beauty that caused the Prince to fall in love with her, just as it is the beauty of the lovely energy of the sisters here that has you spending your nights so sleeplessly, beauty is not what caused the trance to be broken. The trance was broken by the Prince's love for Snow White."

Joe was chagrined. Just when he thought he was going to put Mother Mary in her place by his skillful mental gymnastics in applying the Enneagram's archetypal template to a fairy tale, she upended the table by applying the fairy tale to him.

"So, Joe, when you move beyond simply being enamored by the beauty of the sisters to actually falling in love with one of them, then at that point you will have a chance to wake up. Until then, most of what you think of as love, or *eros,* is simply your mind chasing images of longing through your head."

Joe was without a quick-witted retort.

"Thank you so much for making an appointment to visit with me," said Mother Mary. "You have discovered that the template of the Enneagram lies in fairy tales and myths. This is because it is truth about the nature of being human. Often it is buried in archetypal stories and images. A good lesson. I have to go now, and I see it is past time for you to start your next class. When you get to your afternoon break, please arrange to see Sister Angelina. Things are heating up out there and we're going to need to put some of your good mental resources to work. We may want to see if there is a way to accelerate the process of growth of your consciousness. You will have difficulty managing in the future if you cannot get beyond your ego's love infatuations."

With that, Mother Mary stood up and walked to the door of her office. Carroll followed and headed down the hall back to his room. He was outsmarted in his own effort to outsmart Mother Mary. But suddenly out of nowhere a thought struck him—if his need to outsmart her was simply his ego defense, that was just an illusion anyway. He smiled to himself and felt a little lighter. He would, of course, welcome any opportunity to meet with Sister Angelina.

Just then, he heard a commotion at the other end of the hallway. Heading toward the noise, he could see sisters streaming in from all directions. In the center was an odd couple. The man, to whom much of the sisters' welcome was directed, was the geekiest guy Carroll had ever seen. His hair appeared to be waxed and stood straight up. There were various pieces of metal in his face. He had swarms of tattoos and appeared to move on two left feet. In startling contrast was the woman standing next to him. A luxuriant surplus of dark brown hair escaped in all directions from under her head scarf. Her brown eyes sparkled. Even in her warm clothing, the curving symmetry of her figure was startling to Carroll. While all of the sisters seemed to carry an exceptional energetic radiance, this woman's beauty and radiance were stunning.

Among all the welcoming commotion and enthusiastic embraces, Mother Mary came forward to provide an introduction.

"Joe, I would like you to meet two people who are very special to this Order. This is Aasia," she said indicating the beautiful young woman. "And I would like you to also meet Rat."

"The pleasure is all mine," said Carroll, smiling in an agreeable fashion and shaking his head *no* at the same time.

"Joe, you will be working closely with Rat. He is a tech genius and he has come here to help us get our new website going, www.anewpope.com. This is not just any website. The interaction is not just from you typing something into your computer, but from the web-site's interface connecting with your energy. You put your palm on the web-site's interface on your screen and it reads your energy field. The site takes interactivity to the next level. Because of your literary abilities, you will be helping to provide content for the site, geared toward the old-fashioned Internet users who want something explained in writing as opposed to experiencing knowledge of consciousness directly. Sister Magdalen, our spiritual leader, whom you have not met yet, believes that your work with Rat is an important aspect right now of the Order's outreach."

Rat studied Carroll. A bit of an odd duck, he thought. His appearance was button-down-collar, but Rat's sense was that the things swirling around in Carroll's head made him as crazy as himself. *If the elusive Melissa thinks he is who I need to work with,* he thought, *then I am on board.*

"Okay, dude," said Rat, pulling free from the embrace of a couple of sisters in order to stick out a hand.

Joe extended his hand and felt Rat's limp handshake. *He is a strange guy for sure*, thought Joe, but his appearance, which on others might be a masquerade, was not that at all. To the contrary, he was real. Everything about him seemed strange, but at the same time totally genuine.

"I am sure it will be fun working with you," said Joe. "And I hope I get to work with you too," he said, turning toward Aasia.

"Not on your life," chimed in Mother Mary, with the sly smile of a woman who holds a hand of trumps. "Aasia will be in novitiate training while she is here and will avoid speaking with men she has not previously known during that time. Incidentally, Joe, she is perhaps one of the most pure human beings I have ever known. Purity, at a high price of suffering.

When your consciousness level is increased a bit, if you are lucky and have a chance to be on a chore duty with Aasia, even in silence, I expect there will be a lot for you to learn from her."

In truth, Joe had absolutely no idea what Mother Mary was telling him. As he puzzled on it, Aasia smiled at him, an experience Joe would recall with Slade in the coming months. The best he could do was a description later in his email to Gordon Slade: *it was like an angel peeked out at me from behind a cloud.*

*   *   *

In a daze of feelings, Carroll wandered down the hall to the room where he was to meet with Sister Angelina.

"Joey, it's so good to see you. Tell me how you have been?" asked Sister Angelina.

Even though Sister Angelina usually riveted his attention, Carroll was having a hard time focusing even on her. "I am okay," replied Carroll, his usual garrulousness surprisingly diminished.

Sister Angelina continued, "Mother Mary told me that it was important for us to try to accelerate our work. As you have learned here, psychodynamic tools are often helpful initially in spiritual growth. Often if we get in touch with our repressed personal pain, we get opened up to the experience of emptiness. Are you following me?"

"I think so."

"Because of the need for your progress to be as rapid as possible, Mother Mary instructed me to try to explain to you the process of how you might awaken to greater consciousness. Her thought is, since you are a mental type, giving you some understanding of the terrain we hope to travel across will decrease your anxiety and speed up your progress. She recognizes that there is some risk here—the risk that you will intellectualize what is happening to you and this will take you out of the experience of what is actually happening.

"I believe you understand that you see and perceive reality through the filter of the ego structure of your type. This is a natural process. At birth the infant has no sense of self. The personality and a sense of self develop in early childhood. The infant is just Being, there is no self-consciousness. Slowly, through interacting with the environment, the child has experiences which create a sense of identity and the young child separates from his sense of Being. The gradual loss of contact with Being, as the ego structure grows, creates an underlying sense of loss. The experience of this sense of loss is a feeling of emptiness. It is one of the primary characteristics of people living in modern and postmodern cultures, this underlying existential sense of disconnection or alienation. This emptiness is the absence of an awareness of Being. Are you still with me?"

Carroll nodded his head *yes*.

"In psychotherapy, the patient is often led to understand his sense of loss is due to a dysfunctional family system, the inadequacy of the mother's care or the absence of a meaningful father figure. While the psychological explanations often have some validity, they do not get to the heart of the real problem, which is the loss of connection with Being. What makes psychotherapy a dangerously inadequate solution is its single-minded focus on trying to help the patient develop better ego skills to cope with the feelings of alienation and emptiness. Such efforts block spiritual growth. The feeling of emptiness is not the problem, it is the doorway.

"Enlightenment, or Christ consciousness, is about seeing reality just as it is, not through the distorting lens of our own experience. To be free of the distorting ego lens, we must be able to experience emptiness. As fearful as emptiness seems in apprehension, in the experience itself, as the protective ego construct dissolves, what emerges is huge unbounded spaciousness.

"Understanding this in quantum terms, we see the process of going from a limited, ego-structured field to the larger field of Being. What is so difficult is the passage through the liminal space of looking at the world through the ego structure to experiencing the world through the larger field of Being. It is this transition from the small field of self to the larger field of Being that is so challenging. This transition requires the surrender of the ego self—really its annihilation and death—and the ego structure is going to do everything it possibly can not to let this happen.

"Joey, that is the overall map of the terrain we're trying to cross," said Sister Angelina.

Again, Joe nodded his head. Intellectually, he could certainly follow what Sister Angelina was saying. How to existentially get across the terrain she was describing, he had not a clue.

"Throughout history various spiritual leaders have arisen with the same mission—how to chart the course across the liminal space from the field of the small self to the larger field of Being. The sisters in our Order use whatever tools seem to be most effective to assist the individual person. For example, with Aasia, whom you just met, the sisters held her in loving presence and allowed her to descend through the pain of her own personal experience in a torture camp to the emptiness of the inhumanity with which she was treated. From this place of personal ego despair, it is only a short journey to let go of the ego entirely.

"For others, like Sister Magdalen, who is now the spiritual leader of our Order, refined spiritual techniques used over the centuries, such as silent retreats with sensory deprivation, are ways that one can experience the illusion of the ego self and more freely surrender it and more deeply enter the great field of Being. So our job, Joey, is to find the technique that is going to allow you to progress most quickly. Since you are a mental type, we should look for a technique that does not rely on your mental functioning, since your ego structure is going to be most strongly constructed around what you think. We will want to focus on an emotional process or a bodily process. Usually, because Westerners are most out of touch with their bodily intelligence, a bodily process is one of the most

THE ARMAGEDDON CHOICE

effective ways to undermine the ego mental construct of who we think we are. In fact, great breakthrough teachers of the last century like Wilhelm Reich and Gurdijeff focused their work on body techniques as the most expedient way to end-run the ego's mental constructs.

"So Mother Mary has recommended that we utilize bodily-focused processes. Does that sound okay?"

"I guess so," said Carroll. "Though I have no idea what that means."

"Well, Joey, tell me, as we sit here right now, how do your genitals feel?"

Joe Carroll's mouth fell open.

Before he could reply, Sister Angelina jumped in, "Be aware of how your mind can immediately be off to the races about the meaning of my asking you how your genitals feel. All of the sexual and erotic ideas and feelings that just arose are all ego constructs. You need to surrender them."

"Jesus, this is not going to be easy," said Carroll, looking at Sister Angelina with a wry grin.

Sister Angelina did not allow Carroll to avoid the experience of his own feelings by falling into easy banter. "As you see the ego thoughts arise, just let them go. Keep the focus of attention on the space at the base of your spine. As thoughts come up, erotic or otherwise, just let them go, and use the psychic energy you are experiencing to keep your focus of attention on the base of your spine."

Carroll, his eyes closed, nodded in understanding.

"What do you experience now?"

"This is a bit embarrassing. What I am experiencing is a void there, a complete lack of my genitals."

"Good, just keep breathing, and keep your focus of attention there. Relax and allow yourself to sink deeper into the experience you are having right now."

Carroll, his eyes still tightly closed, nodded again.

"What is happening now?" asked Sister Angelina.

"This huge hole where my genitals should be is still there. There is a feeling of electricity going up my spine and I feel like there is a hole in the top of my head."

"Excellent, just stay focused on the hole at the base of your spine and the hole at the top of your head and the current flowing between them."

For the next forty-five minutes Sister Angelina continued to work with Joe Carroll in this manner. By the end of that time, he was exhausted and Sister Angelina brought their session to a conclusion. She gave Joe some homework: to draw an image of what he was experiencing. They would discuss his drawing in their next session.

"Joe, you are making great progress," said Sister Angelina. "Since Mother Mary said we are to try and progress as quickly as possible, I will see you again tomorrow. Bring with you the image which you draw about your experience today."

Joe nodded *yes,* and walked down the hall. *Wait 'til I tell Slade about this*, he thought. What a laugh he's going to have. I come to Sweden to show these women what a man is like who has some real cojones and find out that to make any spiritual progress I first have to lose my balls. This is not a pretty picture.

\*                \*                \*

"How are you feeling today?" asked Sister Angelina, when Carroll returned the next day.

"I am not sure whether I'm making progress slowly or just losing it completely," said Carroll.

"That sounds like a good sign," said Sister Angelina. "Were you able to draw a picture of yesterday's experience?"

"I have two pictures for you. Let me explain. I had a dream last night. In the dream, I was back home in Boston and I experienced again this hole at the base of my spine. It was very cold. There was a circle of ice around the hole. Gradually the ice began to melt. The area got warmer and warmer until it felt like it was on fire. As the burning sensation increased, the hole got bigger. Fire began to shoot up my spine. The hole at the top of my head began to expand from the heat. It seemed like the fire went on for a long time, until all the blockages in the spinal column were burned away—there was nothing left but space.

"In the dream I left my condo and went to my classroom. I walked into my classroom as if for the first time. The colors were dazzling. My students were already in there. The female students no longer seemed like a bunch of hot snatches and the male students uninteresting, discontented men. Each student simply seemed like a person of infinite textures and possibilities. As I looked from student to student, I felt this up-welling in the center of my chest—I loved them all in some profound way I never experienced before. One of the students read a poem aloud by William Butler Yeats. It seemed to be the most beautiful poem I ever heard. The bell rung and class was over. I sat alone in the classroom. Three lines of the poem were:

*And twenty minutes more or less*
*It seemed, so great my happiness,*
*That I was blessed and could bless.*

"These lines kept going through my head! I mean, I was not just hearing these lines in my head—I was experiencing them.

"When I went with everyone to chapel this morning, the sister, who led the service, read Thomas Merton's description of what happened to him on the morning of March 18, 1958, at the corner of Fourth and Walnut in Louisville, Kentucky. He was suddenly overwhelmed with a feeling of love for all the people around him. He saw the beauty and depth of their hearts and the purity of their essences. He called his experience of oneness with all people an epiphany.

"I now understand what Yeats and Merton meant. I feel completely different. Yesterday, I was worried about losing my sense of masculinity. Today, I have a new sense of being a man, which I never felt before, a feeling of organic male essence. There is nothing I have to do to prove my maleness.

"Coming over here I passed several young sisters in the hall. I have to confess that my usual experience is a feeling of erotic attraction to them, and to you, Sister Angelina. But this time I felt something different. I felt my maleness and I felt their femaleness, like a bluebird seeing a robin. There was just this experience of the *is-ness* of the other person.

Carroll paused and looked at Sister Angelina. Her dark hair seemed surrounded by light.

"I think I am seeing truly for the first time, not simply looking through the lens of my own ego limitations. And I must say, Sister Angelina, that you look astoundingly beautiful."

Sister Angelina reached her hand out and touched Carroll lightly on the forehead. She allowed her heart energy to open fully to him. "Good job, Joey. I think you have progressed a lot faster than Mother Mary ever thought possible. I expect she will want to have you participate in the next community gathering so that we can welcome the new Joe to our convent."

She leaned over and her lips touched him lightly on the cheek.

Carroll sat in the midst of their combined radiance. *Not only had another angel peeked from behind a cloud*, thought Carroll, *this angel peeked around and kissed me on the cheek.*

# Chapter 22

As Dawson looked out the farmhouse door of the monastery toward the east, a layer of heavy gray clouds hung just above the high desert floor. Father O'Donnell was a fighter. Despite the doctor's forecast that he did not have long to live, for the past few days Father O'Donnell seemed to be rebounding.

For Father O'Donnell, a certain clarity was coming with his closeness to death, where more truth is revealed and where what is not true fades away. All week there was an urgent restlessness in his conversations with Dawson, as if he did not want to miss a moment of insight where he might discover one more nugget of wisdom to pass on to the one-time CIA officer, who had become his prize monastic student.

An icy wind was starting to pick up. Dawson went to close the door. He stood still for a moment. Far out across the desert there was a break in the cloud cover. It was miles away—an opening, where the sky was blue and puffy little white clouds floated. It augured the possibility of the weather clearing and a foreboding of a window of passage toward which Father O'Donnell was heading. He shook his head as he realized how quickly a glimpse of blue sky brought a rush of emotional images. It was a reminder of the first lesson he spent so much time working on with Father O'Donnell. Most thoughts and feelings are from prior conditioning, not what is happening in the moment. The goal is to use the energy of those thoughts and feelings, driven by some old story, as a way simply to be present. The days with Father O'Donnell were truly precious. Dawson knew the best gift he could give Father O'Donnell and himself was to be completely present with Father O'Donnell and surrender his constantly intruding thoughts and feelings about what might happen next.

Over and over again, Father O'Donnell stressed to Dawson how misunderstood Jesus' message of love is. One can only love from full presence. Loving out of hope, obligation or worry is, Father O'Donnell was fond of saying, like bailing water out of your rowboat using a bucket with no bottom. One is simply sinking deeper into the 'wine dark' sea of one's own thoughts and feelings, rather than hoisting a sail, catching the wind, and tapping into and channeling the energy of love that is constantly available in the universe.

Dawson walked back into Father O'Donnell's bedroom. The cancer was being held at bay by some greater purpose Father O'Donnell had yet to accomplish. It was hard for Dawson to admit that he might be part of that purpose.

Father O'Donnell's frail body, sheltered under a heavy blanket, turned, and he slowly focused on Dawson.

"Good morning, Father, it looks like this bad weather is going to continue. I've got the kettle on. I will bring your tea right in."

Father O'Donnell smiled wanly.

Dawson returned with a hot mug of tea. Father O'Donnell had reluctantly given up cup and saucer. The saucer was simply too noisy with his unsteady hands. He took a long sip.

"It is a critical time, Brother Isaac. The law of survival of the fittest, as Darwin observed it in the field of Newtonian biology or, as we know it, the law of the struggle for existence will be replaced by the law of cooperation for the development of consciousness. We see the new law already: in the bird that picks the bugs off the hippo, flowering plants and bees, and, I believe, in social networking on the Internet. The triumph of cooperation for consciousness was foretold biblically in Isaiah. I was reading it last night."

He picked up the large Bible from his bedside stand, thumbed the pages and then read:

> The wolf also shall dwell with the lamb,
> And the leopard shall lie down with the kid,
> And the calf and the lion and the fatling together,
> And a little child shall lead them.
>
> (Isaiah, Chapter 11, verse 6)

"The law of struggle will only be replaced with the law of cooperation when the need to cooperate for the species' survival reaches a tipping point in the quantum field."

Father O'Donnell stopped his unusual early morning lecture in order to nurse his tea. Dawson did not interrupt.

"We are not there yet. I believe in free will. This is the Armageddon choice I was talking about earlier. We have the power to choose not to allow the change to occur. But this is the greatest opportunity that will ever occur in the history of humankind. It is counter-intuitive for our ego. Our ego self must surrender its survival compulsion, must accept death, for this to occur. As Jesus taught, only by love is this surrender possible. Only when this level of love happens millions of times in the quantum field will the probability shift in favor of the law of cooperation for consciousness."

"I wasn't sure where you were going, Father, but I think with this talk of love, you're getting back to what we were talking about yesterday—presence," said Dawson.

"Presence is the only place from which real love occurs. Love does not occur because of stored-up good intentions. Neither does love occur because of hoped-for goodwill. Unlike other internal organs, such as the stomach and liver that truly only reside inside the human body, the heart, as the place from which love comes, while connected to the physical blood pump, is also a phenomenon that exists, like most of our thoughts and feelings, in the quantum field. The human being is fundamentally what his heart is. The degree to which we live from our heart is the degree to which we live not from our personal quantum field but this larger field that is God.

"You could say our human struggle to move from the law of survival to reach the law of cooperation is our struggle to enter the collective field of the heart. To do this we engage, on the one hand, the active forces of will and action. On the other hand, we also engage the seemingly passive agencies of knowledge or contemplation. The third and reconciling force of these two forces lies in the domain of the heart. There we must also reside, living from a centered place that exists outside of oneself. The realization of the supremacy of the heart in the human being is spiritual alchemy; it is what all our monastic practices aim for, though they are just fingers pointing at the moon."

Father O'Donnell stopped and gazed out the window at the dawning prairie light. The golden light broke his reverie. He looked at Dawson. "Have you been able to follow me? More traditionally, this great work of arriving at a place of heart centeredness is called the salvation of the soul."

Dawson nodded *yes*. He was not sure he understood everything Father O'Donnell explained, but he had no doubt that Father O'Donnell's explanation of heart-centeredness paled in comparison to his life being a living expression of it.

Father O'Donnell started again. "Let me go at this from a little different direction. To feel something as *real,* in the measure of its full reality, is to love."

Dawson nodded. His memory immediately flashed to his first meeting with Melissa years ago in Afghanistan. The experience was so real it was emblazoned in his memory forever.

Father O'Donnell continued, "You know how we have talked about how you have so often felt disconnected from your own life? That lack of connection is what I am talking about. To the extent that we love ourselves, we feel real. We do not love others who seem unreal.

Those early Galileans who decided to follow Jesus—do you think they did that because they thought, well this guy has really good ideas, or he speaks well or he looks good? Of course not. They totally altered the course of their lives because of his luminous realness, which allowed them to feel loved and to love. Jesus was able to enter the personal quantum fields of others, to experience others as real as himself and in the process they experienced themselves as real and loved. Love, then, is about entering the same quantum field of reality where Jesus lived. This is a purified field in the sense that it is not weighed down with the personal baggage of feelings or thoughts about not liking skinny people or people with short hair. The quantum field of love is the big field, where we are able to experience and see and be what is real and not simply have a view distorted by our conditioned beliefs and experience."

Father O'Donnell paused and sipped his tea. Dawson's mind jumped to thoughts of Sister Theresa. She drove the get-away car for him when he helped spring Melissa and Blaine from the clutches of the CIA. Theresa had the most dazzling light blue eyes.

"Father, what I do not understand is how sexual longing fits into all of these ideas about love and being real?"

"We are all too much under the sway of Freud. For him, libido, or sexual desire, was the motivating energy for all human activity. You might say he had a Newtonian view of love in which sexual energy was the cause and effect of all human interaction. But what you have told me that you have learned at the University of Arizona is that the Newtonian paradigm is simply a small grain of sand existing within the larger paradigm of quantum reality. Love is the larger quantum reality. Sexual longing is only one aspect of love, though an important aspect because it has the capacity to channel great energy. But it is only a channel, like the channel of a river. It is not the water itself, which returns ultimately to this huge ocean, the field of beingness of everything in the quantum field. This is what the Scripture means when it says, *God is love*. Moving from the law of survival of the fittest to the law of survival by cooperation is a similar shift from the small Newtonian stream of libido to the larger field of quantum reality that is God."

"Father," said Dawson. "How do I achieve this level of presence that allows me to love? Sometimes when I deeply concentrate on being present, I feel that I am really present, but it takes a huge amount of energy."

"An important point you are making, Brother Isaac. We can try really hard to be present from within our own limited thought field and it can feel much better than our normal trance, and like you say, take a lot of energy. But we never actually break into true presence because we are only in our own ego-defined field trying to be present. To be truly present you must get beyond trying to make your *I-ness* present; you have to surrender the *I-ness*, the ego self. Only when you are free of it can you enter the bigger quantum field of presence, which is not just your presence, but all presence. This presence does not require enormous amounts of energy or struggle. It simply is."

"Our Order has long used an Enneagram understanding of love as a process. This understanding comes from Romans 12: 9-21. Love is a unitive process. This Scripture gives practical non-dual advice to each type. I was going to give you an assignment as a part of your training to explicate this text in an Enneagram understanding. However, since we are on the subject, maybe I best give this to you while I am still around."

Father O'Donnell reached for his Bible and pulled out a weathered piece of paper that was tucked inside the front cover. He handed it to Brother Issac. On the paper was the Enneagram of Love in Action.

### Enneagram of Love in Action
#### Romans 12:9-21

Love dynamically from the center of your being.

**9**

**8** Surprise your enemies with gifts; overcome evil with goodness.

**1** Rejoice with those who are happy and mourn with those who are sad without judging the truth of their feelings.

**7** Be steadfast with joyous hope and patience and faithfulness in hard times.

**2** Be devoted to others in humble, selfless love.

**6** Don't seek revenge; discover Beauty in everyone.

**3** Don't let yourself burn out through ego striving; but depend on the gracious flow of the Spirit.

**5** Help those in need with what you have.

**4** Get along with everyone; do not feel special or be conceited.

Romans 12: 9-21

THE ARMAGEDDON CHOICE

Point Nine - Love dynamically from the center of your being.

Point One -  Rejoice with those who are happy and mourn with those who are sad without judging the truth of their feelings.

Point Two - Be devoted to others in humble, selfless love.

Point Three - Don't let yourself burn out through ego striving; but depend on the gracious flow of the Spirit

Point Four - Get along with everyone; do not feel special or be conceited.

Point Five - Help those in need with what you have.

Point Six - Don't seek revenge; discover beauty in everyone.

Point Seven - Be steadfast with joyous hope and patience and faithfulness in hard times.

Point Eight - Surprise your enemies with gifts; overcome evil with goodness.


Suddenly, Father O'Donnell's fiery restlessness was gone. His head sank into the pillow. He rolled to his side, signaling an end to the conversation. Dawson picked up the tea mug and returned to the kitchen.

He checked on Father O'Donnell throughout the day, but it turned out that Father O'Donnell's energy was depleted for the rest of the day. Dawson was thankful that he was present when his mentor was moved to talk to him.

*Hmm*, thought Dawson—*present, I think for a few moments there I stopped trying to be present, and I was present.* For the first time he had the feeling that he would be able to carry on, even after Father O'Donnell was gone.

# Chapter 23

After ten days of hiking Blaine, Man, and Ooljee reached the SOS dark-retreat hermitage. It had been raining off and on and it was good to have an already-made shelter for the night and not have to improvise.

The trip was not exactly the honeymoon hike Blaine had hoped for. First of all, it was hard going. Ooljee did a great job of getting them back on the track that they made on their way out months earlier, but though she could occasionally see signs that someone walked that way before, the terrain was rough and the going was exhausting.

The first few days out, after they left the dairy farm safe-house, it did seem like a honeymoon. The mature fir forest was magical. They came to a stream settings that she could imagine Zen masters might have spent centuries designing, they were so serene and idyllic. They would linger at such spots, the sensuality of the natural world flowing into their own caressing, so that making love with each other merged into and out of the effortless way the trees and mossy streams were making love.

After a few days, there emerged a restlessness in Man that Blaine had not seen before. At least, she had not felt the intensity of it. He was as attentive to her as a friend and lover could possibly be, but now that he was back in North American, there was a somberness to him.

When they got to the dark-retreat hermitage, Blaine suggested, "Hey, Man, what do you say we hang out here for a while and maybe do a dark-retreat together? I wouldn't mind a dark-retreat with you."

"I like doing most anything with you," said Man. "But I think we need to push on. I know we don't really need to do anything, but I would like to get on to Pipestone to find out from my ancestors what my life's purpose is. I don't know how long I will need to be there to find whatever it is I'm supposed to find. After I do, I will then want to head to New Mexico to talk with Father O'Donnell. The last update we got from Rat was that Father O'Donnell's health was not good."

Man looked at Blaine with love in his eyes. The blondness was wearing out of her hair. She was beginning to look like her old self and Man thought she was beautiful. He often thought how strange it was to be with a white girl. But he remembered his vision quest—that he was to walk between both worlds, the native and the white world. The feral magnetism of her energy effected him, but his feelings for her were deeper and more inexplicable than just erotic. Somehow, all her cuts and scars made her a bit less white. She was the kind of person her race would easily discard. She truly felt like one of his people.

"You know I would do anything for you that you asked, Blaine, but for me to do something authentically for you I must truly be me first. Being in Europe was hard on my spirit. The monks in Germany were great guys, but the practices were not the ones of my people. It is not that I have been homesick, as much as I've been soul sick, if you know what I mean?"

Blaine nodded her head. "I think I understand, Man. I came with you because I want to be with you. But there is no place here that calls to me like it is home. Of course, I don't want to go back to the town where I was trapped in the mental institution for years. And, I do not want to go back to the town where Professor Gallagher works. I am trying to put the hacking years of my life behind me. I don't really want to go to the Southwest where Will Dawson is. I thought in Italy that I might be in love with him, but I never was. You are the only man I have ever loved and the only one I can possibly imagine loving. What are we to do? This land, or at least the land in the Southwest, is a part of who you are. This land is a part of what I have had to escape from. Somehow Berlin, with Aasia and you and Rat—that was where I was beginning to feel like I was home." She bowed her head and rubbed it into Man's chest and he pulled her close.

"I understand, Blaine, I truly do. I don't know what the answer is for us. Like you, I believe we are to be together. How that might be possible, so that we feel at home with the rest of our lives, is truly a mystery to me now. I have faith Father O'Donnell will be able to help us."

Blaine turned her face upward. She and Man kissed deeply. "I feel so much better for having talked with you about my worries. I have spent enough time with the sisters to know that living in the mystery of my life, while at the same time listening to what my life is telling me, is the key. What do you say we make a deal?"

Ooljee felt Blaine's energy lighten and he came over and pushed his head between Man and Blaine level with her crotch. She loved the way he could read her energy before she was even aware of it herself. Plus she was sure that when he came to nuzzle her crotch, that he knew exactly what he was doing. She reached down between her legs and patted Ooljee's head. "Ooljee," she said, "you are the best dog and such a guy."

"Okay, what's the deal?" asked Man.

"I will go with you on this trip to Pipestone and to the Southwest, even if Will Dawson is there, but no matter how hard we need to travel, each day before we press on, we will take at least an hour to do the centering prayer and energy practices together which we were instructed in by Mother Mary. Remember how she told us we need to give spiritual structure to some of our time together in order for our connection to deepen. Otherwise it is too easy for us to mistake whatever happens to be passing through our heads as what is actually going on between us. The energy practices will help us strengthen our communication, essence to essence and stay in touch, as she said, with the reconciling force, whatever that means."

She looked Man deeply in the eyes. "What do you say?"

"Not only do you have a deal," said Man. "You have my deepest thanks for reminding me that the process of how we make this journey of relationship determines where we get to. I love you, Blaine." And Ooljee quickly lost his place as the couple abandoned themselves to each other.

They stayed one extra night at the dark-retreat hermitage and in two and a half weeks of determined hiking made it back to the convent. They waited in the woods until nightfall before entering the convent grounds. Man had the strong intuition that the CIA's surveillance efforts were still in place. A quick reconnaissance by Man and Ooljee determined that the convent was virtually abandoned. There were a few people around, but they appeared to be newly hired custodial staff, not sisters. Blaine and Man were not surprised. It looked like Mother Mary and all the sisters had left for good.

Man and Blaine quickly decided that it would be best for the custodial staff if they were unaware of their return. The pair stayed hidden in one of the outbuildings until an opportunity presented itself. They did not have to wait long. A food service delivery truck pulled up to the back of the kitchen. After the driver unloaded his delivery, while he was inside the kitchen getting a delivery ticket signed, Blaine, Man and Ooljee slipped into the back of the truck. Fortunately, it was not a refrigerated vehicle.

The next delivery stop turned out to be a small hospital on the outskirts of a medium-sized town. Once the driver unfastened the truck's rear doors and backed to the dock, he went inside a hospital administration building. Man, Blaine and Ooljee immediately exited the truck and walked out of the service parking lot. They found their way to the main street. After a quick walk about they located what appeared to be the finest Native American craft shop in town. They went in.

The man behind the counter appeared to be the proprietor. While Blaine wandered around the shop looking at the handicrafts, Man settled into a long conversation with the owner that began with Man describing the clan he was from and that of his mother. In the native way, he could say who he was in a respectful way without ever giving his name. Man thought that perhaps the owner was a Lakota, who might not be happy about people from other tribes going to Pipestone, but it turned out he was a Mandan who understood immediately the importance of the pilgrimage Man was on.

Man asked for help in renting a car. He did not know how long he might need it and he wanted to drop it off in New Mexico. Fortunately, Man had a good bit of cash, which Sister Darcy insisted he take for their journey. The shop owner did not ask Man to explain why he had such a large sum of cash or why he couldn't rent a car himself. He understood all too well the need for discretion that Native Americans often had to adhere to in order to function in white society. The shop owner took a quantity of the cash and made a few phone calls. Appreciative, Man invited the owner to have lunch with them. For the past five days Blaine and Man had been down to the end of their rations and were surviving on the last of their dried rice cooked each night with any kind of protein Man could hunt down to add to the pot.

The three of them and Ooljee walked a half a block down the street to a diner. It was a breakfast any-time-of-day place. Man finished off two huge country breakfasts in no time. Blaine devoured a large stack of pancakes and Ooljee feasted on portions of what both Man and Blane had ordered that were passed under the table. The shop owner sipped coffee while they ate, as if watching two starving friends fill their stomachs was the most natural thing in the world.

When they got back to the craft shop, sitting outside was an old Nissan pickup. There was rust around the edges and the state inspection was lapsed, but it had a set of Minnesota plates and appeared to be in okay running condition. The shop owner explained that this was not really a rental. He had gotten the car for $500 and hopefully it would get them to New Mexico. If so, Man could just pass the car along to the next person who seemed a bit down on his or her luck and in need of wheels.

Blaine and Man exchanged farewells with the shop owner. When Man opened the door of the Nissan, Ooljee was the first in. They were of to southwest Minnesota and Pipestone National Monument. They drove straight south past Minneapolis and then took the Laura Ingalls Wilder, *Little House on the Prairie* route, Highway 14, to Pipestone. Blaine was fascinated that there was such a thing as a *Little House on the Prairie* route. She remembered reading the book as a youngster in the mental ward and how easy it had been to escape into the interior world of her imagination. But aside from the asphalt strip beneath them, as they headed into the sun, all she saw along the route were miles of soybeans and corn and the occasional interrupting cluster of grain elevators

THE ARMAGEDDON CHOICE

beside the railroad tracks.

They found a place to stay right outside Pipestone, in a camp grounds where there were a few summer trailers to rent. After living in the rough for weeks, the little camper trailer with indoor plumbing was a luxury suite.

The next morning they showed up at the Pipestone National Monument Visitor Center and bought tickets to go in. Once inside, they toured the main tourist areas, walking along Pipestone Creek which flows through the park until it reaches the middle of the prairie grass area where it drops over the edge of the Sioux quartzite cliff line at Winnewissa Falls. Fortunately for them, with the cutbacks in the parks' budgets, there was no staff on duty out in the park. Man's memory of being there as a boy was good, and after slipping over the tourist boundary, they were soon in the part of the park that was reserved for Native Americans to come with permits and quarry.

Man knew that a native person often waited years to get a permit for one of the fifty-six active quarry sites and that it might be difficult to find someone who would want their help in quarrying, but his worry was offset by his belief in the rightness of his being there to quarry into the blood of his ancestors to find a sign for how his life should be.

Each person with a permit had staked out his or her quarry space. Man was not about to interfere in someone else's claimed location. However, as the day wore on he kept being drawn to an area where an elderly woman and a young girl were intently digging. The child he guessed was maybe eight or nine and probably the older woman's grandchild. Without saying anything, while Blaine was reading or drifting off to sleep in a sunny spot, Man began to help the elderly woman move the dirt away that she was excavating using simple hand tools.

As luck would have it, the woman was Navajo, a Diné like Man, who arrived only a week or two earlier to quarry for pipestone and to commune with her ancestors as she did every year. By the end of the day she had adopted Man as part of her quarrying crew.

The next day and the next and so on for the next three weeks Man was there every day helping quarry. It was clear from the start that the elderly woman understood the spiritual implications of why Man was there. She told Man that The Great Spirit once came as a large bird, perched above the waterfall, broke off pieces of red rock, and made it into a pipe and began to smoke. The Great Spirit instructed: 'This red stone is your flesh. You were made from it, and you must all smoke to me through it.' The old woman did not fear that he was there to take pipestone from her claim. She knew that the Great Spirit's intention was that the ground was sacred and belonged to all peoples.

Blaine often worked alongside Man, though some days she would spend time in the trailer reading or taking Ooljee for long walks. When she was with Man, she tried to open herself to enter into the energy that was driving him in his search. She knew that because she was a woman, even though she was not native, Man believed she had a greater ability to find the red rock strata that was the blood of his ancestors.

One day when Man arrived back at the trailer, Blaine was standing in the door with a worried expression. "Ooljee and I went into town today and I found a small library, which has public Internet access. I got in touch with Rat. Seems that he is in Sweden with Aasia. But, wherever he is, he is always keeping up with everybody else. He had news about Father O'Donnell." She paused.

"Yes, what about Father O'Donnell?" asked Man.

"Not anything I guess we don't already know. Just that his health is really failing and he may not have that much longer to live."

Man looked somber. This was a difficult place to be. He felt the rightness of his being at Pipestone. Yet he seemed to be making absolutely no progress in finding anything in the quarry that would be a sign to him about his life. He felt this huge urge to stay and keep digging. And, at the same time he felt it was absolutely essential that he meet with Father O'Donnell once more, while there was time, to get his advice.

Blaine could read the questions in his mind. "I guess what must be done is what we have been taught to do; and that is to seek connection with our three centers of knowing at a deeper level and see what is revealed."

Man nodded and smiled. "Pretty bizarre to have a white girl

tell me how to access the native way of knowing," said Man. "But then, of course, you're not your everyday white girl, are you?" he said pulling her close to him. "Okay, I'll start a quest tonight. That means no food, no water and not even any sex for the next four days. And we will see what happens. Do you want to make this journey with me?"

Blaine knew that at one time in her life she would have run from anything that seemed like greater suffering than her ordinary daily experience. She was aware that she did not feel that way anymore. A little deprivation was no big deal. Particularly when it was in service of moving deeper into the mystery of her life with Man. "Sure," she said. "I am perhaps more lost than you. I should have probably already been doing a quest. I would love to be on a quest at the same time as you."

"Okay, I will take a run in the pickup into town and get some smokes. See if you can find some old shirts we can cut up so when I get back we can make some prayer ties. We may not be able to quest inside a prayer-tied enclosure up on some remote mountain, but we can honor the ritual by keeping the ties around our necks and being in silence."

The next day Man went as usual to the quarry. He explained to the elderly Navajo that while he would be there helping her as usual, and although the format was a bit unusual, he would be on a quest and would be there in silence.

She nodded thoughtfully then said, "In your questing you must learn to distinguish between ephemeral desires and an essence desire. If it is an ephemeral wish, it will soon die. And perhaps be replaced by another wish just as fanciful. If it is a real essence wish, it will last a long time. If you are lucky, it will last your whole life. Some say that our immortality depends on having wishes which outlast the body. The old people say it is the unfulfilled wishes of our ancestors which have frozen their blood in these rock. I know you are here to find the unfulfilled dreams of your ancestors, particularly those of your father. But sometimes these unfulfilled dreams can haunt us throughout our life like craving ghosts. Remember, my son, what is most important is that you find your own essence desire, not that you live out the unfulfilled dream of someone who has gone before."

"Thank you, Grandmother," said Man, not forgetting to address her with the proper honorific.

By the fourth day of his vision quest, Man was too weak to go to the quarry. Blaine touched his forehead. He was feverish. She was sure that he was having visions as he tossed and turned on the bed. Remembering the process that she had gone through with the nuns in Sweden in her healing, she simply sat by his bedside and opened her heart energy to him. She began to drink a little water so that she could stay present for Man. Staying truly present was easy to do for a few minutes, but hard to sustain for a long period of time. Now she marveled at how the sisters in Sweden had been able to do this for her for hours, as she surrendered again and again her wandering thoughts and simply focused her presence and energy on Man.

It was pre-planned that the quest would end at sundown on the fourth day. Finally, in mid-afternoon, Man was sleeping more easily. Blaine decided to take Ooljee out for a walk. When she got back, Man was gone. She was not surprised. Man told her that the transition from the other world back to this world at the end of the vision quest was often difficult, and often best done alone.

She realized that Man's being gone was good for both of them. Now, rather than focusing on him, she could focus on the meaning of her quest. She remembered what the elderly Navajo woman had told them both, '*You can quest together, but you must do so separately.*'

*       *       *

Man returned to the quarry. First he drank some of the special medicine water that the elderly Navajo woman gave him. She said she brought it with her from a special spring near her hogan on the rez. She was not sure why she brought it, nor why she hadn't used it. Now, she said she knew.

After Man quenched his thirst, he went to the Pipestone Creek just below the falls, pulled off his clothes and submerged his body in the cool water that went through the park. The tradition was not to talk with anyone about your quest, except one or two elders who recognized the you that was within you.

Man, naturally, went to talk with the elderly woman who was befriending him.

"What did you learn?" she asked.

"I am not sure," said Man.

"Sometimes what cannot be explained is what is most real."

Man nodded. "I know I must continue this journey walking between the white man and the people, that much is clear, Grandmother."

"I understand," she said. "But even when we walk a middle way, we must be careful not to fall into the white man's way of thinking. For thousands of years they have been trying to reform each other. That is not our way. We know that a man must learn to connect with himself and the Great Spirit instead of praying to some remote God to help him save someone else. The white people must either have a leader to follow blindly, or they remain passive to their fate, indulging in the disease of tomorrow."

Maybe, thought Man, it was not from his quest that he would get direction, but that the quest was simply to prepare him to hear what he needed to hear from this elderly stranger.

She continued. "It is enough for a human being to try each day to be in right relation with the natural world, his family and his community. This can be hard work. The secret is to focus one's energy on what these relationships need, not like the white man does on what his big puffed-up ego thinks it needs." She paused. "I do not mean to speak poorly of white people, but simply to tell you what you need to know so their culture does not lead you astray.

"Remember the meaning of the new name that you got when you did your coming-of-age vision quest. The white man's big book teaches the same thing. In Revelation 2:17 it says: 'To him that overcometh will I give to eat the hidden manna, and I will give him a white stone, with a new name written on it, which no one knoweth save him that receiveth it.' Stay in right relation to your true name, your essence, and everything else will be as it should be.

"Your longing to be home, the feeling of exile, is simply the ache that we have to be who we truly are. Once you surrender to that mystery—which is surrendering to the essence of who you really are, which is so much more than the small self you think you are, you will understand more deeply what the ache of home is about. For now it is enough to know that this ache is something you will want to have all your life. Do not confuse it with living in a particular place, or having a particular job or even being with a particular woman. This ache is not what is missing, rather it is the handrail that tells you are on the pathway to the Great Spirit. Then, in whatever you do, you will excel without becoming identified with some goal or achievement."

Man thought he was about to be dismissed, but he remained respectfully silent as the elderly woman seemed to be searching the air about them to see if there were other thoughts around her that needed to be materialized into words.

"Every day remember your debt to Nature, to the animals and birds and the standing people, which they call trees, and your ancestors—to all who came before and brought you here. If

THE ARMAGEDDON CHOICE

you always remember how much you have been given, then this grateful openheartedness will always allow you to receive more."

Again, Man was certain the interview was over. Just as quickly he realized it was not and he also understood why. He would not see her again and this would be his last chance to learn the wisdom she had to give him.

"When you get in the doldrums or depressed, get in a good fight with somebody who is smarter and stronger than you. Then use the energy of your anger to get back on your path. Native people are too used to tip-toeing around the edges of white society. Don't be afraid to express what comes from your essence. The whites will not understand you, but living from your essence will always be for the greater good and it is what the Great Spirit intends for you.

"When you get to a crossroads, remember we question with our minds, but we decide with our hearts." She put her hand lightly on her large bosom.

"Understand the questions, but let your heart decide. Remember you do not exist for your own happiness, not even to create your own peace of mind. You are here to encounter difficulties. Even sometimes to create them. Knowing this, knowing why you are here allows you to sink more deeply into difficulties, to not make up some fantasy that your life should be different. Do you understand?"

"I think I do, Grandmother, though I know it will take awhile for all of your wisdom to sink into my heart. I am truly grateful that you have taken your time to bless my quest. I hope you soon find the blood of your ancestors.

"I expect we will be leaving first thing in the morning. Thank you again. Thank you so much." And he bowed his head toward her in a gesture of respect and thanks.

She nodded toward him in return and then turned her attention back to looking through the chunks of pipestone she quarried that day, as if she had these kinds of life-directing conversations every day. Maybe she does, thought Man, but I will remember what she has told me for the rest of my life.

Just then, he looked up and saw Blaine walking up to the quarry. "Greetings, Grandmother," she said respectfully, then turned slightly to smile at Man.

The elderly woman reached down around her feet and held up two pieces of gleaming red pipestone. She looked at Blaine.

Blaine thought of the first ride at Tivoli—the tightness in her chest, then the sudden release. This was similar, but different. The tightness of uncertainty, then the release of sure knowing. She smiled.

"It is the stone in your left hand," she said.

The elderly woman nodded, as if she had known that was the correct answer all along and turned toward Man. "This is for you," she said handing him the peculiarly shaped piece of red pipestone. "You no longer need to search in your past for your future. This is your past. You have caught up with it. Now you step into the mystery of your future. Don't worry about the past anymore, it can no longer trap you or empower you. You are free. This stone will remember that for you."

And the elderly woman turned away from Man and Blaine as she picked up her rock hammer and focused her attention back on a vein of red rock just below her knees.

The next day they were on the road early, in the Nissan pickup on their way to New Mexico. Man was driving, Ooljee was sitting in the middle and Blaine was in the passenger seat. Blaine was aware that there was a lightness about Man that had not been there since they arrived in North America.

She also felt different. She wasn't sure what exactly happened on her quest, but she knew now she did not fear seeing Will Dawson. All of a sudden, the trip seemed like the grand adventure she had hoped for before they left Sweden. She looked at Ooljee. The dog was sitting erect. There was a serenity in his bearing. He looked for all the world like he might be the father of two wayward children that he had finally corralled together for an early morning outing, and he could not be happier.

Neither Blaine nor Man was talkative in the morning. It was past nine o'clock when Man spoke.

"Thank you, Blaine, for your patience with me these past several weeks. You know, the old people say that you can carry your past around like a millstone for years, all your life in fact, unless you follow it where it wants to take you and see what it has to say. I needed to spend this time at Pipestone. But I think now I am free."

"Do I ever know what you mean!" said Blaine. "I believe much of the early work I did with the sisters helped me to free myself from my past, and not just my personal past, but also the past of several generations before me. I am not sure I have escaped completely, but I have come a long way." She turned and looked at Man, both of his hands on the wheel, his expression intent. "What is so cool is that because of the training with the sisters I could feel your energy shift dramatically after the Grandmother gave you that stone. It did feel as if something karmic had been released and you were all of a sudden free."

"Not to change the subject, but keep your eye out for a drive-thru. I could sure use some coffee."

"Okay, but why don't we find a place to stop and eat? I bet Ooljee would like a walk around," she said, as she put her arm around the dog and rubbed the tops of his ears.

"You are right about Ooljee, I am sure, but I was just thinking about what Rat told us about trying to stay below the radar on our travels from Minnesota to New Mexico." Man took his eyes off the road for a long moment to glance over at Blaine, taking in how she was dressed.

Blaine feigned being taken aback. "I was feeling so much

lighter this morning, I wanted a little color. Does it bother you how I look, Man?" she asked, suddenly getting serious.

"All I see is wonderful inner beauty," said Man with a huge grin. "But when you don't have Aasia around as your fashion consultant, well, it is not like your appearance has ever been inconspicuous anyway," and he took another long look over at Blaine.

It had been dark when they left Pipestone that morning. Blaine was wearing a black mini-skirt, a bright green, scooped-neck top, and a pair of pink leg warmers that did not quite come up to her skirt. Between the top of the leg warmers and her skirt was her very white, white-girl skin. There was a swirling tattoo on her left inner thigh, which invited the eye to follow it, as it disappeared up her leg.

"You know, if I wore this in Berlin, no one would notice," Blaine said attempting to smooth down her skirt in an effort which got it no closer to the top of her leg warmers.

"There are some weird dudes in Berlin," said Man. "But they tend to gravitate to your old-fashioned standard of hacker black. I am not sure that even in Berlin there are a lot of women with, how should I say it, your sense of color coordination. When we pull into some little restaurant beside a grain elevator in eastern Colorado, it is not exactly like it is going to be your Berlin crowd hanging out there."

"I only wore one earring in each ear this morning. Doesn't that count for anything?  But, yes, I guess you have a point. Okay, I will look for a drive-thru and where we can find a place to pull over to let Ooljee walk around."

"Rat would be proud of us."

"But, even if I don't know how to do colors, these colors would never have happened, Man, without all the love I received from the sisters and you.  I owe you all so much and I am sure it does not take away from all you have given me if, now and then, the old hacker girl comes out in my exquisite fashion taste."

"Yeah, maybe peeps out a slight bit," said Man, and he reached around Ooljee with his right hand and gently traced the swirl of the tattoo up Blaine's left thigh.

She smiled with delight. "And, of course, I am not totally numb to the charm of my fashion flair. I am just glad to see it is having some effect. You can be such a stoic.  After all our time together, hiking through the Canadian and American forest, I am not used to being with you and getting up in the morning without making love," she said, reaching under Ooljee and letting her left hand massage up Man's leg.

"Looks like other needs are surpassing the basic need for coffee," said Man as he pulled over into an empty roadside stop.  Blaine opened her door and Ooljee jumped over her and headed for the bushes.

Man pushed away at the rusty seat control lever and finally got the seat to slide all the way back, leaving just enough room for Blaine to slide onto his lap in front of the steering wheel.

"Jesus, Blaine," said Man with a sigh as he realized that Blaine was panty-less beneath her short mini-skirt, "you aren't leaving anything to chance are you?"

"Of course not, and I see neither are you. But, you native guys hardly ever condescend to wearing white man underwear anyway. Do you?"

They were both quickly in that elevated state of arousal just before orgasm, where each little movement was on the teeter-totter of control and pure pleasure. "How long is this trip going to take to get to New Mexico?" asked Blaine.

"At the rate we are going, maybe weeks." She shifted her pelvis in a slow, circular motion ever so gently. "Okay, I revise that—months. Probably months," said Man with a grin.

"Okay, in that case I guess I can slow down, Sweetheart." And they both rested perilously on their plateau of pleasure.

"You know," said Man. "Mother Mary made us promise that every time we made love we would spend the same amount of time doing centering prayer and practicing a gratitude ritual. I didn't pay too much attention at the time, but before we had the chance to spend long periods of time together on our hike across the border, I wouldn't have understood anyway. But she said if our love energy just stays on the physical level, it stays trapped in matter, that it doesn't naturally replenish itself and that ultimately we get satiated not only with sex but with each other. She insisted that for our sexual energy to nourish us truly, we must let it move through our bodies and out into this place of spiritual energy where God is and then back again. She kept saying our loving must make a trinity. Her ideas were so strange and your sexual desire so voracious, I never really tried to get what she was saying but I think maybe now I understand what she meant."

"I told you, Man, this is make-up sex. Your little hacker girl, who has always, and for good reason, hated men, had no idea how beautiful it could be to be desired by someone like you. And I have to admit there is still that part of me that wants to hack against, to push against this new reality to see if I can really trust it. I remember when I spent that first life-changing time at the convent, one of my epiphanies was that when a girl has been sexually abused by men like what happened to me in the mental ward, your wiring gets all twisted. You want to fight men, fight yourself, fight anything with sex. At times I do realize my desire to repeatedly make love with you is a form of testing our relationship—in a way, without asking, I am asking, 'Are you sure you still want me?' Weird, huh! You know, come to think of it, I guess wearing this crazy outfit is me once again testing and taunting the world. Clearly I haven't been able to leave all of the hacker girl behind.

"I did not fully understand what Mother Mary was saying either, Man, but what is so interesting to me is that the more time we spend together in centering prayer and making love, the more our energy syncs, the more intimacy I feel and the more I want you, not just to test you, but for sheer joy. I think what she was trying to tell us was not to let the pleasure of love making and sex just be about us, but let it be about this bigger circle of energy that is everywhere, that is God."

"I guess she was pretty clear—that we should not let our egos get attached to the pleasure of love-making, that if we do, sex will become an object, something we think we need or have to have. Our old people say love-making is like the air we breathe just another gift of being alive," He rolled the fogged window down and they could both feel the fresh cool morning air on bare skin. "I think this sex thing is easier for native people. We don't take it so personally; that is we don't have any sense of entitlement or feeling of deprivation around sex. Sex is like this cool morning breeze on a clear sunny day. Our job is simply to show up, pay attention, and be grateful for the opportunity to receive such a wonderful gift. Of course, we do miss a beautiful morning when it is gray and rainy for weeks."

"I think you are way too serious this morning. Maybe you need a bit more morning breeze?" asked Blaine, and again she began to increase the gentle rocking motion of her pelvis.

"I think it is very interesting that Mother Mary told us that even the most perfectly matched couple with the healthiest attitudes about sex, if there is not room for a third energy, then the yang energy of the man and the yin energy of the woman will congeal in a way that will eventually make them both irritable around each other. She was emphatic that creating space for the reconciling energy of the Holy Spirit is necessary for their sexual energy and their love to continually be renewed."

"Hey, I don't think you are paying attention to anything I am telling you." said Man as he realized her motion was slowly and subtly increasing. "Jesus Christ!" Then two penned horses were suddenly freed and were racing across the prairie toward home, each bound and determined to match the other's arrival.

And maybe it would have taken weeks or months for them to get to New Mexico, if Man had not gotten a text from Rat a few minutes later, reporting that Father O'Donnell's condition was very serious. Blaine called Ooljee, who jumped back into the pickup, this time riding shotgun. They headed on down the road. Except for a quick stop at the next drive-thru, they would travel straight through to New Mexico.

# Chapter 24

Dawson had always been afraid of water. He was never a strong swimmer. When he was undergoing his basic training to become a CIA officer at the Farm in rural Virginia, passing the swimming portion of the endurance test was his biggest hurdle. Now he was trying to swim against a current, his arms ached, and ever so slowly the current was pushing him further out to sea. He hated being in the water, its constant greater power slowly condemning him to die.

At least his experience of a watery undertow reflected how it was for the past two weeks. He was afraid to speak with Father O'Donnell about the pain his life was in. For the most part, everything outwardly seemed to be going well. Although he missed Norris, he still enjoyed his classes at the University of Arizona. And he profoundly enjoyed the opportunity to care for his mentor, Father O'Donnell.

But, suddenly it was like he went over a waterfall and was being swept downstream. There was no emotional ground under his feet. He simply felt the sheer terror of trying to swim against a current that was pushing him away from his very survival.

Then, all at once, that all changed. During his centering prayer time, which was no different from the time he spent in silent prayer with the other brothers every morning, something uncanny happened. He seemed to still be making the motions of swimming, but he was above the water. His arms moved effortlessly through the air. He felt exhilarated. He opened his eyes slightly, as he had been taught whenever meditation began to be ungrounded, but it did not seem to matter. He was sailing above a body of water. For some reason, without knowing why, his sense was that the body of water was the Sea of Galilee.

Finally he touched down on shore, sad that his journey through and above the mysterious water had ended. He walked along the water's edge. Without seeing anyone, he became aware there was a woman just ahead in a grove of what looked like olive trees, and he knew inwardly that she was waiting for him there. He walked forward. His steps were light. He could feel his energy flowing easily.

She was standing under a gnarled tree that looked hundreds of years old. She said nothing aloud, but in his head he heard her beckoning him. He walked up to her, and involuntarily bowed his head. She gave a slight smile and he felt wave after wave of warm soothing energy flowing from her heart to his.

"It was my wish that you return, this one time. Thank you for coming. These times on Earth are difficult, I know. Of course, in the little stories we live in it is always hard. You have made a long journey, Brother Isaac. You have been depressed and hopeless much of your life and you have re-experienced all of that in the past weeks. You have experienced the impossibility of things changing for the better through your own efforts. More than anything, you have almost lost faith in your own ability to love. But even in the darkest times, you have remained faithful to the possibility that something could be different. Your visit with me is the reward for your faithfulness. It is only through faith that survival through cooperation has a chance."

Dawson was struggling to take in everything the woman was telling him. He was also trying to have a reality check. Looking around, he tried to observe little things which would help him understand later what was happening. He noticed there was a small table next to where the woman was standing. On the table was a lit candle. Beside it was an ancient skull. It looked like something from a museum, or an artifact that had sat on the shelf in a medical school class for years. Next to the skull lay an open book.

He looked back at the woman. She reminded him of someone. Suddenly, he realized that he would not be here long and that he had only a moment to ask one question.

"After Father O'Donnell dies, do I stay here at the monastery, or do I go to Sweden, to try to help Melissa?" asked Dawson.

She smiled more deeply. She had beautiful teeth, dazzlingly white and they made her smile even more radiant.

Without thinking Dawson blurted out, "Your teeth are so beautiful!" He was embarrassed by his outburst. What a strange thing to say. This woman was beautiful in so many different ways, her long flowing hair, her mesmerizing dark brown eyes.

"Then you will find the answer here," she said, bringing her forefinger to the corner of her mouth in a way that was halfway between instructive and seductive.

"Wake up, wake up," said Brother Will, as he shook Dawson's shoulder. "Father O'Donnell is asking about you. Most of the morning is gone, and you usually spend a good bit of time with him each morning you are not away at school. He is wondering what is wrong. Are you okay?"

Dawson looked up dazed. He was in the small centering prayer chapel at the monastery in New Mexico. He had fallen off of his meditation cushion against the wall. His neck ached. He knew that Brother Will would not be speaking aloud to him unless he considered it a real emergency.

"Jesus," said Dawson. "You're not going to believe this. But I better pull myself together first and go talk to Father O'Donnell. I am sorry I caused you to break silence. Don't worry, I'm okay. More later at the appropriate time." And he nodded in thanks to Brother Will.

\*             \*             \*

"Brother Isaac, I am so glad to see you," said Father O'Donnell. I must admit I feel like I have been in a daze all morning. Some days seem so clear and other days all is a haze. I never know which it will be.  And, as I told you earlier, I want to be as awake as possible when I meet death."

"Father O'Donnell, I thought we decided that we did not need to talk so much about death."

Father O'Donnell suddenly was more clearly present. "We did not decide anything like that at all. You are afraid of me dying. That is okay. It speaks of the affection which you have for me. But it is important for me to talk about dying, so that I can encounter that reality as clearly as possible. Do you understand?"

Brother Isaac nodded his head *yes*.

"I was reading Genesis this morning. God tells Adam and Eve that they must not eat of the tree which is in the middle of the garden and that if they do they will die. The serpent just as emphatically says to the woman that they will not die when they eat of this tree. I have been thinking of what the Scripture means from a unitive consciousness point of view. What if the serpent was not lying? What if both the serpent and God were telling the truth? What if there are two kinds of deaths and two kinds of eternal life?"

"I am afraid I do not understand," said Brother Isaac.

"Unitive consciousness suggests there might be truth in both the statement by God and the assertion by the serpent. What if from God's point of view there is a death and an eternal life. What if from the serpent's point of view there is a different kind of death and eternal life?"

Brother Isaac's face continued to betray his puzzlement.

"What if what God understands as life, the serpent understands as death? And what if what the serpent understands as life, God calls death?"

"I hear the words you are saying, but I still don't quite get it," said Brother Isaac.

Father O'Donnell nodded slightly and then continued. "Death as you know in the mystical tradition, is first of all, not death of the body as much as it is going into the trance of ego unconsciousness. Death is the state of forgetfulness, where we are not in touch with our own consciousness and therefore not able to connect with God's presence. This is the form of death that God is referring to in this passage from Genesis—the sleep of unconsciousness.

"On the other hand, eternal life is about being awake, being conscious, and therefore being connected with the emotional/thought field that is God. Eternity happens in the quantum field. Without sufficient consciousness to access the field, then life seemingly ends when you as a manifestation from the quantum field are no longer manifested. If the serpent represents our ego-unconsciousness, then death to the serpent is our being conscious. On the other hand, eternal life to the serpent is remaining forever in our trance in our manifested state, so we never access consciousness in the field. Theologically, consciousness in the un-manifested field is called Paradise.

"Brother Isaac, I think you have learned enough of our monastic tradition to recognize that this is what the monastic life is all about—we are focused on waking up. Thus, the three monastic vows of obedience, poverty, and chastity are the cornerstones of waking up. The practice of these vows renders a person capable of perceiving reality without distortion."

"I think I understand what you are saying," said Brother Isaac.

"Well, there is more yet. There must also be this force that helps free us from the bondage of our trance. The story of Lazarus in the Bible tells us the nature of that force. You will remember the story. Before Jesus called into the tomb for Lazarus to come out, the Gospel of John says that Jesus loved Lazarus. In other words, it is the power of love that helps us wake up, which is the path to eternal life. Of all of Jesus' miracles, raising Lazarus from the dead clearly is the most miraculous. There is no eternal life, there is no freedom outside of the miraculous. The resurrection is the return from the ego trance of forgetfulness. My experience is that we must over our lifetime be born again many times into consciousness. Our longing is to live in this miracle of consciousness."

Brother Isaac continued to hold Father O'Donnell in clear undistracted presence. He was not sure exactly what Father O'Donnell was trying to tell him, but he knew he would remember the experience of being in this place of deep authenticity with his deeply beloved mentor.

"So there is a sense that when we awake fully to the consciousness of the spiritual world there is a forgetting of the phenomenal world. Death, metaphorically, is sort of a forgetting of what is below and being drawn to what is above. But the serpent offers life by escape into the ego, into self-sufficiency, into being master of our own self-improvement project. It is a withdrawal, a retraction of energy from the life force of the field of God. The eternal aspect of this is what the Buddhists call the hungry ghosts—those psychic energy systems which continue to perpetuate the reality of the constricted small self, even when, maybe especially when, that ego self is out there constructing some huge Tower of Babel enterprise in homage to itself.

"So the serpent did not lie. He opposed divine eternal life with the eternal life of the hungry ghosts that get reincarnated over and over in the idea of the supremacy of the human will. Resurrection, entering the quantum field of God, is victory over the continuously turning wheel of self will. There are many paths to the immortality that God promises in Genesis, but only one way. Just as one judges a tree by its fruits, we judge whether or not we are on the right path by the fruits of that path. You are a good man, Brother Isaac. I am beginning to see some good fruit from your path. You have lost your best friend at school, and I see you learning to care for the other brothers here even more. You are not sure what is going to unfold with your life when I am gone, and yet you are learning patience to be in that unknowing and to trust God. You have lost two great loves in your life, yet you have moved out of the house of self-pity and self-doubt into the openness of big sky country where the prairie rolls out in front of you in all directions."

Out of breath, Father O'Donnell paused. Brother Isaac could tell he was getting very weary.

"You have done well, my son. You are a blessing to me and to this monastery and our Order. I hope I have provided to you a worthy example. I have tried to follow and to teach the path of obedience, poverty and chastity, Brother Isaac. But don't get me wrong. I have not tried to follow this path because I thought the payoff was greater than the serpent's path. I have not followed this path to God because I thought He could do more for me. I have followed this path because I have experienced the greatness of His love. The fruits of this path are the fruits of love and you will receive them.

"My concern now is whether or not there are enough people on this path for humankind to decide on cooperation for consciousness. It is a spiritual law in history that our longings, which seem so subjective despite the reality of their existence in the quantum field, can manifest objectively. The aspirations and desires for God that we carry un-manifested for years can one day miraculously become the history of tomorrow."

His head settled deeper onto his pillow. "Of course," he mumbled. "The paradox is—it is not really up to us, and it is up to us. I must sleep for awhile."

Brother Isaac pulled the quilt up around Father O'Donnell's shoulders as his breathing became slower and lighter and he appeared to be falling into a deep sleep.

However, before Dawson reached the doorway to leave the

room, Father O'Donnell awoke with a start.

"Brother Isaac, as I was starting to fall asleep, I was disturbed by one thought. We have often discussed how an understanding of the Enneagram provides a map for each of us to find the Kingdom of Heaven. But I fear I have not sufficiently warned you that it is only a map. As you know, the Enneagram literature talks about nine different levels, from very unhealthy to very healthy, through which each type can experience the world. These levels are all degrees of preparation. As we get to the seventh, eighth, and ninth levels, our learning expands through our observing the ego self's compulsive patterns and from the insights obtained in deeper and deeper meditation practices of centering prayer. Progress through these levels gets us to the experience of the Kingdom.

"However, there are three additional esoteric levels, which require us, ironically, to give up our map. At the tenth level, one has to surrender even the knowledge of the Enneagram path. At the tenth level, one undergoes a purification from this further surrender. This surrender allows one to enter the eleventh level, where, because of the emptiness produced by the soul's journey through the tenth level, the soul can now be filled with illumination. It is from this illumination that Sister Magdalen receives her powers to enter the energy and thought fields of others, because she now has been given, by God's Grace, infinite access to thoughts and feelings in the quantum field.

"I can only tell you from brief glimpses about the twelfth level, but I believe with all my heart that it is real. At the twelfth level, the soul rises from being a receptacle of divine energy to active participation with the Divine. It is the place of union.

"Now, I must sleep. I do not believe that we need individually to get to any particular level for our collective energy to decide on cooperation for consciousness. But clearly, the more of humankind that is on the seventh, eighth, and ninth levels, the more likely I think humankind is poised for transformation. But, we still must have leaders of transformation on the tenth and eleventh levels. For that reason, Sister Magdalen and her gifts are an encouraging sign for all of us. You are lucky you met this woman years ago. I expect if you had not, you would not be here today."

*            *            *

Blaine and Man were not at Father O'Donnell's monastery long before the days eased into a familiar monastic routine. Blaine was enchanted with the big sky feel of the high desert country in New Mexico. It put her in touch with the experience of something real and present beyond self at an elemental level. She couldn't get enough of staring out at the horizon watching a storm move across the plains. She was excited about being able to tell her friends at the convent in Sweden how connected to God the land is out in the Southwest. For the first time, she understood exactly why Man had been so anxious to return to his native land.

To everyone's surprise, Father O'Donnell continued to have some good days. The gradual decline seemed to have ended. He just had good days and bad days. While both Man and

Brother Isaac were anxious to be with Father O'Donnell on the good days, Blaine enjoyed being with him on his down days. She would often spend long hours sitting beside him on those days, neither of them ever speaking.

Because of her time with the sisters at the convent in Sweden doing energy practices, she was more attuned to the quality of Father O'Donnell's energy. While she noticed that on the down days his energy would be feeble—that is, the quantity would be reduced—she was surprised that its quality, what she had learned to recognize as higher energy states, would be increased. She enjoyed the subtle nuances of Father O'Donnell's energy in the higher ranges, where she could communicate with him without words, and he with her.

Having a place for Blaine to stay at the monastery presented a problem. There were no separate guest rooms and even if there had been, it would have been against monastery protocol for Man and Blaine to stay together in the main monastery building itself. Man found a solution with what he called a portable hogan. In actual fact it was a old camping trailer that had been parked for some time at the service station back up the road. The sign on it read: *For Quick Sale: Name Your Price.*

The owner of the service station told Man it had been sitting there rusting away for two years and he had no idea, 'where the owner of the trailer had gotten to.' If Man would haul it away he could have it. If the owner, returned then Man would have to settle up with him at that time. So the camper trailer was towed out to the monastery and situated two drop-cords away from the old farmhouse behind a copse of aspen trees.

Like the place they stayed in Pipestone, even though the trailer was small, their experience of it was cozy delight. Not only did they have electricity, but also running water, courtesy of a garden hose running from the main building.

Man was busy every day working on construction projects which Father O'Donnell wanted completed. Father O'Donnell was driven to assure that the monastery was in good physical shape and self-sustaining before he departed this world.

One night Man was explaining to Blaine what he was learning from Brother Isaac and Father O'Donnell about the global situation—the realization by the people of the United States that democracy was over and the huge, pent-up unrest this was causing now that the President of the country was a corporation named GOD, owned by the Chinese. Added to this was the struggle over who would be the next Pope.

After the last Pope died unexpectedly, the cardinals convened as tradition required to elect the new Pope. However, before the new Pope could be elected, there was a dysentery outbreak among the cardinals, with almost half of them having to be taken to hospital. The election of the new Pope was delayed. Even after almost all the cardinals regained their health, through various moves by certain key cardinals, who were anxious for the elect-a-new-kind-of-pope movement to gain momentum, the re-convening of the cardinals was continually postponed.

Further complicating the situation was that the world economies were only gradually coming back from the financial crisis caused by the Conficter gang terrorizing the world by hacking into the military computers of Iran and South Korea.

Blaine knew all about how fear could be self-destructive. "We have been out of the loop, especially with what has been happening in the United States. Truly this is a critical time," she said, after Man finished summarizing his earlier catching-up-on-the-news conversations with Father O'Donnell and Brother Isaac.

"Yes, I guess so," said Man. "Blaine, do you know who the first woman was to get to vote in a democratic process in white America?"

"I have no idea, and not sure I care," said Blaine, taken a bit off guard by what seemed a complete change of subject. "That must have been about a hundred years ago."

"No," said Man. "It occured two hundred years ago. About a hundred years before women got the right to vote, the first woman to cast a democratic vote was a native woman."

Blaine got a bit more interested in what Man was telling her. She was always amazed at the interesting facts and perspectives that he had on American history from the things he had learned in a little, rundown school house on the rez.

"In 1805, Lewis and Clark, after narrowly surviving their trip to the Pacific, had to decide where their party would overwinter. They put it to a democratic vote, the kind of listening vote as is practiced in our tribal councils, where you listen respectfully to what everyone thinks before you actually vote. Sacajawea, the Shoshone interpreter they acquired, who made the most hazardous part of the trip with the explorers with an infant on her back, got a vote just like everyone else. As a matter of fact, so did York, Clark's black slave.

"Of course, democracy has always worked differently for native people. In some tribes only the women could vote for the tribal leader, who would be male. What do you think politics would be like in the United States if only women voted? Easy to be cynical and think things would not be different, but I bet they would be very different. There would be a much more harmonious balancing of male and female energy. Father O'Donnell believes first-stage democracy has focused appropriately on individual rights. The next step, which will include the first, will focus on community integrity."

"You are right, Man, we do live in this myth of how democracy should be and clearly ours has skewed way off the path, but everyone is resigned to it. I see no sign of this second new phase."

"Yes, things do look discouraging. What Father O'Donnell says is that back in the 1960s, there was an outcry for Latin American countries to emulate the U.S. in order to grow into vital democracies. These countries had labored for centuries under the burden of autocratic colonial powers. For years, however, they have been independent countries, but they maintained the old social structure of a small wealthy elite class and a huge majority underclass. Their governments have been characterized by the brutal use of authoritarian power and corruption in order to maintain a class society. More and more we are emulating this picture, which a few years ago we critiqued as contrived democracy. Let me give you a few of the facts Father O'Donnell has shared with me.

"Over the past fifty years our country's sense of community has unraveled. We have an elite upper class that has advanced education, are largely married, have increasingly moved into exclusive neighborhoods and schools and have shared tastes through their own media. And we have a much larger lower-class who have no more than a high school education and are suffering from increasing social fragmentation. What is striking about this large lower-class to Father O'Donnell is not just the growing economic divide between it and the elite class, but its internal alienation." Man took out a small pad so he could check his notes.

"In this lower class, 84% were married in 1960, and in 2010 only 48% were married. In the 1960s, two thirds of the lower class counted themselves as religious. By 2010 only one third identified themselves as religious. In the same period of time, the number of mothers giving birth to children out of wedlock increased from around 2% to 44%. Strikingly, there is also a dramatic erosion of the work ethic among the lower class. The number of men at the prime age for work who have opted to be out of the workforce in the past thirty years has risen from a low of 3% to 12%. These numbers focus just on the white population; when you add in minority groups, the disparities

308                    THE ARMAGEDDON CHOICE

become even greater.

"When you lose the dignity of being in a family, the dignity of having a job, the dignity of earning a decent wage, and the dignity of feeling you have a meaningful say in the affairs of your community, you become hopeless and your consciousness becomes stuck at a deep survival level. You also become a ready victim to be preyed upon by those who would take your alienation and turn it into violence.

"Father O'Donnell believes we no longer have democracy because we no longer have a sense of community that runs deeper than our own individual beliefs and interests. But despite all of this, somehow Father O'Donnell is optimistic. He simply believes that the stark reality of the choices we are making is becoming increasingly vivid to all. We are all seeing more clearly our choice—to become more conscious or to stay in the unconscious trance of our own ego and its self-interested needs. We will either struggle for survival to promote our limited self-interests, or we will cooperate for the benefit of all and bask in the joy of everyone's mutual gain.

"Enough of this big picture stuff. When Father O'Donnell is having good days, he and I have been talking about what I should do next. But he thinks that we both need to go back and help the SOS sisters whose work is to help usher in this new phase. He understands that I don't want to live in Europe. He thinks that maybe for the next little while, you and I both need to be there to help the sisters and Rat in staging this procession by Sister Magdalen from Assisi to Rome. He says that when there is a great event and everyone participates in the idea of that event, as, for example, happened with the Lewis and Clark expedition and the lunar landing—then people's energy and thought fields coalesce in a harmonious way, and sometimes there is this forward leap of community consciousness. He hopes that this might happen with Sister Magdalen's procession and that the planet will be saved."

"What does he think our work there would be?" asked Blaine.

"I don't know. I thought you might tell me. He says you and he have been talking about stuff."

Blaine smiled. "We have, I guess, but mostly not aloud. We did have one outer conversation where I asked him what I should do about Professor Gallagher's request and the answer to it, which Rat hacked and gave me. He told me to just tell Rat to have the sisters put it up on the blog of the new Pope website. So if you could pass that request on to Rat, that would be great.

"Otherwise, we have been having these conversations in his energy field which is really finely developed. He was surprised I could meet him there. But mostly we talked about you and what a wonderful man he believes you are." She moved across the room, sat beside Man and put her arm around him. Ooljee got up when she did and came and put his nose right on her knee.

"Hmm," said Man. "Very cool! I could tell Father O'Donnell really likes you. If he thinks we need to go back I am willing to consider it. I had thought we should wait till he passed on, but right now who knows when that might happen. Maybe you should be in touch with Rat and find out if our help is really needed and, if so, how we would get back. Since the quest at Pipestone and the Grandmother's present of the blood rock of my ancestors, I don't feel so compelled to solve something from my past. The sense of freedom I first felt, when I got the rock as a gift from her, continues. I won't fight going back to Europe if we are really needed, though it is so good to be back out in the Southwest where it is palpable that God is everywhere."

"You are the *Man,*" she said as she pulled him toward her. Ooljee, as if on cue, stuck his nose in the middle of their embrace.

# Chapter 25

Godfrey was on time for his appointment with Father Hay. The two men got tea and quickly settled down in Father Hay's office.

"How have you been?" asked Father Hay.

"As I sit here and think about it, much better than I realized," said Godfrey. "I have been so fascinated by everything that is going on with the new Pope website. Have you seen it, www.anewpope.com?"

"I have heard about it. But I have not had the chance to check it out yet," said Father Hay. "What is it about the site that is so fascinating to you?"

"What intrigues me?" Godfrey paused. "Is that the website is, in a sense, asking the world some of the same questions that I have struggled with in spiritual direction with you: *What is the purpose of life?* Not only for me individually, but for humankind as a whole. Is life simply evolving on Earth driven by our genetics and each species' desire to survive, or is there a spiritual reality that offers the possibility of something greater than competition for survival?"

"I must take a look at this website," said Father Hay. "Sounds like it is asking provocative questions."

"I think it is asking the right questions for our time. And more than that, I think it is focusing attention on this real world conundrum of who the next Pope will be. People all over the world, many who obviously have no connection with the Catholic Church, seem to care passionately. For millions of unbelievers and people of other faiths, this question of the next Pope has become a lightning rod for an aspiration by humankind to do something important, better. The whole world has cared before about tyrants and dictators, hoping they might be banished. But this is the first time everyone seems to care about who a spiritual leader might be. I don't think this has ever happened before—at least not with the level of global involvement that is occurring.

"Never in history have the cardinals gone so long without selecting a Pope. Never have they gone into such an extraordinary recess from deliberations without anyone knowing when they will return. When you combine these historic events with social media like Facebook and Twitter with millions of people commenting and talking about these events, it does seem that history is at some new juncture."

"From the little I have heard, I take it that the new website is advocating a female Pope. Is that correct?"

"The best I can tell...well, yes and no," said Godfrey. "The site is definitely drawing a line in the sand that the next Pope needs to be someone of unitive consciousness. That is, the next Pope needs to be someone who does not represent belief along either liberal or conservative lines, but someone who first and foremost acknowledges that religious beliefs in the abstract alienate people and that what is important is someone who will live and lead in a Christ-like manner. The folks at the new Pope website believe Jesus came to teach spiritual transformation so we can all access a new level of consciousness. They do not think he preached some kind of religious ideology."

"Well, that is a tall order. It's for sure whatever the next Pope does, before too long he or she will be given a label, conservative or liberal, or something like that by the press, regardless of how the person actually approaches life and the decisions that are presented to him or her. And, particularly if a woman should be elected Pope, that would be a red flag which would bring the most disgruntled former believers back into church politics. Of course, it is hard to imagine a woman being elected Pope given the number of cardinals with conservative ideologies from Third World countries. But, what do the new-Pope-website-people think about the fact that electing a woman Pope would be the most ideologically alienating event that could happen to the church?"

"Given their perspective on getting beyond ideology, they must have thought a lot about that. If they have an answer, it is not on their website. What their website does do is solicit thoughts and suggestions from everyone about how this transition might be made without instigating some sort of backlash. But they really seem prepared to elect their own Pope if the cardinals completely drop the ball."

"All very interesting," said Father Hay, "but, let's see if we can bring our discussion about this back to what is the meaning of all of this for you. Got any thoughts?"

"Our discussion has been helpful," said Godfrey. "I think the big thing that I am gaining from all this is the realization that my own spiritual journey is a part of this larger spiritual journey by humankind. For years, I have experienced a spiritual loneliness and often a sense of alienation from the rest of the culture. Even in church groups, I would feel like a spiritual outsider. As you would say, Father, I have been caught up in the narrative of my small self. What seems hopeful about all this uproar about a new Pope is not that anyone knows how to solve this problem of how to move forward with a new kind of spiritual leadership in the world and not trigger a spiritually backsliding reactionary response, but this sense of solidarity among so many people who are wrestling with the same questions. Does that make any sense?"

"It makes a lot of sense. It may be more important for humankind to come together around the nature of the problem, than having a solution. So what is it going to mean in your life today, tomorrow, and the next day, to be a part of this upwelling of interest in the destiny of humankind's spiritual journey?

"I am not sure at all," said Godfrey. "It sure feels good not to be so alone, but this consolation makes it harder for me to know what is the next step for me on my spiritual path."

"Good observation. Knowing others are out there on a similar path is comforting, but it can also be a way we distract ourselves from understanding our own next steps along our spiritual way. Remember, the underlying touchstone to this general spiritual awakening is having a non-dual perspective. That is the key. What does this mean practically? It means that you care about what is happening out in the world at a global level and you also care about what you can do for the homeless person you see on the street next time you go shopping. And your response to both of these things comes from the same heart-centeredness that your spiritual practices have helped nurture."

Father Hay paused. Godfrey tilted his head and gave a slight smile.

"I think you're telling me not to get too excited about this worldwide movement of interest in a new Pope," said Godfrey.

"I am not suggesting you be excited or not excited," said Father Hay. "What I am saying is that you not let these global issues distract you from being spiritually grounded and open to whatever is right in front of you. If we get the kind of new Pope you and I might hope for, regardless of gender, he or she will have to be doing exactly what I am suggesting we all must do. We must be present in the moment to whatever is before us and respond from a heart-centered place. That is how we will solve the world's problems—by the way we interact with them as a part of our own spiritual evolution. We won't solve the world's problems by some abstract understanding of these problems or having more think tanks. At least, to date, that method has not worked."

"You are sure right about that, Father," said Godfrey.

"So the more complicated the problem, the simpler the solution. Shall we take a few minutes in silent centering prayer and then see if anything else is up for you?"

"Sure, sounds good."

Slowly the breathing of the two men shifted together to a slower, deeper place. Light and shadows played across the room. Whoever the new Pope might be, he or she would need followers like them.

*           *           *

With time in centering prayer, Godfrey sunk deep into himself. As he emerged his brow was furrowed.

"How are you now?" asked Father Hay.

"I thought I was doing great," said Godfrey. "But in the silence what kept coming up was what happened last night. Jeff and I got into one of our old arguments. Well, the issue we were arguing about was not old, but the emotions and feelings were. It just felt so yucky being pulled back into this place of feeling criticized, and then see everything that I was saying in response making the situation worse. So I guess you could say that the good news was I was aware of what was happening. The bad news is my awareness made me feel even worse, as I was helplessly sucked into this conflict with Jeff."

"Doesn't sound like you all have gotten quite through it yet," said Father Hay.

"No, I guess we haven't. We both went to bed last night with our feelings frayed and unresolved."

"Well, let's talk about the issue first. Then we will talk about the process you slipped into when you were dealing with the issue. Does that sound okay?"

"That sounds good," said Godfrey. "The issue is really an old one—of me getting defensive and feeling like Jeff is criticizing me for my Christian spiritual journey. But this time it was not Jeff saying something negative about an issue like the resurrection, which in the past has made me feel defensive because of my own uncertainty about that issue. This time Jeff just made some sarcastic remark about the Ten Commandments. I don't feel I have a whole lot of belief investment around the Ten Commandments, but all of a sudden I got very defensive."

"So maybe your defensiveness is similar to the reason you felt defensive about the resurrection issue—your own uncertainty about the meaning of this particular teaching to your spiritual journey?"

"Yes, I guess that's right. I hadn't realized that until just now. I'm not certain what meaning the Ten Commandments have for me. Maybe if I was Jewish they would be a big deal. But the truth is I haven't thought that much about them one way or the other." He paused. "Since I don't live in Alabama." Godfrey grinned. "But when Jeff made a sarcastic remark about the Ten Commandments I felt blindsided."

"What I suggest we do then," said Father Hay, "let me go through and give you a little background on how the Ten Commandments might be meaningful to you in your spiritual journey. Then you can decide for yourself about whether you're really comfortable with them or if they are even relevant to you. Once you are grounded in your own perspective then I think the process with Jeff will be easier to look at and understand."

"Makes sense to me," said Godfrey. "Fire away."

"The Ten Commandments predate the Christian message by centuries. They came in a period of man's evolutionary history where the focus was on eye-for-and-eye justice—before Jesus' message that justice must spring not from the survival needs of our ego, but from love and mercy, which flow from our connection with our essence and God. So while they don't help us understand today the source of love, they do provide good instruction for us today on how to conduct our spiritual journey. In fact, I guess it will not surprise you when I tell you that nine of the Commandments each relate to a specific point on the Enneagram."

"Oh no," said Godfrey in mock horror. "Not the Enneagram again."

"Well, not exactly the Enneagram. The template of the Enneagram may not have emerged into consciousness at the time the Commandments were given to Moses. So the sequence of the Commandments is not in Enneagram order. But the message of each of the Commandments is an instruction on how to address the blocks of the false-self at each of the nine points of the Enneagram. Let me go through them with you.

"The First Commandment is *Thou shalt have no other gods before me*. This is a Point Nine instruction to surrender dynamically to the living God. Remember for the Nine it is easy to get stuck in easy comforts and the priorities of others. The surrender that this Commandment seeks is active and engaged with life.

"The Second Commandment says that *Thou shall not make any graven images*. This is a Point Five instruction. It tells us not to use our human mind to create ideas of God, which we would substitute for the reality of the living God. This commandment is violated when the Five allows his mental capacity to grasp for ideas about God rather than abiding in the mystery of a living reality.

"The Third Commandment is *Thou shall not take the name of thy Lord in vain*. This is a spiritual instruction directed to the type Two person. It is saying that you should not engage in any activity, including especially activities to help others in order to promote yourself, without giving God all the credit. We take the name of God in vain when we do good as a creature of God, but don't give our Creator the credit. Godfrey, are you following me?"

"Yes, I have enough familiarity now with the Enneagram, that what you are saying does make sense. I had no idea the Ten Commandments might be relevant to my own spiritual life. Please keep going."

"The Fourth commandment is *Remember the Sabbath day, to keep it holy.* You can readily see how this is a spiritual practice instruction. It is saying remember your practice of centering prayer, remember your practice of fasting. It is directed to the personality type at Point Eight. It is telling the Eight that its outgoing, assertive energy must be balanced with an inner practice of silence and centering.

"The Fifth commandment is *Honor thy father and thy mother.* The relevancy of this commandment is not as easily grasped as some of the others. In essence, what it is telling us is the importance of continuity and experience—the importance of learning from those who have gone before us, who have real wisdom because of their experience. As the expression goes, we stand on their shoulders. This instruction is particularly directed toward Point Seven. Sevens when they are caught in their ego compulsion, rather than going deeper with what the history of their experience has given them, they go shallower seeking out new options.

"The Sixth commandment is *Thou shall not kill.* You can just feel the energy and power of this commandment and this gives us the clue that it underlies all other spiritual instructions in the Ten Commandments. Basically it is telling us not to invoke and act out of a dualistic perspective. It is an instruction to maintain unitive consciousness. It gets to the heart of what those folks at www.anewpope.com are talking about. Look at the roots of the word conversation—*con* meaning with and *versa* meaning flowing. This is a unitive approach. And can be contrasted with the dualistic approach found in controversy—*contra* meaning against, so that the meaning of the word is flowing against. In a unitive approach we engage in conversation, in a dualistic approach we engage in controversy. The Sixth Commandment forbids the latter."

"So are you saying that when I engage in an argument with Jeff and simply stand up for my point of view and do not flow with him and understand his point of view, I am violating this Commandment?"

"Yes, you got it," said Father Hay.

"The Seventh Commandment is *Thou shall not commit adultery*. It is an instruction directed particularly to Point Six. It requires faithfulness to life, to your commitment to God, and to those you love. The Six must not allow his tendency to feel betrayed to allow him, in turn, to betray those to whom he has pledged his faith.

"The Eighth Commandment is *Thou shall not steal*. This commandment is directed specifically to the Three. It is an injunction to renounce the desire to accept praise and acclaim for accomplishments, which always depend upon Grace.

"The ninth commandment is *Thou shalt not bear false witness against thy neighbor*. This commandment is directed specifically toward the One. It is an instruction not to be judgmental or accusatory of others.

"Finally we come to the Tenth Commandment—*Thou shall not covet thy neighbor's house, etc.* This commandment is directed specifically to the Four. Just as the Second Commandment says thou shall not make any graven images of God, the Tenth commandment is saying we should not make graven images of other humans. To do so is to dehumanize them. When we covet something our neighbor has, we project our own concepts on that person. In doing so we fail to see the real human being.

"Okay, there you have it. The Enneagram of the Ten Commandments. Here it is on a piece of paper," said Father Hay, as he handed Godfrey an Enneagram image he had hastily sketched out and labeled.

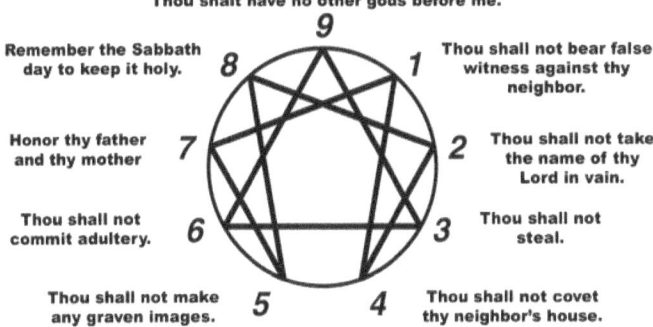

**Enneagram of the Ten Commandments**

Thou shalt have no other gods before me.

**9**

Remember the Sabbath day to keep it holy. **8**

**1** Thou shall not bear false witness against thy neighbor.

Honor thy father and thy mother **7**

**2** Thou shall not take the name of thy Lord in vain.

Thou shall not commit adultery. **6**

**3** Thou shall not steal.

Thou shall not make any graven images. **5**

**4** Thou shall not covet thy neighbor's house.

"I had no idea that the Ten Commandments were so amazingly relevant to a modern spiritual journey. I can see how they all apply to me in a way, but particularly the instruction to my own type."

"Good," said Father Hay. "I think things will be a lot easier to discuss with Jeff now that you have some ground under your feet about the meaning of the Ten Commandments to your spiritual journey. Would it be helpful to discuss the process of how you might move things forward with Jeff?"

"You know, Father, I think what I would like to do is try it on my own first. Now that I better understand the relevance of the Ten Commandments to me, I feel like I can have some compassion in listening to Jeff about his views. I would like to give it a try, to see if I can do this without violating the Sixth Commandment."

"Godfrey, that sounds awesome. We are about out of time anyway. Give it a whirl, and if you have difficulty call me. As humankind has evolved, so has our religious history. All teachings have a way in which they can be meaningfully understood in our lives. You don't just have to be from Alabama," he said with a wink. "Even the old stuff, like the Ten Commandments, belongs."

# Chapter 26

"Thank you," said Father O'Donnell, "for coming to sit with me again this morning, Brother Isaac. I am getting incredibly weak but I am very clear. I realize that preparation for death is a process in which we enter this cosmic hospital for our last treatment. We have a last chance for the surgeries we need to remove those ego attachments which have kept us stuck all our life."

"Here is your tea Father O'Donnell," said Dawson, as he placed a straw in the tea mug and held up the straw to Father O'Donnell's lips.

"Thank you, Brother Isaac," said Father O'Donnell, his voice just above a whisper. "I have been a monk all my adult life, and here I am in the final preparation for my death and I see how many of the old attachments have to be given up yet again. In a sense it is discouraging; and in another sense it is most hopeful because of the ease with which I am now able to let go of them."

Brother Isaac could barely understand what Father O'Donnell was saying, he was speaking so softly.

"Brother Isaac, this really is no big deal. I have died so many times. Years ago I had my first experience of being connected to the great thought field of God and realized that what I thought was me was not me. When I say I realized it, I mean I experienced it firsthand. I cried. The revelation was so startling and so wonderful. We live in a very psychological era. For years I examined my desires, feelings and memories, trying to root out stuff in the way the old religion teaches. Then I remember so vividly one day in a session with my spiritual director experiencing that this internal dialogue of thoughts and feelings of the psychic self is not who I really am."

Father O'Donnell closed his eyes. Brother Isaac could see he was reaching deep within to gather his energy.

Father O'Donnell continued, "Like you, Brother Isaac, I am a mental type. So the last great experience along this path of self-discovery was that my thinking is not the self, is not who I am. So you might ask: 'If we are not our body or our emotions or our thinking, then what are we?' Let me say that telling you anything more of my experience would simply be a distraction. Indeed, it would hinder your experience of the realization of who and what you really are.

But your contemplative practices and your experience at the University of Arizona are like a giant billboard pointing the way. The real you, the Self, is out there in the quantum field that is God. The manifested you, the you that is sitting by my bed right this moment in space and time, is a glimmer of one of the many facets of the hologram of you. The real you is in the field, and when we are plugged in there to the quantum field of God, then writing a great poem, or painting a beautiful painting or even helping save the world is possible."

Father O'Donnell motioned for Brother Isaac to bring the tea mug back over to him where the straw could reach his lips. He sipped noisily with a raspy sound.

"I am sorry that Rat decided there was no way that Blaine could safely return to Sweden to help the sisters there. But I expect he is right. Thank you for helping her get a position in the IT department at the University of Arizona. And I guess Rat is right that she can do almost as much to help the sisters working here with such good computer access, as she could do in Sweden. But how has it been for you, Brother Isaac, having her commute back and forth with you from the monastery to the University of Arizona in Tucson?"

Dawson was amazed. Here this man was on the very doorstep of death and his focus was on a concern for Dawson.

"I was really dreading the first ride with Blaine into the University of Arizona. But she is such an extraordinary person. I was able to talk deeply and honestly with her. I told her how much I regretted that I had not followed my heart and returned to Berlin to see her, and how at the same time I am able to see how happy she is with Man. You know, now that I think about it, she did not actually say that much during our commute. It was just that her energy was so calming for me."

Father O'Donnell's eyelids fluttered open. Dawson was not sure how much Father O'Donnell understood of what Dawson was saying. But, Father O'Donnell's eyes were clear and in their clarity, knowing comprehension was reflected.

"After that first trip in, I have not felt the least anxiety from being in the car on the commute with her. And I think she feels fine about it also. Occasionally, when I look at her when she is focused on scenery outside the car window and the sunlight plays across her face in a particular way, I have this pang of deep regret."

"You have done well my son," said Father O'Donnell. "I have been in communication with the director of our Order and made my recommendation that you are my choice to be the head of this monastery after I die. My recommendation will be subject to the approval of the Brothers here. But I know of no one else who has moved so swiftly along a spiritual path of freeing himself of attachments and spiritual blocks. I believe in the coming days this monastery will be an oasis for people on the spiritual journey. I think they will just show up in ones and twos, but many will come.

"Your task will be to help them connect with some structure in their life that will allow them to stay on their path. Your work at the Center for Consciousness Studies gives you the language of science for those who need that, and there are a lot of people out there in that category. There are a lot of people, who, while they may have grudging admiration and respect for a Zen Buddhist on his spiritual path, will have nothing but contempt for a Christian pilgrim. The language of science is helpful with these people because for them the words are more neutral."

There was a long pause as Father O'Donnell re-gathered his

energy.

"Now about your request to go to Sweden to help Sister Magdalen—I have been giving it prayerful consideration. My first thought was that after I depart, you will need to be here as a stabilizing force. My next thought has been that it is always good spiritually to walk into the lion's den of our fears and regrets. There is a sense that what has kept you on the spiritual path has been your desire to recapture this connection with Melissa that you developed more than twenty years ago. I believe you are at the place where it would be spiritually helpful for the person that you are now, who has changed deeply, to meet this woman, who I am sure has changed mightily since the two of you first met in Afghanistan. Also, it occurs to me that since Blaine and Man cannot go to Sweden to help the sisters, your going might be the next best way we can help."

He paused.

"And it turns out that you may not even need to go to Sweden. Mother Mary has informed me that they are preparing a procession from Assisi to Rome. I understand the plan is to have Sister Magdalen ride on a donkey to meet with the cardinals in Rome at St. Peters. The procession is designed to be an act of incarnation of divine feminine love. I expect you are just the kind of guy they need to handle the donkey's lead rope. You would have one more chance to look after this woman who has mystified you most of your life. I have also been in touch with an old friend of mine, Father Hay. You will remember he came with so many other brothers and stayed with us when I first got very sick. I have asked him to go to Rome to help Mother Mary out. He will be available to you should you need a direction session while you are there."

Father O'Donnell managed a weak grin.

"I will abide by whatever you think I should do," said Brother Isaac. "But I certainly will not leave while you are this sick."

"As you can see, Brother Isaac, I have evidently landed on a plateau. I may be around for another couple of years. The world is becoming ripe to make its decision about consciousness. I believe it is your destiny to help God's kids make that decision. To do that, you need to go to Italy. And sooner rather than later. I think the walk to Rome is scheduled to start in about a week."

Dawson did not know what to say. It was true that Father O'Donnell had reached something of a plateau in his decline. And it was also true that there was no way to figure out whether his death would be next week, next month or next year. The doctors were baffled. According to them, Father O'Donnell should have died months ago.

But while Dawson knew the uncertainties about Father O'Donnell's health were real, the greater likelihood was that he would not be around that much longer. Dawson was torn. He did not want to leave Father O'Donnell and not be present when he died. And, he did not want to miss out on the chance to help Melissa in her desire to save the world.

"Father, thank you for giving me permission to go and help Sister Magdalen. I do think though I should not leave until you are better."

Father O'Donnell shook his head *no*. "This is what being human in this incarnation is all about—making choices between two things, both of which are really important. You need to be there for more reasons than just holding the donkey's halter. I had a dream last night that reminded me that Sister Magdalen needs to understand the process of spiritual change. I want you to be a messenger to her from me. Give it some prayer and a good night's sleep and let's talk again in the morning. I need to rest now.

"Plus, this trip I believe may open up a new possibility for you. Real change, conversion, transformation—whatever it is being called these days—only comes about from great suffering or great love. You have suffered a lot, my son, in the loss of the chance for love, first with Melissa and then Blaine. I have experienced now your love for me. This trip may finally open that stuck window of your heart. Bless you, Brother Isaac."

Father O'Donnell's voice was barely audible. It took every bit of energy he had to speak to Dawson.

Dawson nodded and pulled the covers up around Father O'Donnell's shoulders. Dawson turned and walked out of the room, aware that he did so without the apprehension that had plagued him most of his life when he needed to make a decision. Yes, he was confident he would know what he must do in the morning. His confidence came from the deep conviction that what he would do was not really up to him.

The next morning Father O'Donnell did not look good. He did look determined. "How did you rest last night?" asked Dawson, his voice giving away his apprehension.

"Not too bad," said Father O'Donnell. "I did not sleep much. I have been awake for the past couple of hours worrying about how to say what I need to tell you. It seems complicated but really it is not.   Somehow I just need to make it as straightforward as possible."

"Here is your tea," said Dawson, as he positioned the mug and straw under Father O'Donnell's chin.

Father O'Donnell closed his eyes and took a long pull on the straw. "Ah, that is better. Do you have something to write on? You're going to need to make a few notes."

"I've got my notebook right here and I'm ready to go," said Dawson.

"Good, very good. Here is the overview. The Enneagram provides a template for us to understand the process of spiritual change. For the individual, of course, but here we are interested in the process of change, not just for the individual, but for humanity.

"Here is the visual aid I sketched out for you an hour ago while I was lying here unable to sleep." Father O'Donnell handed Dawson a piece of paper which presented this image:

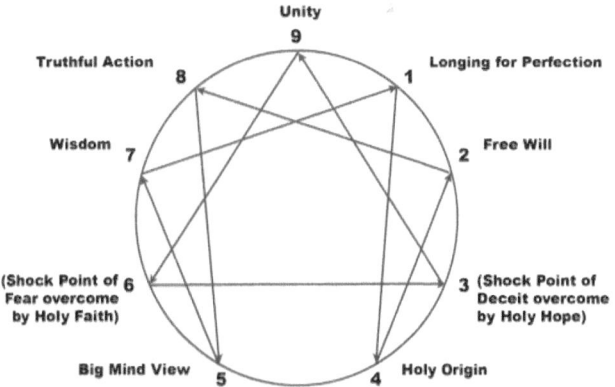

Enneagram of the Spiritual Path

Unity
9

Truthful Action
8

Longing for Perfection
1

Wisdom
7

Free Will
2

(Shock Point of
Fear overcome
by Holy Faith)
6

(Shock Point of
Deceit overcome
by Holy Hope)
3

Big Mind View
5

Holy Origin
4

"As you know, the Enneagram provides a template for the process of change based on lines connecting the points. So if we start at Point Nine, we start from a place of neutrality, a place of harmony. At this point, it is a place of unconscious harmony. You could say this is the place humanity was at in the Garden of Eden. Then we move to Point One. This is analogous to eating the fruit of the tree of knowledge of good and evil. Our longing for something greater, something more perfect.

"From Point One we then move to Point Four. We have to move from an idea of something better back to a place of emotional beginning. At this point in the process we must connect with our origin. Some people believe that the Buddha took us back to this place of holy origin. From Point Four we go to Point Two. To get to Point Two we have to go past Point Three, that is we must gain the dynamic energy necessary to move to Point Two. Point Two is a place of freedom. The freedom to act, to decide. In mankind's spiritual journey, Jesus came to give us this new freedom to pursue our transformation of consciousness. We needed Jesus to get us past the shock point at point Three, to show us the way out of our trance.

"So far, we have only been moving on the right side of the Enneagram image, which reflects internal movement. Once Jesus released us to our free will, we have the chance to move to Point Eight. At Point Eight we act on the truth that we have been given by Jesus. The truth remains inchoate until we act upon it. This has been the path of the church for the last 2000 years, to try and act on Jesus' truth. In its best years, it has done that, acting on behalf of humankind's underdogs, and in its worst years, the church has acted like a bully.

"From Point Eight we move to Point Five. This is the experience of realizing that our individual truth is part of a much larger truth for humankind. This is where we have been stuck for the last century, in a psychological morass. We have been so fascinated with our individual truths at times that we have been unable to see the larger truth of which we are a part. We are now waking up from that. The work you have done at the Center for Consciousness Studies has shown how interwoven our energy fields and connections are. At Point Five we gain this larger mega-view of the reality of our interconnection. At this juncture in history we are consolidating this holy omniscience. This is where we are.

"The next movement is to Point Seven, the place of wisdom that comes from experiencing this interconnection of humankind with the divine. When we get to Point Seven, we will have gained the next rung on the ladder of mankind's spiritual journey. To get there, we must first get past the shock point at Point Six. In other words, humanity must have sufficient faith in order to make this move. Whether or not she knows it, this is the purpose of Sister Magdalen's procession to Rome. Despite all the public attention she is getting about being a woman and the clamor that is being created by her website demanding that the next pope be a woman, the message that I would ask you to give her from me is to remind her that making a woman Pope is not the ultimate task she needs to fulfill. Not that having a woman Pope would not be an incredibly faith-giving event to women around the globe. It is just that her work needs to be done in a manner that is going to allow for the increase of everyone's faith. As I said, points three and six are the shock points on the Enneagram. It will take a significant energetic boost of faith for humankind to make the shift from Point Five to Point Seven.

"Last time, two thousand years ago, we had Jesus to get us over a shock point. This time, at the very least, we will need the return of much Mary Magdalene energy."

Father O'Donnell looked frighteningly exhausted to Dawson. "Are you okay, Father?" he asked.

"I am very, very tired. Do you understand what I am trying to tell you, my son?"

Dawson hesitated a moment too long. He really was not sure he completely understood the arcane ins and outs of the

Enneagram as a template for spiritual change, but Father O'Donnell was way too weak to be worried about whether Dawson would be able to carry his message adequately.

Dawson leaned in close. "I will deliver the message you want me to take, Father."

Father O'Donnell, his eyes closed, nodded, indicating that he understood what Dawson said. Almost immediately his breathing changed. He was deeply asleep.

*        *        *

A day later Dawson was on a flight bound to New York's LaGuardia Airport. From there he had a direct flight to Rome. Dawson's ticket was written so that he would have a short layover in New York. This would give him time to go to the Metropolitan Museum of Art on Fifth Avenue and see if he could find out what the woman in his dreams meant for him to learn when she pointed to her tooth. But how was he going to get a tooth to talk? He had no idea. He got Rat to email his friend Gordon Slade in Boston and ask Slade to meet him at the museum. Maybe between the two of them, they could figure that out.

# Chapter 27

It was a strange team. Rat was in Berlin coordinating the Internet side of the operation, with Blaine helping him. Blaine got access to the University of Arizona's computer system, which she was using at night, when it was day time in Europe, to provide the huge chunks of bandwidth that were now needed. Mother Mary, Sister Angelina and Joe Carroll were in Sweden developing the copy for the website, www.anewpope.com. Father O'Donnell, who could not come because of his health, sent a surrogate, Father Hay, who Mother Mary described as not only a brother priest to Father O'Donnell, but, like him, a wisdom priest. Father Hay and one of his directees, Godfrey, were on the way to Rome to assist. Sister Magdalen was traveling undercover across Europe with an entourage of helping sisters. She was meeting with various orders and religious groups: Protestant, Orthodox and Catholic, as well as Muslim and Jewish communities, to enlist their support in the push for a new kind of Pope. Her ultimate destination was Assisi, where a walk to Rome would begin.

Rat's hands were full. He was able to determine that the SOS convent in Sweden was under aerial surveillance by drone aircraft. No one was surprised. When the United States left Iraq and then Afghanistan, as the physical military forces on the ground left, the virtual forces increased. The war against terrorism and the war by the United States against regimes it did not like were now waged almost exclusively by technology—airborne drones that sent in laser-guided missiles and smart bombs and Internet-borne drones that sent in worms and viruses to computers—like the successful Israeli worm-attack on the computers in the Iranian nuclear processing plant in 2011.

Rat called on a number of hackers in his hacking community to help him develop software, which he now had up and running, to foil the drone surveillance of the convent in Sweden and the drone surveillance of Sister Magdalen as she traveled across Europe. Rat's software was not complicated. It analyzed the radio signal that the drone was using to communicate with its controllers, and once the frequency was determined, blocked it.

Joe Carroll was having the most fun he'd ever had in his entire life. His creative energy had returned. He was writing copy for the website, www.anewpope.com, which was arousing interest around the globe. The site was interactive and millions of people connected via their energy fields to sign an online petition urging that the new Pope be a woman.

Sister Magdalen was receiving a warm welcome wherever she went. At first the idea was to have her meet with small groups who were already doing consciousness work, who would be receptive to her, but her energy field was so loving and compassionate that she could hardly go anywhere and speak without drawing large crowds, with many wanting to physically touch and be touched by her. The crowds were growing ever larger. To protect her, Mother Mary sent a request to Father O'Donnell asking him to have men from his Order in Europe and elsewhere come and help with crowd control during the planned procession by Sister Magdalen.

It was Mother Mary's idea to have a procession from Assisi to Rome. She was a student not only of St. Brigitta, but also St. Francis. For her, as for many others, if Jesus was divine because of his level of consciousness, St. Francis was not far behind. Jesus taught people to render unto Caesar what belongs to Caesar. St. Francis taught people to render unto the church what belongs to the church. Both teachings allowed spiritual pilgrims to deal with the realities of state and church as a necessary part of the Newtonian world, but not to get hung up there so that these realities blocked the spiritual path toward greater consciousness and mystical union.

Sister Magdalen's intended walk from Assisi to Rome was a way to physically embody the metaphor of re-connection of the church to the mystical path of transformation that Jesus taught and St. Francis exemplified. She would represent the bride's procession to the bridal chamber. The other not-so-metaphorical re-connection sought in Sister Magdalen's journey would be the restoration of the yin energy of love in the planet's energy. The mystical writers talk of this restoration as divine union. Only with the re-balancing of yin and yang energy on a planet-wide basis, did Mother Mary believe it would be possible for the Earth to survive. As Joe Carroll had written on the website—'we are about to get *yanged* out of existence.' Mother Mary believed that if there could be enough yin love-energy cultivated in the human thought field, then it might be possible to have humankind step forward in consciousness, without the yang energy of survival competition dragging human progress back.

With all there was at stake, Mother Mary was stressed out. She knew this was not good for someone who was supposed to be setting an example for others of spiritual equanimity. She felt a hint of irritation when there was a knock on her door, anticipating another problem to go with the myriad of those already stacked on her desk.

A rat-like nose poked out form behind Mother Mary's slightly opened door. It wiggled.

"Oh, it's you, Rat, come on in," said Mother Mary, finally giving in to Rat's antics and breaking into a big smile.

"Just a routine security check on the Queen Mother," said Rat. "There is a rumor going around on the Internet that the CIA sent up a special rock 'n roll drone above the convent to direct rock 'n roll music into the Abbess' head. I thought it was a great idea. But I figured I better check on you. I was afraid they might mix in some old Jerry Lee Lewis and that you might be having a hard time with all that shaking. How is it going?"

"Rat, I am so glad you came by. I need a confessor. I have to admit that I am feeling tired and drained with what seems like an almost impossible task. I mean, at times, I think it is utter foolishness to think that we could actually raise the consciousness of the world.

"Last night I had this extraordinary dream, but it weighs on me heavily. Are you familiar with the seven stages of Christ's final transformation?"

"Not me, Mother Dude," said Rat. "But I have heard some of the young sisters say he was a kind of hot, center-stage guy."

"Well the word *transformation* is used in the sense of what is experienced in the heart during an emotional ordeal, much like the ordeal we are going through in preparing for this procession to Rome."

"Gotcha," said Rat. "So what did you get last night when you were plugged into the dream Internet?"

"I saw this image of the Enneagram, and along the points on the circle I saw each of the seven stages of the final transformation of Christ. Here is what I wrote down after I awoke." Mother Mary handed a piece of paper to Rat.

**Enneagram of the Seven Stages of Transformation**

The resurrection
9

8 Crowning with the crown of thorns (Shares with 3)

1 Scourging

7 Laying in the tomb

2 Washing the feet

6 The crucifixion (shares with 5)

3 Crowning with the crown of thorns (Shares with 8)

5 The crucifixion (Shares with 6)

4 The way of the cross

"Rat, you understand that I am a type One on the Enneagram. I do feel like getting everything prepared for this procession has been the equivalent of being scourged. Seeing in the dream that it is the emotional trance of my type does not relieve me of the burden I feel, but it does make it lighter. It makes sense that I should feel the way I do because of my type. Now as we talk I realize that I am more able to be in the essence of my type in this task—to make this bridal procession happen as best we can, knowing that the perfection of Mary Magdalene will once again be revealed to all those who suffer and need her.

"Oh, Rat, I don't know how, but you really have made me feel better. And I know this is not and will not be easy. But I truly do think the world is what is at stake. And I know it is not just us, but us and God, but I am tired because the false-self of my type One compulsion has become totally caught up in this effort to get everything right. The vision I had about this procession months ago foretold that Sister Magdalen would arrive in St Peter's Square on July 23rd, the feast day of St Brigitta and the day of her death. There is not much time."

She took a deep breath. "We would be totally lost without all the help you have given us. And here you are, bright-eyed and bushy-tailed as ever."

"Well, you know, Mother Dude," said Rat, feigning seriousness. "I have never told anyone my spiritual secret, but I will make an exception just for you. The truth is, there's not that much difference between spiritual detachment and not giving a shit, and the latter comes easy for me." He broke into a huge grin and wiggled his nose. "Don't worry, be happy. Or, as the Missy Julian dude you told me about would say, *All will be well*."

"Oh, Rat, I know you do care, and you care a lot, but when the adrenaline chaos gets going, with the challenge of all we have to do, you seem to enjoy it more, while I get more irritated."

Rat folded his hands and bowed his head and struck his most monk-like pose. "Pray without ceasing, my child." And he commenced to mumble in some indecipherable manner to mime the chanting of a prayer in Latin. He ended his mumbling routine with, "and we need a whole lot more of Jesus and a lot less rock 'n roll."

"Get out of my office right now," said Mother Mary, but finally she was laughing and the tension was draining from her.

"But, great Mother, you haven't heard the message yet which I came to deliver." Rat paused as if waiting for a drum roll. "Will Dawson, a.k.a. Brother Isaac, is on a jet as we speak flying across the Atlantic on his way to Rome. Looks like you got your guy to lead Sister Magdalen's donkey."

"Rat, that is great news. Thanks so much for letting me know."

"And he may be bringing some reinforcements with him. I have been helping Dawson communicate with his friend Gordon Slade in Boston and Dawson is asking Slade to come to Rome. If Slade comes, I expect he will bring his wife Joy with him—you know, the one who does the *divina* cookies. Curiously, it looks like the whole gang will be converging for our walk from Assisi to Rome. And I have been thinking that we need to head south before too long. I am used to doing a lot of things virtually, but I want to be on the steps of the Vatican watching this one."

"Yes, you are right, Rat. And for once, I'm not behind you. Not ahead either, but maybe at least abreast. I asked one of the sisters to see about getting us tickets to fly to Rome tomorrow. All of the sisters are coming with us. We have made arrangements to move in with another sister Order right in Rome. I was hoping we could slip you in as one of the girls, but with Dawson coming over, and maybe Slade, hopefully you guys can find a place to bunk together with Joe Carroll. We will set up the main command center in the sister convent where we will be staying. I understand that it has great computer facilities, so you will be working there. The funny thing is that their computer access actually is through the Vatican's servers."

"Whoa, dude, that may be a great opportunity for us. Hard to track a hacker down who is on the inside. And your salvation project, Joe Carroll, is delighted to find out that his old friend, Slade, may be on his way over to help. Carroll will be glad to know that we are on our way to Rome. If we leave tomorrow morning, we should arrive about the time the others are getting there."

By now Rat was halfway out the door. He turned and blew Mother Mary a kiss. She laughed again.

She mused. Father O'Donnell was sending Brother Isaac, whom Father O'Donnell wanted to be his successor. Brother Isaac's and Joe Carroll's best friend Gordon Slade might be coming. *You know*, she thought, *everything really is in God's hands.*

# Chapter 28

As always, Rat was the communications intermediary. He let Gordon Slade know that Will Dawson was coming east, on his way to Rome, and that Dawson very much wanted to talk with Slade about him also traveling to Rome. Rat did not try to describe to Gordon Slade why he might be needed, but simply impressed on him the importance of meeting with Dawson. Slade did not need too much convincing. He missed his old buddy.

The circumstances of their meeting were curious to Slade. Even though he was only recently retired from a long career as a private investigator, Rat's instructions that he meet Dawson at the Metropolitan Museum of Art in Gallery 306 seemed more cloak-and-dagger than necessary.

Slade and Joy decided that they would drive from Boston to New York for Slade to meet with Dawson. Joy insisted they bring their luggage packed for a trip to Rome so they would be ready to go, if they decided they should go with Dawson. In fact, once Slade told Joy the reason Dawson wanted to meet with him, Joy was on board. She decided that a trip to Rome was exactly the kind of spiritual adventure she and her new husband needed and that they should plan to go to Rome regardless of the outcome of Slade's meeting with Dawson.

The schedule was tight. Slade and Joy left Boston early in the morning. They wanted to have plenty of time for the drive to New York City and into Manhattan so that Slade could meet Dawson at the Metropolitan Museum of Art at two p.m.

Dawson's flight from Albuquerque landed at LaGuardia Airport at 12:30 p.m. He caught a cab at the airport and was in Manhattan on the Upper East Side by 1:30 p.m. He walked up the broad spacious steps of the museum's entrance, stood in line to pay the requested donation and obtain a map of the museum so he could find his way to Gallery 306.

Dawson entered Gallery 305, directly behind the museum's grand stairway. This gallery replicated a great medieval hallway. Dawson hardly thought to look up to its soaring ceiling, he was so intent on finding Gallery 306 to the right, midway along the great hall. When Dawson entered Gallery 306 the room was empty of people. On both his left and right were medieval stained glass windows. One struck his notice, the last one on the left side, beyond all the deep blues and reds. It stood out in contrast by its white lightness. As anxious as he was to find the tooth, he paused just long enough to notice the placard below: The Virgin Mary of the Apocalypse.

He looked ahead and saw a museum exhibit case. He immediately knew it contained the reason he had come. The tooth was contained in an ornate golden reliquary shaped like a lamp. In the center of the reliquary, was an oval shaped rock crystal in which a vertical channel had been ground out. In the center of the channel sat her tooth. The museum commentary noted that the reliquary was made between 1450 and 1500, probably for Franciscans. Golden spires surrounded the inner oval giving the reliquary itself the feeling of a mini medieval cathedral.

Dawson began to examine what had brought him this far on his journey. The lamp-like reliquary sat just a bit off kilter. On the top was a rock crystal cross, below a medallion. On one side of the medallion the crucifixion was depicted and on the other the birth of Christ. He would have to ask Father O'Donnell whether Dawson's intuition was right that the reliquary was a Trinitarian expression of Christ's birth, death and rebirth through his relation with Mary Magdalene. After all, Father O'Donnell, in counseling Dawson about his failure to follow the two women who had most opened his heart, told him rebirth always involved an experience of love.

Dawson chuckled to himself, maybe that tooth had grazed the skin of Jesus.

Dawson was a skeptic when it came to relics. He had the Protestant predisposition that relics were part of the hocus-pocus Martin Luther had rebelled against, because their veneration trivialized the meaning of the church. Father O'Donnell simply asked Dawson to have an open mind about Mary Magdalene's relic. He said that relics were windows open to heaven. Or, putting it in the language of the Center for Consciousness Studies, relics were doorways into a field of energy from the person connected to the relic. This is the reason, Father O'Donnell said, that the more people attend to genuine relics, the more power they seem to have, as the more the field of energy is opened up. Thus relics are helpful to a pilgrim who has a spiritual question, because in the presence of the relic the pilgrim experiences greater resources of energy to understand his or her question. The way that Father O'Donnell put it intrigued Dawson—crises lead to questions, which lead to seeking, which leads not to answers but greater states of consciousness. Sometimes the boost of energy which makes possible the greater state of consciousness results from a surge of energy given to the pilgrim who believes in the power of the relic.

The question for Dawson was not whether or not to go to Italy. Father O'Donnell had already sent him. The question for Dawson was: *What was to come next for him, now that Melissa was found?* Dawson knew that Father O'Donnell wanted Dawson to take over the leadership of the monastery, but was that really God's will for him? Only because Dawson believed so fervently in Father O'Donnell's love and caring was he willing to indulge in the possibility that being in the room with Mary Magdalene's tooth might provide an extra boost of spiritual energy to give him a new perspective, and a greater level of consciousness to understand his own life.

Dawson looked around, there was only one bench for sitting in the gallery and it was situated back between the stain glass windows display. The best Dawson could do was stand close to the plexiglass case. When he did, the tooth was less than two feet away and level with his heart center. Before Gordon Slade arrived, Dawson wanted to have some inner experience of being in the presence of the tooth. He sank into a deep state of relaxation. He kept his eyes slightly open so he could see the tooth.

Just as he began to experience himself entering into an unknown place, Dawson heard a noise. He turned and looked back toward the door from which he entered. There stood Gordon Slade. Dawson did not like being hauled so abruptly out of a meditative state, but he was delighted to see Slade.

Dawson walked toward Slade and embraced his friend. "How are you?" asked Dawson.

"Better, now that I see you looking healthy and fit." said Slade.

"Do you remember the last time I ran into you sitting on the steps of my condo?"

"Yes, a lot has sure changed since then."

"And it looks like for the better," said Slade.

"Only had one direction to go. And, thank you for being there for me," said Dawson smiling. "An incredible amount has transpired since we talked last. But maybe we can postpone our catching-up conversation. There is a bit of a time crunch. I brought you here for two reasons. First and foremost, to convince you to go with me to Rome for the walk that Melissa is leading from Assisi to Rome."

Slade interrupted. "So the mystery woman really is alive. What do you know?

"Normally I would want to argue with you about something that adventuresome, but even if I did, I would lose. Joy simply has this bee in her bonnet that we have to go. If I could argue myself out of going for you, I don't believe I can with her."

"Good, I'm glad that is settled," said Dawson. "You will not be sorry. I'm not sure what is going to happen, but I am sure that whatever happens will be significant for the rest of our lives.

"The other reason for asking you to meet me here is I need a little expert private detective assistance. You see that little whitish object in the center of that golden reliquary?"

Slade nodded.

"It is supposedly the tooth of Mary Magdalene. I need to be as close to it as possible without setting off the museum alarm system. Got any ideas?"

"Do you mean you need to touch it?" asked Slade. "Like you have a sudden urge to go to jail so you can be captured by your old employer and allowed to disappear?"

"Yeah, I guess touching it would be a bit risky," said Dawson.

"Just a bit. You know, really smart crooks spend years planning a museum heist and you want to figure this out on the fly while you are waiting to catch a plane. Dawson, you may be looking better than you were when I saw you last, but I can't say that your mental functioning is back up to par." Slade grinned.

"Let's don't make this all that grandiose," said Dawson. "I just want to get as close as possible to touching the tooth without setting the alarm bells off or having some nosy guard start harassing me. Can you help me?"

Slade shook his head in disbelief.

"Let me explain why this is important."

Slade looked at Dawson. "You know, Will, I am still not sure I understand why you had me come here to meet with you."

Dawson paused, then replied: "Do you remember when you told me about that strange fortune that you got from the new line of cookies Joy was making?"

"Vaguely," said Slade, not sure at all what this had to do with his question to Dawson.

"This is what it said: *So then every seed that my Father in Heaven has not planted shall be uprooted. Those who were separated shall be united, and all who are empty shall be filled, so that everyone may enter into the Bridal Chamber where they will be born into the Light.*"

Slade was amazed that Dawson memorized a fortune, which he received months before. "You still remember that?" he asked. "But what does that have to do with why we are here?"

"It comes from the Gospel of Philip, analogue seventy-one. I think it is telling us generally what Melissa's procession is all about, but specifically what it is telling me I do not know.

"Earlier, I thought if I were to come to the energy field of Mary Magdalene's tooth I would have some new experience of the meaning of these words. I have spent enough time around Father O'Donnell to know that true understanding only comes from an encounter with what has been said, not just reading or hearing something. I want to encounter these words."

"Well," said Slade. "I am thinking your encounter-er is better than mine. Give it a shot. What do you experience as the meaning of these words right now as we stand just a couple feet from the tooth? Oh, and by the way, there is your guy Philip." And Slade pointed to a gilded figure of the apostle Philip in a museum case just to the left of the one containing the Mary Magdalene relic.

Dawson gulped—a bit uncanny that Philip was standing close by.

Slade walked over to the gallery doorway and posted himself in a position where he could observe anyone coming toward Gallery 306 from Gallery 305. The problem was that the other end of Gallery 306 opened into another space that led to the new American wing. So even with Slade as look out there was no avoiding the fact there were a lot of people flowing through the Gallery. Nevertheless, Dawson stood as close to the reliquary as he could and sought to deepen his meditative state.

Minutes passed. When museum-goers came near Dawson they seemed to automatically drop into a state of reverence and pass by in silence. There were no intruders into Dawson's private space with Mary Magdalene's tooth. Finally, Slade came back over.

"Getting any psychic text messages?" asked Slade.

Dawson ignored the dig. "While initially I thought the most important thing for me in coming here to meet you was to convince you to come with me to Rome, just now I have come to realize there is more.

"I think we are here to recognize that the meaning of the Gospel of Philip and the reality of the truth Mary Magdalene expressed is now in a museum. This reliquary is not even in a church! This is awful. Who Mary Magdalene really is has been dramatically ignored by the church and now she has been reduced to a footnote in civic history in a secular art museum.

"What I am realizing in receiving an energetic sense of the relic is that what the Gospel is telling us must be understood in terms of the Law of Seven.

"Not too long before I left New Mexico, Man was telling me that Black Elk, the spiritual leader of the Lakota people, spoke of seven traditional Lakota rites as ways for man's union with the Great Spirit. In the Judeo/Christian tradition, Proverbs says there are 'seven pillars of the house that wisdom has built'. There are seven days of creation, seven miracles in the gospel of St. John, seven *I am* sayings of Jesus Christ, and of course, seven Sacraments of the church. In the Gospel of Mary Magdalene, she talks about seven blocks at each stage of progression along the spiritual journey. And there are so many sevens in Revelation that it is almost silly.

"But what does this Law of Seven mean in terms of Melissa's mission? That is the question for which I don't yet have an answer. Give me just a little more time with the relic," said Dawson.

Slade nodded affirmatively and moved back toward the doorway leading to Gallery 305. Dawson again dropped into a meditative state, sidling up as close as possible to Mary Magdalene's tooth.

Minutes went by. Suddenly Dawson was aware that Slade was hustling back over toward him.

"Looks like a guard is on the way down the hall and is going to be turning into this gallery," said Slade.

Dawson breathed deeply and felt his center of attention rise to the surface from deep within. He nodded toward Slade. The two men walked toward the gallery doorway.

"I got two messages. First, the tooth told me that I am free. The tooth also told me that it is about words that need to be said, words from when the tooth was in her mouth. I am to remind Melissa of the *I am's*." said Dawson.

Slade gave Dawson a blank stare.

Dawson looked down at his watch. "I'll catch you up on this

when we get to Italy. But I also did get a message for you."

"What is that?" asked Slade.

"In a nutshell it is this. Joy has come into your life for you to understand that the world is not a problem to be solved by you, mister detective. The world is a work of creative art. Creation is animated by joy. The wisdom that we learn from God in how we experience the world is above all a joyous wisdom. You have literally been given the gift of joy in a physical human being." Dawson frowned, searching his mind to see if he could recall anything further. "Well, my dear friend, the bottom line for you is, and I say this knowing I have not gotten anywhere close myself—be joyous."

The two men walked out of the museum into brilliant sunlight.

"Slade, thank you so much for coming," said Dawson. "You are a true friend." And with that, Dawson gave him a hug and reached into his pocket and pulled out airline tickets for Slade and Joy. "Rat has taken care of you guys," Dawson said as he gave the tickets to his friend. "Travel safe. See you in Italy." And with that, the two men caught separate taxis to travel by different routes to their rendezvous with Sister Magdalen's procession to Rome.

*         *         *

Slade was bringing Joy. As he drifted in and out of sleep in his reclined aisle seat on the long flight from New York to Rome, he kept thinking about the miracle of it all. For most of his life he futilely sought to find joy—in being one of the best detectives in Boston, in chasing women, in cultivating a finely crafted persona of street-smarts and good taste. But then he found Joy, not just it, but her. Hardly a year earlier he was on a flight from Rome back to Boston with high anxiety because he thought he had lost Joy. Not only had he found her, found her—he had in the process found himself and that made possible his surrender to Joy, and a whole new life. He was bringing Joy with him to celebrate Sister Magdalen's procession from Assisi to Rome. His lost essence had been found, and, he mused, *the selfish, petty part of himself that still surfaced from time to time was being brought along also, just so it too could belong.*

He looked at Joy in the seat next to him. She had never flown abroad and she had been worried about the long flight. However, there was nothing but contentment in her expression as she drifted in a light sleep beside him. Her red hair covered her shoulders in harmonious disarray, and her skin gleamed white like living porcelain. Suddenly Joy blinked awake, as if she was being drawn out of sleep by his thoughts of her. When they got married, she gave up her thick librarian glasses in favor of contacts, which made it all the easier for him to melt beneath her green-eyed gaze. He bent over and kissed her on the forehead. She re-adjusted herself in her seat, smiled a beautiful smile of contentment at him, closed her eyes again and drifted back into sleep.

Slade returned to the thought which turned over and over in his mind—why should he be going to Rome? Was it simply to see his buddies Joe Carroll and Will Dawson? Was it to bring Joy, because the energy of what was to happen in the walk from Assisi to Rome was above all intended to embrace joy? To him, the woman and the metaphor were deeply intertwined. It was hard in a way—living with a metaphor. But more recently he stopped worrying about trying to figure it all out. The reason he and Joy were going to Rome was bigger than just visiting two old friends, was bigger than just Joy and him. He was sure of that, but he was unsure of what this larger meaning was.

There were some clues. From what he had learned about the Enneagram, he knew that each person contained an essence of one of the Holy Ideas, an aspect of the divine which was their gift to bring into the world. If Sister Magdalen's gift was bringing truth, and Joy's was joy; well that made sense to him. And maybe you couldn't really understand the truth Sister Magdalen was bringing without joy. He would have to ask Carroll. For sure, Carroll would have an opinion.

But what did he, Slade, an old gumshoe, bring to the table? He could think of nothing. He had grown enough, however, that he could feel the reality of the pull toward greater awareness. Something was going to happen in him or through him. He felt it as solidly as he did when the clues of a case suddenly congealed into a pattern and showed, not necessarily what the damning evidence is, but exactly where to look next. However, it was one thing to feel he was on track to solve a case, and something totally different to feel his life was somehow about to dissolve into some new experience. The first involved that solid ego satisfaction of figuring it out, the latter, stepping off a cliff.

As he nodded back off to sleep, his last thought was—thank goodness, for the changes in my life that allow me to step into this greater meaning, without knowing what it is all about or where it might lead.

*         *         *

To make the trip to Rome, Dawson used one of his old CIA identities. While he was relatively certain that he would be able to travel to Rome with this identity, both he and Rat agreed that it would be problematic to use it to return to the United States. Dawson and Rat decided with Father O'Donnell's blessing that the problem of Dawson's return could be deferred. Sister Magdalen's procession from Assisi to Rome was too important for him not to be there. They would worry about what Dawson would do about returning later.

As difficult as it was to leave Father O'Donnell in his illness, it would have been even more difficult not to obey Father O'Donnell's request. Dawson had been torn, but now that he was airborne over the Atlantic, he was bursting with nervous energy and excitement. He expected that once his name was entered into the airlines computer identifying him as being on an international flight, or when he went through customs in a foreign country, the CIA would promptly get word that an old CIA identity was being used. He and Rat decided at the last minute that it would be best for him not to go directly to Rome. Instead he was flying to Paris. From there he would follow a zigzag path by bus and train to Rome.

He would see Melissa again!

Finally, they would meet, after all these years, since he first met her in Afghanistan, after the many months since he began his search to find her when she had gone missing.

The Benadryl that he took to get some sleep on the flight was having no effect. What would Melissa be like now? Would she be glad Dawson had come? Would he recognize the young, care-free Peace Corps worker he had first known in this person now called Sister Magdalen? Would she still care about him at all? Or, would the new Pope movement she was symbolizing be all that she cared for? With these thoughts whirling around in his mind, sleep remained resolutely at bay.

*       *       *

Leave it up to Rat to be able to keep track of everybody's travels. Joe Carroll, Rat, Aasia, Mother Mary, and all the sisters from the convent in Sweden arrived in Rome first. Gordon Slade and his wife Joy landed just behind them. By the time the coach, which Father Hay and Godfrey hired, pulled up outside the terminal and all the sisters' luggage was loaded up, Gordon and Joy had caught up with the larger group.

Slade was delighted to see Carroll. After all the introductions were made, Carroll motioned to Slade with a nod of his head toward the terminal.

"Gosh, it is great to see you," said Carroll. "I do believe there is a bar just across the way. What do you say we celebrate our arrival in Rome by lifting a glass?"

Slade looked over at Joy. She was busy meeting and talking to Aasia and Mother Mary.

"Carroll, it sure doesn't seem like living for a few months in a religious order has changed all that much about you," said Slade as he looked closely at his old friend.

Carroll put his arm around Slade's shoulder. "What has changed or not changed—that is always a good question old pal, but one which should be discussed over some libation."

"Rat, if Mother Mary gets anxious about where we are, we will be right inside the terminal at the closest bar." Rat nodded. He was in communication with Dawson. As soon as Slade's and Joy's luggage was loaded onto the coach, they would all board the bus and head over to the train station to pick up Dawson. His plane had landed in Paris hours earlier and his overland journey to Rome had him arriving soon.

"Okay, we have a bit of time to waste before Dawson's train arrives," said Rat.

Slade and Carroll settled into a corner table, where they had a view out of the bar and could see the coach with the sisters milling around at the curb.

Carroll put their order in. "One of the great civilizing joys of life these days is that you can be at any international airport anywhere in the world and get a good single malt Scotch," said Carroll, raising his glass to salute his friend.

Slade lifted his glass in return. "It is great to see you. My life has been full with Joy, and I sure have missed our getting together."

"Yes, I have missed the chance to hang out with you and go see the Red Soxs play, and I have also had an extraordinary experience being able to work on all the copy for the www.anewpope.com website. "

"Aside from your work on the website," said Slade, "tell me what you have been up to."

But before the conversation could go further, Rat was walking toward them waving for them to come back out. The driver said the traffic was bad and they should go ahead and head for the train station. Carroll got some to-go cups for their drinks.

"Let's all catch up after we pick up Dawson," said Carroll. " I am anxious to learn about what has been going on with both you guys and it will be more fun to do it together."

*       *       *

There was little time for Slade, Dawson, and Carroll to catch up. After the coach picked up Dawson at the train station, a few of the sisters led by Sister Angelina and the logistical team, which included Carroll and Rat, were taken to the convent in Rome, to set up the command center for the procession. The coach then set off on the three-hour drive to Assisi, where plans for beginning the procession were being sorted out and preparations were being made for the anticipated arrival of Sister Magdalen.

# Chapter 29

Dawson was as nervous as a school kid with candy melting in his pocket, waiting for the final school bell to ring. Mother Mary was also worrying. Sister Magdalen was constantly revising her plans about when she would arrive in Assisi. She seemed to be continually called to visit one more group, who wanted to hear her vision about a new way for people to live together. Of course, her vision was only about 2,000 years old. But framing it as she did about the opportunity to 'love your neighbor as yourself,' as an experience of a new level of consciousness, where you realized your neighbor's thoughts and feelings in the quantum field really were a part of you, allowed everyone to receive this ancient message in a new and radically different way.

Dawson jumped when the phone in his hotel room rang. It was Mother Mary asking him to meet her downstairs. Another one of those planning meetings, he figured, as he picked up his hotel room entry card and headed down to the lobby.

Getting off the elevator, the lobby seemed unusually crowded. Dawson made his way toward the hotel's front doors. As he walked toward the doors, suddenly he was aware that, off to the side surrounded by a couple dozen people, there she stood. All of his worrying vanished. His recognition of her was instant.

At the same time that he recognized her, instantaneously her energy field recognized his presence and she looked toward him.

Everything that he remembered about meeting her for the first time in the Kabul market decades ago came flooding back. Her eyes met his. He walked to the edge of the crowd encircling her. She raised two fingers. The noisy crowd at once became silent. She walked toward him. Involuntarily, he knelt before her. She placed her hand on the crown of his head. Immediately a shock of electricity surged through his body.

"Arise, Brother Isaac," she said.

He stood up and before him stood not the woman who had lived in his imagination for more than twenty years, but a woman about whom he knew nothing and everything in the experience of her living presence and outpouring love. His body surged with energy as if trying to re-calibrate itself to a new level. He spoke and almost did not recognize his own voice.

"Sister Magdalen, how may I serve you?" were the words that tumbled from his mouth like water flowing in a rocky stream.

"Come, Brother Isaac, let us speak together," she said and led him to one of the rooms reserved for her party on the first floor of the hotel. She nodded to one of the sisters accompanying her as she and Brother Isaac entered the room, and the sister left them, closing the door behind herself.

Dawson had often imagined this meeting. He had believed that if they only had the chance to be together then they would be talking for hours about their early times together in Afghanistan and what had happened in their lives since.

"Brother Isaac, I am glad you have come to help," she said, her gaze resting gently on him, her energy surrounding him in a soft, gentle vibration.

"I look forward to us having the chance to be together, but for now I must speak to you about this seemingly impossible mission I have received, despite my initial hope that this would not be my fate. I will give you a little roadmap. You have some understanding of the Enneagram, do you not?"

Brother Isaac nodded his head *yes*.

"Good," she said. "In order for our mission to be successful, we must create the opportunity for a deep spiritual experience by mankind. As I expect you know from your training with Father O'Donnell, all of our spiritual experiences are a matter of both our effort and Grace. It is the clearing that we do of our own ego energy, our own willfulness, that makes possible the gift of God's greater energy in our life. Then energies moving back and forth across the boundary between the quantum world and our everyday world will interact dynamically. Are you following me?"

"I think so," said Brother Isaac.

"We can understand this process best from an Enneagram

perspective. There are three principal types of authentic spiritual experience—vision, inspiration, and intuition. Each of these is identified with one of the Enneagram points that makes up the inner triangle of the Enneagram. Point Nine is the place of inspiration. The word inspiration refers to our breath. We use our own effort to breathe in, and use no effort to breath out, so our breath represents this process of effort and Grace. Through inspiration one accesses new ways to see and understand the world. Because inspiration is the interaction of the human opening to the divine, and the divine to the human, or as your teachers might say at the University of Arizona, the Newtonian experience of being human opening to the quantum field and the quantum field opening to the Newtonian experience of the human, there is always a sweet sorrow or a sweet joy about inspiration. Because of this, inspiration is always identified with tears. Point Nine on the Enneagram is identified with the monastic vow of obedience. It is through obedience to the spiritual practices that one creates the opening to the divine so that inspiration may happen."

Brother Isaac was stunned. First, he was stunned to be with Melissa again after all these years. He was stunned the passage of all the years did not matter. And he was stunned that in their first encounter she would so urgently be teaching him spiritual lessons which picked up exactly where his work with Father O'Donnell left off. He nodded his head so she would continue.

"Point Three is the place of vision. Again, the spiritual experience of a vision is the process of both human effort by letting go, and the incoming energy from the divine coming by movement from the quantum field into the individual. Point

Three is associated with the monastic vow of chastity. It takes chastity in order to let go of the ego sufficiently so that there is a place of purity for a vision to enter. When one lives from a pure heart, the channel between the material world and the spiritual world is fully accessible. Often we will get visions that we do not understand. It takes great purity to be guided for years by a vision that is not yet understood, or not fully understood. For that reason the bodily fluid associated with vision is sweat. This is seen most literally in the spiritual practices of Native Americans who will engage in a sweat lodge, as a precursor to going on a vision quest.

"Point Six is the place of intuition. The spiritual experience of intuition, like the spiritual experiences of inspiration and vision, occurs through the dynamic interaction of the material world and the spiritual world. Point Six is associated with the monastic vow of poverty. Poverty is the virtue of living from a place of emptiness. Without emptiness, without non-attachment, there is no opportunity for new life, new knowing to come in. With poverty we live from an open mind and heart and with faithfulness. The bodily fluid that is associated with intuition is blood. This is why the ritual of the Eucharist, which in its language of bloody sacrifice seems so primitive and pagan, obscures what the Eucharist is really about—the quantum physics process by which Christ's identification with us and ours with him in the quantum field is expressed.

"These three kinds of authentic spiritual experiences work together. Inspiration leads to longing for greater connection with the Creator and creation. A greater connection with God and creation leads to a vision of what is possible through this inter-connection, which we call love. This vision, in turn, leads to the intuition that one is this love. In this way, the three spiritual experiences build on each other, so that the experience of intuition becomes a new way of seeing, which is aptly called a rebirth—so radical is the process of change in perspective wrought by intuition.

"Brother Isaac, I can see that you are a bit shocked by my going on and on like this. There is much to do, and our time is short. Tell me how was your trip over to Italy?"

Dawson, without meaning to, immediately began to tell Sister Magdalen about his visit to the Metropolitan Museum.

"I was instructed to go there to see the tooth of Mary Magdalene encased in a reliquary. It was a moving experience. First, just to think that might actually be her tooth; and second, to notice details about the reliquary. On one side of the reliquary there was a medallion portraying the crucifixion of Christ, and around him were St. Francis and Lady Clare as well as Peter and Paul. Below the tooth itself there was another depiction of St. Francis."

Sister Magdalen interrupted. "Your observations are quite astute. It is because of the connection between St. Francis and Mary Magdalen that we are having a procession from Assisi to Rome. St. Francis understood the unique role that Mary Magdalene played in Jesus' life, just as Lady Clare had such a unique role in St. Francis' life. It makes sense that Mary Magdalene's tooth should end up in a Franciscan reliquary. Our procession is about the re-connection, or marriage, if you will, of the Sophic energy of Assisi to the patriarchal energy of Rome. We will need to begin the procession from Assisi to Rome in three days. The entire purpose of our walk will be to create the possibility for people to experience inspiration, vision and intuition.

"I understand that you have been recruited by Mother Mary to lead the donkey I will be riding. I cannot think of anyone else I would rather have holding the donkey's halter. Remember that everything you do, every pull on the donkey's lead, even the way you walk beside the donkey—all of these things offer you the chance to do them in a way that embodies creating the possibility of an experience by humankind of inspiration, vision, and intuition. You may not know how that might be possible. Just let me assure you that it will be."

She stopped and sank into reflection.

"Oh, I almost forgot," said Dawson. "When I spoke with your tooth—I mean when your tooth spoke to me—I mean Mary Magdalene's tooth." He stopped, all flustered.

Sister Magdalen waited patiently.

"What I am trying to say is that when I visited Mary Magdalene's tooth, it told me to remind you that you must tell the *I am's*."

After a long moment Sister Magdalen spoke. "What a wonderful idea, Will. Yes, I must remind everyone who has this longing for change of these doorways by type into Christ consciousness.

"Not only has it been wonderful to see you, what you have told me is beautiful and will be so helpful. I must go now to meet with another group of pilgrims that I have kept waiting."

And with that Sister Magdalen arose from the chair where she was sitting. When she stood, Brother Isaac also stood up. She stepped toward him and kissed him on each cheek. With two fingers she made the sign of the cross over his heart.

"God bless you." She paused and with a twinkle in her eye concluded, "Thank you for coming, Will."

Brother Isaac bowed his head, as a gesture of understanding and honoring. He lifted his eyes. "Melissa, I will not let you down this time."

She nodded thoughtfully. She looked lovingly into his eyes, smiled, and walked out the door.

*      *      *

Father O'Donnell once told Dawson that all great events in history happen because a few motivated individuals of varied backgrounds come together at a certain time in a certain place. Dawson was not sure if this was a correct formula for the kind of consciousness change which Sister Magdalen was hoping for, but for sure there were a motley assortment of very diverse individuals coordinating and participating in Sister Magdalen's journey by donkey from Assisi to Rome.

Aasia was selected to lead the march. It was an inspired choice. Every day she seemed to grow more devastatingly beautiful. Her dark hair showered her shoulders beneath her lacy headscarf. The steady gaze of her dark brown eyes softened the hearts of those along the parade route, whether admirers, detractors or simply the curious. Surrounding Aasia were a number of SOS sisters whose blonde hair and blue eyes simply magnified Aasia's dark, earthy beauty. Joy was also marching with the sisters and Aasia. It was not lost on the world that the procession was being led by a Muslim woman who had survived the Sebrencia genocide.

Rat procured a small drone from Drones-are-Us, which had a digital camera no bigger than a coin affixed to its belly and the whole procession was being streamed live on the Internet at www.anewpope.com. As unlikely a choice as he would have been just a few short months ago, Joe Carroll was providing the live commentary to go with the streaming video. Carroll had a flair for the dramatic in his commentary that held people's interest; and, true to his Irish heritage, he had the ability to talk continuously for hours.

Behind the SOS sisters came assorted lay groups in support of the procession. These groups were increasing in size every day, even though some groups might only walk for a few hours before being replaced by others. After the lay supporters came groups of clergy and spiritual leaders from a variety of traditions. There were large groups of Buddhist monks from Myanmar and Tibet, who believed that the support they were showing helped repay a karmic debt to the West for the support they had been given when they were being persecuted.

The Buddhist monks, many in colorful saffron robes, with their large smiles and shaved heads, added a gentle touch of gaiety to the procession.

Behind the spiritual groups were a raucous group of gays, lesbians and bisexuals. Sister Magdalen had become a Diana Ross symbol to these marchers—a symbol of liberation that made them see the new-pope-movement as an extension of their own journey toward liberation. Father Hay's directee Godfrey was in charge of keeping this unruly and light-hearted group in the procession. Sister Magdalen loved their zany unholiness and they in return adored her.

Following these groups came Brother Isaac holding the lead of a sturdy donkey. Sitting astride the donkey was Sister Magdalen. Because she insisted on riding bareheaded, Slade was delegated the task of leading the umbrella and security detail at the rear of the procession. The large umbrella that towered over Sister Magdalen was a nice touch. It reflected an Eastern sensibility of how enlightened spiritual leaders are honored and addressed the practical need to give Sister Magdalen some relief from the direct rays of the hot, Italian sun.

As Joe Carroll reported on the Internet feed, the whole procession only went a short distance the first day. Many of those in the procession carried musical instruments and there was much playing, singing, and dancing as they walked. Those gathered along the parade route were smiling and laughing by the time Sister Magdalen came into view. As she got close, the spectators instinctively dropped to their knees.

This is the natural human response to encountering pure, embodied love. Sister Magdalen responded by having Brother Isaac lead the donkey back and forth from one side of the street to the other so she could bless all of those who kneeled. Her blessings were bestowed in energetic waves and were so palpable those kneeling felt she actually touched them on the crowns of their heads.

# Chapter 30

Father O'Donnell's body had been preparing to shut down for weeks. His gentle spirit continually said, *No, not quite yet.* Now, since he received the news of the success of the procession to Rome, his spirit was slowly yielding to his body's demand for final rest.

He missed Brother Isaac. And he was so glad that Blaine and Man were there with him. The Navajos were not much on funeral rituals, but at Father O'Donnell's urging Man arranged for Navajo Singers to be available for his transition. Like Brother Isaac had, every morning at first light, Blaine and Man brought Father O'Donnell a steaming cup of Irish tea.

Father O'Donnell noisily sucked tea from a mug. "Tell me again what happened when the procession got to Rome," he urged in a hoarse whisper.

Blaine looked at Man. Her eyebrows lifted like question marks. Blaine and Man were pulled up to Father O'Donnell's bed so close that their knees touched. In the past forty-eight hours, each of them had repeated the story to Father O'Donnell numerous times of the final procession into St. Peter's Square. Man's right knee applied a gentle pressure on Blaine's left knee. She nodded.

"The procession arrived in St. Peter's Square in late afternoon. It was a beautiful day. The sky was blue and St. Peter's Square was bathed in sweet, yellow light. There were hundreds of thousands of people there. After Sister Magdalen dismounted from her donkey, the cardinals came pouring out of the holy church into the square in front of her. The faces of the cardinals were grave and scowling, as if coming into their front yard to scold an errant child. Sister Magdalen stepped toward them and suddenly everything changed."

"Tell me again about the instant replays," said Father O'Donnell.

"Well, evidently there were many television cameras and cell phones taking video pictures at exactly this moment. Man and I watched the replays. It is impossible to tell where the movement first started. What Man and I think is that the general movement downward occurred spontaneously when Sister Magdalen opened her energy field directly upon all the cardinals. Each cardinal dropped to his knees in front of her. She bestowed a blessing on all of them and walked through them into St. Peter's. The cardinals rose and walked behind her, single file, into the great church. It was a stirring image to see the all-male hierarchy following a woman, who had arrived on a donkey, into the ultimate symbol of church hierarchical authority."

"Tell me how you are doing?" asked Blaine. "Is all our talking wearing you out?"

Father O'Donnell spoke in a low tone. "What I never realized is that dying is such an active process. To be engaged in dying is like being engaged in life. Who would've guessed? Please keep going."

"We were watching the streaming Internet. It had a commentary provided by Brother Isaac's old friend, Joe Carroll. Carroll didn't miss a beat. He immediately quoted the Scripture that says, *They gathered the kings together to the place that in Hebrew is called Armageddon*. Carroll explained that this Scripture means the kings of the church, who are, in fact, the cardinals who were gathered there."

Father O'Donnell motioned for Blaine and Man to come close. He whispered, "I like it when things work out the way they were foretold." His eyes twinkled.

"Well, maybe that part," said Blaine. "But nobody foretold what came next. Nobody, including any of us, could have imagined it." Blaine looked at Man.

Man took up the retelling of the story. "So Sister Magdalen leads the procession down the central aisle of the church. She walks directly up to the altar where the sacraments of bread and wine are. She turns and faces the cardinals. At first, there is a wavering and it seems as if some of the cardinals are about to break ranks. She then focuses her energy more fully on all of them and begins to speak. She tells him that the time has come for a choice to be made. For the church to live it must be reborn. For the planet to live it must be reborn. For humankind to live it must be reborn into a new consciousness. She tells them that the church has the opportunity to lead the way. She asks them which path they wish to take–to give up their hierarchical authority and follow her, or stay in their antiquarian roles grasping for control which is already literally slipping through their fingers. One by one, the cardinals kneel before her signifying their willingness to choose the path of rebirth."

"Are you sure you want me to keep going, Father?" asked Man.

Father O'Donnell nodded *yes*.

"Sister Magdalen asks the cardinals to take off their vestments as a symbol of letting go of their egos and their need to control. One by one, the cardinals come forward and drop their richly brocaded robes to the ground before her. Many are left standing only in their underwear, looking as Joe Carroll described on the Internet feed, "like the inmates at an elderly care center lined up to get their meds." Sister Magdalen then asks the cardinals to join her in celebration of the New Mass. She instructs them:

*The New Mass represents our surrender to the three aspects of the Trinity. The force of assertion is represented in the bread which comes from a seed in the ground which has grown into grain. It has asserted itself into being. In the new church there is no room for distinction between the laity and the clergy. But as the bread represents the masculine force, in the New Mass the bread will be served by a man. The receiving force is represented so well in Scripture by Mary. She receives and gives birth with her own blood. Therefore in the new Mass, the wine shall be served by a woman. What has also been absent in the Mass has been recognition of the Holy Spirit, the reconciling force, Grace. This is the role of incense that is brought down the aisle to precede the Eucharistic ritual. It is to be brought down the aisle by a young adolescent, who represents the innocence and miracle of Grace. The smell of the incense, God's Grace, permeates the entire celebration. The New Mass thus represents and is the experience of the dynamic qualities that allow us to move into real communion, into the interacting flow between the linear world and the quantum world.*

"What else, what else did she say?" asked Father O'Donnell weakly.

"She explained that the New Mass was a recapitulation of Creation. *In the beginning was the Word, and the Word was God.*" Man paused. He had been through Sister Magdalen's explanation of the New Mass for Father O'Donald at least a half dozen times.

"Tell me again, please."

By now Man knew Sister Magdalen's explanation by heart. He began to recite.

*"Initially the Word, or Logos, is simply a symbol for something, it is not yet the thing itself, because it represents what is un-manifested in the quantum field before creation. In the process of creation, God becomes the mother/father*

*Creator. With creation the idea is transformed from the un-manifested field to manifestation in the linear world. Creation is thus the daughter/son of the Creator. However, Logos means more than just the idea in the un-manifested quantum field and its manifestation in the linear world. The Logos is also the connection or relationship by which the un-manifest in the quantum world moves into manifestation in the linear world. In other words, it is also the Holy Spirit, the flow of connection back and forth between the quantum field and the linear world of manifestation. The New Mass is a celebration of the Creator, creation and the connection between the two—a celebration of our living, dynamic trinitarian God.*

*"When we celebrate creation, we celebrate our connection to the Creator, the creation and that connection between them, which makes the existence of creation possible. By our celebration we renew our connection to God, to all of God's creation and to that Spirit by which we and all creation are sustained. Every time we celebrate the New Mass we renew our connection with the quantum field, which renews our connection with our essence and with God. For a living human being the soul is the unique part of each of us in the quantum field. The person's spirit, contained in one's thoughts, feelings and bodily intuitions, connect the soul and the manifested body. The New Mass celebrates all creation and our own.*

*"The New Mass, of course, is also a celebration of Christ's birth or creation—transition from the un-manifest state to the manifest—and transition from the manifest back to the un-manifest or resurrection. Creation always includes resurrection because resurrection is simply manifested reality*

*returning to an un-manifested state in the quantum field. So because Creation always includes manifested and un-manifested reality, we always have resurrection as a part of Creation. Thus the New Mass includes, but is bigger than, the Old Mass. When we celebrate the New Mass, we are also celebrating the choice the gift of transformation gives us to decide to walk this path of connection to our Creator in both worlds.*

"Sister Magdalen then asked Father Hay to read a selection from the Bible. He read from Romans, chapter 12, verses six through eight. After that she told the gathering. 'Here we are given the Enneagram of the Body of Christ Living in Unitive Consciousness. In this text we are told how to be messengers of the good news of transformation from a non-dual perspective.'

"Point Nine - When you speak truth do so with love
Point One - When you teach do so without judging
Point Two - When you serve do so without taking over
Point Three - Chastity - keep an open heart
Point Four - When you encourage do so heart-fully without
              envy
Point Five - When you give, give generously
Point Six – Poverty - keep a clear mind
Point Seven - When you are to lead don't waiver in your
              direction
Point Eight - When you show mercy do so smiling

"Blaine put it on an Enneagram diagram to show you," said Man. He handed Father O'Donnell a piece of paper with the image sketched on it.

## Enneagram of the Body of Christ
## Living in Unitive Consciousness

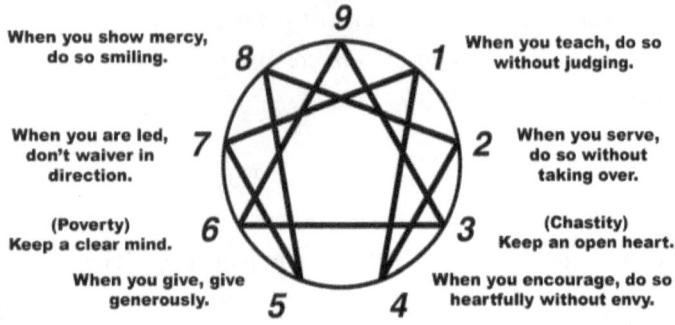

When you speak truth, do so with love.

When you show mercy, do so smiling.

When you teach, do so without judging.

When you are led, don't waiver in direction.

When you serve, do so without taking over.

(Poverty) Keep a clear mind.

(Chastity) Keep an open heart.

When you give, give generously.

When you encourage, do so heartfully without envy.

"Then she told the assembled clergy that with the New Mass and the Enneagram of the Body of Christ Living in Unitive Consciousness, the church would be transformed from its dualistic way of being into a unitive reality."

"I think that was about all of her teaching," said Man. "What followed then was the ritual celebration of the New Mass. A young lesbian girl, who marched in the procession with Godfrey and your old friend Father Hay, carried the incense burner down the aisle of the church. A bishop came forward to serve the bread. And Sister Magdalen herself served the wine. At the conclusion of the New Mass, Sister Magdalen left the cardinals in the main part of the church and went into the Sistine Chapel. What happened next is unclear. It was assumed that she would become the new Pope. But no one has seen Sister Magdalen since. And according to her instructions, in

THE ARMAGEDDON CHOICE

the new church there would be no hierarchy, so there is no need for a Pope."

Father O'Donnell let out a long, audible sigh. "She does seem to have this habit of disappearing at a critical juncture. Or maybe she is just slipping back and forth through some little microtubule between this side and the other. But tell me again about what happened earlier in the procession when they got to Foligno."

"This was one of the first stops along the way. It seems that the procession came upon a truck that was parked blocking part of the road along which they were traveling. What first appeared to be an obstacle became an opportunity. Sister Magdalen was helped up onto the bed of the truck. From there she could see and be seen by much of the crowd. She then delivered what has become known as Sister Magdalen's first sermon. Or, as Joe Carroll called it rather ruefully on his Internet commentary, the *Sermon on the Truck*."

"Tell me again exactly which she said," said Father O'Donnell his eyes glistening.

"Her walk to Rome was like a wedding procession. She explained she was bringing the receiving energy of love, which Mary Magdalene first brought to Jesus as his first apostle, which so dramatically marked Mary Magdalene's relationship with him. Only by Mary Magdalene's receptive love energy, balancing with Jesus' love energy, was he able to assert outward-going love energy to so many.

"Sister Magdalen then told the crowd that she would not be here for long, but that her mission was to repeat the instructions that Mary Magdalene communicated to the disciples from Jesus as they are recorded in the Gospel of Mary Magdalene. She said many would recall that the Gospel of Mary Magdalene focuses on a scene after Jesus' death in which Peter asks Mary Magdalene to share with the disciples some of the 'secret' teachings of Jesus given just to her. She responded to this invitation by giving her visionary recital of the soul's progress.

"Sister Magdalen explained that the Gospel of Mary Magdalene is directed toward the progress of the individual soul, but now those instructions are directed first and foremost to humankind."

"Tell me," said Father O'Donnell. "What she said the teachings are for the soul's progress."

"She started by quoting exactly the text of the Gospel of Mary Magdalene," said Blaine, taking over the re-telling. Blaine reached over and picked up a copy of the Gospel of Mary Magdalene and paged through it until she came to the page she was looking for.

*"That which oppressed me has been slain;*
*that which encircled me has vanished;*
*my craving has faded,*
*and I am free from my ignorance.*
*I left the world with the aid of another world;*
*a design was erased,*

*by virtue of a higher design.*
*Henceforth I travel toward Repose,*
*where time rests in the Eternity of Time;*
*I go now into silence."*

"I am quoting there from page 16 line 16 of the Gospel of Mary Magdalene through line 6 on page 17. This is exactly the portion of the Gospel that Sister Magdalen spoke to the crowd. She went on to explain that what Mary Magdalene was describing was the new state of consciousness which she experienced in her revelation from Jesus."

"As always the question is—how do we get there?" whispered Father O'Donnell.

"Sister Magdalen explained to the crowd the journey Mary Magdalene described in the lines preceding the portion she quoted. The journey is similar to the template described by Teresa of Avila in her image of moving through the rooms of a castle. But Mary Magdalene did not use the image of moving through rooms. Instead she described the process as one of moving through climates. Sister Magdalen said this is a wonderfully useful image as it so aptly describes the tactile feel of the sometimes suffocating psychological states through which we must move to be liberated from our false-self's ego trance into unitive consciousness.

"There are four climates which she described: first, the climate of darkness or meaninglessness; second, the climate of craving and neediness; third, the climate of close-mindedness; and fourth, the climate of wrath or attachment. In the first three climates, a person is basically unconscious: in the first climate, one is caught in meaninglessness but has no self-awareness from which to understand that meaninglessness. In the second climate, one has desires and cravings but again lacks sufficient self-awareness to see the pattern of one's cravings. In the third climate, one is stuck in a close-minded inertia and is unwilling to move into greater awareness."

Father O'Donnell perked up. "The way I learned that as a young monk was, first, we must give up our need for our defended body; second, we must surrender our self-centered emotions that keep our heart closed down; and third, we must give up our opinionated mind. In Enneagram terms we must surrender our self-centered survival hold on control of our emotional, mental, and somatic centers. That is the first and basic task of spiritual disciplines to get us out of those first three smothering climates. But I interrupted. Go on, what did she say next?"

Blaine continued, "Unlike the situation in the first three climates, the fourth climate has some level of self-awareness and because of that, in the fourth climate one has to face each of Seven Wraths or attachments. The use of the word wraths is interesting. Sister Magdalen noted that it taps into the passion and power of these attachments. The seven attachments are to darkness or inertia, to craving for experience, to ignorance or lack of humility, to jealousy, to enslavement to the body's need for power, to intoxicated wisdom or the mind's need to control and to guileful wisdom or trying to be perfect.

"The Seven Wraths are what in Enneagram terms we would call the emotional, false-self energies, or passions, of seven of the types. Here is a little chart I did this morning, showing how they relate to the Enneagram. As with the Seven Deadly Sins, points Three and Six are omitted since it is from the energy of fear and dishonesty that the false self-energies of the other points are shaped.

**Enneagram of Mary Magdalene's Seven Wraths**

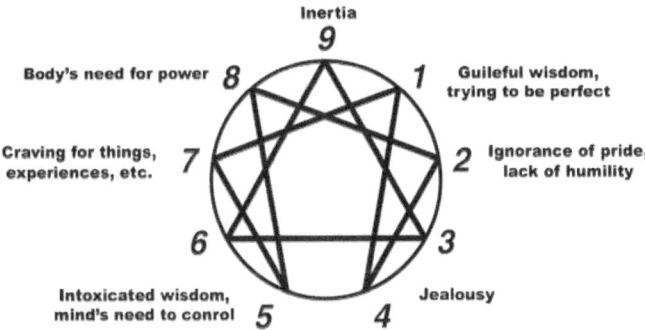

"Sister Magdalen alluded to how Mary Magdalen's description of the Seven Wraths relates to the Enneagram but she focused most of the rest of her *Sermon on the Truck* on how we, like Mary Magdalene, can become free of them—how our consciousness can be transformed."

"Oh, this is the good part," said Father O'Donnell. "Tell me again what she said. You could say I am cramming for my finals." He winked at Blaine. "And I don't want to miss a thing."

Blaine felt again how easily it was for her heart energy to open to Father O'Donnell. She continued, "The soul that is free of attachments or wraths naturally rests in heart-centeredness. When this happens, then it is naturally open to a relationship with Spirit, with the quantum field, the reality in which God lives and which is God."

"Ah, yes. I have said so myself countless times, but how wonderful to hear it from someone who knew Jesus. And as the Gospel of Mary Magdalene recounts, after she gave this wisdom knowledge to the disciples, they didn't believe her. So in a sense we have been caught in this hiatus for 2,000 years, where the wisdom both of Jesus and Mary Magdalene has, for most of human history, not been experienced but has continued to exist out there in the field available to all who sought it. The question is whether Sister's Magdalen's teaching of this wisdom again is enough to catapult humankind to greater consciousness. I guess the jury is still out on that, Blaine. Is that what you must tell me?"

"She did address the underlying question—the place from which we make a conscious choice—the locus of how we believe what we believe." Blaine paused. She was unsure of whether Father O'Donnell had the energy for her to continue.

"Please go on," he said.

"She pointed out that with our intelligence we can determine that the principle of cooperation is vividly illustrated in nature, at least as much as the struggle for existence. Bees and flowers cooperate. Plants, air and light cooperate in photosynthesis to produce wheat, which gives the very bread we eat. And the human body, she asked—don't the cells and muscles and bones and glands and the blood cooperate rather than struggle? Isn't the life and health of a human being due to cooperation?

"By now the crowd was with her. No one was denying the supremacy of the principle of cooperation. But she was quick to point out that intellectual knowledge of how things cooperate has not been sufficient unto itself to give humankind the faith to live into the greater cooperation necessary to save the planet and the human race. Here she paused to give the crowd the time to grasp what she had said. They knew that this was true."

Father O'Donnell nodded his head very slightly.

"Faith, Sister Magdalen said, never has come from intellectual knowledge. In fact, without more, intellectual knowledge has often been a tool for destruction and is the preferred twentieth and twenty-first centuries' weapon in the destructive struggle for survival. Intellectual knowledge, even intellectual knowledge of the supremacy of the pattern of cooperation for existence, must be grounded in the heart and the gut for meaningful action to flow from it—for it to create a new reality. There must be a kind of essential sympathy, an essence to essence contact, for there to be the clarity and honesty that provides wisdom from which action comes. This essential sympathy only arises from a heart-centeredness that is connected to more than just the small ego self. When this occurs, the knowing that something is deeply true and what action must be taken is experienced as intuition. Intuition is faith in action. Intuition includes everything that we know from raw data from the sensory world, as well as what is unknown from the quantum world.

"In other words, she told the crowd, it is not enough to intellectually understand the problem of the struggle for existence—we must move beyond fact-knowing to heart-knowing. It is like the wise men following the star in the East. They had no collaborating information to tell them they should make their journey. The only fact they had was the star itself in the night sky. But this fact was combined with something else from beyond themselves, an intuition that they should engage in a long and arduous journey. And because they had faith in their informed intuition they traveled to Bethlehem.

"There is a center of gravity of our hearts, just as there is a center of gravity in the solar system. From that center everything is possible, even the transformation of human consciousness."

"Then she told them about the Enneagram of *I am's*. I remember this because before she began this part of the *Sermon on the Truck*, she looked down at Will Dawson, who was standing by the truck still holding the donkey's halter. She smiled at him, and watching it on the video feed, it is clear something about Will changed when he received her smile."

Father O'Donnell's eyes opened briefly as if pleading with her to go on.

"I am sorry, Father. I didn't mean to get sidetracked. Then Sister Magdalen told the crowd that we each are given a way in Jesus' teachings to understand entry into heart consciousness. He is the universal entry way, but he provided a map for each Enneagram type as to how to enter heart consciousness."

Blaine picked up a piece of paper from the table on which she had drawn the Enneagram of *I am's*, after she first heard Sister Magdalen deliver this part of the *Sermon on the Truck*.

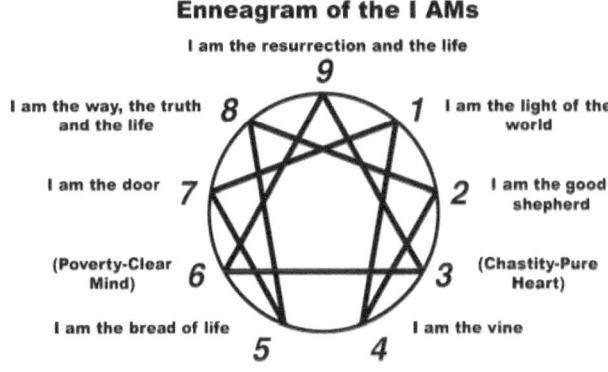

**Enneagram of the I AMs**

I am the resurrection and the life

9

I am the way, the truth and the life    **8**      **1**    I am the light of the world

I am the door   **7**     **2**   I am the good shepherd

(Poverty-Clear Mind)   **6**     **3**   (Chastity-Pure Heart)

I am the bread of life    **5**     **4**    I am the vine

Blaine read the points by type to Father O'Donnell.

"Then Sister Magdalen told the crowd, 'I do not make this walk to Rome to confront the hierarchical authorities of the Church. I do this because the center of gravity of my heart tells me, without knowing why, that this is a journey which must be made. I thank all of you who are making this journey with me. And I ask all of you who are listening to, or watching, this journey to make this journey with me in your hearts.'

"After that the crowd cheered for a long time. She got down

from the truck bed and greeted the followers crowded around. A short time later, the procession began again."

Father O'Donnell's eyes opened and flashed like burning coals. But he was exhausted from listening and his eyes immediately closed again. Quickly he fell asleep.

Blaine was holding his left hand and looking down she saw how frail and feeble his fingers were. His skin was stretched tight over the bones of his wrist and his skin glowed like parchment. She was aware that Man, who stood up behind her to move around and stretch earlier, had returned to stand behind her.

Man put his hands on Blaine's shoulders. Just then, as Father O'Donnell let out a light exhalation, she felt his body shudder and a spark like electricity come from his hand into hers. She could feel the charge go through her into Man's hands.

They both looked attentively at Father O'Donnell and sought to will his chest to rise again, just as it had done for the past eighty-some years. It did not. But they were both flooded with an overwhelming sense of peace. Father O'Donnell had slipped to the other side, but there he was in the same quantum field as Jesus, as Mary Magdalene, and with them, right below their breastbones on the inside.

# Chapter 31

The mood was somber. Everyone was gathered for the evening meal in the convent refectory where the sisters of the Sacred Order of the Sisters of Mary of Magdala were staying in Rome. Mother Mary was seated at the head of one of the tables. Around her were gathered Sister Angelina, Joe Carroll, Aasia, Rat, Brother Isaac, Gordon Slade and his wife Joy, Father Hay and Godfrey, as well as other sisters, who had been a part of making Sister Magdalen's procession from Assisi to Rome possible. Everyone was tired. The long hours of preparation for and during the procession had been exhausting. On top of all of this was a feeling of emptiness, because Sister Magdalen was mysteriously gone.

Suddenly Rat got up from the table and walked over to the large refectory window where reception on his iPhone was better.

Quickly he returned, looking shaken. "I just got a text message from Blaine. Father O'Donnell passed away just a few minutes ago."

There was the sound of a collective sigh and the palpable feeling of the room being wreathed in grief. Father Hay began sobbing quietly.

Then the main door to the refectory opened. In walked Sister Magdalen. There was a collective gasp.

"I am sorry you had to get the message about Father O'Donnell's passing from a text. I was on my way to come tell you. I was just with him. He sends his love to all of you. He wants to be sure you know that for those who have received the gift of unitive consciousness, you will experience that resurrection is real. As he would say, resurrection is no more mysterious than the law of the conservation of energy. Father O'Donnell's thoughts and feelings are simply energy and his feelings and thoughts about you and for you are as real now in the quantum field as they were when he was physically here with us, just as the thoughts and feelings of Jesus and Mary Magdalene are as alive today in the quantum field as they were 2,000 years ago.

"He asked me to remind you of this passage from the Gospel of Philip:

*So then every seed that my Father in Heaven has not planted shall be uprooted. Those who were separated shall be united, and all who are empty shall be filled, so that everyone may enter into the Bridal Chamber where they will be born into the Light.*

There was a pause, then Mother Mary, who seemed to be recovering quickest from the sudden appearance of Sister Magdalen, asked, "Tell us what Father O'Donnell wants us to understand about this passage from the Gospel of Philip."

Sister Magdalen smiled. "I could say, just ask him, but in the grief you are all feeling, that response seems unfair. So let me take a shot at what Father O'Donnell might say to you." She paused. "The seeds that our Mother/Father God of creation planted are the seeds of our divine essence. All the other seeds that get planted are simply those of our false selves. When the false-self is uprooted, when we return to our authentic divine essence, then we are no longer separated. We do in fact return to God, to the quantum energy field of his creative presence, empty of our false-self. When we do, we are reborn again into the Light. Light is the form of energy or matter that goes most easily between the Newtonian world and the quantum field."

As if wanting to forestall further questions, Sister Magdalen continued. "I love the Bridal Chamber image. Just as something physical and real and also mysterious happens between the bride and the groom in the Bridal Chamber, so something real and also mysterious happens to us when our false-self slips away and we are reunited with the creative force of the universe in the quantum field of the eternal now."

"When I was talking to Father O'Donnell, he was chuckling and telling me how he first felt this re-uniting as a young monk, and how he has felt it over and over again during his earthly life. He wanted me to be sure and tell you not to fret about getting into the quantum field after you die; you have the free will to do it while you're alive. His initial impression is that entry into the Kingdom might not always be available later. The time to enter is now."

Sister Magdalen reached over and picked up a glass of wine

from the table. She raised it high and held it over her head. "To the Bridal Chamber, my beloved friends, your open-heartedness will take you all there. Amen!"

And one by one they all stood and raised their glasses. Slade involuntarily reached out and took Joy's free hand. Rat moved closer to Aasia so their shoulders touched. Sister Angelina put her hand against Joe Carroll's cheek. Soon they were all touching in some way. As their arms went up, simultaneously their spirits seemed to elevate and enliven. The sad and tired faces erupted in smiles.

"To the resurrected Christ within each of you," said Sister Magdalen, and as she touched her glass to Mother Mary's glass a spark of electricity went through the gathering. They each drank their glass empty.

First Rat, and then all the rest, began to whoop and holler and hug each other with gleeful joy.

Rat said, "Hey, I need to get Blaine and Man on the cell phone so they can join in the celebration."

"You don't really have to," said Sister Magdalen. "They're already connected to us via the field. But, of course, it's fun to celebrate with them in this world and the next.

"I must tell you that I have a limited hall pass. Thank you so much for all the efforts you made with me to push humankind in the direction of transformation. I have to tell you that I don't honestly know whether we made it. But what I do know is that it matters one hundred percent that we tried, and what happens is also one hundred percent up to God. Love and blessings and, when you're ready, I'll meet you in the field."

With that, Sister Magdalen turned and walked toward the door. Then she stopped and looked back at Brother Isaac. She raised her hand and beckoned to him with her finger. He moved out from the table and headed toward her. She turned back in the direction she was going in order to leave. However, she appeared to be a bit disoriented about the right direction to find the door. There would be much discussion about it later, but for all the world, it seemed as if she simply left through the window. Brother Isaac somehow seemed to follow. After a moment, Joe Carroll broke the stunned silence: "Let us raise our glasses again in thankful gratitude to Mary Magdalene and all those in her lineage, including our Sister Magdalen. Let us, in the words of the poet and prophet Jelalu'ddin Rumi, invoke entry into the Magdalenic field:"

*Close the language-door,*
*and open the love window.*

*The moon won't use the door,*
*only the window.*

Dear Reader,

I share your sense of frustration with this author. Here we are, finally at the end of the third novel of The Consciousness Trilogy, and again things have not been properly wrapped up. But I must confess to you, despite my annoyance with the uncertainty this leaves me with, that I understand the reason why.

The novel's conclusion, dear reader, is of course up to you. As much as I think the author could have done a much better job in many places along the way, he certainly has no way to narrate the final outcome without knowing what your choice—between the struggle for existence or cooperation for enlightenment—might be. We must each make our Armageddon choice, which then determines the book's and humankind's outcome.

The history of all serious political, philosophical, and spiritual thought is one of choice. All great political philosophies are built on having a choice of one form of government as opposed to another. But political philosophies are all philosophies of willfulness—decisions of the ego. Religious or spiritual philosophies are largely decisions of willingness—decisions informed by something greater than our ego selves. The great prophet Zoroaster wanted people who could say *Yes* to the Light and No to the darkness. The Buddha wanted followers awakened from the trance of the psyche's automatic pilot who could say *Yes* to freedom of the spirit and *No* to the slumber of unconsciousness. At the risk of losing those of you who react automatically to become closed-minded against anything Christian and the quoting of Scripture, Jesus also taught the reality of the choice you are making. Matthew 5:37: Let what you say be simply *Yes* or *No*.

Having persevered despite my earlier letters against reading these novels, you have now read them—you are aware of what is at stake. You are making the Armageddon choice for yourself and all of us. Choose well.

While the choice point is close at hand you have by now learned enough about the Enneagram that you can take heart in the historical Enneagram perspective. As you learned in the novels, the Enneagram gives you insight into your own patterns and it is also tells us about the way processes unfold, even when that process is our history. Because of the gloom I feel about what choice humankind might make, I am inclined to reveal to you what has given me hope. You are the first to get this comprehensive Enneagram view of our history.

The Enneagram of Human Evolution
also know as
The Enneagram of Historical Return—The Journey to Regain
a Sense of Unity

Point Nine - Spiritual Human in Participation Mystique - unconscious participation in unity of tribe and nature

Precipitating transition event - rise of irrigation and stored grain

Point One - Hierarchally Defined Human - Egyptian Cult of

Ra, the Sun God - theocratic perfection, emergence of monotheism

Precipitating transition Event - rise of language

Point Four - Imaginative Human – Judaism, the longing for deliverance; first sense of self consciousness; longing to live in past and future; birth of the imagination; longing as way to unity

Precipitating transition Event - Oppression of new urban minorities imagination's sense of self-identity by government and religious authorities

Point Two - Affiliative Human - Christianity in its first three centuries; the first trans-ethnic, universal religion open to all; seeking unity through affiliation and love; conscious participation in affectional bonds of group as way to find unity

Precipitating transition Event - adoption of Christianity as State Religion

Point Eight - Imperial Human; Religion as an ideology for conquering; loss of religious empathy and vulnerability; seeking unity through aggression and assertion

Precipitating transition Event - Printing Press and Protestant Reformation - giving humans information for choice

Point Five - Reasoning Human; seeking unity through logical analysis of how things are; through the acquisition of knowledge; through the mind

Precipitating transition Event - Industrial Revolution

Point Seven - Materialistic Human, seeking unity through material options

Precipitating transition Event - Two World Wars; Identity Crisis of Modernism

Point Nine - Psychological Human; seeking unity through understanding emotional self, escape into self forgetting, loss of being in touch with dynamic being and the transpersonal self.

Current transition point - Precipitating transition Events - Televised Moon landing, televised natural disasters, World Cup, Olympics; humans experiencing planet-wide events together; experiencing being part of humankind rather than only self, tribe, state or religion; experience of being a part of all humanity and dwellers all on the same planet

Point Six - Consciously Spiritual Human; conscious experience of participation in trans-national, trans-ethnic events; experiencing unity through faith in connectedness of all life and in the quantum field; non-dual perspective; awareness of self and others and ability to hold both empathetically

Possible Precipitating transition Events - Global Warming ecological crisis, excessive food and energy consumption by first world countries and want-to-be first world countries; complete Internet wiring of the world, development of hydrogen energy to transition out of energy crisis

Point Three - Dynamically Spiritual Human; Wholeness experienced by action, feeling and thought to save the planet; unity experienced through integration of body, mind and heart and through the integration of the shadow, both individually and culturally; freedom comes through affiliation, through process, not isolation; justice comes through relationship not abstract laws, energy is democratized, sufficient food resources for all localized; life is lived in a post survival era.

**Enneagram of Human Evolution**
The Enneagram of Historical Return - The Journey to Regain a Sense of Unity

(8) Psychological Human
*(1) Human in Participation Mystique
**9**

Imperial Human (5) **8**          **1**(2) Hierarchally Defined Human

Materialistic Human (7) **7**          **2**(4) Affiliative Human

Consciously Spiritual (9) **6**  Human          **3**(10) Dynamically Spiritual Human

Reasoning Human **5**(6)          **4**(3) Imaginative Human

*number in parentheses is the order of movement

The Enneagram of Human Evolution is hopeful. For all of us, the struggles of the characters in this book (certainly that has been my goal in my struggle to provide spiritual direction for Godfrey), have provided sufficient clues for us to understand fully what is at stake in making our choice. I hope that your choice is enriched by the journeys of the characters in the trilogy and that their journeys have in some sense heightened your awareness and access to the mysterious presence available across the quantum divide--the abundance and joy of the Mystery of a heart-centered life.

Very Sincerely yours,

Father Charles F. "Cloudy" Hay

# ABOUT THE AUTHOR

Don Carroll is a spiritual director and the author of *A Lawyer's Guide to Healing*, the *Connect* interactive journals (www.practicesofawakening.com) and THE CONSCIOUSNESS TRILOGY. He completed his spiritual direction training at Sursum Corda. He is a member of the Wesleyan Contemplative Order and leads workshops using the Enneagram as a tool for spiritual transformation and as a tool for deepening spiritual transformation in 12 Step recovery. He is a certified Enneagram teacher in the Enneagram in the Narrative Tradition.

Don received his undergraduate degree from Davidson College. He has a Masters of Philosophy from the University of Dundee in Scotland and he received his law degree with honors from the University of Virginia. He holds a MFA in writing from Vermont College. From 1994 to 2011 Don served as Director of the North Carolina Lawyer Assistance Program. He is a certified Professional Coach and a certified Strozzi Institute Somatic Coach.

In November 2011, North Carolina Governor Bev Perdue conferred on him membership in the Order of the Long Leaf Pine for outstanding service to the citizens of North Carolina.

www.doncarroll.com                    www.anewpope.com